The Alabaster HIP

THE
Regency Romp
TRILOGY
BOOK THREE

THE ALABASTER HIP
THE REGENCY ROMP
BOOK 3

Copyright © 2017 by Margaret Cooke
ISBN-13: 978-1546356936
ISBN-10: 1546356932

All rights reserved. Except for use in any review, the reproduction or utilization of this work in whole or in part in any form by any electronic, mechanical or other means, now known or hereinafter invented, including xerography, photocopying and recording, or in any information storage or retrieval system, is forbidden without the written permission of the publisher.

This is a work of fiction. Names, characters, places and incidents are either the product of the author's imagination or are used fictitiously, and any resemblance to actual persons, living or dead, business establishments, events or locales is entirely coincidental.

Printed in the USA.

Cover Design and Interior Format
© THE KILLION GROUP, INC.

THE
Regency Romp
TRILOGY
BOOK THREE

The Alabaster HIP

MAGGIE FENTON

ALSO BY MAGGIE FENTON

REGENCY ROMP TRILOGY
The Duke's Holiday
Virtuous Scoundrel

WRITTEN AS MARGARET FOXE:
Prince of Hearts
A Dark Heart
Thief of Hearts

To the late Dr. Sin-Hsing Tsai, an incredible concert pianist, teacher, life coach, and ally, gone too soon. I am heartsick every time I sit down at the piano bench and think of you . . . scowling at me for messing up my scales. Rest in music.

Deceiving others: that is what the world calls a romance.
—Oscar Wilde

CHAPTER ONE

In Which A (nother) Peer of the Realm Sweeps Miss Minerva Jones Off Her Feet

THE HONORABLE MISSES BEATRICE AND Laura Leighton, spawn of the notorious Viscount Marlowe (not the devil himself—an alarmingly common and *unsurprising* misconception), were going to be the death of Miss Minerva Jones, teacher of grammar and composition at West Barming School for Recalcitrant Young Ladies. The coroner was sure to write that in his report when her body was discovered tangled up in the remnants of the little terrors' latest experiment in torment.

If her body were ever discovered at all, which was doubtful. Between the remoteness of the academy in the wilds of Kent and the twins' terrifyingly Machiavellian intelligence, archaeologists two hundred years in the future might very well be the first to come across her remains . . . if she was lucky.

And the twins claimed to *like* Minerva. She could only imagine what they did to their enemies.

Well, she didn't have to *imagine* at all. She glanced over to the half-finished woolen mobcap she'd been unenthusiastically knitting for Fräulein Schmidt for days and winced. The poor woman's head had been as bald as a baby's bottom after the Leighton twins—and a straight razor—had finished with her.

The only reason the woman was still on the premises and not halfway back to Heidelberg was because she was too embarrassed to leave her room. And the fräulein, like most of the school's female staff, didn't really have anywhere else to go. That thought alone had made Minerva hold in the completely inappropriate laughter that had bubbled up inside of her when she'd seen the twins' handiwork.

For this particular crime, however, she could hardly bring herself to blame the twins, for Fräulein Schmidt was one of the most unpleasant people Minerva had ever come across. It was no justification for shearing her bald in her sleep, of course, but . . . well . . .

Minerva made no claims to being a particularly nice person herself, especially when it came to feeling sympathy for a woman who had been blackmailing her for months. Perhaps Minerva should have rid herself of her Christopher Essex collection after her last employer, Lady Blundersmith, had sacked her for it, but while she wasn't all that nice, she *was* stubborn. And Essex was a genius—she didn't give a fig how scandalous he was or how the starchy headmistress was sure to have a conniption if she found out.

So she'd let the fräulein bully her out of a few pence a month to keep her post *and* her secret library and silently cursed the woman to high hell.

In Minerva's most mean-spirited moments, she inwardly applauded the twins' rough justice, for Fräulein hadn't demanded her blood money from Minerva since her shearing. And the *look* on the woman's face that Boxing Day morning after the deed was done . . . well, it really was worth all the pence Minerva had paid to her over the past year and a half.

No, she was not particularly nice.

She could only be thankful that she was on the twins' good side. For now. They'd not been happy after she'd lost her temper with them tonight, though she *had* been elbow deep in frog entrails at the time . . .

Minerva collapsed on her small cot with a weary sigh and tried to rub the burgeoning headache from her temples. She may have secretly admired the twins' handiwork with Fräulein Schmidt, but tonight had crossed a definite line. It was well past midnight, closer to dawn, and it had taken hours to sort out the latest calamity, which the twins had claimed was in the pursuit of science.

West Barming did not even teach science.

And this so-called experiment had involved dead frogs. A great deal of dead frogs. And their innards. How the twins had managed to procure so many of the creatures when they supposedly never left the academy gates was beyond Minerva's ken at the moment. She wouldn't be surprised to learn that the little hellions had sprouted wings. More likely they had taken a page from Fräulein Schmidt and blackmailed one of the staff into their service. It had already happened more than once in the three months they'd been in residence.

Normally Minerva was able to be more sanguine about the trials and tribulations of West Barming, but tonight she was just so bloody *tired*. The Honorable Misses Leighton were getting worse, their reformation not even a speck on a distant horizon, and she could only pray that their next "experiment" didn't involve fire.

Rumor had it that they'd been packed off to the academy by their grandfather, the Earl of Barming himself, for burning down half a city block back in London. Minerva hadn't believed the ridiculous rumor at first—the twins just looked so innocent at first glance—but that was before Fräulein Schmidt. And the rats. And the frogs . . . and that one time with the manure . . .

Dear Lord, the *manure*.

For one brief moment, Minerva actually missed Lady Blundersmith. But that moment was very, *very* brief. Five soul-crushing years at the beck and call of that hypochondriacal, self-righteous frigate of a woman was quite enough for Minerva. She'd take the Honorable Misses Leighton, the frog entrails, razors, and a disturbing predilection for fire any day, even though it often felt like she was merely trading one circle of hell for another.

She supposed the twins hadn't stood much of a chance, considering their parentage. Minerva had rather firsthand experience with the walking disaster that was Evelyn Leighton, Viscount Marlowe. She'd carried the bruises around for months afterward to prove it.

The one rare ball Lady Blundersmith had deigned to attend the last year of Minerva's employment had ended with two peers of the realm—the notorious viscount himself and his supposed best friend, the equally notorious Sebastian Sherbrook, Marquess of Manwaring (the "Most Beautiful Man in London" according to the *Times*)—brawling in the Duke of Montford's giant sponge cake over a woman. Montford, the viscount's other best friend (though Minerva had no idea how a man as reputedly fastidious as Montford could possibly be friends with someone as . . . *calamitous* as the viscount), had managed to sustain a concussion in the ensuing fracas, sending the rest of the guests into a titillated bumblebroth.

Minerva's fate had been even less pleasant than the duke's, as she'd been buried under the immovable Mont Blanc that was Lady Blundersmith in a swoon. Minerva wouldn't soon forget the boorish Viscount Marlowe, with his broken, bloodied nose and uncensored tongue who had been the cause of all of the chaos. Nor those bright, too-intelligent brown eyes, so at odds with the rest of his rumpled, cake-smudged appearance.

Beatrice, from the top of her unkempt head of coal-black curls to the tip of her too-sharp, too-long nose, was her father's child. Laura's softer beauty and quieter nature must have been a gift from her dead mother, but Minerva had learned the hard way not to be fooled by that innocent packaging. They may not have been identical, but both girls had their father's preternaturally bright brown eyes, after all, and his penchant for trouble.

After quickly undressing for the second time that night and scrubbing *amphibian* from her hands, Minerva tried to settle under her blankets and steal at least a few hours of sleep before sunrise. But between the gruesome image of murdered frogs lingering behind her eyelids (what had those girls even *done* to those poor beasts?) and the persistent suspicion that her life had become completely ridiculous, sleep proved elusive.

She kicked away her blankets and turned her eyes toward the ramshackle desk tucked under the tall casement windows. She had enough moonlight streaming in from them to finish her letter to Inigo without wasting paraffin, and if anything would put her to sleep, it would be that.

The doctor was too conscientious for his own good, his letters of polite concern arriving in the post every month like clockwork. If she failed to respond in a timely fashion, his letters and concern increased exponentially, so she had discovered it was easiest to send back a response as fast as she could to save him the worry. She might grumble about his high-handedness on occasion—not to mention feel perpetually guilty for being yet another weight upon his shoulders—but it *was* rather nice to have someone in the world who cared whether she lived or died. He was as close to family as it got for her these days.

But he was half the reason she'd left London after Lady Blundersmith had sacked her.

She'd planned to marry his brother Arthur . . . up until Arthur had run off to the war, despite her protests. After Waterloo had taken him, she had given up on the whole idea of marriage. She hadn't the heart or the courage to attach herself to another man after all of the ones in her life had failed her so spectacularly—not that she had offers pouring in, considering how small, plain, and poor she was. Arthur Lucas had been her one shot, and she'd completely failed to hit that particular target.

Inigo, however, had somehow come to the conclusion that the best way to fulfill his promise to his dead brother to see to her welfare was to marry her himself. He'd thought it a perfectly sound idea when he'd broached the subject. *She'd* thought it was complete lunacy. As much as she admired and cared for Inigo, her feelings for him went no deeper than his for her.

She couldn't deny that Inigo's proposal had nearly swayed her resolve, though, for he was one of the best men she knew and unquestionably attractive underneath that ridiculous facial hair he was so fond of. And perhaps some nights she did lie awake regretting turning him down.

But it didn't seem right to accept his proposal, fond as she was of him, for she knew his persistence on the matter was only because of his grief at losing his own fiancée, Yvette, around the same time as his brother. He had never recovered—never would enough to seek out love again—and she couldn't blame him. After losing first her father and then Arthur, she herself had not been able to bring herself to risk her heart again. Although . . .

Well, she'd have to admit that she would certainly *consider* encouraging one particular gentleman, but so would most of the female population of the country. She doubted even Lady Blundersmith would have the strength to turn Christopher Essex away, despite her crusade against the man's poetry. The woman had blushed to her toes after Minerva had made the mistake of reading a passage from *Le Chevalier d'Amour* to her one evening years ago. But Lady Blundersmith was convinced that anything that got her blood up had to be unhealthy, and she'd quickly added Essex to a long list that included music by Beethoven, fresh air, regular bathing, and unnecessary exercise.

No one knew Christopher Essex's true identity, but that

mystery, along with his verse, was enough to gain him a following even more rabid than Byron's. Minerva had been no more immune to his siren song than any other female under the age of one hundred. After she'd calmed Lady Blundersmith down following that failed recitation, she'd smuggled *Chevalier* to her own room and devoured it for days. She'd been addicted ever since.

Essex's poetry had made her feel . . . well, *not* alone for the first time in years. Made her feel like anything but the pragmatic, sensible woman she'd always prided herself as being, transporting her outside of her narrow reality. She thought herself deserving of this small indulgence, this small thing of beauty, in a life of diminishing prospects and poorly paid drudgery.

She didn't dare lump herself with the poet's more . . . overzealous followers—the so-called Misstophers, who swooned at the mere mention of his name (or that one Bedlam-bound fanatic who'd threatened suicide in a letter to the *Times* if Essex didn't marry her). But Minerva was only human, and she couldn't say she wasn't guilty of a little daydreaming of her own when it came to the secretive poet. Anyone who could write such exquisite poetry was surely just as exquisite a man.

She groaned inwardly at her fancifulness, casting off her dressing gown and cracking open one of the casement windows over her desk. Even though it was only February, she was absolutely boiling. She had no idea how the rest of the academy was a frozen mausoleum, yet her room felt like it was in the bloody tropics year-round.

She unbuttoned the top of her nightdress, revealing a shocking expanse of chest. But she *was* in the privacy of her own room. It wasn't as if anyone was going to fall out of the heavens, notice her dishabille, and report her to the headmistress. Fräulein, the odious snitch, who could always be counted upon to catch Minerva at the most inopportune moments, was quarantined by her own wounded vanity, after all.

She sat down at her desk and glared at the half-written letter to Inigo on the blotter. She sighed, opened another button on her gown just because she could, uncapped her inkpot, dipped her quill, and continued to write one of the most boring letters in the history of boring letters. In order to spare poor Inigo apoplexy, she ended up having to censor anything even remotely interesting that had happened to her in the last few months. So she did not tell Inigo about the frogs or the manure.

Or Fräulein's haircut.

Or the blackmail. *That* would necessitate admitting to him that she had managed to rescue her book collection from Lady Blundersmith's wrath. He'd never approved of or understood her weakness for Essex and would only be even more disappointed in her than he already was to learn she had kept the "instruments of her downfall," as he'd called them in his last letter.

She did not tell him she was going out of her mind with boredom, stuck in the gray walls of the academy.

Nor did she tell him she missed London desperately, even though she used to complain constantly about Lady Blundersmith's refusal to leave the city . . .

"*Bollocks!*"

Minerva dropped her quill midstroke and nearly fell backward in her chair at the sound of the loud, deep voice drifting in through the open window. She'd often heard the caretakers' voices echo up to her tower in the early morning hours, but it was still much too early for the day's work to begin.

She stood and peered out the open window into the gloom. The moon was nearly full, so she could just make out the lawn far below her window. She scanned it for the owner of the voice, but could see no sign of life. She held her breath, listening hard for a moment, but she heard nothing but the howl of the wind and the occasional groan of the weathervane on the rafters above her attic room.

Perhaps that was all she'd heard, though she'd never known it to creak out the King's English in the past.

She ducked her head inside after casting a bewildered glance toward the roofline, and turned back to her letter.

"Motherfu . . ." *That* word was cut blessedly short with a strangled sound and heavy thud. "Bloody buggering bastard, it's bleeding high up here!" the gruff voice continued after a pause.

Not the weathervane, then. And not the groundskeepers, a father and son team with a broad, nearly indecipherable Kentish accent. No, this speaker was all drawling, growling public school underneath that foulmouthed London cant. And it was definitely a man, a strange man. At her attic window. Five stories high.

Two large hands suddenly appeared, gripping her open windowsill, and Minerva stumbled back with a gasp, knocking her hip against her desk and sending the contents flying to the floor.

"What the devil?" that masculine voice growled again, the hands stilling at the commotion she'd caused.

On a sudden inspiration, Minerva rushed forward and stabbed at the man's hands with the quill still clutched in her fingers. This did nothing but stain the man's knuckles with black ink and turn his growls into full-fledged cursing, the likes of which Minerva had heard only from her late sailor father . . . and from the foulmouthed Lord Marlowe at that horrible winter ball two years ago.

In fact, the intruder's voice rather resembled the rumbling baritone that had been so unfortunately etched into Minerva's aural memory that fateful night.

Minerva tossed aside her broken quill and searched around the room for something more substantial with which to defend herself, for a man climbing into an attic window in the dead of night could hardly be up to anything good. But before she could make a move across the room, the man was hoisting himself up onto the sill with a groan.

He was an extremely tall and disreputable-looking specimen, whose broad shoulders blocked out the moonlight and cast a menacing shadow over Minerva from top to toe. She didn't manage to make out much more than a pair of dark, glinting eyes and a head of equally dark, shaggy hair—and oddly, what appeared to be a man's red silk dressing gown—before he was tilting in her direction, his massive arms spreading wide to brace himself.

In sheer panic and having no wish to become like a heroine in those dreadful gothic novels Lady Blundersmith had secretly enjoyed (the hypocrite), she pushed at the figure with all of her strength.

Two huge pawlike hands wrapped around hers, holding tight, and for a moment she feared he meant to take her with him out the window. Death by defenestration was not at all how Minerva had envisioned her life ending. The Leighton twins weren't involved, for one—unless this was yet another one of their pranks gone very, very awry.

She screamed in terror, for that was what one did when plummeting from old Norman keeps with strange men, and tried in vain to jerk her hands away as clothing ripped and her feet left the floor.

It took no more than a blink of an eye for her to realize that she wasn't falling forward, but rather backward, and just another blink before she was slamming into the floorboards, the wind knocked out of her body at the impact. One last blink, and the intruder landed on top of her, whacking the rest of her breath from her lungs.

Twice in two years! How was it possible that she'd ended up squashed like a bug under someone twice in two years! Granted, the intruder was not Lady B's size (that is, the size of HMS *Victory*), but he was no butterfly either. He was the approximate weight of a blacksmith's anvil, and just as immovable.

And his hands had landed in as rude a place as possible upon her anatomy. If he had expected to find some padding there to cushion his fall, he was out of luck, for her chest had all the variation in landscape of East Anglia. But it was also rather exposed since she'd shucked her dressing gown and loosed all of her buttons earlier, thinking herself quite safe from molestation in her own room. All of the tussling about hadn't helped either, and the ripping noises she'd heard as she fell must have been the rest of her bodice.

He was fondling her naked breasts.

Even Arthur had never gotten so far.

She would have screamed again had he not squashed all of the air from her lungs. She brought her knee up, just as her father had taught her, and aimed for the seat of his masculinity. He shifted to the right just in time, and her knee only managed to catch at his hip. His balance was thrown off by the blow, however, and he moved his hands from her breasts to the floorboards on either side of her head to brace himself.

Her breasts, at least, thought this a much better arrangement.

"Oi!" the man said, indignant, warm breath gushing over her forehead, eyes flashing with indignation. "No need for *that*, madam!"

She tried kneeing him again but only succeeded in causing him to collapse even more fully across her chest. He was hot as a furnace—unnaturally so, as if he were fevered, though she hardly made a habit out of taking the temperature of men's bodies. And he smelled strongly of leather, bay rum, something almost medicinal—spirits, most likely—and a fair bit of mannish sweat.

Ugh.

She began to struggle in earnest, and so did he, although he didn't seem in any particular hurry to molest her again. In fact, she couldn't figure out what he was doing with all of the tugging and grunting on his end, but he did seem to be going out of his way *not* to touch her, despite the fact that they were hopelessly tangled together. "Would you please remove yourself!" she finally managed to breathe out once his bulk shifted from her chest.

"I am *trying*, madam," the man growled. "But my banyan is stuck beneath your bony arse!"

She gasped in outrage and shoved at his shoulders before she gave in to the urge to claw out his eyes, as she so desperately wanted to do. He reared back, as if reading her desire to maim, and the moonlight finally revealed his face. A crooked, bladelike nose that had been broken one too many times. A broad forehead hidden beneath a messy fringe of brownish curls. Hawklike, rough-hewn features more startling than truly handsome. Full, mobile lips so at odds with the rest of his stark angles. And those eyes. Oh, she remembered those eyes. She'd seen them just hours before in duplicate, gazing up at her with false contrition amid piles of dead amphibians.

Though he looked a bit changed from the man she recalled from two Novembers ago—too thin, too pale, nearly a shadow of that bear of a man who'd brawled and cursed his way across the Duke of Montford's ballroom— there was no doubt in her mind that she was squashed beneath Lord Marlowe.

She'd only had to *think* of the devil, it seemed, for him to drop out of the heavens—and onto her bosom.

"You!" she breathed.

His craggy, bushy-eyed brow furrowed. "Me?"

Clearly he had no recollection of her. And why should he? He'd doubtless been in his cups that night, if not concussed from the Marquess of Manwaring's coshing, and would never remember the wallflower he'd inadvertently caused Lady Blundersmith to faint upon, even though she'd told him how to stop his bloody nose.

She had half a mind to remind him, but before she could

get another word out, the door to her room swung open, and half the school's staff—including the baldpated Fräulein Schmidt, wielding a candlestick—burst through the room.

Minerva glanced between the gathering, gasping throng—Fräulein Schmidt was starting to smirk, the cow—to the half-dressed viscount hovering above her, and then on to her exposed bosom, and groaned.

She couldn't even begin to fathom why the viscount was climbing the walls of West Barming in a red dressing gown at three in the morning, but she knew without a doubt that it meant trouble.

This was *not* going to end well.

CHAPTER TWO

In Which Our Hero Rescues Damsels in Distress

AFTER HAVING AT LONG LAST wrangled the feral creatures he called his daughters into the carriage and escaped past the front gates of West Barming School for Recalcitrant Young Ladies—an establishment that had all the grim allure of Fleet Prison—Evelyn Leighton, Viscount Marlowe, thought he was at a safe enough distance to make one final grand gesture. He cracked the window and leaned out to shield his actions from his daughters—who, God forbid, should pick up any more of his bad habits—and gave those cold, bleak Norman walls the good old-fashioned two-fingered salute they deserved.

Newcomb chose at that moment to swerve around some imagined obstruction, nearly tossing him from the carriage window and into the muddy lane. There was no shielding the girls from the litany of curses startled from his lips as he clutched at the window frame for dear life. After the night's—morning's?—excitement, he hadn't much strength left, and Newcomb, the shifty bastard, had to know this.

Montford's head coachman had been gently bullied into his current assignment by the duke, since nearly all of Marlowe's own malingering staff had deserted his employ during his protracted illness. The overbearing duke always turned into a clucking mother hen when one of his friends fell ill, so Montford had thus seized the first opportunity he could to set Newcomb upon him, ostensibly to see to it that Marlowe did not get himself killed on his journey. But Newcomb, an ex-prizefighting Liverpudlian, was hardly an exemplar of deferential servitude. The bastard was taking every opportunity to remind Marlowe of how little he wanted to be here, in the arse end of Kent, on this fool's errand.

Well, Newcomb could bloody well join the club. It wasn't as if Marlowe wanted to be here either, in a region of the country that was perilously near the family seat and his thrice-damned sire. He was hardly in any fit state to be out of bed at all, but he was damned if he was going to let his children molder and rot for one moment longer in that ludicrous excuse for a school. And after the morning he'd had dealing with the headmistress and her staff, it seemed his haste had been justified. Frigid, parochial beast of a bureaucrat! He'd had to invoke his damned title before she'd even let him see his own daughters.

He was still working out what the bald Teutonic woman sneering in the shadows had to do with anything, but the whole thing smelled a bit too much like Bedlam for his taste.

He himself could admit to impaired judgment to think it a good idea to climb into that woman's open window last night—on the top floor, no less, of that extremely *tall* old Norman keep. But his instinct to sneak inside and kidnap the twins under the cover of night had been the right one, judging from the trouble it had been to extract them from the school's clutches in the light of day. He'd make no apologies for his actions, as ill conceived as they'd been.

He'd been chastised enough by that hellcat who'd greeted him. He scowled down at his punctured, bruised, and ink-stained hands. She'd tried to stab him to death with a quill, not to mention push him out of her window. Her *attic* window. She could have killed him had she weighed more than six stone and had all the fighting strength of a guppy. But she'd been tenacious in her quest to knee him in the family seat, he'd give her that. He had the bruised hips to prove it.

He rubbed at said bruises and finally turned his full attention to his girls. They sat on the seat opposite him, their matching sets of brown eyes fixed on him with an intensity that made him squirm.

So, no warm embraces yet, if ever again.

"What?" he grumbled.

Laura just sniffed at him, crossed her little arms over her chest, and turned her head toward the window in a snit. He would have blamed her proclivity to sulk on his late, unlamented wife, Caroline, but alas, the behavior was pure Leighton. His own twin brother, Evander, had been the undisputed master. Marlowe himself was not too shabby at it either, though from an early age he'd learned to do it behind closed doors, away from the taunts and threats of his family. Evander, that sly fox, had somehow always been able to evade those deprecations—had always, in fact, been able to avert all the attention and blame in *his* direction when anything went pear-shaped.

Not that he was comparing Laura to his brother—also late and *very* unlamented. But sometimes it was so hard.

So hard to look at Laura and Bea both, and not see himself and Evander as they were at that age. The two of them had been so happy then . . . well, as happy as one could be with the Earl of Barming for a father.

And Bea, who may have looked like him but was so much like her mother at that age that it hurt—so brash and brave and *bright*—just deepened her scowl, knocking him out of his head once more.

Definitely no warm embraces.

"How *could* you, Papa?" she cried, sounding supremely

disappointed in him.

"*What?*" he repeated. What had he done now? Had they *not* wanted him to rescue them from that armpit of a school?

"How could you send us to such a dreadful place?"

Ah. So that was the problem. He crossed his arms like Laura and mimicked Bea's disgruntled expression. "That was your grandfather's work, Bea, not mine."

She sniffed, unconvinced. "He said you knew. He said you *wanted* us gone."

That cruel, manipulative old liar, banishing his own flesh and blood to the blind cheeks of his holdings and then blaming Marlowe for it. Oh, when he next saw his sire, there was going to be hell to pay, his vow not to rise to the earl's bait be damned. "I was too sick to know my arse from my elbow, Bea, you know that. Didn't even know he'd sent you here until a few days ago." He cocked his eyebrow. "Or the *reason* he'd sent you here."

Bea and Laura both had the good sense to squirm in their seats at the mention of their transgressions while guests at Montford's London palace.

"It was all Antonia and Ardyce's idea," Bea declared firmly.

"I'll bet it was." The younger two Honeywell chits were hellions of the first order (unsurprising, considering their older sister was the impetuous Astrid Honeywell, now the Duchess of Montford, who had beguiled the normally straight-laced duke into matrimony through some alchemy of mischief and misadventure Marlowe had yet to understand), but Marlowe knew his girls only too well to think them completely blameless. Having the four children tossed together had been begging for trouble. He'd made the mistake of doing so a few years ago when the duchess's sisters had first come to London. When the nurseries of Montford's London house had begun to resemble 1789 France, however, Marlowe had thought it best to keep his daughters as far afield from the Honeywells as possible.

But he had not given this bit of sage wisdom to his older sister Elaine, Countess of Brinderley, who, unable to cope with the twins *and* her own five (or was it sixteen now?) children, had shipped the twins off to Montford's at some point during Marlowe's illness. Marlowe had not discovered this until he'd come out of his delirium enough for Dr. Lucas to decide he was not going to cock up his toes.

By then it was too late.

Weeks too late. Barming had already "intervened," and not even Montford had been able to fight off his claim. Marlowe doubted the duke had even wanted to after what the twins had done to his gardens.

"You're lucky no one was injured or killed. What were the two of you thinking? I expect you've learned your lesson, stuck in that dreadful place," he said.

Laura just huffed out another breath and continued to glare out the window. Bea continued to look a bit contrite, which was a start, at least.

"We were there for Christmas, Papa! Christmas!" Bea said mournfully, her eyes wide and pleading and just begging for his forgiveness. His anger over their antics, half-hearted at best to start with, began to fizzle quickly. He'd been too worried about them to muster up much outrage. And they'd been punished enough, God knew, in their exile.

He'd never been able to resist Bea's puppy eyes—or Laura's for that matter, though it had been an age since Laura had looked at him like that. She barely looked at him at all these days, and he was beginning to wonder if it were she, and not Bea, who would give him the most trouble when she was older.

It was always the quiet ones.

But just the thought of that—his twins *older*, of *marriageable* age—was nearly enough to send him swooning back to his sickbed.

"You did almost succeed in burning down London," he

pointed out, for though he wasn't cross with them, he was prepared to give them an extremely hard time about their bad behavior for the foreseeable future.

Bea immediately began to negotiate. "It was one *small* building—"

"Two," he corrected. "The groundskeeper's cottage and the greenhouse." Both of which had been built by Sir Christopher Wren . . . but Marlowe doubted a string of short-lived governesses and West Barming School for Recalcitrant Young Ladies had equipped the twins with an appreciation for fine architecture.

"And it wasn't as if the duke will miss it, as he never used it anyway—"

"Not the point, and there were *two* buildings." He thought it rather important to stress that. "And I'm sure the groundskeeper missed his home. That you burned down. With Chinese rockets. On a dare. With *Honeywells*."

"Ugh. *Christmas!*" Bea reiterated. "With no one for company but Fräulein Schmidt and Miss Jones. It was dreadful!"

Laura nodded her agreement, the first sign of life he'd seen from her since they'd left the school. She held out her hands, which were covered by a rather poorly made pair of chartreuse-colored woolen mittens. Beatrice wore a matching pair in canary yellow.

Well, he said *matching*. The stitchwork was as appalling as the color choices.

Had they been forced to make their own clothing? Was that what they were implying? Had the earl sent his precious babies to a glorified workhouse? Oh, good God, he knew it had been bad, but not *that* bad.

The memory of that hairless woman kept flashing through his mind. He'd begun to write it off as a fever dream, *hoping* it was a fever dream, because he really, *really* didn't want to have to call out his own father.

Well, he did. He'd always wanted to call out the old Tory pig, but that was beside the point. He was *not* a violent man. Aside from his war record. And all the dueling. And the brawling he'd done all through school. *And* the notorious and surprisingly sticky fight he'd had with Sebastian just two Novembers ago at Montford's ball. Though in his defense, the latter had just been a ploy to get Sherry to come to his senses and admit he was in love with Katherine.

Never let it be said that he wouldn't suffer utter social humiliation—and a broken nose—for the sake of his best mate's happiness.

But he was absolutely not willing to hold against himself the ridiculous kerfuffle that had landed him on his deathbed for the last four months. It was absolutely *not* his fault some angry bastard had taken offense when Marlowe, walking the streets alone after a night in his favorite gambling hell—and minding his own bloody business, thank you very much—had tried to stop the man from picking his pockets with a fist to his jaw. It wasn't *his* fault the bastard had then knifed him in the back, stolen his valuables, and thrown him into the Thames. It was the Thames's fault. That polluted cesspool had given him a fever. And the knife wound had certainly not helped.

Well, perhaps he needed to reassess his life choices a bit, since even he could see a worrying trend developing.

Whatever the case, it would be, alas, some time before he was well enough to kill his father for sending his children to live in a workhouse with baldpated bedlamites. While he was over the worst of the fever, it had left him about as capable as a kitten. He still couldn't quite work out how he'd managed to scale the side of the school—or precisely why he'd thought it such an excellent idea last night. There had admittedly been several more sensible points of access on ground level.

Perhaps the fever was returning after all.

"Miss Jones *did* give us the mittens," Bea allowed, jerking him back to the present. Oh yes, the mittens. "It was the only redeeming part of the holiday. And they are hideous."

"It's the gesture that matters, Bea," he reminded her, as a good father was supposed to do—or so he'd been told. Many times. By Elaine, who God knew had enough children of her own to know what she was talking about.

Bea rolled her eyes as if that were obvious. "Well, Fräulein Schmidt made us listen to sermons all Christmas day. In *German*."

The pieces suddenly slotted into place in his fevered head. The German woman. Sermons. His daughters. That bald, bald head.

Oh, dear Lord.

"Is that why you shaved that poor woman's head?" he asked.

Bea exchanged a wary glance with her sister, no doubt telepathically attempting to get their stories straight. He used to do that with Evander all the time when they were young enough to still like each other, so he was on to their scheme.

"She made us eat soap whenever we cursed," Bea said.

So, quite a lot of soap, then.

"She rapped our knuckles with a cane whenever we were naughty," she continued.

Not acceptable. The soap was one thing—laying hands upon his children was quite another. Their knuckles had to be black and blue underneath those terrible mittens, since the twins were perpetually doing something wrong.

He hoped he never ran across the bald woman again, for he was afraid he might have to return the favor. With his fists. Not that he was a proponent of hitting women or anything so incredibly callow. But he was still not quite sure that creature *was* a woman.

He braced himself for their next complaint, dreading tales of further corporal punishment. He still had nightmares of the lashes and beatings he'd received in his childhood at the hands of both his father and those bumbrushers at

Harrow. They'd nearly succeeded in breaking his spirit, and if he'd damned his girls to a similar fate while he was too sick to keep them safe, he'd never forgive himself.

"*And* she was blackmailing Miss Jones," Bea finished.

Marlowe's eyes, clenched shut in preparation for the next blow, shot open in surprise. This was an unexpected and rather fascinating development. Who knew West Barming School for Recalcitrant Young Ladies was such a hornet's nest of intrigue? "Blackmail?"

"We like Miss Jones," Bea said. "She's not very good at knitting, but she's nice to us. Unless we've done something naughty. Then she gets a bit piqued. But not in a mean way. *She* never rapped our knuckles."

Marlowe rather liked the sound of this Miss Jones, despite the mittens.

"Why was the fräulein blackmailing her?"

Bea shrugged. "Miss Jones likes naughty poems. She has a secret stash of Christopher Essex books under her mattress, and the fräulein found it and threatened to tell the headmistress about it."

He thought it best not to inquire exactly how the twins knew about this stash. But . . . "You know who Christopher Essex is?"

Both twins rolled their eyes in tandem, as if Marlowe were as thick as treacle.

"Of course, Papa. Who doesn't?" Bea said in exasperation.

He wanted to know just when the devil his nine-year-old twins had metamorphosed into cheeky thirteen-year-old girls. Surely he'd not been on his deathbed for that long. He could only pray they hadn't gotten their paws on *The Hedonist*. And—if they had—that they didn't understand any of the double entendres in it.

"Not that we've read any. Poetry is hideously boring," Bea continued.

Marlowe didn't know whether to be relieved or insulted.

He'd settle for relieved. He didn't fancy having to explain (i.e. lie convincingly about) what a dew-kissed woman's secret bower symbolized. It was just too early in the day.

"So you shaved the fräulein's head because she was blackmailing this Miss Jones for reading poetry?" he prompted, endeavoring to stay on a safe-ish subject.

"Yes?" Bea said a bit uncertainly.

Well, never let it be said his twins were not humanitarians. But he did not praise them for their actions. Even he knew this would be a terrible idea. Though he wanted to. Very much. He settled on a noncommittal grunt.

"Well, all of that bother is over now," he said. "No more blackmailing Huns or knuckle rapping." Just as long as the twins didn't set fire to Parliament next. He wouldn't exactly be shocked by that development, but he was fairly certain that even *he* would not be able to rescue them from the wrath of the British government.

Bea seemed about to give up their ridiculous verbal wrangling and give him the hug he'd been waiting for all morning, but Laura nudged her sister in the shins—well, *kicked*, to be more precise—and sent her a weighted glare.

Bea's scowl quickly resettled upon her brow, and her arms crossed again. "We're not forgiving you so easily, Papa," she said scoldingly.

When the devil had they turned the tables on him so completely? Why was *he* being chastised like a child when *they* were the ones who had committed arson?

"Oh, and what else have I done to incur your wrath, brat?" he demanded.

"You got poor Miss Jones sacked," Bea said, as if this, like every other thing they'd spoken about, should have been perfectly obvious to him.

"What are you on about?"

"Miss *Jones*, Papa," Bea replied exasperatedly. "We heard the headmistress yelling at her . . . when we were absolutely *not* listening at the door to her office . . . and we heard all about what you did to her."

He was totally at sea on this one, and it must have shown, because Laura just rolled her eyes at him again and huffed.

"Papa! You were found *in fragrant delicious* with her!" Bea cried, outraged he didn't understand what she was trying to say.

He still didn't.

Until he suddenly did. Oh. *Oh*, so the little hellcat from last night was the infamous Miss Jones of the chartreuse mittens. "Ah. *In flagrante delicto*," he said. God, he hoped that they didn't understand what *that* one truly meant.

"That's what I said," Bea muttered back. "They found you *on top of her*, Papa."

"I was trying to sneak in and find you lot. I . . . er, fell on her by accident?" He cringed. Just hearing himself say that out loud sounded absurd. Of course the headmistress—and half the school, who'd gathered outside Miss Jones's bedroom—would have believed the worst.

"Well, the headmistress thought Miss Jones was your fancy woman."

He could feel his cheeks grow warm with a blush, his skin crawling with the wrongness of this conversation. Bea was nine. Nine! She was not supposed to know about fancy women, not until she was at least a hundred years old. None of Elaine's nauseatingly perfect children did. How had he gone so wrong with the twins?

"And then Fräulein Schmidt told the headmistress about the books, hateful old bat," Bea continued. "So the headmistress sacked Miss Jones. And it's all your fault."

Marlowe huffed and crossed his arms defensively. "Probably the best thing to ever happen to her," he muttered. He'd not wish employment at West Barming on his worst enemy.

"But, Papa, Miss Jones is an *orphan*, and now thanks to you, she is a lewd woman without references. What is to become of her now?"

So they'd paid more attention to the German woman's sermons than they'd let on, apparently. "Why do you know anything at all about lewd women without references?" he demanded.

Another tandem eyeroll. "Papa, we've just spent three months in a school for *recalcitrant girls*. All we *learned* was what happens to lewd women. Now Miss Jones is going to burn in hellfire, no thanks to you, Papa."

Oh, yes, he was definitely going to murder his father.

After he had Montford and his ducal influence raze the School for Recalcitrant Young Ladies to the ground.

"No one's going to burn in hellfire, brat," he growled. "Especially your Miss Jones, who is, by the way, *not* a lewd woman."

Definitely not. He rubbed at his bruised hips and banged-up hands and thought about those outraged gray eyes, that long, prim braid of sable hair, those pursed lips and sneering button nose, and that flat, unspectacular chest beneath the ripped muslin gown. No one would ever mistake her for a lewd woman. A hissing, spitting she-kitten with claws, but not a lewd woman.

"Miss Jones will land on her feet; don't you worry about her," he muttered.

Bea looked somewhat appeased by his platitude—enough, at least, to leave off her scold. He mentally breathed a sigh of relief, though those eye-searing mittens now seemed to be staring back at him accusingly from the twins' laps.

He did not squirm in his seat from his guilt. Much. But he did nearly leap to his feet despite the carriage's low roof when Laura shouted in surprise and mashed her face up to the window. "It's Miss Jones!" she cried. It was more life than he'd seen from her all morning.

Bea scrambled over the seat and tussled with her sister for a view out the window. Their argument ceased abruptly as both girls gasped, their eyes going wide at whatever they'd witnessed.

"What is it?" he demanded, reluctantly moving toward the window as well.

The pair turned to him, their hands on their flushed cheeks, half-horrified, half-amused expressions on their faces. It was the same look they wore whenever they'd done something hilarious but very, very naughty.

"I think the carriage startled her so much she jumped into a ditch," Bea whispered.

Newcomb *was* rather cracking along.

"We must turn back for her, Father," Bea said with those puppy eyes of hers.

Ugh. The last thing he wanted to do was play knight in shining armor. Though if Newcomb had run the creature into a ditch, he supposed it was rather on his head to see if she were still alive.

It took him rapping on the roof five times before Newcomb deigned to even listen to his request. Only with a very insolent groan and something mumbled under his breath about his wife wanting him home for the evening meal did Newcomb finally stop the carriage and turn around.

The only indication that someone had once been in the lane was an abandoned portmanteau and half-empty carpetbag perched on the cusp of a ditch. Marlowe bid his daughters to stay after assuring them he would rescue their teacher and stepped out of the carriage to investigate.

Something creaked under his bootheel, and he looked down to find a very familiar-looking book in the mud. A volume of sonnets—*Christopher Essex* sonnets. It must have fallen from the eviscerated carpetbag he spied not too far away, along with a trail of books leading into the ditch. He bent down and retrieved the book, shaking the mud off as best he could.

Midway through the action, however, he froze as the voice he remembered from the previous night drifted up from the ditch.

"Bloody buggering sheep-shagging bollocks."

Ooh. How delightfully filthy.

He walked to the edge and peered down at Miss Jones, crouched over a growing pile of books, soaked through top to toe in muddy rainwater and looking ready to spit fire. "If I ever see that bloody son of a devil-spawned donkey, I swear I'll scoop out his eyeballs with a meat hook."

Something in Marlowe's chest dropped to China and back at the sight—and sound—before him. It seemed that he'd been mistaken entirely in his assessment of Miss Jones. The evening before, it had been too dark for him to appreciate what he'd stumbled upon. And what he'd stumbled upon was . . . delightful. Either his fever was making him hallucinate, or he was in the presence of an actual fey creature—piskie or elf, or perhaps even a selkie, what with that pelt of sable peeking out from beneath her sodden bonnet.

Miss Jones may have been a small, pale little thing beneath all that tatty muslin and mud, but that was all that was small about her. This one, with her storm-cloud eyes flashing like lightning and alabaster skin, had an adamantine spine and the temper of a Greek god, of that he had no doubt.

And the *mouth* on her. Where the devil had a prim, proper schoolteacher learned such a delightfully creative vocabulary? He would have asked her, if he thought she wouldn't attempt to claw his eyes out. As she crouched over her books in the mud, she wore the precise look Monty had worn at Harrow right before he'd punched out Marlowe's back molars. That had been the start of a beautiful friendship, but Marlowe didn't really have any more molars to spare (though he had a feeling that this one would focus her attentions below the belt, should they come to blows. And not in a fun way).

He was suddenly very glad he'd had Newcomb turn back. And that the carriage had not trampled her. He could already tell that Miss Jones was anything but boring, and he'd been nothing but bored for years. Instead of trying to relieve his ennui in every pit of vice and sin from London to Paris, perhaps he should have been keeping company with spinster schoolteachers in the arse end of Kent. A bit counterintuitive, it seemed to him, but then the best things in life usually were.

He began his descent, a clever plan formulating in his mind.

CHAPTER THREE

In Which A Ditch Attempts To Eat Our Heroine

MINERVA WIPED HER DRIPPING FACE with the back of her sleeve, the only place on her person not covered in muck, and glared at the rear end of the oversize carriage careening down the lane and out of her life. The viscount, no doubt. No one else in this godforsaken backwater would be driving in something so grand and in such a disreputable manner. He'd probably hired a highwayman for a driver just for the bloody hell of it.

She cursed with all the foul language her late father had used when he thought she couldn't hear him and gave the carriage a two-fingered salute—also a remnant of her father's unintentional influence. She didn't even care if the girls saw her . . . well, not much, anyway. Perhaps a little.

Fine, more than a little. *They* didn't deserve her wrath. *They* hadn't fallen on her or groped her bosom. *They* hadn't sacked her and thrown her out on the coldest, wettest day this month. *They* hadn't run her into a ditch and strewn all of her belongings in Kentish sludge so thick and stubborn it might well have been sentient.

She stared down mournfully at her mud-covered feet, where her entire collection of Mr. Essex's works lay fallen in the muck like wounded soldiers on the battlefield. The old carpetbag she'd used to transport them had not stood a chance against the weather or her final, inelegant blunder into the ditch.

She would not cry. Even though those books were the only reason she was able to carry on some days. And if *that* wasn't the most depressing thought she'd had all day, she didn't know what was.

She crouched down, her boots squelching alarmingly in the mud, and began to gather up the volumes. She wouldn't cry, damn it, but she was a sailor's daughter, and she'd damn well put her unique education to good use, especially since there was no one around for miles to disapprove.

"Bloody buggering sheep-shagging bollocks," she muttered as she wiped off a blob of filth from the spine of *The Hedonist*. "If I ever see that bloody son of a devil-spawned donkey, I swear I'll scoop out his eyeballs with a meat hook."

She felt better already.

"That sounds painful. But creative," a deep baritone drawled above her.

Startled, she jerked backward, but her feet refused to move from the mud's stranglehold. Instead, she fell on her arse in the mire, clutching the volume to her bosom. She peered in front of her at a pair of giant feet clad in muddy hessians, and her startlement began to transform into something else. She knew those boots from the previous night's misadventure.

Her gaze rose over a pair of overlarge buckskins precariously cinched around a narrow waist, a billowing lawn shirt half tucked into said buckskins, and a wrinkled cravat with a suspicious, mustard-colored stain near the collar, all wrapped up in the dreadfully garish red Chinese silk banyan that was sure to give her nightmares for years to come.

Her gaze finally settled above the distracting muddle of his attire, onto a gaunt face with a stubborn, stubble-coated jaw and deep, dark, bruiselike marks ringing tired eyes. The man had either been in a tavern brawl or was in desperate need of a decent night's sleep. With someone like the Viscount Marlowe, however, it was probably both.

And it *was* the Viscount Marlowe, even if, in the light of day, he barely resembled her shadowy attacker from last night, or the bloated, drunken specimen she'd encountered at the Montford Ball two Novembers ago—a man who had been living testimony as to why she could almost sympathize with the Jacobin cause to eradicate the aristocracy altogether. No, this man, rail-thin and pale, was a different beast altogether.

Though she'd recognize the eyes anywhere. And that battered Roman nose. It was impertinently prominent. Poor Beatrice had inherited both, along with his shaggy mahogany mane and devilish brow. Luciferian was not a good look on a little girl, but on the viscount . . .

Well, she refused to ever call him an attractive man for so many varied reasons—one of them being her present circumstances, for which he was entirely accountable. And if he'd stopped the carriage to confront her over the rude hand gesture she may or may not have made after being bullied into a ditch by his careless driver, she'd damn well stand her ground.

She really had no other recourse, for she was sunk into the mud past her ankles. Running away was literally not an option.

She glanced behind him to the top of the ditch, where the carriage had circled back. She'd not heard its approach at all, though she supposed that incendiary rage had a way of limiting one's senses. The twins' heads poked out of an open window, and they observed every movement she made with mischievous grins. They waved at her. She waved back half-heartedly before turning her attention back to the viscount, who was suddenly crouching in front of her and gathering up the books himself. The tops of his hands were covered in ink stains and angry red welts.

Which she refused to feel guilty for inflicting. Especially when he was pawing at her most private possessions. She reached for the books he'd gathered before he could read the titles, but she could tell she was far too late for that from the unholy gleam in his eyes. His lips quirked into what was probably the singlemost disconcerting smile she'd ever seen, all blindingly white teeth, sharp incisors, and something almost . . . wild. Definitely uncivilized. He truly looked like the devil. Or perhaps the devil's creature: vulpine and predatory.

Not attractive at all.

"You're a Misstopher!" he cried, sounding far too delighted.

"What?" she said flatly, her pulse spiking.

"A Misstopher," he insisted. She knew very well what a Misstopher was, and she refused to be embarrassed to be called one.

Even though she was. Horribly embarrassed. Judging from the warmth she felt in her cheeks, she was halfway to scarlet by now.

She scrambled to collect the rest of her books before things could get any worse—though she didn't see how. She didn't even dare to meet his eye.

He reached behind him and retrieved a rather limp edition of *The Italian Poem* and attempted to shake off some of the excess mud. A blot of it landed on her cheek. He didn't appear to notice. Nor did he seem to notice the scowl she settled on him.

"A Misstopher is a young lady obsessed with Christopher Essex," he persisted, as if she needed the clarification.

"Obsessed?" She jerked the book from his hand and slapped it on the top of her pile. "Who's obsessed? I'm not obsessed. That's utterly ridiculous." She didn't sound defensive at all.

He arched a skeptical brow as he glanced at the ruined volumes stacked precariously high in her arms.

"And I am *not* a young lady," she said as haughtily as she could muster.

"You look young to me," he countered, eyeing her from top to toe. She flushed even further under the scrutiny. "Seventeen? Eighteen?"

"Impertinent," she snapped. "I'm seven and twenty."

His brow furrowed. "You don't look seven and twenty to me. Although I don't know what seven and twenty is supposed to look like."

"It's supposed to look like me," she gritted out.

He studied her for a moment longer—it felt like an eternity to her—then finally shook his head and leaned back on his haunches. "No, no, it is impossible you are seven and twenty . . ."

"I know my own age, sirrah!"

"Unless you are a changeling. You have that look about you."

"Look? What look?"

He narrowed his eyes at her in a contemplative manner. "The look of the fey. All pale and small." He waved his hand in the general direction of her face. "It's either that or malnourishment."

She was very sure her head would explode if he continued talking in such a vexing manner. "I can't believe I'm having this conversation. Why is this happening to me?" she muttered, banging her forehead on her pile of Essex.

"Ah, yes, what *are* you doing on the road in this dreadful weather? My driver almost trampled you, I'll have you know."

"I am well aware," she said, standing up with as much poise as she could while clutching a mountain of books, her boots shackled to the mud. He stood with her and grabbed hold of her arm when she began to list backward. When she glared up at him for the further impertinence, the words froze in her throat, for she had not realized quite how tall he was until now—taller than Arthur or even

Inigo. It was an actual strain to her neck to meet his eyes.

And he was standing much too close to her, the collection of Essex the only thing separating their bodies other than the mud.

Before she could gather her careening thoughts and demand her release, he let go of her forearm. But the reprieve was short-lived, as he abruptly wrapped both of his enormous hands around her shoulders. She squeaked in response.

"What are you . . ." she began, sounding breathless and a bit too much like a swooning Misstopher for her taste.

Her protest was cut short by another embarrassing squeak as he lifted her off the ground, her boots making the rudest sound imaginable as they were released from their muddy prison. He carried her out of the ditch by the upper arms as if she weighed nothing, her legs dangling like a rag doll, and deposited her in a relatively mudless patch of grass next to her abandoned portmanteau and disemboweled carpetbag.

The whole ordeal was over before she could decide how she felt about it. On the one hand, she was very glad she was no longer in danger of drowning in mud that was determined to eat her. On the other hand, she was no damsel in distress, and the last thing she wanted was to feel indebted to the viscount.

She wouldn't have even *been* in the ditch if not for him.

"I beg your pardon?" he said, looking startled.

She'd said that last bit out loud, hadn't she? "You heard me. And what do you mean, why am I out here in the rain? You know perfectly well why."

The viscount's brow furrowed, as if he were truly perplexed. "You've lost me, Miss Johnson."

"Miss *Jones*, you . . . you . . ."

"Devil-spawned donkey?" Either he really was a lackwit, or he was toying with her. She had a sinking feeling it was the latter, especially when she noticed the corners of his mouth twitching, as if he were fighting back laughter.

Devil-spawned donkey indeed.

She shoved the stack of books in his arms and unbuckled the straps of her portmanteau. She reached inside the already overstuffed compartment and pulled out her third best dress to make room for the books. She'd only have two gowns left to her name, but this one—a scratchy black crepe disaster left over from when she'd been mourning her father—was ready for the dustbin anyway. She balled it up angrily and tossed it toward the ditch with as much rage behind it as she could muster. Which was quite a lot.

The wind caught it, and it floated gently to the earth about two feet away from where she stood.

She growled in fury, plodded over to the dress, and threw it again.

As if on cue, the wind picked up abruptly and whipped the billowing skirt back in her face and around her neck. She struggled for several fruitless moments before she finally managed to untangle herself from the fabric. She decided to abandon her initial plan, since the wind seemed quite set against her dramatic gesture, and threw the gown straight down at her feet. She stomped on it until it was dead and buried under a layer of fragrant mud. Then she stomped on it some more.

It was surprisingly cathartic.

Chest heaving and temples throbbing with the beginnings of a spectacular headache, she turned back to the viscount, daring him with her eyes to say one more ludicrous thing. Just one thing, and she was more than willing to stomp on him next, his title be damned.

She *may* have inherited her father's temper, along with his vocabulary.

The viscount just stared at her with wide eyes and a slack jaw, the stack of books cradled protectively against his breast as if to shield them from her wrath.

"That was . . ." He broke off and swallowed, a strange,

feverish flush anointing his cheekbones. "That was brilliant. Absolutely brilliant. I think you'll do quite nicely." Then he broke into another grin—that shining, unnerving baring of his teeth that sent chills down her arms and a fire through her belly.

She glanced away before she went blind from such an unseemly display and stalked back to the portmanteau.

"I have no idea what you're talking about," she muttered. She shifted half the books from his arms and began stuffing them inside. They were going to make an absolute mess out of everything else she owned, but she'd just have to sort it out later. Good poetry was far more important than clean stockings.

Murdering her third best dress had taken most of the fight out of her. Her anger over her whole hopeless situation had fizzled away enough to make room for her rising despair. She'd have to make it to the village before the mail coach to London came. She couldn't afford to miss it—could barely afford the fare to London, where she could only hope Inigo would be willing to help her. She hated having to rely on his charity yet again, but she had no other recourse.

His offer of marriage was sounding better by the minute, though she knew she could never go through with it.

"Well, you're such a small human I just worry if you could hold your own against the little beasts," the viscount answered as he watched her pack, as if every move she made were absolutely fascinating.

She could feel her self-pity receding in the wake of the viscount's continued gibberish. She shook her head in disbelief. "Small *human?*" Who even talked like that?

He nudged her aside with his elbow and stuffed the rest of the books inside the trunk himself. When he straightened to his full, unnerving height again, she wrinkled her nose at the streaks of mud on his shirt and cravat. He didn't look like he even noticed—not that she expected a man wearing a dressing gown in public to give much of a damn about his toilette.

He was studying her too closely once more, and she wanted to punch him in the nose more than ever for the way those brown eyes made her blush. "You can't be more than four stone soaking wet. That's small," he finally said.

"I weigh more than four stone!" she scoffed.

"In those skirts, perhaps. But out of them, I'm not so sure."

"I am a lady, *sirrah*. How dare you speak of me without my skirts."

"But you said you weren't," he countered, looking baffled.

"I beg your pardon?"

"You said you weren't a lady not ten minutes ago."

"I said I was not young."

"Then you're an *old* lady?"

"Yes!" she cried. "No! Wait. Oh, God, what is *happening* right now?"

He looked at her despairingly, as if *she* were the lackwit. "I am attempting to hire you as my governess. But you won't allow me to finish a single train of thought," he replied.

She laughed a bit hysterically. "What?"

"Gov. Er. Ness. For the brats," he elucidated.

"I *must* be having a nightmare," she muttered.

"I almost didn't stop; you were such a pathetic sight down there in that ditch. I was not convinced from that sorry display that you could handle my girls. It would have been more merciful to leave you behind. The twins can be quite a handful."

She thought *that* was a bit of an understatement.

"But you have convinced me," the viscount continued. "You're a vicious little thing, aren't you? I think your claws will be sufficient to keep the brats in line."

She stared at him for a long, long time as she struggled

to come up with words to counter such brazen insolence.

"Do you even realize that you've insulted me? And who calls their own children such names?"

"I do. They love it."

"Demon-spawn? Hellions?"

His brow darkened. "They're terms of endearment, Miss Smith."

"Jones! Miss *Jones*. Miss Minerva Jones, who you just got sacked from her post after falling on her and *groping* her . . ."

"I was trying to regain my balance," he interrupted loftily.

"On my breasts?" She cringed at the volume of her voice, especially on that last word. She glanced toward the carriage to find the girls giggling their evil little heads off as they watched her. Even the driver, who had propped himself up against the side of the carriage to shamelessly eavesdrop on the proceedings, smirked at her.

The viscount's pale cheeks grew rosy, but she doubted it was from embarrassment at her *faux pas*. He looked more than ever as if he were trying not to laugh at her.

If he did . . . oh, if he did, she *would* punch him.

"It was dark?" he finally managed to strangle out. He didn't look contrite at all.

Unbelievable. "I was sacked with no references. The headmistress said I was a threat to the moral sanctity of the entire school. That I must have *tempted* you to fall through my attic window and onto my bosom."

He guffawed, unable to restrain himself any longer. She stalked in his direction, hands balled up, ready to deliver her blow. "My father was a navy captain. He taught me how to fisticuff," she bit out, closing the distance between them.

His eyes widened, and he actually shifted back a step or two. He raised his palms in surrender. "First of all, fisticuff is *not* a verb. Second of all, if you punched me like that, you'd break your thumb." Without warning, he took her hand and moved her thumb to the outside.

Damn it, she always got muddled on that point.

And he was still holding her hand. His own was big and warm and surprisingly rough for a pampered aristocrat.

It did *not* feel nice at all.

She jerked away. "I'm surprised you even know what a verb is," she muttered.

He scowled at her, as if she'd finally succeeded in ruffling his feathers. But she didn't feel bad for her scathing tongue. She was a *vicious creature*, after all.

"I suppose a *Misstopher* is allowed to feel superior about grammar," he drawled.

Ouch. He was surprisingly quick for a legendary wastrel. And tenacious.

"I *am* a grammarian. It is my job." She tried to end her retort there and then, but she found herself unable to hold her tongue now that the subject of her favorite poet had been broached once more. "And while Christopher Essex *is* a genius, the likes of which has not graced English letters since the time of the Bard, a grammarian he is not."

"What?" he strangled out, his expression wounded, though his eyes still danced with something that looked very much like glee.

"His verse plays fast and loose with the English language in ways that would appall Dr. Johnson. It is his greatest talent, as well as his most annoying . . . and why am I talking about this with you?"

"You used *fisticuff* as a *verb*," he said flatly.

"I stand by my use of that word," she stated haughtily, though she really, really didn't. It was just that he was so infuriating he seemed to render her incapable of proper speech.

"Miss Smith . . . Smythe?"

"Jones. That wasn't even close."

"Will you accept the position or not?"

She snorted. "You have got to be having me on."

His scowl metamorphosed into a smirk. "Oh, you'd know if I was having you on."

She was so gobsmacked by his effrontery that it took her a few moments to recover enough to speak. "Was that innuendo? Are you hurling *innuendo* at me now?" she cried, appalled. "And you want me to be a governess to your children? Tell me, Lord Marlowe, do you treat all females under your employ in such a libidinous manner? We are human beings, sirrah, not your playthings."

"Tell that to my last mistress. Though I rather think I was *her* plaything," he muttered, rubbing his backside for some reason.

She spluttered, unable to find words.

"And I should have known you were a bluestocking," he continued, immune to the vicious glare she sent his way.

"You make it sound like a bad thing," she retorted, crossing her arms over her chest in challenge. Perhaps she'd get to punch him after all.

He matched her stance and gave her what very much resembled a pout. "It is, Miss Jones. It means m'sister and the duchess will try to snatch you out from under me for their own brood. And I'll not have it."

"What are you even talking about?"

He rolled his eyes impatiently. "Governessing. I've been talking to you about governessing for the past four hours . . ."

"Half an hour *at most*."

"But you keep interrupting me to talk about dreadfully dull things like grammar and Dr. Johnson and *mistresses*."

What? "*You're* the one . . ."

"You'd be miserable with m'sister's bunch. I think there's eight of 'em now. Or eighteen." He shuddered. "She keeps breeding with Brinderley at a revolting rate. And the Duchess of Montford's sisters are even worse than the twins. I am near convinced that they were the ones to burn down that castle in Yorkshire, not Aunt Anabel's wig, but Monty refuses to listen."

He was, in a word, exhausting, and most of what he said made no sense whatsoever. Aunt Anabel's wig indeed. She had no idea what he was going on about. "Yet didn't your own daughters burn down Montford's property?"

He snorted. "Who do you think put them up to it? The Honeywells make excellent ale, but they really do belong in Bedlam."

Oh, *someone* belonged in Bedlam, and he was standing in front of her in a red dressing gown.

And she herself would indeed belong in a madhouse to even contemplate accepting the viscount's offer for one second. She would be insane to agree to play mother hen to the Leighton twins. The destruction they had wrought at Barming in their short tenure had been as impressive as it had been bloodcurdling—though the fräulein *had* rather deserved her fleecing and the headmistress that drawerful of rats. And that awful cook, who had served the charity girls table scraps and half-rotted meat, really had deserved the load of exploding cow manure in her oven. The whole school had to suffer the smell for a week, but it had been worth it.

But this—*this*—could never work. While the twins seemed to like her well enough, she doubted their goodwill would last forever. One day she would wake up, bald and naked, in a field full of cows with digestive problems. That wasn't even touching on the issue of having Lord Marlowe as an employer. He was without a doubt one of the most aggravating human beings she'd ever met.

"You called me a vicious little thing," she gritted out.

"I'll double your salary at Barmy."

She shut her eyes and refused to be swayed by filthy lucre. She was better than that. "You called me a *Misstopher!*" she hissed.

"A spade is a spade, Miss Jones. I'll triple it."

Well, that settled it. A lady had to eat. But she didn't have to be happy about it. She picked up her portmanteau and stalked toward the carriage as fast as the mud would allow. She didn't make it two steps, however, before the added weight from her sodden library made her nearly topple straight back into the ditch. Lord Marlowe tugged her upright by the collar of her damp redingote and snatched the portmanteau from her hands. He smirked victoriously at her one final time before bounding off toward the carriage.

She sighed and followed at what she hoped was a much more dignified gait, wondering just how much of a disaster this was going to be.

CHAPTER FOUR

In Which The Viscount Reveals His Poetic Prowess...Sort Of

JUST WHEN MARLOWE THOUGHT HE'D arrived back in London unscathed, he discovered Dr. Lucas lurking about the townhouse, no doubt waiting to scold him. This was *not* the happy homecoming he'd imagined. One moment, his housekeeper, Mrs. Chips, was giving Marlowe her usual taciturn greeting, and the next, the vision of salt-and-pepper whiskers and a judgmental frown was assaulting his eyeballs from the doorway to his library. He ducked behind a corner, out of the doctor's view, and glared down at Mrs. Chips.

She was, as usual, totally unruffled by his pique, from the top of her graying head to the tip of a nose that was as sharp edged and perpetually unimpressed with the world as the rest of her.

"He's been here since dawn, Your Lordship," she said in the same tone of voice she'd used when mold had once had the effrontery to invade her pantry. "It seems the duke told him of your trip."

"That traitor," he muttered. Montford, the meddler, had never been able to keep his gob shut when Marlowe needed him to.

And for some misplaced reason, Montford had a great

deal of faith in the medical profession. But then again, Monty had not had the dubious honor of witnessing the British Army's Medical Services at work during wartime. Even men with flesh wounds had rarely survived their stay in the medical tents on the Peninsula.

Marlowe had to grudgingly admit that Dr. Lucas was a cut above the rest in his profession, though. He'd yet to bring out the leeches.

Nothing would ever convince Marlowe that leeches had any place in a sickroom.

The sound of the twins clattering in the front door, followed by a suspicious crash and Miss Jones's shriek, rose up behind him. Mrs. Chips's left eye twitched, as it always did when the twins broke something, and Marlowe tried to hide his amusement, lest the woman finally decide she'd had enough and retire to Cornwall, as she'd often threatened.

He had to give old Chippers credit for holding on as long as she had. Marlowe had always had trouble retaining servants, and indeed, most of the current staff had fled en masse during his illness and the twins' reign of terror. Yet Mrs. Chips had soldiered on as she always had. He suspected she had a soft spot for the twins underneath that India rubber exterior—deep, *deep* underneath. For as much as the twins made Mrs. Chips's left eye twitch, they also tended on occasion to elicit a brief twinge of the lips that was a very close approximation to what someone might call a smile. Maybe. In the right light.

It was the same twinge Marlowe remembered from his own childhood, when Mrs. Chips had been employed in the earl's household. He and Elaine had often been the recipients of that same look. Mrs. Chips had always been too smart, though, to have been taken in by Evander's false charms or the earl's haughty posturing, which was the reason Marlowe had poached her for his own household after the twins were born.

Well, not the only reason. He'd enjoyed the look on his father's face when he'd learned of his best servant's defection. He suspected Mrs. Chips had enjoyed it too. Her contempt for the earl nearly matched Marlowe's own.

Mrs. Chips had been with him ever since, and the only explanation for that had to be a reluctant sentiment on her part. He didn't dare accuse her of such a thing to her face, however, since she'd have the kitchens serve him nothing but pea soup and mutton for a week, or claim the laundresses had "misplaced" all of his favorite banyans. She tended to take out her grievances on the household, and in that she was rather like the twins. Sometimes he wondered if Mrs. Chips had taught his daughters everything they knew about sabotage. Which was a great deal.

Something else shattered in the hallway behind him. Mrs. Chips's eyebrow twitched again.

"I hope that was nothing important," he murmured.

"It was a copy. They broke the original last year."

Ouch. "Well, don't despair, Chippers, I've brought a governess with me."

"It sounds like she has everything well in hand," Mrs. Chips said, deadpan, after another shriek from Miss Jones rent the air. Then with a heavy sigh and a final twitch, she whisked her way down the hall to defend the household honor, leaving Marlowe to face the firing squad alone.

Dr. Lucas was one of those rare people who could make Marlowe, a man with very little shame left, feel like a naughty infant with a single look. Marlowe blamed it on the doctor's lethal combination of lightning-blue eyes and facial hair: one mesmerized his patients, while the other made him seem like he knew what he was doing. In Lucas's case, that was more or less true (e.g. the lack of leeches in his medical bag, healing more patients than he killed, etcetera, etcetera). Though Dr. Lucas looked as if he wanted to stick Marlowe with a hundred leeches at the present moment.

Marlowe pretended not to notice the doctor's disapproving gaze as he strode briskly into the library, trying to project an aura of good health. It failed spectacularly.

"A week ago, you were on your deathbed, Lord Marlowe," Lucas chided. "Where you'll be again if you continue such foolhardy behavior. Your definition of convalescence leaves much to be desired." Then the wily bugger managed to maneuver himself close enough to feel Marlowe's brow and take his pulse before he could even attempt to evade his clutches.

Marlowe glared him off and retreated to the sideboard. He poured the doctor a dram of the Scotch whisky but stayed his hand before he poured himself the same. Excessive drinking had led him into his present fix, and he'd be damned if he let his daughters down again. Tea sounded like a much better idea, and he'd have Chippers fetch some for him just as soon as she rescued the household from the twins' incursion.

Tea. His illness had transformed him into his Great-Aunt Agnes.

The doctor didn't turn away the whisky, however, as the man was clearly not a fool. He threw it back in one go with barely a grimace, which was rather impressive for stodgy old Whiskers (though Marlowe suspected that underneath all of that facial hair the man was not nearly as old as he seemed).

"You've a fever yet. I'd order you back to your chambers if I thought you'd actually go," the doctor said in a much more agreeable tone now that he'd had a fortifying dram.

Marlowe waved a hand in surrender. "I'll go. I'm pigheaded, not an idiot. But my errand couldn't wait. You'll just have to patch up what's left of me."

Lucas looked as suspicious of his easy acquiescence as he was surprised. Marlowe hadn't been this agreeable since he'd been unconscious, which was doubtless a shock to the doctor's system. Now that his daughters were safe, however, Marlowe was feeling magnanimous.

And feverish. Lucas was right about that, unfortunately.

A rap sounded on the door, and Miss Jones poked her head around the edge. She looked even worse than she had in the ditch—unsurprising, since they'd driven straight through to London without stopping for anything other than the twins' distressingly small bladders. Her sable hair was almost entirely fallen from its moorings, and her gray redingote—hideous to begin with—was brown now. It creaked when she moved, little flecks of dried mud marking her progress across the parquet. She looked half-vexed and half-dazed, as she had for most of the journey, as if she still couldn't believe she'd agreed to their arrangement.

He couldn't either, for he'd not made things easy for the woman, but *he* wasn't vexed about the outcome at all. There was something about Miss Jones that was absolutely riveting underneath the mud and frump and righteous indignation, and he planned on figuring out what it was.

He must have been staring at her too long, for she was beginning to look impatient. "My lord? Your housekeeper has disappeared with the twins, and I'm not sure what I'm supposed . . ."

"Minerva?" Dr. Lucas interjected, sounding shocked.

Miss Jones's eyes widened almost comically at the doctor. "Inigo?" she breathed as the doctor came forward and kissed her knuckles. Her cheeks flushed in a much too charming manner at Lucas's gallantry.

Well, *this* was an unexpected development.

Marlowe cleared his throat, but they ignored him completely.

"What are you doing here?" Miss Jones demanded of the doctor, who was now smiling in delight. Marlowe hadn't seen Lucas look so pleased with himself since the doctor's short-lived courtship of the Marchioness of Manwaring a few years back.

"I'm here for my patient," the doctor said, indicating

Marlowe with a rather dismissive gesture, all of his attention now focused on the muddy schoolmarm. "What are *you* doing here?"

Miss Jones's blushes faded quickly, and she grimaced, obviously not relishing having to recount the events of the past few days.

Marlowe cleared his throat again, louder this time. The pair jumped apart as if they just remembered there was a real, sentient being in the room with them. "You know each other?"

"Miss Jones is a close family friend," Lucas said, giving Miss Jones another indulgent grin.

"A *friend*?" Marlowe said. Did he sound disgruntled? Judgmental? He must have, for Miss Jones's eyebrows slanted at him warningly.

"I was to marry Dr. Lucas's brother, but he died in the war," she said in a manner that dared him to put one foot out of line about *that*.

That took all of the wind out of his sails, though he was still not quite sure where all the wind had come from in the first place.

"I'm sorry to hear that," he grumbled.

"Thank you, but it was long ago," she grumbled back, turning her glare to the parquet at her feet as if embarrassed by his sympathy.

"But I don't understand why *you're* here, Minerva," the doctor pressed, apparently uninterested in enlightening Marlowe any further on the subject of their acquaintance. "The last time I heard from you, you said you were quite content in your new position."

"I was," Miss Jones began, too carefully, and Marlowe had to cough at this glaring bouncer, for there was no way on earth anyone with a soul could have been content at West Barming School for Recalcitrant Young Ladies.

Miss Jones flashed him a warning look, as if she could read his mind. "But the viscount has offered me a position as governess to his daughters, and I have accepted it."

That recounting rather left out all of the interesting bits, but Miss Jones seemed determined to give the doctor as close to a Banbury tale as she could.

Lucas, who, as the family sawbones, had both met the twins and become quite familiar with the long laundry list of their misdeeds over the years, valiantly managed to keep his expression mostly blank. He was too much a gentleman to express his true opinion of the twins in front of their own father, but the judgment was nevertheless apparent in the pursed lips and slightly alarmed widening of his eyes. The doctor clearly thought Miss Jones had lost her mind.

"Governess? Are you sure . . ." he began.

"Absolutely," Miss Jones lied once more with a grin that was too wide to be at all believable. "I shall enjoy being back in London, and the twins are . . ." She faltered a little, God bless her, and Marlowe supposed he should be indignant that Miss Jones couldn't manage at least one halfway positive adjective to describe his girls. She was a grammar teacher and a Misstopher, for heaven's sake. She couldn't be lacking in vocabulary or imagination.

"Well, anything's better than West Barming, honestly," Miss Jones finished briskly. And she wasn't wrong about that.

Lucas wilted. "You should have told me if you were unhappy, my dear Minerva. You know my offer still stands. I wish you would consider it instead of . . ." He gave Marlowe a sidelong look that was anything but subtle.

Marlowe gave the doctor his most shameless grin. He was beginning to regret offering the doctor that whisky.

Miss Jones's cheeks went crimson at the doctor's cryptic words, which was interesting. He wondered what the doctor's offer could possibly have been to warrant such a reaction. "Thank you for your concern, Inigo. But you had my answer years ago, and it hasn't changed."

"Arthur would have wanted . . ."

"I doubt that very much, and as I've said, it only matters what you and I want," Miss Jones cut in, sounding a bit weary, as if the two of them had had this conversation many times before.

"Of course," the doctor said, though he sounded like he was merely humoring her.

Miss Jones obviously thought the same, for her jaw clenched and a vein pulsed in her temple. Marlowe braced himself for the explosion, for he already knew Miss Jones's tells when her temper was stretched to the breaking point. That poor frock of hers had met as violent an end as any he'd ever seen.

But the fight just drained straight out of her, and she gave the doctor an affectionate smile.

Soon after, the doctor took his leave, and Marlowe found himself alone in the library with Miss Jones. He decided to poke at her to see what happened.

"The two of you seem quite close," he observed. "Inigo, was it?"

She scowled at him. "If you must know," she said in a tone that made it clear he mustn't, "Inigo asked me to marry him."

Well, *that* was unexpectedly blunt. And all of a sudden, his stomach felt very sour. Something else clenched tight in his chest—something that couldn't possibly be jealousy.

Ha! That would be ridiculous, since he'd known Miss Jones for barely a day.

"But of course I couldn't accept," she continued.

"Of course," he murmured. "Though it seems he is very agreeable with the idea."

Her look made it clear how very little business it was of his. "He is a dear friend," she said insistently. "Though how my matrimonial prospects are of *your* concern at all is unclear to me."

"My concern is that my children's governess will abscond for greener pastures at the first opportunity. And after all the trouble I've gone through to hire you."

Her brow rose in disbelief. "Trouble *you've* gone through?"

"You are very difficult to reason with, Miss Jones."

The disbelief transformed into angry incredulity, her pale cheeks flushing, her whole small body vibrating with barely contained rage, as if she were one step away from attacking him.

He wasn't sure whether to feel worried or flattered, since he seemed the only one so far capable of inciting Miss Jones to fisticuffs. But he was certainly entertained.

"And you . . . you . . ." she began, but then broke off, her attention caught by something beyond him. Her brow furrowed at first, then her whole face seemed to go slack with astonishment. She turned in a circle, gazing around the room, looking astounded.

"What is it?" he demanded, alarmed by her sudden shift in behavior.

"Your . . . *this* . . . I had not noticed until now," she murmured, walking toward one of the nearest shelves with a covetous look.

"Noticed what?"

"Your library," she said. "I've never seen one quite so large."

He manfully restrained himself from pointing out the double meaning in her words. It was just too easy. And inappropriate, of course.

Instead, he followed her lead and surveyed his library. It *was* rather splendid. He'd bought the townhouse because of the massive room. The last owner had used it to display his taxidermy collection (Marlowe still shuddered every time he remembered walking into *that*), but with a little work, Marlowe had turned it into a repository for his books. It was nothing compared to the size of many country house libraries, but it was big enough, especially for London living.

He followed her stunned gaze to the second level, reached by a winding, wrought iron staircase, and heard her gasp, "It's two levels!"

It was indeed, and her enthusiasm for his library was doing funny things to his heart. Either that, or his fever was worsening.

"I've got poetry—Essex and the like—somewhere around here," he said, gesturing vaguely across the room, though he knew very well his very extensive poetry section was to Miss Jones's immediate right.

Her brow furrowed with disbelief. "You don't even . . . ?" she spluttered. "Do you even *read* any of these books?"

How to reply to *that*. "Er . . ."

His hesitation seemed to confirm her worst suspicion. "How could you have all of these books and not . . .?" It appeared from the horrified look she was giving him that he might have broken her brain box just a little bit.

He attempted a reassuring grin while simultaneously fighting down what Monty would doubtless have called an inappropriate amount of glee over his governess's discomfiture. From the way her eyebrows rose nearly clear off her face, his attempt was less than successful. It was probably all the teeth. Even his last mistress had asked that he refrain from smiling while in her company, citing his resemblance to a murderous hyena—and he'd *paid* her to be nice to him.

He scaled it back, though her eyebrows remained aloft. "Oh, no, Miss Jones, I like words well enough."

"Words?" Oh, the scorn she managed to breathe into that single word was inspiring.

"A bit of verse. Poetry and the like."

"Poetry?"

She was very good at repetition, which he supposed was a good quality for a teacher to have. Lord knew the legion of tutors and professors who'd plagued his formative years had been very good at putting him through his paces when they weren't rapping his knuckles . . . or caning his posterior.

"Poetry," he repeated. "You know, limericks and a bit of bawdy verse here and there."

"Limericks."

He cocked his own eyebrows to match her own. "Limericks, as in '*There was a young fellow from Kent / Whose anatomy was very bent . . .*'"

"Yes, yes, I know what a limerick is. Thank you," she interjected primly, her eyebrows finally dropping into a fearsome scowl.

"Wrote that one myself," he murmured.

"I have no idea what I'm supposed to say to you right now." She sounded either awed or in pain. It was a hard one to call.

He shrugged. "Since you like Mr. Essex, thought you might appreciate a bit of my own talent."

"You are . . . this is . . . are you *actually* comparing your . . . your highly offensive crudity to Christopher Essex's genius?"

"Well, we do both enjoy a bit of bawdy verse."

"You're calling Essex's work bawdy verse?" she cried, eyebrows climbing once again.

He felt justified in calling it whatever he damn well pleased, especially when it was eliciting such a delightful response in Miss Jones. But he thought it best to move the situation along before she started hurling books at him.

"My library is at your disposal, Miss Jones," he said, "since you have such a high opinion of its worth."

She looked as if she wanted to scold him further, but she was so surprised by his offer that she managed to restrain herself. "Thank you, Lord Marlowe," she said instead, sounding both bewildered by his generosity and irked by his ignorance.

"Well, someone should enjoy it," he said briskly. "And if

you do decide you might enjoy a bit of bawdy verse, *that* section is on the balcony."

Her marble-pale face turned a delightful shade of red at that. "That will . . . not be necessary, my lord," she said primly.

From the way her eyes kept drifting upward, he did not believe her for a second.

Just then, the sound of something else crashing in the hallway—and Mrs. Chips's indignant yelp—startled them both.

"I suppose I'd better . . ." she began, backing out of the room with one last longing glance around the shelves—and the balcony.

He waved her off while gifting her with his most infuriating grin and sat down at his desk, contemplating his newest acquisition to his household. Perhaps when the fog of his fever cleared, Miss Jones would reveal herself to be as ordinary and as short-lived as every other governess he'd ever hired, but somehow he doubted it. He had a feeling that he was going to enjoy having Miss Jones around, if only to vex her every chance he got.

His grin didn't fade for a very long time.

Chapter Five

In Which Another Damsel In Distress Rescues Herself

IN THE YELLOW LIGHT OF a gas lamp turned low, at an hour when most reasonable people were abed, Marlowe, who had never been reasonable when it came to his work (or anything else, really), scribbled out one last word and scowled down at the foolscap on his library desk, unsatisfied. Half the words he'd written were marked out, just like the page before, and the page before that one.

Come to think of it, the entire stack of paper at his elbow was one giant inkblot. He balled up all of the wasted pages and threw them one by one toward the smoldering, half-dead fire. Most of them fell far short of the hearth, but he really couldn't be arsed to pick them up and dispose of them properly.

He knocked his forehead against the desktop in the futile hope of knocking out some decent verse.

It did not work.

He didn't know what he had been thinking, anyway. The muse had abandoned him long ago and showed no signs of returning, even though he'd felt unaccountably inspired after his trip to West Barming. The epic that had been languishing on his desk for months had also been relegated to the flames (it had been even more insipid than usual), and he had started a new one that may or may not have featured a petite, gray-eyed enchantress with sable hair.

But while the urge to write was there, as it hadn't been in months upon months, his output was as dismal as ever. The wellspring of inspiration in his mind had dried up, and try as he might, even he could not wring water from the stones of a barren creek bed, no matter how much he wanted to. Having never before been faced with this problem, he had no idea how to fix it. He hadn't in nearly three years, not since he'd finished *The Italian Poem*.

He stared unblinkingly at the blank page before him for so long his eyes went dry. He reached for the bottle beside him and paused as his fingers closed around empty air. The habit had become so engrained over the years that he'd forgotten his self-imposed vow for a moment.

He glanced at the sideboard on the other side of the room, fully stocked and taunting him. The cut glass decanter full of his favorite port sparkled in the moonlight streaming in from the open window beside it, the liquid inside gleaming like a precious jewel. For one second, he was tempted, as he'd been tempted too much in the past three years when troubled by a blank page.

His appetite for excess had always been the worst during the night, when most of the world was either asleep or hidden away enjoying its secret pleasures, and everything was too still, too quiet. Sleep for him had been elusive as far back as the war and his disastrous marriage, and his pleasures were few outside the bottom of a bottle. The only thing to assuage his sleeplessness besides drink had been his verse, but that too had abandoned him.

For so long, his despair and outrage and hate of the world had fueled his poetry, but that toxic phoenix had burned to ashes far too quickly, leaving him a soused husk shattered by the war and his wife's betrayal. The words that had flowed from his pen as effortlessly as rain from a storm cloud—as effortlessly as the rage and sorrow that had flowed through his veins—had been gone for years now. He didn't think it was a coincidence that he'd become wordless around the same time as he'd begun to forgive— his family, the war, Caroline, himself—but he did think it terribly ironic.

Now that he couldn't even write one decent couplet— not one, for God's sake!—he had no shield between the nightmares and regret but the drink, even after he'd let go of the worst of his anger and grief. He'd become a hypocrite, for after railing at Sebastian for years over the man's self-destructive habits, he'd nearly succumbed to his own vices and lost the two most precious things in his life: his daughters.

Well, he'd not do so again.

It was shockingly easy to shift his eyes from the sideboard to the window when he thought of Laura and Beatrice.

Easier still to do so when someone was climbing over the open sill, swathed in shadows and a heavy cloak, distracting him completely from his brooding. Since he'd not bothered with any lighting other than the small gas lamp on his desk, the intruder obviously didn't see him at first, tumbling into the room in a flurry of curses and flailing limbs.

Marlowe's momentary alarm quickly faded into exasperation. He recognized that voice. The intruder was hardly a threat . . . a threat to his sanity, perhaps, but not to the sanctity of his household.

He sighed wearily, for just when everything in his life had begun to take on some semblance of normalcy again, trouble had to tumble into his life. Literally. He supposed it was rather poetic, though, considering the nearly identical way he'd tumbled into Miss Jones's life . . . though he'd rather steer far clear of any bosom groping in this particular instance.

He cleared his throat pointedly and turned up the flame on his lamp, flooding the room with light. The intruder let out a loud, high-pitched yelp of surprise and flailed even more, one arm knocking into the sideboard so hard that it sent his prize decanter of port to the floor. The sound of shattered glass pierced the quiet room for a moment, and a pair of wide, familiar brown eyes caught his and held.

He sighed again and shook his head at the puddle of port spreading at the girl's feet. Even though he was a bit abstemious these days, it didn't mean he couldn't mourn the waste of a premium beverage.

"Elizabeth Leighton! What the devil do you think you are doing?" he demanded.

His little sister shoved the cowl of her cloak back and revealed a mass of dark brown curls falling out of its pins. Her shock at being discovered quickly faded, for the next thing he knew he was being gifted with a roll of the eyes. As if *she* were the one exasperated with *him*.

"It's *Betsy*," she hissed. "And you weren't supposed to be awake."

He raised an eyebrow at her. He was always awake these days.

She was unimpressed, as usual, by his silent posturing. "And what are *you* doing, lurking in the dark? Humans have invented these things called candles, you know," she huffed, stepping over the remains of the port and loosening the ribbons of her cloak, her native forwardness—and cheek, apparently—now totally restored.

He indicated his desk lamp—a piece of technology that was far more advanced than a mere beeswax candle, thank you very much. "I was writing." Not that he needed to explain himself to a sixteen-year-old girl. "And again, what do you think you're doing?"

"Running away, obviously," she said briskly. She slung an overloaded carpetbag off her shoulder and aimed it at a divan. It hit the edge and fell to the floor with a heavy thunk.

"What's in there?" he demanded. "Rocks?"

She scowled at him. "Books, for one. Not that *you'd* know the difference, you philistine."

He glanced pointedly around his library but said nothing to her ridiculous statement.

"And clothes," she continued. "I may have run away, but that's no reason to wear the same frock every day. I'm not a street person. Though I shall need to visit a modiste soon. Space was limited, and I could only bring my best ball gown."

Of course. Only his flighty half-sister would think it sensible to run away with a sack of books and a ball gown—only his sister would think it sensible to *run away*.

He pinched the bridge of his nose and prayed for patience. "Tell me you didn't travel here from West Barming. Unchaperoned."

"I didn't travel here from West Barming unchaperoned?" she said with a much too innocent expression.

"Except that you did."

"Of course I did!" she said brightly, tossing her cloak in the same direction as her bag. It slithered to the floor as well. Underneath, she seemed to be wearing a ratty old gingham dress more suited to a milkmaid than an earl's daughter. Well, at least she had attempted some sort of discretion.

"I couldn't very well run away in Father's chaise," she continued. "I caught the mail coach in the village. Never has my nose been so offended in my life. I swear, does no one else but me understand the purpose of soap?"

"Most people can't afford soap, Elizabeth," he growled.

She scoffed and waved away his comment as if it were ridiculous. "How can one not afford soap?"

He pinched the bridge of his nose to try to contain his annoyance. She reminded him so much of Evander at that moment—though blessedly without the cruel streak. But he was not about to educate his sister on the myriad injustices of the English class system and the bloody soap tax at such an ungodly hour. Besides, she would have listened just as well as Evander would have—which was not at all.

"And once you reached London, how did you find your way here?"

She arched her brow at him as if she thought him quite dim. "A hack, of course."

"Of course. You hired a hack in London in the middle of the night. Do you know how dangerous that was?"

She waved her hand at her clothing dismissively. "I borrowed my maid's dress . . . well, I *say* borrowed . . . No one recognized me, I assure you. My reputation is intact."

He ran a hand through his hair in exasperation. He hoped to God his daughters did not grow up to be so damned bird-witted.

"I don't give two figs about your reputation," he said. "I care about your life. At any point you could have been accosted or abused by those unsoaped, unwashed men who couldn't care less whose daughter you are."

Her expression went slack with surprise, as if she'd not once considered this. Which she probably hadn't. Damn his father for raising his daughter in such a rarified bubble.

But then Elizabeth pulled a knife from one pocket and a pistol from another. She brandished both at him with a wicked grin. He ducked when she waved the pistol's barrel a little too cavalierly in his direction.

"I'm not an idiot, Evie," Elizabeth said briskly. "And I resent the implication that I am some completely helpless female who needs the protection of a man. Honestly, you're as bad as Father." She wiggled the gun at him again, and he ducked once more.

"Would you put that down before you shoot me?" he hissed.

She shrugged and set the pistol on the edge of his desk with less care than he thought wise. She returned the knife to her pocket, however. He decided to pick his battles and let her keep the blade. With the trouble she was likely to get into, she'd probably need it. He snatched up the pistol, unloaded it, and shoved it in his desk drawer. "Do you even know how to shoot this thing?"

She sniffed haughtily. "Of course. What else is there to do in West Boring but hunt? I am an excellent shot. Cracking, in fact."

He was afraid for England. Truly. The idea of Elizabeth—clumsy, impulsive, flighty, little *Betsy*—shooting at things was a frightening prospect indeed.

He scowled at her. "I don't care how prepared you thought you were, it was still dangerous to travel alone," he said, coming around the edge of his desk and leaning against it.

She just smiled and patted his cheek. "You're just soft and fluffy underneath all of that bluster, aren't you? And I'm sorry I compared you to Father. You're nothing like him. You couldn't care a whit about damage to my reputation, while I'm sure that is all he'll think about when he realizes I've run off. He couldn't give a toss about my safety."

She was, unfortunately, not wrong.

But . . . soft and fluffy indeed! She was getting as bad as Elaine.

He cleared his throat. "You better have a good explanation, Elizabeth."

"Betsy," she corrected. "*Please*. Do I look like a three-hundred-year-old monarch?"

"You *look* like you traveled by mail coach across the country, *Elizabeth*," he said, refusing to grant her any ground. At least not yet. He knew from bitter experience that Betsy would eventually wear him down to the point where he'd agree to anything just to get her to stop talking, just like Elaine did, but he didn't want to make it easy for her. And if she insisted on calling him Evie, he was damned if he'd concede on her own name quite yet. "What the devil has brought you here?"

"Can't I visit my favorite brother?" she asked, the picture

of innocence.

He ground his teeth. Her cow eyes and compliments would not sway *him*. Besides, it was hardly a compliment, as the only other option was moldering in the family mausoleum.

"You could have arranged a visit. Properly."

She snorted. "That is never going to happen. Father would never allow it. He hates you, you know."

Oh, did he ever. He refused to give in to that small niggling hurt in his heart he felt at hearing the truth so blatantly pointed out to him. He'd never understand his father's enmity, though—how the earl could have loved one son so utterly while loathing the other. "The feeling is mutual, I assure you," he grumbled.

"And I'm stuck in West Boring anyway. Father never lets me go to London. I was supposed to have my debut this Season, you know. But he decided it was unnecessary."

"Is that what this is about?" he demanded. "You're upset about your coming-out? Really, Elizabeth, did missing a few parties and balls warrant running away?"

Her glare deepened. "He canceled my coming-out because he has found me a husband. A completely odious specimen, might I add. And I refuse to tie myself to that toad for the rest of my life. The banns were begun last Sunday, Evie, and there was nothing I could do to stop it. I couldn't stay a moment longer."

Marlowe's heart sank to his toes at this news. Surely even his father wouldn't be so callous. "You're only sixteen!" he cried.

"That argument did not work on Father," Betsy said wearily, throwing herself on the divan dramatically. "He reminded me that plenty of girls my age have husbands."

"It's archaic."

She shot him a knowing look. "Our father *is* archaic. He also reminded me that Elaine married at my age."

"He forgot to add that Elaine pursued poor Brinderley

until the man had no choice but to concede to her will," he muttered. "And still I say she was too young."

"It was a love match," Betsy said firmly, as if this excused everything, which showed how distressingly young she was. His had been a love match too. Or at least *he'd* thought so. "Whether she was too young or not, she and Brinderley are very happy. But I most certainly will never be with the Duke of Oxley."

His blood ran cold with horror, then immediately began to boil with fury at his father.

"Poxley Oxley?" he cried. "He's sixty, if he's a day!" And one of the most depraved men Marlowe had ever had the misfortune of knowing, even if only by association.

Oxley had certainly come by his nickname honestly. His perversities were legendary among certain circles, and if rumor could be believed, he'd been barred from every halfway reputable establishment due to his propensity for breaking his playthings. Marlowe would not let his sister anywhere near such a brute. Oxley had already gone through three wives, and Marlowe shuddered to think what that monster had put them through in the marriage bed before they'd died.

There was no way Marlowe's father didn't know these same rumors, as he was Oxley's confederate (another reason to loathe the earl). And yet he was willing to give his sixteen-year-old daughter to that villain. Marlowe shouldn't be surprised by anything his father did at this point in his life, but this was a new low, even for the earl.

"Tell me Poxley didn't touch you," he demanded, taking her by the shoulders and examining her as closely as he could in the moonlight, looking for any sign of abuse.

"I'm fine. He has never touched me," she said, enduring his inspection grudgingly. "Though I certainly don't like the way he looks at me." She shuddered. "He would be a perfect villain for a gothic novel. Besides, I am perfectly able to take care of myself. Cracking shot, remember? So you see why I've run away. I can't marry him."

"No, you cannot," he agreed. "What is Barming thinking?"

Betsy snorted. "He's thinking about Poxley's deep pockets, what else? Father's a bit low tide these days, and Poxley's offering a settlement that would keep him solvent—and Uncle Ashley in port—for years to come. I would be flattered I'm worth so much, though I'm certain Poxley wants me for a broodmare and nothing more. He has no heirs, you know. The other day he mentioned how much he hoped I had Elaine's fecundity. *Fecundity!* He *actually* used that word. Over tea. With Father listening on as if it were the most normal thing in the world to say to me. I wanted to cast up my accounts all over the both of them then and there, but alas, I have too strong a constitution."

He'd forgotten just how much his little sister could talk.

"You cannot marry Poxley," he reaffirmed with a shudder. "He is *definitely* a gothic villain."

"I knew you would agree," she said smugly.

"When Father finds out you are here, though, there will be hell to pay. The law is on the earl's side, Betsy."

Suddenly Betsy looked a lifetime older than her sixteen years, all of her flippancy cast aside. "I know. But I can't marry that man. I'll die, Evie," she said quietly.

For once, Marlowe didn't mind the nickname. And he feared that her death would be a less than metaphorical event should she wed that reprobate.

"You won't have to," he said grimly. Over his dead, cold corpse, would she be marrying Poxley. Though how he was going to manage this, with the banns begun and his father on the warpath, he hadn't a bloody clue.

She threw herself at him and wrapped her arms around his torso, squeezing hard. "Thank you," she cried. "I knew you'd help me."

He wasn't used to embracing anyone in affection but his children, and they came in a much smaller package. But after a moment's hesitation, he wrapped his arms around the girl and held her tight. He hadn't had much to do with Betsy over the years, had seen her only a handful of times since he'd gone off to the war. She'd only been four when he'd left, and even before that he'd not been around her a great deal, as she'd been sequestered at the earl's estate all her life.

He'd liked his father's second wife about as well as he'd liked his father, which was to say not at all. He'd, thankfully, avoided having much to do with either of them over the years, since he'd spent most of his time away from the family seat, first at Harrow, then at Cambridge.

He'd seen Betsy on the unavoidable holiday visits and tolerated her attentions as well as any impatient young man could the attentions of a small girl-child. Though to her credit, even at such a tender age, she'd had the rare good sense to prefer his company to that of Evander.

But Marlowe had learned to be wary of his family the hard way, and after his return from the war and the fall out that had followed with Caroline, he'd rather lumped Betsy in with the rest of the Leightons as People to Avoid at All Costs.

The handful of times he'd been in her company in the last few years on her rare visits to Elaine's, she'd done very little to convince him otherwise. She'd reminded him either too much of Evander with her manic enthusiasms, or too much of his stepmother, one of the most vapid, frivolous human beings he'd ever encountered.

But he'd never stopped loving her. Just as he'd never stopped loving the earl or even Evander, despite his best efforts to exorcise them from his heart.

Maybe he *was* too soft and—good Lord—*fluffy*.

He now realized it had been a mistake to have kept his distance from Betsy. He shuddered to think what would have happened if she *hadn't* turned up on his doorstep . . . or windowsill, as the case may be. He would have never even known about her marriage until it was too late—his father would have seen to that. Betsy had shown a surprising amount of sense in running away, despite the risks she had taken on the road. Perhaps he'd been mistaken in her character.

She lifted her head and smiled up at him sunnily. "You won't regret helping me, Evie."

He rolled his eyes. "I already do," he said without heat, feeling a surprisingly strong surge of affection for her.

"I have a plan, you see," she continued.

That didn't sound good. "Really."

"Father can't marry me off if I'm already married. And I have the perfect candidate. Someone so scandalous that father will disown me altogether."

Not good at all.

"You're not marrying anyone," he said firmly. He'd thought that was the whole point she'd been trying to make by running away. "Not until you're at least thirty."

She pulled away from him with a pout and crossed her arms stubbornly. She looked shockingly like the four-year-old girl he remembered. He feared he'd not been totally wrong about her character after all.

"You'll not stop me from a love match, Evie. You didn't stop Elaine."

"I was thirteen. And nothing short of the Apocalypse could stop Elaine," he grumbled.

Betsy shook her head at him as if she didn't understand how he could be so dense. "Do you think I would be any different?" she asked as if she truly wanted an answer.

He narrowed his eyes at her. Perhaps she was more Leighton than her mother after all. More like *Elaine*.

That was *not* reassuring.

"Who is the other half of this love match, then?" he demanded, praying that she had not progressed so far in her scheme that she had chosen her groom. "It's not Sir Thaddeus Davies, is it?"

"What?" she cried, aghast.

"Well, weren't he sniffing around Barming last year?"

"It is not Sir Thaddeus. Good grapes, I think I might prefer Poxley over that squint."

"Then what poor soul have you decided upon?"

She huffed and pretended to smooth out the wrinkles in her dress, her cheeks heating in what he hoped was embarrassment and not some other frighteningly passionate emotion. "Mr. Essex, of course," she said.

"What!" he spluttered. It was the last name he would have ever suspected.

Her cheeks grew even ruddier at his reaction, and her brow wrinkled in annoyance. "Christopher Essex," she said slowly, as if talking to an imbecile. "The poet. Surely even *you* know who he is."

"I know who he is!" he said, his voice strangled. "And that is a *terrible* plan!"

Her scowl deepened. "I don't see how."

He did. Very much so. "He could be anyone!" Like her much older half brother, for instance.

"He is perfect. I don't care what he looks like. One only has to read his verse to see the beauty of his soul."

Oh, for the love of . . . To be sixteen again. "He could be worse than Poxley!" Or, again, her *much older half brother*.

"No one could be worse than Poxley," she retorted.

Well, she had him there. But still. His skin crawled at the idea that his little sister was . . . infatuated. With Essex's beautiful soul. *His* beautiful soul.

"You're a Misstopher!" he hissed. He knew he sounded like a scandalized old maid, but on this occasion it seemed appropriate. It was horrifying enough to know Essex had such a strangely devoted following—the majority of them distressingly impressionable, distressingly *young* women— but knowing his own sister was among them was . . . wrong. Wrong, on so many, many counts.

Not for the first time, he regretted letting Sebastian talk

him into publishing altogether.

He prayed she was like Miss Jones and only read his poetry and not those ridiculous, disconcertingly explicit works of fiction his more rabid followers wrote and circulated about him . . . or rather about Essex and his . . . conquests. Marlowe had made the mistake of reading one too many of those, and he'd been horrified . . . then aroused . . . then horrified at his arousal.

The thought that some young miss fresh from the schoolroom—Lord, he'd prayed that she was, at the very least, out of short skirts—had written smut that would rival any act committed at the most disreputable brothel in the city was life-altering in the worst way.

He wondered if Byron had to put up with this shit.

Though Byron, the narcissistic little fop, would doubtless enjoy such attention. Marlowe, however, did not. His poetry was scandalous, but not *that* scandalous. And he really didn't want sixteen-year-old girls lusting after him . . . or rather Christopher Essex. Who was him. Sort of.

The whole thing was extremely confusing. And nauseating.

But one thing was certain. Marlowe had to nip *this* particular problem in the bud.

"You are *not* pursing Christopher Essex, and that is final," he intoned, wincing inwardly. He'd sounded just like his father then.

Betsy obviously thought so too, for she snorted at him and cocked her chin at her most stubborn angle. "We'll see about that," she muttered.

"Yes, we will," he said. And then he wondered why he was even arguing with her. He, more than anyone, knew her little quest could never succeed.

She could spin her wheels all she liked on her scheme, just so long as it was on a man who didn't exist. She was going to be a handful in the meantime, though, and that wasn't even taking into account the drama that was sure to come when the earl discovered exactly what had become of his errant daughter.

He was cursed. It was the only explanation for the way he seemed to be accumulating stray females lately—and Misstophers at that. First a governess, and now a sister. Between his all-female staff (he really needed to hire more servants) and his family, his house was overrun by the opposite sex.

Though now that he thought about the governess, however, his panic receded slightly. Miss Jones was proving to be a more welcome addition to the household than he could have ever predicted. She had managed, after a few rough patches toward the beginning, to wrangle his daughters into some semblance of a routine in just a few month's time—a feat no one had ever accomplished before.

She had also proved a distraction for him as he'd convalesced. He'd been taken by her unabashed wit and sharp tongue from the beginning. Few women—other than his sister Elaine, perhaps, and Astrid, Montford's unconventional duchess—had ever challenged him so completely as Miss Jones did.

He'd never met anyone like her before, so buttoned down and plainly packaged on the outside, but with a hidden passion that he could glimpse burning bright behind her eyes—a stodgy grammarian on the one hand, and a secret Essex fanatic on the other. It was a fascinating contradiction, and he was self-aware enough to admit the gray-eyed enchantress of his current project looked an awful lot like his governess in his mind's eye.

Miss Jones had inspired him when he thought inspiration out of his reach, and though he only had a pile of ruined foolscap to show for it so far, he had more hope than he'd had in years of finding his voice once again on the page.

And he also had a feeling that if anyone could bring

Betsy to heel, it was the indomitable Miss Jones.

"Do you know, Betsy," he began with a wicked grin, "I believe you are going to *love* my governess."

CHAPTER SIX

In Which Misstophers Of The World Unite

WHEN A MONTH HAD PASSED without Minerva losing a body part, she almost let herself relax into her new position. But she knew the twins better than that. Even though they seemed to genuinely like her and half the time deigned to obey her—a small miracle, considering the viscount and dour old Mrs. Chips never fared much better—they'd surely have their way with her eventually. They couldn't help themselves.

But when yet another month passed, and the worst they'd done to Minerva was leave a frog under her pillow and steal her unmentionables—her sole pair of newfangled pantaloons had mysteriously disappeared just that morning—she began to truly believe that she might come out of the other side of her present circumstances without being maimed. She'd long since resigned her patience and sanity to the dustbin.

But then Mrs. Chips ambushed her in her bedroom one morning before the sun was even up with a summons from the viscount, throwing back the draperies and clanging about the room as if it were (a) her own and (b) *not* arse o'clock in the morning.

Not that Minerva was able to appreciate it at the time, considering her hatred of mornings in general, but it was the most the housekeeper had interacted with her directly in one go for the entire time she'd lived there. Mrs. Chips was not a verbose woman at the best of times, and her expressions were so inscrutable that Minerva had started to seriously wonder if the woman turned to stone at night.

Apparently not, since Minerva had yet to see any evidence the sun was even up at the present moment.

Mrs. Chips, despite the inscrutability, had also made it perfectly clear through cold teas, stale biscuits, and that truly vile pea soup she'd served to Minerva her entire first week in the household, that she didn't like her and trusted her even less. Minerva suspected that had something to do with the legion of governesses who had tried and failed before her. But she'd thought Mrs. Chips was beginning to thaw, since the breakfasts she now received in the morning had become suspiciously edible.

The chilliness factor was now somewhere around a Scandinavian winter—nowhere near a warm Mediterranean spring, but better than the arctic blast of the first few weeks. Minerva had learned to take what she could get. And she'd take Mrs. Chips, pea soup, and her frigid disapproval any day over West Barming and the fräulein.

But this loathsome early-morning awakening, without even a tray of cold tea or stale biscuits in sight, seemed a step back to the early days of their acquaintance. Even though Minerva could read nothing on the housekeeper's impassive face, Mrs. Chips was enjoying Minerva's obvious misery far too much from the way she unhesitatingly turned up the oil lamp and flicked back Minerva's draperies.

And, oh yes, there it was: a bit of wretched sunlight leaking over the sill. Morning, after all.

She put her pillow over her head and tried to ignore it.

FIFTEEN MINUTES LATER, Minerva was reluctantly dressed, halfway conscious, and en route to the viscount's library, cursing her employer in her head every step of the way. And when she arrived there, she began to fervently wish she'd never left her bed in the first place.

Minerva had always considered herself a pragmatist. As the motherless daughter of a naval officer, she'd had very little choice otherwise. She had never doubted her father's love, but no one would have ever called him a warm man.

Nathaniel Jones had found himself the sole custodian of his daughter after his wife died of childbed fever just a few months after her birth; he spent the remainder of his life shuffling Minerva from one distant relative to another while he was off fighting Napoleon's endless war.

When he was on leave, it was obvious even to Minerva that he had no idea what to do with her. Sometimes—the best times—he'd seem to forget she was female entirely and would teach her things Minerva was rather certain were more suited to a son: how to shoot a pistol, how to swear like a proper navy man (these lessons tended to come after Captain Jones had been well lubricated by his Madeira in the evenings), how to fight dirty, and how to tie a proper sailor's knot.

The impromptu lessons—even the drunken ones—had ended around the time the captain had returned home to find his daughter in the possession of a nascent bosom and a few other unmistakably female attributes that could no longer be overlooked. Minerva remembered being crushed by what she saw as her father's rejection. The things she had loved most about having him at home were suddenly stripped from her, and for the longest time she'd not understood why.

It took one of her cousins—a rather mean-spirited boy who had lived to torment her for the six months she'd had to stay with his family—to point out the obvious: her father had lost interest in her because she was a girl. Of course, she'd always been a girl, but she'd just grown to an age where her father could no longer pretend she wasn't. That realization had hurt.

All she had left by the way of fatherly reassurance was the occasional gruff pat on the shoulder or—and she still shuddered at the memory—that awkward lecture on the dangers of men—perhaps the most mortifying moment of her life. Her father had delivered that one to her with the look of a man who'd rather be having his teeth extracted—exactly how she'd felt having to listen to it. The captain had loved her, but he'd never forgiven her for not being a boy.

In the two months living under the viscount's roof, however, she'd discovered something unexpected about her employer: Lord Marlowe, for all his dogged efforts to exasperate her at every encounter, was the sort of father to his daughters that Minerva had always wanted for herself.

In her experience, men rarely spent so much time in the company of their children—especially girl children. That was what they hired nurses and governesses for. But the viscount seemed the exception to the rule. She knew he was far from perfect (his daughters had ended up at West Barming School for Recalcitrant Young Ladies for a reason). But she would have gladly taken all of his failings to have a father who'd loved her as unconditionally as the viscount loved his girls.

Perhaps in the past the viscount had not been as present as he might have been, but it seemed this last illness of his had done more than trim away his waistline. Since they'd arrived in London, the viscount had been surprisingly . . . well, *normal* was definitely not the right word to apply to the viscount *ever*. He'd come far too close to death, according to Inigo, and that tended to change a person. He rarely drank and spent most of his time either with his daughters or closeted in his library conducting business.

The most reckless he seemed to get these days were his morning rides, a habit he took up after he'd finally shaken off the lingering fever that had plagued him since West Barming. He'd come back from these rides bright-eyed, damp, and smelling of fresh spring air, giving Mrs. Chips fits from the mud he tracked in over her clean floors.

Despite his clear affection for his daughters, however, Minerva remained skeptical of his apparent reformation. Life had taught her the hard way that a leopard couldn't change its spots. The viscount may have been an extraordinarily attentive father, but a saint he was not.

Still, the last thing she expected to find when she stepped into the viscount's library was a milkmaid dozing on the divan—though perhaps she should have known better than to be surprised by anything that happened in this haphazard household.

She was not exactly pleased to not only be summoned at the crack of dawn but also be confronted by this: proof of the viscount's low character. She'd suspected he'd soon tire of his reformation and revert to his old ways soon enough, but not in so blatant a manner.

In this instance, though, she truly hated being proven right, and as she studied him in the weak morning light, her indignation was overshadowed by a deep-seated disappointment. She had started to like the man and all of his idiosyncrasies—like him perhaps too much, judging from the tight, unhappy knot that had taken up residence in her stomach.

He sat scribbling at his desk, unkempt and disreputable as ever, his ubiquitous red silk banyan thrown carelessly over irredeemably wrinkled clothes, his rough-hewn jaw covered in at least a day's growth of beard, and his mahogany curls at sixes and sevens, as if he'd spent the entire night running his fingers through them. She doubted that he had slept a wink, judging by his present company. And that he thought it appropriate to summon her while looking so disreputable, and while his . . . fancy piece still dozed not five feet away, just confirmed how much of a rogue he was.

He could have at least had the courtesy to keep the sort of thing that currently occupied the divan in his bedchamber.

She held her tongue—barely—but gave him her most disapproving scowl as he looked up from whatever he was scribbling.

He seemed immune to her disapproval, however, giving her one of his crooked grins that absolutely did not make her feel weightless, or her heart flutter, or anything so absurd. He just looked so unfairly . . . innocent and . . . attractive—damn it, broken nose and all—when he smiled like that, but she was on to him.

"Ah, Miss Jones! Just the person I wanted to see," he said, as if her presence in his library had surprised him.

"You *did* send for me," she reminded him. "Before dawn." *Way* before dawn.

He looked out the window, where the sun was still only barely making an appearance, then back at her. His smile grew a bit devilish at the edges, which boded ill for her. She'd not been subjected to *that* particular smile since the ditch in West Barming. She braced herself.

"My apologies. I know how much you love to sleep in, Miss Jones."

She narrowed her eyes—how did he *know?*—and struggled to come up with a suitable retort, but her mind came up blank, as it tended to do before she'd had at least four cups of tea.

She really, *really* hated mornings. And this was shaping up to be one of her worst yet.

She knew his weeks of good behavior had been nothing more than a ruse, lulling her into a false sense of complacency. Though he was right, obviously. Usually the twins had to literally jump on her to get her out of bed even when the sun was fully risen. It was a habit she knew she needed to change, for it wouldn't do to continue to allow the girls to behave in so uncivilized a manner.

But she had never liked mornings, no matter how hard she'd tried to overcome her weakness. It was bad enough that he knew about—and mocked—her love of Christopher Essex. Of course the viscount would call her out on the other area of her life over which she had no discipline.

The viscount barreled on without bothering to wait for her tongue to catch up with her brain. "But no time to waste. I've a bit of a situation."

He gestured toward the little baggage on the divan, who had begun to snore rather unattractively. And really, what sort of dowdy costume was the girl wearing? Minerva would have thought that even the viscount would have more refined tastes in his women—and ones that weren't so reprehensible. Her stomach soured even further as she took in the girl's obvious youth.

"She looks as if she's still in the schoolroom," she scolded in a harsh whisper.

He gave her a strange look. "Of course she is. Or she should be, though I'm rather shocked my father even allowed her to be taught how to read and write."

This was worse than she could have ever imagined. His *father*? The Earl of Barming? Did they . . . share?

"Allowed!" she cried, truly alarmed. "Is this girl some sort of prisoner?"

The viscount snorted. "That is rather one way to put it. But she has come to me for protection now."

Minerva gasped in outrage at the implication. Protection indeed! "You cannot involve yourself in this . . . wretched business."

His brow creased in confusion. "Whyever not? I'll not turn her away. What sort of unfeeling churl do you take me for?"

"Someone who would not engage in such licentiousness with your children under the same roof. It is repugnant. This girl cannot be much older than they are!"

His confusion was fast transforming into irritation.

"She's sixteen. And I don't see what is so repugnant in this business. Unless you are referring to my father, for it shall indeed be extremely repugnant having to deal with him when he discovers she has come to me."

He was a despicable, utterly amoral villain who couldn't even see how wrong his behavior was. Minerva wondered how she'd ever thought him capable of basic human decency.

The viscount, however, seemed blithely unaware of her disapproval. "Now I need your help with her. The chit will need a firm hand while she settles into the household."

"I will not be your . . . procurer!" she gasped, utterly appalled at the idea.

He gave her an incredulous look. "What the devil are you talking about?"

"I think it obvious!" she scoffed.

He ran a hand through his hair, disordering it even further, looking totally perplexed by her outrage. "It really isn't, Miss Jones."

"But it is, Evie," drawled an amused, sleep-roughened voice from the divan. Minerva froze at the sound of it, realizing she hadn't heard snoring from that corner for some time. Slowly, she swiveled her head at the sound of rustling and met a pair of very amused, very familiar brown eyes peeking out of a tumble of brunette curls. The girl sat up and threw her legs onto the floor in a swirl of patched gingham skirts.

"She thinks I am your ladybird," the girl said, sounding far too gleeful for the hour and the subject.

"What?" the viscount cried.

"A strumpet," the girl clarified with relish. "A barque of frailty. A bawd. A. . ."

"Yes, I get the idea," the viscount said, suddenly looking distinctly green about the gills.

The girl continued, unrepentant. "You failed to mention who I was, though you did a cracking job of implying that our father has been imprisoning me against my will for rather nefarious purposes. Which I cannot entirely disagree with, since that is *exactly* what he has been doing. Though not quite in the way Miss Jones has implied."

The girl rose to her feet and bounded over to Minerva, looking much too awake for someone who had been snoring five minutes ago. And much too like a Leighton for there to be any doubt in Minerva's mind that she'd made a terrible mistake. Alongside those distinctive eyes, the girl had the viscount's same rangy build, long, unruly limbs, and all the grace of a bull in a china shop.

It was rather unnerving to see the viscount's demeanor translated onto someone of the opposite sex. Minerva was still struggling to get used to the viscount.

The girl smiled sunnily at her and then proceeded to shake her hand as if they were blokes at a sporting match. "Lady Elizabeth Leighton. But you may call me Betsy."

Minerva could feel her face heating, and when she dared to glance over at the viscount, he seemed to be faring no better. He had his palm pressed to his forehead as if he couldn't believe what had just happened. Well, she couldn't either.

"This is my *half sister*," the viscount finally managed, waving at the girl half-heartedly. "Not my . . ." He looked as if he were near to casting up his accounts.

"Yes, yes, I think I understand now," Minerva said quickly before he could finish that thought and make both of them sick.

Lady Elizabeth looked from her brother to Minerva and broke into giggles. She laughed so hard she had to sit back down on the divan. "The look . . . on your faces!" she gasped out.

Minerva had a sneaking suspicion that Lady Elizabeth was going to be as much a handful as her nieces. And her brother.

"Betsy," the viscount said, trying his best to ignore his

sister's giggles, "this is Miss Jones. She's the twins' governess."

"Oh, I'm sorry," Lady Elizabeth said commiseratingly, not looking sorry in the least.

The viscount scowled at his sister. "And now, she is to be yours as well."

"What?" Minerva and Lady Elizabeth cried simultaneously. It was really much too early for this.

"I am too old for a governess," Lady Elizabeth declared.

"Companion, then. Chaperone," Lord Marlowe said. "Whatever you want to call it. You're both rabid Misstophers, so I'm sure you'll have enough in common to muck along together."

Lady Elizabeth's disdain quickly gave way to delight. She turned to Minerva with a bright, hopeful smile. "You're a Misstopher?"

She looked so pleased and young that Minerva hadn't the heart to deny it—though she wanted to. Vociferously. "I admire Christopher Essex's poetry," she allowed primly.

"She's a Misstopher," the viscount confirmed to his sister. "And while you're under my roof, you are to mind Miss Jones, Betsy."

Lady Elizabeth rolled her eyes. "Fine." Her expression lightened as she turned back to Minerva. "What is your favorite work?"

"Wha . . . ? *Le Chevalier*, I suppose," Minerva answered when her brain had finally caught up with the girl's abrupt change of subject.

Lady Elizabeth looked as if she approved. "Mine is *The Hedonist*, but only by a small margin. I can already see we shall get along famously."

Perhaps. But perhaps one more strong-willed Leighton would be just enough to tip the scales against her. "Are you here for long?" Minerva inquired as innocently as she could.

"My sister has run away," the viscount intoned before

Lady Elizabeth could answer.

"Oh, dear," Minerva said, though she was hardly surprised, considering the consistently naughty behavior of Lady Elizabeth's nieces. She could only hope that the twins didn't get any ideas from their aunt while she was here.

"Oh, don't worry," the viscount continued breezily. "We have decided that this is a good thing, as our dear father is attempting to marry her off to the Duke of Oxley."

"Poxley Oxley!" Minerva exclaimed, horrified.

"You've heard of him, then," Lord Marlowe said dryly. "I usually hate to give credence to gossip, but in Poxley's case, everything you've ever heard is probably all horribly true. So Betsy will be staying with us until we can sort this business out."

"Don't worry; I have a plan," Lady Elizabeth assured Minerva, sounding so confident of herself that Minerva knew she was just the opposite.

Lord Marlowe wore the same tolerant look he employed when the twins were being particularly trying. "We shall see about your plan," he murmured doubtfully. "In the meanwhile, Miss Jones, if you would make sure she stays out of trouble, I would be most obliged."

"Of course," she agreed. For the absurd amount he paid her, she could have hardly done otherwise, though Minerva could already see this ending in disaster. *Three* Leighton charges. And a viscount. She wasn't sure she'd survive it.

Lady Elizabeth grinned wolfishly at her. "Don't worry, Miss Jones. I won't do anything you wouldn't do."

That was not as reassuring as one might think.

☾

MINERVA SOON DISCOVERED that Lady Elizabeth certainly made life interesting—though she'd thought it interesting enough, between corralling the twins and bickering with their father. However, far from being the hellion Minerva had expected, Lady Elizabeth seemed reasonably rational . . . unless she was waxing poetic about Christopher Essex. Minerva had thought herself embarrassingly immoderate in her own regard for the poet, but Lady Elizabeth took things to a whole new level of insanity. She truly was a Misstopher—not only that, she was one of those extreme cases who wrote *stories* about the poet. In compromising positions.

One of which Minerva found herself reading just a few hours after their meeting in the study as they sipped tea in Lady Elizabeth's new room, waiting for the twins to awaken.

> *"Oh, Elizabeth!" the poet gasped into his beloved's dew-kissed shoulder. "I have waited so long."*
>
> *"No longer, dearest Christopher," she murmured tenderly, caressing the rough, granite-hewn line of his jaw.*
>
> *"We mustn't," he murmured, even as his long, elegantly masculine fingers began to undo the buttons of her bodice and slip beneath. "We are not yet wed."*
>
> *"We shall be in Gretna Green by dawn. What's a few hours? Who is to know?" she whispered, coaxing him into continuing his caresses on silken skin.*
>
> *"I shall know," he breathed. "God shall know. I may be a hedonist, but I love you too much . . ."*
>
> *"Then don't stop; don't ever stop!" she cried as his fingers touched her naked, quivering br . . .*

Minerva slapped the commonplace book closed, her cheeks burning, and shoved it back in Lady Elizabeth's direction as if burned.

Lady Elizabeth—Lady Hedonist to those who'd read her stories, whose ranks now, unfortunately, included Minerva—just laughed at her and winked. She looked so much like her brother in that moment that Minerva wondered how she could have ever mistaken her for anything other than a Leighton.

"Don't tell me you've never dreamed something similar," Lady Elizabeth said slyly.

Minerva cleared her throat and tried to look suitably disapproving. She couldn't defend herself from the charge and stay honest. But an elopement to Gretna Green? And . . . *that* in the back of a carriage? She supposed to most sixteen-year-old girls that would seem romantic, but to her it just sounded dreadfully uncomfortable. She'd spent far too much time in overcrowded, bumpy mail coaches for it to ever sound like a good idea.

She decided to avoid reading anything else Lady Elizabeth offered her in the future, for it seemed wrong to read about the heaving bosoms and dewy flesh inhabiting the mind of a sixteen-year-old girl.

But she had to admit the writing itself was surprisingly well done, if just a tad too salacious for polite company. It seemed the earl had, in fact, allowed his daughter some schooling after all. Minerva would thus not judge the girl for her taste in hobbies, but rather praise her for her industriousness. And good grammar.

But Minerva nearly spat out her tea when she was next introduced to Lady Elizabeth's plan for avoiding her marriage to Oxley. She probably shouldn't have been so surprised that it involved Christopher Essex, since even she had a few idle daydreams about meeting the man, but really . . .

Marrying Christopher Essex?

It was hard to tell if Lady Elizabeth were serious or not. She announced her intentions so teasingly and lightly that Minerva doubted she was in earnest. How could she be? Lady Elizabeth was only sixteen, but she seemed anything but naive. Surely she had enough sense to know how highly unlikely her plan was to succeed.

Even if she were to unmask Essex—which no one had done in a decade—there was little hope he'd fall in line with Lady Elizabeth's matrimonial plans—or that he was any more suitable a candidate for marriage than Poxley Oxley.

Then again, Lady Elizabeth, under the secret guise of the notorious Lady Hedonist, was practically the leader of the Misstophers, so perhaps Minerva overestimated her level-headedness on this particular matter.

Whatever the case, one thing was certain: Lady Elizabeth could not marry Poxley Oxley. The only reason he'd not been thrown in Newgate long ago was his title and vast wealth. Even Minerva had heard the whispers about the fate of his past three wives, and though she hoped the rumors were exaggerated (for otherwise her faith in humanity was in danger of being severely compromised), she could not wish such a husband on the kind, exuberant treasure that Lady Elizabeth had turned out to be in the few short hours of their acquaintance.

She vowed in that moment to be Lady Elizabeth's friend—though she drew the line at calling her Betsy, as the girl kept insisting upon—and to aid the viscount in any way she could to help him extricate his sister from Oxley's clutches.

For the girl was going to need all the help she could get if her only plan of action was to marry a man who didn't even exist.

Chapter Seven

In Which Miss Jones Bemoans The Loss Of Her Pantaloons

MINERVA SOON REALIZED THAT LADY Elizabeth wasn't to be the only new addition to the household when strangers in livery began appearing in the hallways. The viscount had apparently lost most of his staff—not just the governess—during his long illness, and Mrs. Chips, through a judicious application of lukewarm tea and cold bathwater, had finally convinced the viscount to let her replace them.

Expanding the household staff was a task Mrs. Chips threw herself into with great alacrity—or so Minerva presumed by the improved temperature of her tea. The day after she'd received her orders, Mrs. Chips had already brought in two chambermaids, a scullery maid, and two bewigged footmen, leading Minerva to suspect that the housekeeper had been storing them in the attic somewhere, just waiting for an opportunity to give them an airing.

Mrs. Chips had even thrust upon the viscount a valet by the name of Pymm, a small, scrupulously turned out man who eyed the viscount's dishabille with the look of a general preparing for battle. Marlowe had responded to the incursion by hiding in the nursery the entire first day of the man's employment, grumbling about Pymm's threat to burn all of his banyans (which Minerva privately thought an excellent idea).

Minerva had finally called in reinforcements (i.e. the housekeeper), and one glimpse of Mrs. Chips's twitching left eyebrow and thinned lips was enough to cow both men into standing down. Once Pymm had grudgingly agreed not to burn his banyans, the viscount had even submitted to visiting the tailor with his new manservant. He'd looked as if he'd rather have all his teeth pulled out at once, but Minerva called it progress.

Needless to say, the twins did not get their lessons done that day, but Minerva didn't begrudge them the time with their father, even if he were acting like a five-year-old. She'd not seen the twins happier, and twins who were happy were twins who didn't put toads under her pillow (really, where did they find such an endless supply of amphibians in *London*?) or hide all of their mathematics lessons. Or steal her pantaloons. She still had no idea what they'd done with the things.

Minerva herself couldn't say she minded the viscount's frequent visits either. She thought Marlowe's reasons for lurking about the nursery had less to do with dodging Pymm's brushes and cravat pins and more to do with being in her company, not just the twins'. Just like Lady Elizabeth, he seemed intent on pursuing a friendship with Minerva in his own awkward way, which usually involved running circles around her in their conversations until she wanted to bite off his head (that is, behaving as he always had since the day he'd pulled her out of the ditch).

Minerva wasn't sure how she felt about this development in their relationship. But though he was still perhaps the most aggravating man she'd ever met, she'd come to a conclusion over the past few weeks that was as unexpected as it was in retrospect completely obvious: Lord Marlowe was a good man masquerading in wolf's clothing.

Or rather, vagrant's clothing, though Pymm's elegant hand was starting to show, as the viscount had begun to venture out into the world in nankeens that actually fit those long, rangy legs of his. After that initial triumph, smart cutaway jackets molded to the viscount's broad shoulders and newly trim waistline began to appear, followed by snowy-white, cleverly tied cravats that could have rivaled Brummell's in his heyday.

However, Pymm had still not broken the viscount of the habit of lounging around in his Chinese silk banyans and bare feet on the days he didn't leave the house. Minerva doubted Pymm ever would. Or that she even wanted him to. She was growing rather fond of the viscount's idiosyncrasies—either that, or she'd been steadily losing her mind over the past two months without realizing it.

That could very well have been the case, especially when she woke up one morning to the twins piled on top of her and one of Lady Elizabeth's naughty stories (which she'd not been able to resist after all, any more than the second floor of the library) plastered to her cheek, and came to the stunning conclusion that she didn't want to be anywhere else in the world.

Oh, God, she was actually *happy*. Which made it even more likely she'd gone insane.

But then the duchess came to visit.

It was Minerva's sacred day off (for though she'd truly grown to love the twins, she frankly needed her one day a week to recover from their antics), and she had every intention of hiding in Lackington's Temple for the afternoon, browsing the new books. She had only made it as far as halfway out the back servants' entrance, however, when she felt someone catch the door behind her and swing it wide.

She feared for a moment that it was the twins, for they'd developed an uncanny ability to know just when she was leaving the house on her day off—and an even more uncanny knack for manipulating her into staying with them instead.

It was, thankfully, just Mrs. Chips. Minerva had become fluent enough in the housekeeper's cryptic body language, however, to know that twitch in her left eye meant trouble. And it was twitching particularly fast today.

"You can't leave," Mrs. Chips said without preamble. "The duchess has come calling with the Countess of Brinderley."

"The duchess?" she prompted, since Mrs. Chips seemed to assume she knew what that should mean and why it should cut short her day off.

"The Duchess of Montford."

Mrs. Chips's tone was as flat as ever, but the name was enough for even Minerva to understand. The memory of Lady Blundersmith's dead weight tackling her to the ballroom floor of Montford House swam through her mind, followed by the memory of the flame-haired duchess standing off to one side and loudly ordering everyone around with far too much glee for someone whose husband had just swooned into the refreshments. Trouble indeed.

"Ah," she said diplomatically.

"She has brought her sisters."

She had a sudden, horrifying vision of her standing in the ruins of a smoldering house while four cackling imps danced around her.

She stepped back into the house, abandoning her plans for the day. "What would possess her to do that?"

"I believe His Grace is out of town," Mrs. Chips said, as if that explained everything.

"And?"

Mrs. Chips's eye twitched even faster, which was answer enough. It seemed a bored duchess, the Honeywell sisters, and Lady Brinderley rated higher on the alarm scale than the twins playing lawn tennis in the drawing room. Which they'd done last week. On her *last* day off.

Speaking of which . . .

"My day off . . ."

"Will have to wait. The children are in the garden. I must . . . see to tea for the duchess and countess."

Mrs. Chips would have stared down to the death anyone who had the nerve to accuse her of skulking, but that was exactly what she did, abandoning Minerva in the servants' hall for the sanctum of the kitchens.

Something told Minerva that Mrs. Chips had made up that last bit in order to avoid the chaos sure to be in progress in the garden.

Minerva sighed as she shrugged out of her redingote and bonnet, tucking her gloves into a pocket and stowing the whole bundle away for later retrieval. If the stalwart Mrs. Chips was afraid of the duchess's sisters, then perhaps what the viscount had told her about the Honeywells inciting the twins to arson last winter had been true.

Whatever the case, the four children together boded very ill indeed, though surely the few minutes it had been since their arrival could have hardly been enough time for them to cause too much trouble.

When she reached the back gardens and discovered the fate of her lost pantaloons, however, she realized just how wrong she was.

☙

FIVE MINUTES EARLIER, IN THE VISCOUNT'S LIBRARY . . .

JUST WHEN MARLOWE thought his life could not possibly get any more ridiculous, the Duchess of Montford and his sister—the meddling older one with a nursery nearly the size of a Roman legion, *not* the Misstopher currently tucked up in her bedroom—decided to pay a call on him just as he was sitting down at his desk to write one morning. He had vague memories of the pair visiting when he was on his sickbed, but he'd successfully avoided them ever since. He should have known his luck would run out.

The first time Marlowe had met the Duchess of Montford, she was in the middle of the King's Highway having her way with the duke—an image he very much wished he could excise from his brainbox. Very little had changed in that respect over the last five years besides the location: Astrid led Montford around by his nose, and for some inexplicable reason, Montford adored her for it.

Usually Marlowe was happy to let his friend enjoy the dubious rewards of wedded bliss, for he'd never seen Montford happier. But he secretly dreaded it whenever the duke traveled out of the city on estate business and left his wife behind. For an idle duchess was a social duchess, and a social duchess schemed with certain marchionesses and countesses to "improve" the lives of their husbands' unmarried acquaintances.

The only low she'd yet to stoop to was outright matchmaking, but Marlowe knew it was only a matter of time, for the insinuations had already begun.

He cursed himself anew for making the disastrous mistake of introducing Astrid to his older sister. Then he cursed Sebastian for getting himself married off, for now the full brunt of Elaine's and the duchess's attention had landed on him. How they could think Marlowe was even remotely adequate husband material was quite beyond him. Elaine herself had witnessed his spectacular failure the first time around.

Then again, the two women's judgment on the subject of men was questionable at best. Astrid had married Montford, after all, a man who to this day indexed his stockings by a complicated algorithm of fabric weight, color, and age, and still fainted like a maiden at the sight of blood.

And Elaine had married *Brinderley*. Who indexed his *coin collection*.

Their standards were skewed, to say the least. Marlowe had been hoping his drunken blunder into the Thames would have been enough to scare them off the hunt, but he should have known better.

"I have brought Ant and Art to see the twins," the duchess declared as she breezed into his library unannounced, his sister, eight months gone, waddling in behind her. Mrs. Chips was on their heels, her left eye quivering. Even she hadn't stood a chance guarding the gates against the two women. "I told them to play in the gardens so we can have a nice little chat."

Marlowe's wide-eyed look of panic was enough to send Mrs. Chips straight back through the door, hopefully in time to intercede before the Honeywell chits reenacted the Great Fire with the twins. Again.

"Elaine, Astrid," he muttered in greeting, reluctantly rising to his feet to receive a kiss on each cheek . . . and a hard punch to each shoulder.

He rubbed at the injuries. "What was that for?"

"Worrying us to death for running off to Kent when you were still so unwell," his sister sniffed.

"That was two months ago!"

"*I* would have come over here sooner to clout you," Astrid said, "but I was giving birth. This is the first chance I've had to give you a proper scolding."

"And I've been dreadfully sick with this one," Elaine said, patting her round stomach.

He got that nauseated feeling every time he came too close to thinking about how his sister and the spindly, myopic Brinderley had made—and continued to make—all of those babies.

Astrid eyed him up and down approvingly. "I must say, though, being on your deathbed has improved your waistline, if nothing else."

His hands shot to his midsection defensively, cradling it much like Elaine was cradling hers, and he scowled at her.

"I have given up Honeywell Ale. *Something* in it was disagreeing with me," he said loftily. Ha, *that* ought to stick in her craw. Astrid's family had proudly brewed the ale for centuries, and any slight upon it was a slight upon the Honeywell name—something that never failed to get the duchess's blood up.

Astrid scowled back at him. "Just for that, you shall not get your shipment of reserve this autumn."

Damn. He'd made the decision to reform his profligate ways, not consign himself to a completely joyless existence. And that was exactly what his life would be in a world without Honeywell Reserve. But he figured he had half a year to get back into Astrid's good graces.

In the meanwhile, he refused to let the woman run roughshod over him in his own house. Much.

"When does the duke return?" he asked, much too idly.

Her eyes narrowed. "Soon."

"Thank God."

"Humph. In his absence, I thought it best I check in on his best mate. I have heard you've acquired a new governess," she said, much too innocently.

Every instinct he had told him to duck and cover. He had a feeling she wasn't there to matchmake him after all, but something far, far worse. "You can't have her," he declared preemptively.

The duchess gave him an enigmatic smile that he didn't like at all. "She has been here two months, I hear. And she's still alive. Who *is* this miracle worker?"

"The twins are fond of Miss Jones, and I won't have you poaching her to corral those two hellcats of yours." He turned to his sister. "And you can't have her either. She'd waste away running after your horde."

Elaine lowered herself gingerly into a chair and waved her hand dismissively at the subject. "I have no need of your governess. But where is our sister, Marlowe? She has been avoiding me ever since she arrived in London."

"She's sixteen, Elaine, and it's ten in the morning. Far too early for anyone to be paying or receiving calls," he said, glancing pointedly at both of his unwanted guests. "We'll be lucky to see her before the afternoon."

Elaine ignored his hint entirely. "Father has already written me several outraged letters on the subject of Betsy."

"He's trying to marry her off to Poxley Oxley, Elaine."

"Well, we cannot have that," Elaine said crisply.

The duchess, impatient as ever to be the center of attention, inserted herself into the conversation. "Elaine and I have been talking about Lady Elizabeth's situation." Which didn't bode well at all, in Marlowe's opinion, especially when he noticed that secret gleam in her mismatched eyes. "And I have managed to procure these for you," she continued, pulling three small cards out of her reticule and depositing them in his hand.

It took him a moment to truly believe what he was beholding. His palms started to sweat, his stomach began to churn uneasily, and his heart raced so hard he was afraid he was having some sort of traumatic episode. All he could clearly think was that he was too young to die.

"Vouchers. To Almack's," he said flatly. "What the devil am I to do with these?"

"Escort Lady Elizabeth to the Assembly Rooms," Astrid said as if she were being perfectly reasonable. The duke had definitely been away for too long if Astrid had managed to convince herself that this was a good idea.

"Me. At Almack's."

She rolled her eyes. "You make it sound like the seventh circle of hell."

"Isn't it?"

He turned to his sister for help, but Elaine was looking far too entertained. "This moment was worth the miserable carriage ride over here," she said with a grin.

He harrumphed and shot her a glare that promised some future retribution . . . perhaps when she was not so pregnant. Which could very well be years at the rate she reproduced.

Astrid set her fists on her hips and regarded him with a rare, sober expression. "The trouble with Poxley and your father is not going to go away. How long before the earl tries something? Better to head him off at the pass."

"By attending Almack's," he said flatly. He would never understand the logic of a Honeywell.

"By demonstrating to your father that you have no need of his particular brand of matchmaking," she said, as if she were having to explain something very simple to a very small child. "If Lady Elizabeth is out in society, your father may be more inclined to back off, if for no other reason than to avoid airing the family's dirty laundry in public. There will be questions enough about why she is being brought out by you and not Barming, and he will be afraid how you might answer these if he presses the issue."

Marlowe hated to admit that Astrid's argument was sound. If there was one thing his father hated more than him, it was appearing anything less than pristine in the eyes of the ton. As badly behaved as the earl was behind closed doors, in the public eye, he was the image of sober respectability (the hypocrite).

It was another reason the earl despised Marlowe so much, for Marlowe had done his level best to be the cause of one public spectacle after another since his brawling days at Harrow.

The earl, as much as he wanted to marry Betsy off to the highest bidder as quickly as possible, wouldn't dare put a foot out of line if Betsy were officially out on the marriage mart. Barming was trying to sell her to Poxley before she could be introduced to society at all, for he must have feared how it would have made him look if it were widely known. The Upper Ten Thousand made the institution of marriage look like the auction block at Tattersall's, but surely even the worst cynic would have frowned on marrying off a sixteen-year-old girl to such a man.

Marlowe had never thought he'd live to see the day he'd be thankful for London society's judgmental high-sticklers. But Almack's?

Almack's?

He shuddered.

"They'll never let me in," he said.

"Your name is on the vouchers. Let's just say that Lady Cowper owes me a very big favor," the duchess said briskly. She eyed his attire with a grimace. "Just don't turn up in a banyan, or the Countess Lieven will kick you clear to Hampstead Heath."

"But why must *I* be the one to do this?" he cried, growing desperate as his fate loomed closer. He felt as if an invisible noose were tightening around his neck.

Astrid gestured toward Elaine. "Your sister is about to burst any day now, and do you honestly want your father and stepmother involved? You need to bring out your sister as soon as possible and present it to your father as a *fait accompli*. Besides, you need the practice of acting like a normal, upstanding pillar of society for when your daughters are presented."

The noose tightened even further, and he could barely see through a moment of blind panic. He may have crumpled the vouchers in his fist a bit at a sudden, soul-crushing vision of his daughters, grown and tarted up in the ridiculous, filmy silk fashions of the day, on an auction block, a slavering mass of young dandies gathered at their feet.

"The devil you say!" he cried.

"You have a decade at most to prepare yourself," the duchess declared bluntly.

"Two decades. Three. I am in no hurry," he said vehemently. "And why can't *you* escort Lady Elizabeth if you're so keen on this plan?"

Astrid laughed as if he'd said something amusing. "Me? At Almack's?" she scoffed. "I'd rather be run through with a hot poker."

Marlowe wondered if Montford would still be his friend if he murdered his wife.

He doubted it.

"Now let us go find the children," Astrid said breezily, helping to tug Elaine to her feet, "before they manage to find trouble."

Marlowe was certain that they were already too late for that.

CHAPTER EIGHT

In Which A Greek God Sweeps Miss Jones Off Her Feet

THE VISCOUNT WAS RIGHT. TROUBLE had indeed been found . . . then played with, tied to a trident, and flung aloft by the time Minerva located her charges and their companions. The unnecessarily grandiose marble fountain of Poseidon, set in the center of the garden, had become a castle, the basin of water a moat. Both of the Honeywell girls were chanting something about vanquishing Norman invaders while dancing around the perimeter, faces painted with what Minerva feared was the sludge from the bottom of the fountain.

Other than a difference in height—one was a slightly taller, auburn-haired demon, compared to the other—it was even harder to distinguish between the two Honeywell girls than it was between the twins. But she didn't need to tell them apart to know she was doomed. The Honeywells, with their war paint and battle cries, made her charges seem almost tame.

Or maybe they were merely the lit fuse on an already unstable powder keg. She came to this conclusion when she glanced up at Beatrice's shout of "Die, you Saxon filth!" to find the girl clinging to one of Poseidon's muscular alabaster thighs and flinging a bucket of water in the

Honeywells' direction.

Somehow, most of the brackish water landed on Minerva's bodice.

She tilted her head heavenward to gather her fraying nerves...

And spotted her missing pantaloons billowing in the wind off the spikes of Poseidon's trident.

When she recovered enough to tear her attention away from that particular beacon of humiliation, she found four pairs of wide eyes fixed on her. She couldn't fathom why they'd gone so suspiciously still and quiet so quickly until she realized she'd just shrieked like a banshee.

The water had been extremely cold, after all.

She decided not to look a gift horse in the mouth, thankful she didn't have to resort to more physical means of subduing the siege in progress.

She stabbed her finger in the direction of her pantaloons. "What is that?" she demanded.

Beatrice, feet planted on the pedestal rising out of the center of the fountain, had the good grace to look sheepish. Laura just looked defiant, as usual. Minerva didn't even bother gauging the Honeywells' level of contrition, since it would doubtless be nonexistent anyway.

"It's our pennant," Bea said.

"Are you sure? Because your pennant looks just like my new pantaloons," she said flatly.

The Honeywells snickered at the edge of the moat, and Minerva began to reconsider her stance on corporal punishment. She settled for a stern glare—to little effect.

Bea glanced up at the unmentionables, then at her sister, and then the pair of them gave Minerva a synchronized shrug. "I don't see it," Bea said.

Minerva set her hands on her hips and gave Bea The Look that was successful at least half of the time.

Bea looked for a moment as if she might set her heels in, but she finally sighed, her tiny shoulders slumping. "Fine," she said, as if Minerva were being a huge imposition. "If you want them back so badly you'd interrupt the Siege of Exeter, I suppose you can have them."

Well, at least Bea paid attention to her history lessons. But if she thought she was going to guilt Minerva into letting them continue their ridiculous behavior, she was wrong.

Bea started scaling up one of Poseidon's overly developed calves, and Minerva's stomach dropped. She didn't want to even imagine how the twins had managed to plant their flag in the first place, but Bea was certainly not going to attempt the climb to the top of Poseidon's trident again in *her* presence. The twins may have been half-feral, but that did not make their tiny skulls any more immune to being cracked open from a fall.

Minerva rushed forward, climbed into the fountain, and gritted her teeth at the frigid water soaking her up to midthigh. She splashed through the water, wincing all the way, and pulled Bea from Poseidon's pedestal without preamble. Bea looked shocked at the manhandling but remained surprisingly quiescent all the way back across the basin.

"Don't you dare climb up there again, Beatrice Leighton," she scolded, hoisting the girl over the edge of the fountain and depositing her next to her sister. "I'll not have either of you cracking your heads open."

"I'll go," one of the Honeywell chits said, bounding toward the fountain with a much too gleeful expression.

Even though she had lost all feeling in her legs in the frigid water, Minerva felt her heart sink to her toes at the very idea. The only thing worse than the twins' skulls cracked open were the Honeywells' skulls cracked open—and the Duke of Montford out for blood. *Her* blood. Though he'd probably faint at the sight of it.

She leveled her best glare at the girl, channeling her father at his most autocratic. It seemed to work, for the girl's cocksure expression faltered, and she stepped back in line.

Minerva transferred her glare to her billowing pantaloons and considered her next move, shivering when the April winds picked up and bit through her drenched skirts. The thought of leaving her unmentionables flying high for the new footmen to find—or God forbid, the viscount or Mrs. Chips—made her want to punch someone in the face. There was nothing for it but to retrieve them herself, though how she'd arrived at such an impasse in her life boggled the mind.

She gathered up the weighted bulk of her wet skirts and slogged up to the marble pedestal where Poseidon was half kneeling in his altogether, looking on the verge of smiting his foe with his trident. She grasped a marble shin and heaved onto the ledge, slowly dragging herself up the line of Poseidon's body until she was hugging him around the waist, her face smashed against the cold, damp marble of his breastbone.

Something poked her in the stomach, and she glanced down to find Poseidon's . . . attributes . . . staring back at her from far too intimate a distance.

"Oh, for the love of . . ." she muttered. She could feel her face heat at the ridiculousness of her position. The Honeywell chits must have realized her predicament, for she could hear them giggling below her.

The only bright spot in what was quickly becoming a terrible day was that the twins were still too young to understand what the older girls found so amusing. They took her long pause for a case of nerves. Thank heavens, for the only thing that could make this day worse was having to explain male reproductive organs to them instead of reading their usual bedtime fairy tale.

"Do be careful, Miss Jones!" Bea called, almost sounding concerned for her safety. "It's a bit wobbly up there."

"Nonsense," she began briskly with all the false confidence she could muster through her chattering teeth.

Then she placed her wet boot on Poseidon's bent knee and felt the entire statue list ever so slightly forward.

She threw her weight against the god's torso, and the statue shifted back into place with a creak and groan. The sinking sensation in her stomach stopped, and she rested her head against Poseidon's throat, wondering how her life had come to this utter abandonment of decorum.

A saner person—one who'd not spent five years tending to Lady Blundersmith's imaginary agues, a year in a remote girls' reform school with Fräulein Schmidt as the closest thing to a friend, and then two months governessing for Viscount Marlowe—would have at that moment abandoned the venture altogether. And since she was not quite ready for Bedlam, she did actually consider climbing back down to earth, swallowing her mortification, and fetching the one lone footman the twins had yet to scare off to retrieve her unmentionables.

But then she heard the deep baritone growl of the viscount's voice drifting from the entrance to the garden and the light, teasing tones of what she assumed were the duchess and countess, and she froze. The voices were growing perilously close to the fountain. She could even see the flash of the duchess's infamous Honeywell Swirl chignon and the matching siren-red of the viscount's favorite red silk banyan through the rosebushes.

The thought of the viscount discovering her pantaloons flying high on Poseidon's trident—the thought of the *look* on his face, that same smug amusement he'd worn the entire journey from West Barming to London—was enough to overrule the last of her common sense. She hoisted herself onto Poseidon's knee once more, ignoring the gentle sway of marble beneath her, and strained upward toward the leg of her pantaloons, billowing just out of her reach.

"You have to prop yourself up on his shoulder, Miss

Jones!" Bea called.

"Shhh!" She motioned at the girls to keep their voices down—or at least she tried to. The movement seemed to make the statue wobble even more. She clutched at Poseidon's head until his wobbling slowed down, then took Bea's dubious advice and lifted her left foot onto the god's shoulder, trying to arrange her wet skirts so she too wasn't revealing all of *her* attributes to the world. She wound up having to drape most of her skirts over Poseidon's head, her splayed legs stretching the fabric.

For some reason, this seemed to set off the Honeywell girls again—perhaps because of the position of the Greek god's head.

Well. At least Poseidon was the only one seeing up her skirts, however awkward.

After a bit of contortion, she was finally able to grab the leg of her pantaloons, but the fabric snagged on the trident and refused to budge. She tugged on it again, to no avail.

"Oh lud, what have we here?" came the duchess's amused voice from much too close.

She cursed inwardly. Too late. She was *too late*.

Minerva chanced a glance downward and saw the duchess's flame-colored hair, freckled face and startlingly mismatched eyes beaming up at her, looking as if Minerva had done something miraculous rather than scale Greek statuary in a wet dress. Next to her was an extremely pregnant woman with the Leighton coloring—Lady Brinderley, she presumed—who was laughing outright.

The viscount stood just behind his older sister, but the smirk Minerva had been dreading was not there. Instead, his jaw hung slack, and his big brown eyes were popped so wide they seemed incapable of blinking anymore. He looked as if he'd run into a wall, and when she finally looked down and caught sight of her legs, bared to midthigh with nothing but her sagging stockings to cover them (she really could have used those pantaloons right about now), she understood why.

Cheeks burning, she jerked at her unmentionables—now the least of her worries—one final time, and the force she used was so great the statue creaked forward, causing her boot to slip from Poseidon's shoulder. The front of her skirts was still thrown over Poseidon's head, and so as she slipped down his torso, her skirts rode up even higher.

Below her, the viscount cleared his throat, his face the same color as his banyan, and attempted to look anywhere but at her. The duchess seemed to be caught between glee and concern. "My dear, are you all right?" she called.

"Quite," she bit out, jerking her skirts from around Poseidon's head and pushing them down her legs with one hand. But just when she'd nearly restored her dignity enough to clamber down the pedestal, something cracked—Poseidon's thigh underneath her foot—and the wobbling became a relentless tilt forward.

She scrambled to remove herself from the god's path of destruction. Somehow she managed to jump into the fountain and make it over the edge with her pantaloons in one hand before the statue could fall down completely. But once again she was too slow to completely avoid catastrophe.

She saw the viscount's panicked expression as he rushed toward her . . .

But he was too late to save her from Poseidon's clutches. She spun around and shrieked as she saw the god of the sea bearing down on her from above. She had just enough time to slow the statue's creaking descent with her hands to Poseidon's sculpted breast before the statue's weight had pinned her to the ground, but she wasn't quick enough to save her head from banging against the flagstones.

The last thing she could think before everything went blank was at least she'd managed to salvage the pantaloons.

SHE CAME TO a moment later and found the god of the sea between her legs, her skirts rucked up scandalously high once more, and the viscount hovering over her, looking as if he didn't know whether to push the statue off her or keep it there to protect her dignity.

Her dignity, however, had long since abandoned her.

The duchess and Lady Brinderley loomed into her line of vision, both trying to look appropriately serious, but failing miserably. Somewhere behind her, all four of the little imps who had begun this whole debacle were cackling with hilarity.

The duchess turned to Marlowe. "*This* is your governess?"

"It would appear so," he murmured, trying and failing not to ogle her naked legs. The wretch.

The only upside to the situation that she could see was the heated blush she could feel spreading through her blood as she noticed the viscount's gaze. At least she wasn't cold anymore.

"If you wouldn't mind," she bit out.

The viscount startled, looked puzzled for a moment, but then finally snapped into action. "Yes, of course," he said gruffly, still blushing like a schoolgirl, and lifted the statue away from her. There were advantages to being a giant, after all, for he showed little strain in hoisting Poseidon into his arms and carrying it away from the scene of the crime.

She just managed to tuck her skirts back over her legs by the time he turned back to her. Her attempt to climb to her feet ended in disaster, however, her head spinning and her eyes crossing. She fell backward once more—though she would categorically, positively deny it was a swoon—and was caught in warm, strong arms.

Minerva opened her eyes and discovered the viscount peering down at her from only a few inches away, his brow creased in concern. From so close, his thick, luxurious hair gleamed in the midmorning light, and his brown eyes glittered. She could see the bump on his nose clearly, right between his eyes, and the way his full, mobile lips were parted as he panted slightly with his exertion. His body was warm beneath his rumpled layers and fragrant with bay rum and sandalwood.

She couldn't breathe for a long while, and it had nothing to do with the bump on her head or the chill in her bones. In fact, she wasn't chilled at all anymore. Not in the viscount's arms.

And *that* thought was worrying enough to make her push away from him entirely. She wobbled a bit but miraculously remained upright this time. She glared at Poseidon, now in a nearby flower bed, staring blankly up at the sky, his *attributes* also pointing the same direction.

Twice now, she had been struck down by a member of the peerage. She had not thought to guard herself against Greek statuary as well.

Minerva turned back to the viscount. He was holding his hand over his eyes while his sister and the duchess chortled behind him. She glanced down and discovered why. She may have covered her legs, but the fountain water had made her gown utterly translucent.

"Bollocks," she muttered. She crossed her arms over her breasts.

The duchess's eyes lit up at her crudity. "Oh, I *like* her." She removed her pelisse and offered it to Minerva, who wrapped it around her shivering shoulders. "If you're ever in need of employment, my dear, you are welcome at Montford House. I have a feeling you could keep up with my sisters quite nicely."

"Astrid," growled the viscount warningly, "no poaching the governess!"

Minerva side-eyed the Honeywell girls, who were standing over the fallen statue, poking it with their sticks. When their sticks reached Poseidon's groin, she cleared her throat and thought it best to avert her eyes. She'd had quite enough of *that* today. "I shall keep that in mind," she said, intending to do anything but.

"Well, the offer stands," the duchess said briskly, then started to herd Minerva from the garden, leaving Lady Brinderley and Lord Marlowe to corral the children. "Now, let's get you inside and out of those wet things. And you can tell me all about how you came to be climbing Poseidon," the duchess said with such enthusiasm Minerva had no choice but to follow her orders.

Minerva glanced over her shoulder at Lord Marlowe, who was hauling his two damp, squealing children up by each arm—no easy feat, for the little hellions were heavier than they looked. He made it look as effortless as he had lifting the statue, though.

Which of course it was for him, with all of that brawn at his disposal. Now that he wasn't encumbered by the bloat of his excesses, the viscount was all raw muscle beneath those ridiculous Chinese dressing gowns of his. She knew this well, for she'd felt the strength for herself when he'd fallen on top of her at their first meeting.

She wondered if the Leightons came from Viking stock. It would certainly explain those shoulders. And the proclivity for brawling. *And* the easy way he'd lifted her out of that ditch in Kent, or caught her in his arms just now, as if she'd weighed no more than a feather . . .

"And," the duchess said, watching Minerva with far too much interest as Minerva watched the viscount, "you must tell me how long *this* has been going on."

Minerva jerked her attention back to the duchess, blushing—though she wasn't sure why. "What? I have no idea what you're talking about, Your Grace," she said. And that was the truth. Mostly. Though she didn't like the secret little smile that graced the duchess's lips. Or the way her eyes gleamed as she looked from Minerva to the viscount and back again calculatingly.

The duchess merely patted her hand as if humoring a child. "Of course you don't," she said soothingly. "But let's just say my task has become a thousand times easier."

"Task?" Minerva asked, suspicious.

Her Grace didn't bother to explain herself further and bustled them both inside.

☾

A HALF HOUR later, the duchess had somehow managed to bully Minerva into dry clothes, charm a piping hot pot of tea and fresh scones and butter out of the uncharmable Mrs. Chips, and corral not only Lady Brinderley but also a bleary-eyed Lady Elizabeth into Minerva's small bedroom to enjoy the refreshments. Minerva thus found herself tucked into her bed like an invalid, surrounded by titled ladies, sipping Earl Gray as if they were at a tea party, and waiting on Dr. Lucas to come and check out the bump to her head.

It was one of the strangest moments of her life.

Then Her Grace proceeded to pull most of Minerva's life history out of her as threatened—including her employment with Lady Blundersmith, which she hadn't even mentioned to the viscount. But the duchess spoke no more of her strange insinuations in the garden, for which Minerva was grateful. Minerva was not prepared to let her mind even touch upon the implications of *her* and the *viscount* . . .

No. Just—

No.

But when Lady Elizabeth somehow let it slip that Minerva was a Misstopher—which she *wasn't*, for heaven's sake, though she'd yet to convince Lady Elizabeth otherwise (or herself, deep down)—that calculating gleam returned to the duchess's eyes, and she grinned like a cat that got the cream.

And a nice plump mouse.

And a few unsuspecting birds.

Minerva had absolutely no idea what that was about, and she thought briefly about demanding an accounting from Her Grace—even though the woman was one of the most powerful duchesses in the realm. But then the subject turned away from Minerva completely—thank hell—since Lady Elizabeth was off on her favorite subject: Essex, and her intention to wed him instead of Poxley Oxley.

Both the duchess and Lady Brinderley thought this so amusing for some reason that they were overcome by laughter for several minutes. Lady Brinderley finally gripped her belly and moaned, "No more, or I shall give birth right here."

That prospect was one of the most horrifying things Minerva had ever heard. She was glad the ladies calmed down enough a few seconds later to avoid such a messy outcome, but she gripped her saucer with white knuckles in the meanwhile, thankful Inigo had been summoned in case the worst happened.

"I don't see why you think that is so funny," Lady Elizabeth said haughtily, stung by the ladies' reaction. It *had* been rather excessive. "I know you think me silly and I know it is likely never to occur, but I am determined to have my silly little hopes. Otherwise, I am liable to give into despair."

Minerva's heart promptly sank at the bleak look on Lady Elizabeth's face. So too did the other ladies', if their contrite expressions were anything to go by. That had certainly taken the wind out of their sails.

"Of course you should have hope," the duchess said firmly. "And never fear. We are all on your side. You won't have to marry that odious man."

Lady Elizabeth's smile was tight. "I hope you're right."

"Of course I am," the duchess said briskly and with full confidence in the matter.

Minerva could only wish for Lady Elizabeth's sake that

the duchess was right. At the very least, the girl deserved a husband that wasn't half a century her senior. At best, she deserved to have many, many more years to grow into herself before she even contemplated marriage. But women were allowed few choices when it came to such matters—especially for someone in Lady Elizabeth's position, who had a father determined to barter her off to the highest bidder at the first opportunity.

Minerva may not have had the ideal upbringing, but she'd be forever thankful the captain had never sought to marry her off. She'd had the chance, however short-lived, to marry for love—a rare occurrence indeed for any woman.

Minerva's fate had been proscribed almost entirely by her sex and her father's limited income, and her only real option to escape penury—or worse—was marriage or the sort of half life lived by governesses or companions (both of which were as near to penury as to make no difference). When she'd met Arthur, however, she'd decided that marriage might not be a terrible thing if she could marry a man like him, a man who could steer the helm of his own fate and offer her a place at his side.

Though the chances were slim indeed, Minerva hoped Lady Elizabeth would one day be given the same opportunity.

"But I don't think it wise to set your hopes on Mr. Essex," the duchess continued gently. "He could be anyone. A haberdasher from Cheapside with five children and a fishwife. Or Poxley Oxley himself. *He* could even be a *she* for all we know."

"Or Marlowe," Lady Brinderley murmured, eyes dancing.

Lady Elizabeth shuddered, and they all laughed at the absurdity of the idea, the mood restored.

Marlowe indeed. *That* seemed more unlikely than a haberdasher.

CHAPTER NINE

In Which Marlowe Gets His Muse Back

IT ONLY TOOK MARLOWE ONE night to finish the ode—his first half-decent work in nearly three years—and it was just going on midmorning by the time he was penning the final draft at his library desk. Only a few more lines were left before it was done, and he held his breath as he wrote them out . . .

> . . . *The nymph who warmed my bed, to me it seems,*
> *The frigid stone of winter after all.*

He applied the final full stop with aplomb.

Perfect. His eyes felt like sandpaper, his mouth tasted as if something had crawled in it and died, and his shirtsleeves were stained in ink. But despite all that, he felt better than he had in months—in years. He'd been half-afraid he'd never write another decent word, but it seemed that his dry spell had, at last, ended.

All it had taken, then, was seeing his governess's naked legs.

He'd had a momentary pang of guilt about his choice of material sometime after midnight and halfway through the second stanza. He knew it was wrong of him to be so exploitative, but he couldn't seem to help himself. The inspiration had been just too good, and he knew even before he put the pen to paper that it would be the best work he'd done in years.

But while it wasn't complete rubbish, he doubted he would be submitting this one to Waverley, no matter how desperate his avaricious little publisher was to sink his teeth into a new manuscript. For one, the ode had ended up a bit too self-pitying for his taste, even for a poet known for his hyperbolic angst. For another, he'd used his governess's *naked flesh* as inspiration, and even though he was the only one who'd ever know the inspiration for the poem's nymph, it just didn't seem right exposing her to the public eye.

Though he'd had little problem exposing his bleeding heart and broken soul in his past works to his readers—albeit anonymously—he couldn't do the same with his latest creation. It was too private, too fragile—just like his feelings for Miss Jones altogether.

He'd admired her from the start, adored her vicious tongue and unfiltered banter. She wasn't afraid to speak her mind or challenge him, that was for sure. Perhaps she was sometimes quick to judgment, as she'd seemed to have made up her mind about him long before their meeting in Kent, but she was not inflexible and not afraid of being proven wrong. But she wasn't all prickly bits: she was kind to his daughters and deferential to Chippers, despite the housekeeper's gruff manner, and had even managed to wrangle Betsy into something resembling good behavior.

He liked her. He liked her more every time he saw her, and though he'd never found himself drawn to pocket-size brunettes in the past, he'd been attracted to her from the moment he saw her half drowned in that Kentish ditch. Perhaps it had been those flashing storm-cloud eyes, or the angry roses in her alabaster cheeks, or the selkie grace of her small body even in the throes of a pique. Perhaps it was all of her.

But the lust—pure, consuming, and shameless—had not come until her ignominious fall by the fountain. He was a red-blooded man, after all, and there had been a rather lot of naked flesh on display. He had a vivid imagination, but none of his secret daydreams could have ever prepared him for the reality of what was underneath all of those drab muslin layers.

He had discovered, to his delight, that her skin was flawlessly alabaster from top to toe—and when she blushed, she blushed *all over*, infusing all of that gorgeous marble with the prettiest, most delicate rose glow. It had made him want to put his hands all over her with an urgency he'd never felt before.

He couldn't very well attack his governess in broad daylight (or at all), or even bring himself to more covertly seduce her—though the thought had crossed his mind once (or a hundred times). She was his employee and the first capable minder of the twins he'd ever found. It would be positively criminal to act on his desires—to tempt a decent woman under his protection into sin, no matter how much he wanted her.

Besides, he doubted he *could* tempt her. Despite their banter, despite her grudging acceptance of him as a friend in recent weeks, she would never want him like that. No matter his attempts at reformation, he would always be, to her mind, the buffoon in a banyan who'd fallen on her breasts and gotten her sacked.

No, he could not seduce her. But Christopher Essex could, on a sheet of foolscap, for the duration of four stanzas, at least. And though she'd never read the poem, he'd have the cold comfort of knowing she'd like it if she did.

She liked everything Essex wrote, he thought sulkily . . .

And apparently he was jealous of himself—of her steadfast and uncomplicated admiration of an unknown poet.

Yet another reason—childish as it was—to keep the ode to himself. Knowing Miss Jones would read the poem but have no idea it was about her—or that *he* had written it—seemed the worst sort of torture.

His good mood in finishing the ode promptly ended, however, when Mrs. Chips had the effrontery to announce a visitor. The last person he wanted to see cross the threshold of his library was Nigel Waverley . . . well, the second to last, as his father would always hold pride of place in Marlowe's private pantheon of undesirables. But when his sire was in West Barming, his publisher definitely moved to the top of the list—especially in the midst of his endless creative drought. And especially *now*, when the drought had finally ended.

He wanted to bang his head on the desktop as Waverley marched into the room, but he manfully restrained himself despite his exhausted irritation. It was as if the man knew precisely how Marlowe had spent the night, damn him.

"You know, harassing me won't make me magically pull a sonnet out of my arse, Waverley."

"A man can hope," Waverley said shortly. He was a small, whippet-thin man with the face of a hungry weasel and gold spectacles perched on a thin nose. Marlowe's previous works had made Waverley a rich man, but like everyone who'd had a whiff of success, he wanted even more. Judging by the expensive cut of the man's jacket and his Hoby boots, he'd developed quite expensive tastes over the past few years.

Marlowe had given him *The Italian Poem* two and a half years ago, and doubtless his coffers were running low. Hence the last year of increasingly urgent visits. But Marlowe couldn't give Waverley what he didn't have—and he certainly wasn't prepared to give him "The Alabaster Hip."

"But what's all this?" Waverley demanded of Marlowe's cluttered desk and stained fingers. His beady eyes had a rather maniacal glint to them behind his gold spectacles. "Have you been writing, then?"

"No," Marlowe lied, covering "The Alabaster Hip" with

his hands, wincing inwardly at himself for being so very unsubtle. Waverley gave him an appropriately doubtful look. "It's a letter to . . . my, er, father."

Waverley looked even more suspicious. "You hate your father."

"Don't mean I don't write letters to him," he grumbled. "Estate business and all."

Waverley didn't believe him for a second but seemed willing to indulge in the lie. "Fine. But please tell me you're working on something."

"Of course," he hedged. He was always working on *something*, even if it was a blank page.

"Because it's been three years."

"Two and a half," he corrected.

"I need *something*, my lord," Waverley said, frustrated. "Murray is running us to ground with Byron's new cantos. And I don't have to tell you about the absolute splash *Adonais* has made."

"And yet you just did," he muttered.

"For God's sake, *Keats* is outselling you, and he's dead!"

Marlowe winced at the reminder. The young man's death had shaken him—had made the last year even more unbearably dreary than the ones before it. In his humble opinion, Keats had put him and all of their contemporaries to shame, and it was a tragedy to have lost him so soon. Shelley might have turned his grief into a masterful elegy, but Marlowe had buried his in the bottle and abandoned the pen entirely.

"Perhaps I should cock up my toes so you may reap the profits," he groused.

"That would be a wonderful idea," Waverley said, completely bloody serious. "But no one *knows who you are*."

Unfortunately, Marlowe could see where this meeting was going. His continued anonymity had been a long-standing bone of contention for Waverley.

"If you're still . . . struggling . . ." Waverley began much too innocently.

"Struggling?" Marlowe scoffed, offended. He hated it when Waverley talked about his unproductivity in such honest terms. "I'm not struggling. I'm taking my time."

Waverley clenched his jaw in annoyance and forged onward. "While you're 'taking your time,'" he said dubiously, "why not announce publicly that you are Christopher Essex? We might reissue your whole catalogue then. The number of people clamoring for your work when they know you, Lord Marlowe, are the poet, would be . . ."

"No," he said flatly.

"But . . ."

"No. And if you even think of doing so without my permission, I will eviscerate you."

Sometimes Marlowe was grateful for his pugnacious reputation, for Waverley's protests died immediately, and he paled slightly at the threat.

"I don't understand you," Waverley grumbled. "Why are you so determined to remain anonymous?"

Frankly, Marlowe wasn't quite sure he had a good reason for it anymore, but at first, publishing as Christopher Essex had been a strategically defensive move. He'd endured years of his family's mockery and abuse, and he'd been quite certain he'd not survive the world's, not when it came to his poetry and the intimate, inner world inside of him that it exposed.

And while Marlowe was usually quite keen on sticking it to Barming, he'd never wanted to publish his work simply to spite the old man. He'd not make his poetry—that one part of himself he'd held completely inviolable—part of his feud with his father. It was too sacred, too essential to the maintenance of his soul, to be sullied by the earl's inevitable denigration.

As a child, Marlowe would have lived in the library if he could have gotten away with it, but his father had done his level best to beat out what he saw as his heir's failure to be properly masculine. The earl had a distressingly medieval view on manhood. Books and learning weren't to be enjoyed—they were to be tolerated only until they'd served their purpose. Real men—like the earl, like Evander—enjoyed hunting and gambling, brawling and wenching, not Shakespeare and Milton and Donne.

So he'd learned to hide that part of himself from an early age and instead became quite adept at the manly pursuits endorsed by his father—especially brawling, for he'd been, unsurprisingly, a very angry child.

Things had not improved. An adolescent Caroline, who'd been raised by a man with similar opinions to his own father, had laughed the first and only time he'd tried to give her a poem. He probably should have taken that rejection as a sign of things to come, but his puppy love had blinded him to all of the ways they didn't fit together.

Later on, after things had completely fallen apart between them, she'd mocked his work—early drafts of some of his sonnets—when he'd been stupid enough to leave it out on his writing desk. She'd called him names that didn't bear repeating, as unimpressed as his father had been with his "hobby."

After the war, after Caroline's and Evander's deaths, when he'd finally worked up the nerve to publish the sonnets—if only to exorcize those demons from his soul—he'd never even thought to do so under his own name. He'd long stopped caring what his father thought, but still that deeply ingrained fear that he'd carried around since the first time his father had jerked a book from his hands must have remained. Perhaps he was a coward to still be hiding behind his nom de plume, but he'd yet to find a reason for courage.

Enough he was published at all—though sometimes he regretted even that.

"I couldn't care less what you understand," Marlowe finally said in his best lord-of-the-manor tone.

Waverley's shoulders slumped, as they always did at the end of one of their tiffs about Essex.

"You've nothing then? No small work we might sell to the broadsheets?"

Marlowe narrowed his eyes and wondered if Waverley had set spies on him in the night. "You must be in dun territory to even think of selling to the broadsheets."

Waverley scowled at him. "Business is slow, my lord. I'm tempted to drop *you* completely and spend my time on someone who actually produces."

Marlowe shrugged, completely unbothered by the empty threat. He wasn't writing or publishing for the money anyway, and Waverley's badgering hardly made him want to cooperate. Besides, Waverley would murder his firstborn if he thought it would bring him Essex's next manuscript, and they both knew it.

"Do what you like, Waverley. *I* am quite content to look elsewhere as well. Do you know, I met Murray just last year at Tatt's. I found him quite an agreeable fellow."

Waverley's cheeks grew ruddy at the mention of his nemesis. Of course, Marlowe had absolutely no intention of approaching Murray, but Waverley's constipated look was priceless.

Marlowe stood up from his desk and began to herd the man from his study. He did not have time to deal with any more of Waverley's nonsense.

"Now if you don't mind, I'm busy."

"But . . ."

"Soon, Waverley," he promised, and this time he actually meant it. Now that he'd produced an ode, he felt absolutely invigorated.

Waverley, red-faced and spluttering, finally conceded to Marlowe's demand and stepped back out into the hallway.

Marlowe slammed the door in his publisher's face and returned to his desk to reread the ode with satisfaction. His muse had finally returned.

And she was currently in the nursery somewhere above his head, teaching grammar to his children.

☾

WHEN MARLOWE WAS sure enough time had passed for Waverley to find his own way out, he left his library in search of something more fortifying than his lukewarm tea, tucking "The Alabaster Hip" in the top drawer, away from prying eyes.

In his haste, he didn't notice the Hoby boots lurking beneath the draperies at the end of the corridor.

When he returned to the library an hour later—fed, shorn, bathed, and forced into a cravat, hessians, and cutaway by Pymm—he thought it odd to find his inkpot unstoppered. He could have sworn he'd put it up before he'd left. Then again, he'd been awake for over twenty-four hours, so his mind could very well have been playing tricks on him.

He moved the ode to the bottom drawer and locked it up with the rest of Essex's work, just in case Waverley did indeed employ spies.

☾

WHEN "THE ALABASTER HIP" appeared on the front page of the *Morning Chronicle* the following day, Marlowe nearly spat out his eggs.

Waverley.

The bloody little bastard had copied the poem while Marlowe had been out of the room. It was the only explanation.

He *knew* he'd put that inkpot away.

He abandoned his breakfast, stormed over to Albemarle Street, slammed into Number 51, shouldered into Nigel's office, and punched the little thief in the jaw.

☾

THE FOLLOWING MORNING, when he grudgingly opened the *Morning Post*—an insufferably Tory mouthpiece he only read to keep abreast of the enemy—he was met with a headline that took up nearly a quarter of the page and stoked his still-smoldering ire:

"ALABASTER HIP" SHORTAGE SPARKS RIOT
ON N. BOND STREET:
DAUGHTER OF DUKE OF D—— INJURED IN
STAMPEDE

Waverley.

Marlowe left his poached eggs congealing on the china, stormed over to Albemarle Street, slammed into Number 51, shouldered into Nigel's office, and punched the little thief in the jaw yet again.

CHAPTER TEN

In Which The Morning Chronicle Presents

(With the Exclusive Cooperation of Nigel Waverley,
Of Waverley & Sons Publishers,
51 Albemarle Street, Mayfair)

THE ALABASTER HIP

AN ODE
By Christopher Essex
Author of *The Hedonist* and Other Works of Poesy

ONE EVE BEFORE ME WAS *a vision seen*
    With rosy lips and eyes of silver'd cloud;
And off her dais the vision step'd serene
In naught but the Springtime winds did enshroud;
She moved, this nymph, with potent grace and charm,
To dew-dripped bower there to pass the night;
She turned to me, her tender flesh once more
Bedamp'd by rain, to seek my trembling arm;
And she was then as fair to me as light
Upon a fiery sheath of golden ore.

A third time pass'd my hand on marble turn'd
As warm as woman's secret flesh interred;

THE ALABASTER HIP

Then burn'd did she, and follow her I burn'd
And ached for words to sing my love for her;
Yet many moons had pass'd since last I'd had
Calliope's sweet favor in my hand;
So still my tongue in praise did hesitate,
My lust, my love, in plain truth still unsaid
Beyond caresses in our bow'r; and then
Her praises sung rose from my heart too late.

She cooled as my sweet words remained unforged;
Oh desire! How soon it fled from her lips,
How brief the fire lit tender flesh engorged
And left naught but an alabaster hip;
Cruel Galatea holds no love for me
Nor I for her—a maid encased in ice
With heart of stone and lips of wintry chill;
Oh for the heated press of dewy knee
And slick, sweet slide of skin that ever lies
'Neath moon and roof of fragrant bougainvill'.

So, fair nymph, farewell! I cannot desire
A nightly defeat on false pleasure's wing,
For I so sapped of Poesy's strength'ning fire
Ne'er could withstand another broken ring;
Go from my lonely vigil, quick, and be
No more than what you were before my dreams,
Atop a fount, stillborn, in Spring's first thrall;
You are, no less, a goddess' parody:
The nymph who warmed my bed, to me it seems,
The frigid stone of winter after all.

TO BETSY LEIGHTON, Lady Hedonist herself, it was as if Christmas, Easter, her birthday, and her father's future funeral had all come at once the morning she found "The Alabaster Hip" among the discarded broadsheets covering the breakfast table. It was definitely the first time anything good had ever come of rising before noon. Breakfast forgotten, she stole the *Morning Chronicle* before her brother could return from wherever he'd stormed off to, closeted herself in her room, and began to read.

Two days later and twenty readings in, she had nearly memorized the entire poem, transcribed it twice (once for Miss Jones, who was still recovering from being squashed by Poseidon, and once for Mrs. Chips, who liked Essex despite what her eyebrows said), and ranked it among Mr. Essex's other works—somewhere above *The Italian Poem*, yet still falling short of the genius that was *The Hedonist*. Alas, a mere four stanzas, however prettily done, could not unseat that masterful narrative poem in her affections.

Nevertheless, Betsy was not complaining. Four stanzas in nearly three years was better than *no* stanzas in three years. And while the ode hadn't the playful irony of his longer works, it was wonderfully morose and deliciously, tragically romantic. Just what all the Misstophers were gasping for at the moment.

Even Prudence Potts, daughter of West Boring's vicar, had been in alt over the ode in her recently arrived letter, and that tasteless philistine usually found everything wanting in comparison with Lord Byron's verse—even that abysmally dreary "Prisoner of Chillon." It was as if Essex had read the minds—or perhaps the secrets contained in their commonplace books—of every one of his female followers.

Betsy sighed into her pillow, clutching the much-loved broadsheet to her bosom, and thought about reading it again. No doubt all of the females in the English-speaking world—and some of the males, at that—had swooned when they'd read the poem. Betsy herself had done so quite dramatically upon her counterpane halfway through the first stanza.

She'd done so again at the titillating vision her mind conjured upon reading of "tender flesh engorged" in the third stanza. She wasn't quite sure what the author intended to suggest by this, but she had a fair idea. What she lacked in experience, she more than made up for in her imagination.

By the end of her first reading of the poem, she had been burningly jealous of whoever this woman was who had inspired the ode. If Essex were writing about anything other than a theoretical hip, if some other woman had sunk her claws into him . . . well, she was a Leighton and would not be pulling her punches any more than her father ever did. Which was never.

She could only hope that the owner of the alabaster hip was merely the symbolic *every woman* of Essex's other works, but after several days of trying to convince herself of this, she gave up. She may have been only sixteen, but she knew what a man sounded like when he was in love. It was how Brinderley sounded when he spoke to Elaine, how Montford sounded even when he was bickering with the duchess. It was even how Evie had begun to sound whenever he spoke of Miss Jones . . . though the man was too much of a muttonhead to ever realize how transparently enamored of his governess he had become.

But she had Lady Hedonist's rather rabid following slavering for her next work to keep her from brooding too much over Essex's love life (for brooding was quite all right for poets, but not for young ladies determined to avoid wrinkles). And "The Alabaster Hip," with its Greek allusions and mouthwatering sensuality, was ripe for the plucking. She had no less than a dozen plot ideas in need of pursuing already.

But first she needed some foolscap, and for that she needed to raid Evie's desk. He always seemed to be hoarding it, which never made sense to her, considering how allergic to letter writing he was. She waited until late afternoon when she knew Evie would be out of the house, then slipped inside the empty library, quietly shutting the door behind her and tiptoeing across the parquet to his cluttered desk. Betsy wasn't sure why she felt the need for such subterfuge, as if she were doing something criminal. Then again, Evie had always been overparticular about the oddest things.

Though his visits were increasingly rare as she grew up, then nonexistent after Evander's and Caroline's deaths, Evie had been her only ally in a house full of bedlamites. There had been Elaine, of course, but her older sister had been married and living in London long before Betsy's memories even began. For all of his tarnish, Evie was pure mint underneath, and she had not even hesitated over whom to go to when she'd run away from Kent.

That didn't mean he wouldn't have an attack of apoplexy if he caught her going through his desk. The one time in her childhood she remembered him losing his temper with her had been because she'd decided to use one of his journals for her watercolors.

His anger had made him look exactly like Evander, who was always in a temper about one thing or another, and it had frightened her so much she'd vowed never to go snooping about her brother's things again. He'd never laid a hand on her, of course—even at his angriest, Evie just didn't have that sort of maliciousness in him (unlike his twin)—but she'd never wanted to see him look at her like that again.

But desperate times called for desperate measures, and now was not the time to run out of foolscap, not when she was bursting with the perfect inspiration for her next story. It featured one delicious Mr. Essex, of course, and a young brunette, brown-eyed maiden who may or may not have been the runaway daughter of an evil earl, the pair of them trapped in a cave during a thunderstorm. In the shadow of the Parthenon, of course.

Betsy's enthusiasm waned, however, when she spotted a letter from the earl, half-crumbled, under a pile of bills. She slumped in Evie's chair and sighed at the dread reminder of her father. Evie could only hold off the earl for so long, and just being here was asking a lot—maybe too much—of her brother.

His relationship with Barming was already tattered enough without him shouldering the burden of her situation as well. The stubborn idiot would fight to the bitter end for her on principle alone, and that was both why she'd run to him and what scared her the most. Their family had already cost Evie too much. He'd shouldered the worst of their father's abuse and Evander's heartlessness—and she didn't know precisely what had happened with his dead wife and Evander, but she had imagination enough to guess it was beyond horrible.

Besides, why should she wait around for her brother to solve her problems? Legally, he could do nothing if the earl chose to retrieve her. Her father practically owned her until she was owned by a husband. She damn well hoped she lived to see the day when such ridiculous, archaic laws were changed, but they were not going to be soon enough to help her. Her only recourse, it seemed, was to find herself a husband more suitable than Poxley Oxley.

She still held out hope where Essex was concerned, however. Despite what everyone thought, she was not so naïve as to think Essex would fall in love with her at first sight. She'd not want him if he did, for only fools—or people under the spell of a sorcerer's potion (exactly what had happened to Essex in the Tristan and Isolde–inspired short story she'd written last year)—did that.

Second or third sight would do just fine, and would give her enough time to weigh whether she could love the poet as much as she loved the poet's words and her own fantasies. She was rather sure she could if the only other option were Poxley.

In her nightmares, Essex turned out to be something horrible, like the corpulent haberdasher from Cheapside with five children and a fishwife, or even worse, Poxley Oxley himself, as the duchess had so horribly suggested. Though it seemed unlikely. Betsy seriously doubted Essex could be anything other than a beautiful man, for beauty did beget beauty, and she could think of nothing as beautiful in the world as Essex's verse. "The Alabaster Hip" had done nothing but confirm what she already knew.

But while Betsy remained certain she could win Essex's affections if given half the chance, she also understood full well that being swept away by Essex—much less locating him—was likely to remain a mere daydream. It was a conclusion she'd reached after countless unanswered letters to the poet's publisher (and a few covert trips to Albemarle Street, about which Evie remained oblivious).

She had the daydreams, at least, and her stories, and these things would just have to suffice until she either met a halfway decent fellow or turned twenty-one and came into her grandmother's bequest (her father had, so far, been unable to touch his mother-in-law's funds, despite his best efforts). She'd set up her own household in London, become a novelist, and have ten cats instead of a husband.

She rather hoped for the latter option, honestly, though it was the most unlikely, considering her father's recent machinations.

Too bad Evie's best mates were taken. Christopher Essex had worn the Marquess of Manwaring's perfect countenance in quite a few of her early fictions, but that had been before he'd eloped with Katherine Manwaring. Betsy was no adulteress, not even in the written word, and not even for the most beautiful man in the kingdom.

That ruled out Montford as well, though she didn't think she'd take *him* even if he were in need of a duchess, despite his noble profile. If she wanted to marry an old curmudgeon, she'd make sure he was at least an octogenarian with one foot in the grave.

Which wasn't a half-bad plan, actually. She'd be a merry

widow soon enough, and as free as she'd ever get.

She just needed to find one of those, then. Octogenarians—or *any* unattached man who wasn't related to her—were rather low on the ground, however. She only knew of two prospects so far, and one was Sir Thaddeus Davies. The squint was rather disconcerting, and something she was not sure she'd be able to tolerate across the breakfast table for the next fifty years. His estate, in the Outer Hebrides, where she'd never be able to escape the squint, made him even less appealing.

Betsy's other prospect, which was even more abysmal, was Miss Jones's sawbones friend, who'd been summoned to check on the governess after Poseidon had fallen on her. He was, according to Miss Jones, quite unattached and even younger than Evie, despite the steel in his beard—not that Betsy had *asked* about him after he'd left or anything. But Dr. Lucas seemed as stodgy and unbending as Montford. *He'd* never let her get away with anything.

Besides, he was a *sawbones*. They were even less solvent than Cheapside haberdashers. Just because she was desperate didn't mean she'd consign herself to a lifetime of abject poverty. Not even for those distinguished whiskers. Or those shockingly blue eyes. Or those broad shoulders and well-turned calves that obviously needed no padding to perfect their shape . . .

Perhaps in her next work, Essex could be a physician with premature salt-and-pepper hair and blue eyes, and she could be the languishing consumptive whom he cured through the amazing healing power of his . . .

She coughed and tried to push down the sudden flood of heat at the parade of lusty images that had just filled her head. Oh, the fun she'd have writing that one. The mere thought of imagining Dr. Lu . . . er, rather, Dr. *Essex*, "examining" her was . . .

Well, totally inappropriate, especially while sitting at her brother's desk, holding her father's latest rant in one hand.

What was she here for again?

Oh, yes, the foolscap. She tossed aside the letter and rummaged through the drawers without any luck, though her brother seemed inordinately well stocked with inkpots and quills. She pinched a few of those for herself and tried the middle drawer, which only held the household ledger, judging by its utilitarian leather binding, and a stack of business correspondence addressed to the viscount.

Betsy gagged at how *boring* her brother had become. He'd not been embroiled in one good scandal since she'd arrived in London. Of course he would have *reformed* before she could enjoy any of his roguish ways firsthand.

Ugh.

The least he could do was leave something interesting on his desk. She remembered a time when her brother's desk had been filled with books of all sorts, both printed and written in his own hand, even though she'd been too young to read them. She wondered when he'd stopped, when the earl's distaste for a bookish heir had become yet another thing that had beaten down Evie's spirit until he'd changed.

Her father had a lot to answer for.

Betsy tested the large drawer on the bottom right-hand side of the desk, but the handle wouldn't budge. She jiggled it a few more times, but it held firm, locked tight against intruders. She beamed at the drawer, delighted. Finally, something interesting. What could warrant locking up when Evie didn't even bother to do the same to his ledgers and financials?

Not even the memory of the scolding Evie had given her years ago over his ruined journal was enough to overcome her curiosity. She'd cultivated that particular aspect of her character into a well-hewn weapon over the years, and it had served her well. Her skill at poking and prying into places she didn't belong had been what had saved her from her father's most recent plot, after all.

After that first reading of the banns—which had come as a total surprise to her—she'd spent that following night reading all of her father's correspondence out of the false bottom of his bureau. She'd discovered precisely how much he was in debt and precisely how much Poxley had promised him in exchange for her hand, and knew that she was doomed. The next night she'd fled to London on that dreadfully malodorous mail coach.

For all of his reticence about the disastrous end of his marriage—which seemed more to do with common decency than a desire to truly conceal anything—Evie was an open book . . . or so she'd thought. For good or ill, he'd always been easy with his tongue, even when he probably shouldn't have been. He'd always called a spade a spade, even when that spade was himself. He made no bones about his failings and had no problem pointing out the failings in others. He was as honest as Evander had been devious. She didn't at all like the thought of Evie having secrets.

And locked drawers definitely contained those.

Likely it was merely the sort of illicit material men generally sought to keep out of the hands of the fairer sex. She'd discovered such things while snooping in her uncle's rooms growing up—and her father's, though she had to perform a mental scrub every time she remembered *that* particular, ill-advised invasion of the earl's privacy—but Evie was being embarrassingly obvious about it. Those sorts of things were usually in stocking drawers or pressed between volumes of old sermons that no one wanted to read, on the top shelves of the library. Not in locked desk drawers.

Perhaps the contents were not so lascivious, but she was definitely determined to find out one way or another. Evie was just *begging* for her to open it.

So Betsy did just that . . . and recalled the tale of Pandora and her box much too late for it to do her any good.

❦

TWO HOURS LATER, Marlowe turned up the gaslight on his library desk to find Betsy sitting in his chair, her cheeks ghostly white and her mouth hanging open like a dead fish.

He nearly jumped out of his skin at the rather unexpected—and unattractive—sight. He definitely jumped far enough to ram his hip into the edge of his desk and send a pile of books and papers clattering to the floor.

When Betsy didn't react at all to the commotion or the curses that followed, he waved a hand in front of her face and called her name to make sure she was still alive. Only when he shouted her full name and title did she come to, her unfocused eyes finally snapping to attention on his face. When she recognized who it was, her dead fish expression was replaced by one of dawning horror.

His skin crawled with foreboding.

"What the devil are you doing sitting in the dark at my desk?" he blustered, for giving way to his irritation was a hell of a lot easier than giving way to concern.

Her pale cheeks flooded with a sudden heat, which was not reassuring at all. Could he not go one week without someone in his household falling ill or blundering into catastrophe? Sometimes he felt as if he were trapped in some Minerva Press disaster of a novel—and he wasn't even cast as the hero, just one of the bumbling minor characters who got murdered early on and sealed in a cupboard to molder for centuries.

He had a feeling *that* wasn't going to change until all of the females in his life were wedded and bedded—which meant he was stuck like this for the rest of his life, since he didn't see himself letting any man wed and bed his daughters. Ever. Not while the blood still pumped through his veins.

"Are you ill?" he ventured warily, not looking forward to the prospect of yet another visit from Dr. Lucas and his judgmental gaze. The sawbones visited his residence even more often than Lady Blundersmith's, and that was just embarrassing.

Betsy pulled a face and groaned. "If only I were of a weaker constitution, I'd have cast my accounts ages ago and felt the better for it."

Then she proceeded to glare at him as if it were all his fault. He had no idea what "it" could be, however, so he just glared back in silence until she would crack and explain herself. *She* was the one behaving like an overwrought damsel, after all.

But then out of the corner of his eye, he caught sight of just what he'd knocked off his desk earlier. All of his letters from Waverley and all of his books and notes on the project he'd abandoned for "The Alabaster Hip," along with the ode's various drafts, lay across the parquet floor like limp, wounded soldiers. There was no mistaking the evidence for anything other than what it was, but just in case he was imagining things, he glanced at the desk drawer—The Drawer—and found it hanging open and empty.

He cringed and faced Betsy once more. She waved a paper she had been clutching with white knuckles. It was from his latest effort—the damnable *fairy* epic he'd been too embarrassed to acknowledge he was writing, even to himself.

"I can explain . . ." he began.

She held up a hand to halt his words, looking even more pained. "Don't even try to lie to me, Evelyn. I've sat here for hours reading *everything*. I know."

"Whatever you think you know . . ."

"You're Christopher Essex. *You*."

He was a little offended she found the idea so incredible. "Don't look too surprised," he muttered.

"Surprised? *Surprised*?" Her red cheeks started to turn an alarming shade of purple-green. "You're my brother! The stories I've written about you and . . . and *me* . . ." She broke off, looking as if her constitution might finally fail her. He certainly felt as if *his* might as her meaning sank in through his shock. He'd known she was stupidly infatuated with Essex, but not . . . this. Worse than a mere Misstopher, it seemed she was one of those fanatic *commonplacers* who wrote *stories*.

He felt his gorge rise.

"You're one of those, then," he said as calmly as he could, which was not calm at all.

"Oh, I'm definitely one of those," she cried, equally frantic. "What part of me telling you I wanted to marry him—*you*—*him*—Oh, dear *God*—didn't you understand?"

He scoured the room for a receptacle just in case both of their Leighton constitutions failed them. He'd read some of those stories. Women sent Waverley those stories, Waverley sent them to *him*, and he had made the mistake of opening those letters one too many times.

He squeezed his eyes shut and prayed as he hadn't prayed in years. "Please tell me you didn't write to me."

"I'm Lady Hedonist."

He gagged and collapsed on the edge of his desk. "Not the one about the love potion and the wand." Dear Lord, the wand.

She looked both proud and slightly queasy. "My Tristan and Isolde tribute. My best work."

He did the arithmetic in his head and gagged again. Nothing came up, but it was a near thing. "You couldn't have been more than fourteen when you wrote that."

Silence. "What can I say but that it runs in the family?" she offered.

"Fourteen! *The wand*, Betsy. How could a fourteen-year-old schoolgirl even know . . ."

"My imagination is very fertile, Evie," she said dryly. "But it certainly doesn't extend to incestuous fantasy. I leave that to Byron's followers." She paused. "And Byron, for that matter."

He decided not to even touch that one. "*You* are Lady Hedonist," he said again, just in case she might deny it this time around and spare them both.

He was not so lucky.

"Not anymore," she said with a shudder. "I'm burning every single story I've ever written just as soon as my abject horror fades enough for me to be able to walk again."

"*You're* Lady . . ."

"Yes! Lud, Evie. How could such a muttonhead like *you* be Christopher Essex?"

"Maybe I'm just a very good actor."

She snorted. "Not that good. You're *definitely* a muttonhead. Why didn't you tell me?"

"No one knows." She snorted again and crossed her arms over her chest, her brow arched at such an obvious falsehood.

"Except my publisher," he allowed. "And Sherry…"

"Sherry?" she demanded suspiciously. "Is that one of your fancy women?"

"Oh, for heaven's…it's Sebastian! The Marquess of Manwaring now," he clarified. "And I've told Montford."

She leaned back against her seat and waited.

"And Astrid," he grumbled. "She'd have squeezed it out of him by now."

She tapped her foot.

He sighed. "And Elaine. That's all."

"So everyone you love. Except me."

"Betsy . . ."

She picked up a quill off the desk and chucked it at his head. It bounced off his temple.

"You are unbelievable. I can't even . . . You're Christopher Essex!"

Marlowe held his breath as Betsy's face underwent a series of contortions he doubted even the most skilled linguist could decipher. He feared spontaneous combustion at any moment. Or tears. Oh, he was done for if there were tears.

Instead, she started to laugh. She laughed so hard she doubled over in her chair and slapped the desktop hard enough to make the inkpot bounce. The tears started to well up in her eyes, but they didn't seem to be tears of someone who had been traumatized for life—thank hell. He held his breath nonetheless until she finally wiped at her cheeks, her laughter disintegrating into quiet giggles. She held up the paper in her hands again.

"Fairies?" she gasped. "Really?"

Damn it. "Keats did it." It wasn't as if he were gasping for her approval . . . except that he was.

"Keats could have brought off a fairy epic. I'm not so sure you could," she said.

Now he was just confused. "And you call yourself a Misstopher," he mumbled.

"I know your strengths," she retorted. "Though I have to say I'm pleasantly surprised your main character is female for once. Less surprised that she could be Miss Jones's twin."

He could feel the blush creeping down his neck. "That is . . . ridiculous," he spluttered. "And completely false . . . How could you even think . . ."

"'Ebon hair bejeweled by the stars,'" she quoted, "'stormcloud eyes and marble-pale skin'?"

"Nevertheless, I deny the accusation," he grumbled.

"'*Marble-pale skin*,'" she enunciated, just in case he hadn't heard her the first time, "'from the alabaster mines of Italy's ancient hills . . .'" A light went off in her eyes, and he knew he was in even more trouble. "Oh, oh! 'The Alabaster Hip'! You wrote it about Miss Jones, didn't you!" she cried.

He seriously contemplated strangling his sister, or at the very least gagging her until this was over. If it ever was over. He was beginning to fear she was going to torment him over this for the rest of his life. "Perhaps you might try that again. I don't think the residents of China heard you properly," he bit out.

She jumped up from her desk, smiling in delight. "Oh, good grapes, it's true!" she breathed. "You didn't deny it."

He slouched down into his vacated seat and buried his face in his hands.

"Oh, Evie, you *must* tell Miss Jones," Betsy said next, just as he'd been dreading.

"I know," he murmured, tugging at the ends of his hair in frustration. "But how?"

Betsy's glee faded as she saw how pained he was, and she slumped against his desk, considering his question. "You mean, how do you do so without her being extremely put out with you?" she asked.

"Yes."

Betsy grimaced. "Well, I don't see a way around *that*. But the longer you put it off, the worse it will be. She needs to know the truth about who you are."

Betsy was right, but he'd been two different people for so long that *he* wasn't sure who he was anymore. He wasn't sure he'd ever known. He'd played the slightly belligerent, slightly oblivious court jester for years, first to protect himself from his father's abuses and slights, then later as a preemptive shield against the rest of the world. If he'd not let Barming see his pain, then he'd damn well not let the rest of the world.

He'd become Christopher Essex for the same reason.

Along the way, he'd lost sight of who he was . . . or perhaps more accurately, he'd forgotten who he wanted to be. And he didn't want to be just a buffoon or a navel-gazing poet. Of course, part of him would always be these things, but they weren't all he was.

The longer he put it off, the harder it had become to tell the truth. Or more precisely, the truth had become something different—*he'd* become different. Besides, for the first time in his life, he was beginning to like who he was—*all* of who he was. With Minerva, who had little patience for his title or public opinion—and who had seen him at his worst and was, amazingly, *still here*—he was simply a man, without anything to recommend him other than his own character and strength of purpose. He was, at last, the man he'd always wished to be. And though their acquaintance was based on a lie, one single lie, he felt that he was more honest with her than he'd ever been before, to himself, to others.

It was self-deception perhaps. Obsession. But at night, before his head hit the pillow, he wished to wake up to a world in which the debauched Viscount Marlowe of his youth had never existed, and the war—and his hideous family—took up no space in his brainbox. He wished nightly, as his eyes closed and he prayed for pleasant dreams, that he'd wake up to discover Minerva next to him, that they had met years ago, before the war and Caroline's betrayal had a chance to cripple him, and that she loved him as much as he'd already come to love her—for he was afraid that was what this was. Not merely *like* or lust, but love.

Sometimes, when the outside world intruded and he felt strangled with guilt, he went to bed at night with a different fantasy. He told Minerva the truth of who he was, and instead of hating him, she forgave him on the spot and took him in her arms. In this fantasy, they had dozens of children and lived happily ever after. Well. Maybe not dozens. One or two more. He'd leave repopulating the earth to Elaine and Brinderley.

But he knew, were she to find out the truth, that her reaction would be much different. She would *hate* him. The mere thought of her rejection made him sick and clammy all over, and he wondered if it were better to never let her know the truth.

Which was absurd, of course.

Sooner or later, she would find out. Because eventually he would slip up, as he'd done with Betsy. Eventually it would become just too unbearable to continue the charade.

Well, he'd never made things easy for himself.

Betsy patted his shoulder. "Don't worry, Evie. She's bound to forgive you. Eventually."

She sounded much too doubtful for her words to be any sort of consolation.

Chapter Eleven

In Which The Viscount Braves Almack's And Lives To Tell About It

MINERVA WAS QUITE SURE THAT most governesses were not called upon to attend Almack's with their employers' families. Neither did she think the fearsome patronesses were likely to let someone like *her* through the door, even with the guest voucher the duchess had procured for her. Unfortunately, the knot on her head—and the mild cold she'd contracted—from the fountain incident had healed, so she was unable to cry off playing chaperone, though she still attempted to. All her protests did nothing to deter Lady Elizabeth in her determination either. Minerva was quite stuck.

Literally. With pins. From perhaps the clumsiest seamstress in London.

"You look splendid," Lady Elizabeth proclaimed as she observed said seamstress fitting one of her gowns to Minerva.

Minerva winced as another needle pricked her waist, and didn't bother to argue with Lady Elizabeth's wild claim.

But as little as she enjoyed being poked and prodded by the seamstress—or the thought of the evening ahead—she had to admit she rather liked the gown Lady Elizabeth had insisted she take. It was a dark jeweled blue silk—far too extravagant a fabric for Minerva's station in life, but of a sober enough cut and color not to make her feel too much like an imposter. She was no youthful debutante bound for the marriage mart, and she had no desire to pretend otherwise. If she were to attend the Assembly Rooms, she'd do so as unobtrusively as possible.

Though there was nothing unobtrusive about the puffed sleeves. Or a paid companion attempting to run the gauntlet of the lady patronesses. Minerva flicked at one of the sleeves and sighed. "I shall not make it past the guard dogs," she muttered.

Lady Elizabeth scoffed. "You are our particular guest and the daughter of a navy captain who died a war hero. Surely that shall bear weight. It's Marlowe I'm worried about."

Lady Elizabeth did have a point. Hopefully Marlowe would be distracting enough to the patronesses that they wouldn't even notice Minerva trying to slip by.

"The duchess says we must put forth the effort of attending, and she's right," Lady Elizabeth said, sounding much too practical for her years. "My only hope of extricating myself from Father's alliance with Poxley is to be seen publicly. At the very least, it may hold him off from acting until after the Season is done, for fear I should kick up a public fuss—which I am quite prepared to do, mind you."

Minerva thought this a rather tenuous strategy, but she supposed they had no other at this point.

"And if I am to attend this horrid farce, I want you at my side and no one else," Lady Elizabeth continued. "Besides, I need a chaperone, and Elaine is indisposed. The patronesses shall not begrudge me one, I am sure."

Minerva hoped—and doubted—she was right.

The seamstress finished her stitching with one last prick, and she was finally allowed to turn to face the mirror. She sucked in a surprised breath. The gown was the loveliest thing she'd ever worn. The sapphire color made her pale skin look fetchingly dewy and her black hair less like an animal's pelt. She wasn't completely hideous after all.

Lady Elizabeth bounded up behind her with a sly grin. "Didn't I tell you the sapphire would suit?" she said, fussing with the sleeves. She narrowed her eyes at Minerva's uninspired chignon. "Though we shall have to do something about your hair."

"It won't hold a curl," Minerva warned as she noticed Lady Elizabeth glancing thoughtfully toward her iron. Her hair had always been as thick, straight, and stubborn as a hedgehog's quills. Lady Elizabeth was more likely to burn it off than make it curl.

"We shall see about that," Lady Elizabeth said with an ominously determined tone to her voice and began to take down Minerva's hair.

"Who knows? Perhaps Mr. Essex shall be in attendance tonight," Minerva said teasingly, hoping to lighten her friend's unusually somber mood. "And he shall indeed fall in love with you."

Lady Elizabeth's reaction was not at all what Minerva was expecting, however. The girl's expression went curiously blank, and a blush crept on her cheeks. "Yes, well, I have quite abandoned that particular hope," she said after a moment, sounding strangled.

Minerva was shocked at this about-face. The girl had been extremely committed to her objective not two days ago. "What? When did this happen?" she demanded.

Lady Elizabeth refused to meet Minerva's eyes in the mirror. "Er… when I read 'The Alabaster Hip.' It is patently obvious the poet's affections are already engaged."

Though privately Minerva thought the poem was, at heart, more a lament about the poet's inability to write—which explained the last three fallow years—it was hard to deny Lady Elizabeth's claim. It was indubitably a love poem. Essex hadn't penned one of those since his early sonnets—though even then, those had been about heartbreak more than anything else.

"The Alabaster Hip" was different from anything else the poet had ever written: overt eroticism without even the pretext of a heroic epic surrounding it, and a melancholic longing for romantic love he'd long since seemed to put behind him in his other works. It was at once the saddest thing she'd ever read and the most utterly romantic. The Misstophers were doubtless flinging themselves on divans with mournful sighs all across London. Even she'd felt like doing so just a tiny little bit, but she had so far restrained herself. She'd settled for a mental swoon. And another reading. But as for the poet having fallen in love . . .

Well, that seemed a rather large leap for Lady Elizabeth to have made. Something deeper was at work here.

"I'm not so sure you can tell that from one poem," Minerva said doubtfully.

"Perhaps not," Lady Elizabeth murmured, though she didn't sound the least bit convinced. "But though I will always be a loyal admirer of Essex, I have decided to move on to more . . . realistic goals."

"That sounds . . . practical," Minerva said, feeling oddly disappointed about the girl's sudden show of maturity. She'd hoped that Lady Elizabeth would come to her senses on the matter of her infatuation, but now that it had come to pass, she was surprised to feel little relief. She didn't like seeing Lady Elizabeth so subdued.

"It is what I must be, until I am free of Poxley," Lady Elizabeth said firmly.

"I do hope this works, then," Minerva said, infusing as much optimism into her voice as she could. "And surely Lord Marlowe shall discover some way to warn off Oxley."

Lady Elizabeth's wry smile revealed her doubts on the matter. They both knew the earl had the upper hand, and Minerva's heart sank over her friend's bleak future. "Perhaps. The viscount's willingness to subject himself to an evening at Almack's shows that he is at least trying."

THE VISCOUNT WAS indeed trying, for he joined Minerva and his sister in the front hall that evening looking like a true disciple of Brummell. His broad shoulders were stuffed into a midnight-black tailcoat that clung to his powerful body like a second skin, a snowy-white cravat folded into an elaborate waterfall and pinned by an enormous jewel at his throat. His long, lean legs were encased in tight white trousers, his usual scuffed hessians had been traded for shiny black dancing pumps, and his usually untamed locks were pomaded and shaped into something more fashionably tousled.

He held a *chapeau bras* in one hand and white gloves in the other, and he looked as if he were about as comfortable in the rig as a wolf might be in sheep's clothing. Only the admonishing—and rather teary—looks from Pymm, who trailed after his master with a clothes brush as if unwilling to abandon his masterpiece, kept the viscount from pulling at his cravat and ruining the whole effect.

Minerva hoped he managed to restrain himself for the night, for he looked . . .

Well, he looked rather delicious. Just when had the debauched Lord Marlowe transformed himself into such a fine specimen? Or had it been there the entire time she'd lived in his household, underneath all of his cant and banyans?

She felt that same hot, slightly queasy feeling she had in the gardens when the viscount had caught her in his arms, and she suddenly knew what it was—finally let herself acknowledge it.

Attraction.

Oh, good Lord, she was *attracted* to the viscount. More than that, she feared she had already tipped over into fullfledged infatuation, judging from the way she couldn't seem to tear her eyes away from him at the moment or control the blush that was sure to be evident on her cheeks.

At first, she'd thought her feelings toward the viscount

were purely those of exasperation and, on occasion, utter bewilderment at his eccentricities, but over the past few weeks, it was hard to ignore the shift toward . . . something else. Though she had tried. Valiantly.

So yes, she was a bit thrown. At one time, she'd not expected to last a week in his employment, yet now she was wondering if she should leave not because he annoyed her, but rather because he did something even worse: he made her feel things she never thought were possible.

She'd no doubt that he loved flirting with her, but beyond that, she could never quite read him. He was surprisingly inscrutable for all that he presented himself as a transparent buffoon. So whether he was truly attracted to her remained to be seen, but the way he was looking at her right now, as if he too could not help himself, despite everyone else gathered in the hall, told her that maybe . . .

Maybe.

Which was dismaying and electrifying in equal measure, for even if it *were* a mutual attraction, what good could possibly come of it? Aristocrats were not in the habit of marrying their governesses, and *she* was certainly not going to become his latest light-o'-love (and she was not naive enough to think he hadn't had his fair share of those).

The only way she could see this ending was in a stalemate, at best, and her departure, at worst. But she was nevertheless unable to completely quell her own hidden excitement at the thought of having her regard returned, as inappropriate as it was.

She was, quite possibly, doomed.

☙

MINERVA HAD HOPED Lady Elizabeth would reclaim her usual high spirits, but she hadn't counted on the girl smirking meaningfully at both of them the entire ride to the Assembly Rooms, as if they were being horribly transparent. Minerva knew she was. She couldn't seem to stop looking at the viscount. But she certainly didn't need Lady Elizabeth pointing it out.

Minerva was still reeling from her revelation in the hallway and would have much rather been thousands of miles from Mayfair at the moment, for the things she was beginning to feel for the viscount—inappropriate, dangerous things, toward an inappropriate, dangerous man—were as terrifying as they were baffling. Somehow, through some strange alchemy of word and deed, he had worked his way under her skin in a way that Arthur at his sweetest and even Christopher Essex at his most eloquent had never done.

She glared at the back of his head (which had been suspiciously turned out the window the entire journey), for it was all his fault. It had to be. He was rather like hookworm, really: dangerously catchable and annoyingly persistent. But unlike with hookworm, she wasn't at all sure she wanted to be rid of him.

Which was the most frightening thing about the whole situation.

Lady Elizabeth finally cleared her throat and resolved to break the silence at last.

"Isn't Miss Jones looking fetching tonight, Evie?" she asked with far too much mirth in her voice for Minerva's liking.

Marlowe grunted rather rudely, his cheeks flushing, which was response enough, and refused to turn his head.

Minerva gave Lady Elizabeth a quelling look, but the girl continued, undaunted. "Perhaps while we're there, we might find a suitable match for Miss Jones as well. She can't remain a governess forever."

She could, thank you very much, and that was just what Minerva intended to do, unless . . .

Well, there was no use in thinking of what could never be.

"She'll be too busy fighting off your swains to find her

own," Marlowe muttered.

"Then perhaps we might find *you* a wife," Lady Elizabeth continued teasingly. "I am sure we'll stumble upon one or two tonight. Pymm has outdone himself."

Marlowe flushed even more, looking as if he might take to clawing at his cravat after all. His squirming was not adorable. Not at all.

Though it was.

Oh, God, she was even worse off than she'd feared if she found his *pouting* attractive.

"No one is finding a wife. Or a husband tonight," he lobbed out a bit desperately. "I cannot believe Astrid talked me into this ridiculous idea. *Almack's*." He shuddered eloquently.

Lady Elizabeth patted his hand. "Miss Jones and I shall protect you."

"See that you do." He glanced out the window when the carriage stopped and paled. "Oh God, we're here," he muttered. "So *quickly*."

Minerva tried to put the last half hour from her mind completely, though that was rather hard to do when the viscount handed her down from the carriage and she could feel the warm strength of his grip even from beneath two layers of gloves.

But tonight wasn't about her, she reminded herself sternly. It was about Lady Elizabeth, after all, and their campaign to save her from Oxley. Revelation of her own mad infatuation aside, she had a mission tonight, and it didn't involve being distracted by the viscount's broad shoulders. Or eyes. Or legs. Or derriere, though *that* was looking particularly spectacular tonight in his new trousers.

Not that she was looking. Much.

She raised her eyes to a more appropriate level and followed her charge and the viscount past the front door, held open by a liveried servant. They were immediately hit by a wall of heat and reluctantly began down a long entrance hall lit by gaslight. The sound of a slightly out of tune orchestra drifted in the air from the ballroom at the corridor's end, along with the overwhelming stench of stale perfume and sweat. A queue of guests trailed down the corridor, waiting for entrance, and all three of them let out a collective groan at the sight.

"I can already tell I'm going to hate it," Lady Elizabeth muttered. Minerva had to agree with her prediction. It already looked dreadful, and they'd not even been inside the ballroom.

They joined the end of the line and were immediately scrutinized by their neighbors. Marlowe had obviously been recognized, for the ladies began whispering behind their fans, and the gentlemen gave him gruff greetings, which he even more gruffly returned.

"I suppose you should start introducing me," Lady Elizabeth said to her brother in a low voice.

"Let us get past the dragon first," he muttered, nodding toward a tall, brown-haired lady in a glimmering ice-blue silk gown holding court just inside the ballroom door, two ostrich feathers sprouting from the top of her head. "Damn. It's the Countess Lieven. She has never liked me."

"What did you do?" Lady Elizabeth asked.

"Nothing. Why do you assume I did something?" he protested much too innocently.

Lady Elizabeth and Minerva both just leveled him with a knowing look until he finally cracked. "I may have, *possibly*, called out a man at one of her house parties," he admitted in a rush.

Lady Elizabeth rolled her eyes. "How were you even invited in the first place?"

Marlowe side-eyed Minerva and blushed. "That's not important," he muttered.

Lady Elizabeth's eyes widened. "One of your mistresses was invited, wasn't she?"

Marlowe's cheeks were scarlet. So were Minerva's. "Keep

your voice down, for heaven's sake, Betsy," he hissed. "And how could you . . . no, don't even bother answering, for I know all too well how *your* mind works."

Lady Elizabeth grinned unrepentantly.

"And for the record, I do not have a mistress," he continued lowly, glancing at Minerva as he did so. "Not anymore."

Well, at least he was honest, though Minerva was sure that she didn't care. The feeling of relief that flooded through her at his denial made it hard for her to pretend this was true, however.

Lady Elizabeth threaded her arm through Minerva's and grinned far too knowingly down at her companion. "You have become so boring these days, Evie. Perhaps you really should just get a wife and have done with it."

Before he could stop spluttering long enough to respond to that, they were standing before the Countess Lieven, a sweating, liveried servant handing her their vouchers and looking seconds away from passing out from the heat.

"Lord Marlowe," the countess intoned rather sourly. "I hardly recognized you."

He gave her his best leg. "Countess, it has been too long," he said.

"Not long enough, I daresay," she said.

Minerva thought the woman rather rude for being a leader of society, though knowing Marlowe, he probably deserved it.

He politely pretended not to hear the countess. "May I present my sister, Lady Elizabeth Leighton," he forged on. "And her companion, Miss Jones."

They both took it as their cue to curtsy. The countess's ostrich feathers bobbed on her head as she studied Lady Elizabeth top to toe. The girl must have passed inspection, for the countess was all too soon turning her attention to Minerva. She held her breath as she was scrutinized. This was the moment she'd been dreading all night. She was sure to be barred entry, and then they'd all have to go home, for even the viscount knew he couldn't be his sister's only escort.

It was a foolish idea anyway. She couldn't begin to fathom what the duchess was thinking to give the third voucher to her.

But all of her worry was for naught, it seemed, for in the end, the viscount managed to bungle things all on his own. The Countess Lieven, done with her inspection of Minerva, turned her attention to Marlowe. She took one look down her long nose at Marlowe's legs and winced ever so elegantly. She folded her fan with the snap of her wrist and held it up to her left cheek.

It wasn't an encouraging sign.

"Oh dear," Lady Elizabeth murmured, sounding more amused than anything else.

"What?" Marlowe demanded of the patroness with his usual forthright tactlessness when he finally sensed something was wrong. "What's happened? Why are you doing that with your fan?"

"You are wearing trousers, Lord Marlowe," the countess said as if it pained her to have to explain herself.

"What's wrong with trousers?" he demanded. "They're all the crack, ain't they?"

"Gentlemen must wear silk knee breeches, or at the very least pantaloons, Viscount, or one cannot enter the Assembly Rooms," the countess replied loftily.

Marlowe glanced down his long legs. "That would explain why Pymm were in tears when I wouldn't wear the silk breeches tonight," he murmured. "Are you sure there is no way to . . ."

"Even Wellington himself was not allowed an exception, Viscount," Countess Lieven snapped, her accent becoming more pronounced. "I *certainly* won't make one for you." Her expression softened somewhat when she noticed the curious audience that had gathered around the exchange. She was a politician's wife, after all. "But should you come back next Wednesday suitably attired with your charming sister . . ."—she paused, ran her eyes over Minerva once more, and pointedly did not include her in the invitation—"I am sure you shall be allowed entry."

"I look forward to it," he said, though he sounded as if he'd rather eat glass.

A few moments later, they found themselves in the corridor once more. Marlowe and Lady Elizabeth both were looking relieved more than anything else, but Minerva didn't know how to feel. Other than vaguely irked. She couldn't regret not having to spend the rest of the night in that greenhouse of a ballroom, sweating through her lovely gown and avoiding being trampled by waltzers.

"Thank hell *that's* done with, then," the viscount murmured.

"At least I might breathe out here," Lady Elizabeth said, fanning herself. "How could anyone possibly enjoy themselves in such a stink?"

"I don't think anyone's supposed to be enjoying themselves," Minerva replied.

Lady Elizabeth began to giggle. "Oh, the duchess is going to murder us," she cried, though she didn't sound the least bit bothered. "We didn't make it past the door!"

"Breeches!" the viscount muttered. "Can't believe it were over breeches!"

"Next time, don't bully poor Pymm. He obviously knew what he was doing," Lady Elizabeth said pertly.

"He's the bully," Marlowe retorted like a child, then yanked on his cravat as he'd wanted to do all night. He sighed in relief as the complicated folds gave way.

Minerva wondered not for the first time how she had managed to lose her head over such a man.

"Don't worry, my dear. We shall find other ways to keep the earl at bay," Marlowe said, though Lady Elizabeth seemed anything but upset to have been turned away. "Almack's ain't the only way."

Lady Elizabeth patted her brother's hand. "That I managed to haul you even to the Assembly Rooms' entrance is a small miracle. Besides, being turned away at Almack's will make us more popular than if we actually attended. If this doesn't make the papers, I shall be shocked."

"Never let it be said I don't try," Marlowe said with a smirk.

"I don't think that shall matter to Elaine and the duchess when they hear of our failure," Lady Elizabeth said.

"Then perhaps *they* ought to escort you the next time."

Lady Elizabeth made a face. "I shall endeavor to make sure there isn't one," she murmured.

So would Minerva. One moment more under Countess Lieven's scrutiny, and she probably would have punched the woman.

"*I* should be more than happy to be your escort tonight, Lady Elizabeth," said a smooth, silky voice behind them, and Minerva immediately felt a chill go down her spine. "Since I hear the viscount is having trouble with his toilette tonight."

"Oh, good grapes," Lady Elizabeth muttered under her breath. Her good cheer dropped away immediately, along with all the color in her cheeks. Lord Marlowe looked as if he'd smelled something rotten. Which he probably had. It really was appallingly fragrant inside the Assembly Rooms.

"Poxley," Marlowe said with grating politeness.

The man in question glared at Marlowe but did not call him out on the slip of the tongue—if it was indeed a slip of the tongue, which Minerva rather doubted. "Marlowe," he sniffed. A large gold signet ring embedded with an enormous ruby gleamed on one of his bony, shriveled fingers, announcing Someone of Import had just entered the room louder than any cornet flourish ever could. His toilette was impeccable, his reptilian expression just as cold, and every instinct Minerva had recoiled.

The duke looked just as she'd imagined the treacherous

Montoni in *The Mysteries of Udolpho* might look, though he was perhaps a few decades past his villainous prime. But he made up for his lack of diabolical aura through his sheer repulsiveness. He wore an old-fashioned chestnut periwig and so much lead paint it was difficult to tell what his true skin might look like underneath it—but it couldn't be good, judging by the lesions covering his wrinkled neck beneath his cravat.

Minerva felt compelled to take a few steps back from the man in case he was contagious.

She felt immensely sorry for Lady Elizabeth, who shuddered as the man bowed over her hand and kissed it lingeringly. He then proceeded to openly leer at Lady Elizabeth's bosom before straightening to his full height.

The viscount looked as oblivious as ever, but there was a light in his eyes that made Minerva shiver where she stood. She knew then that the only reason he did not lay the duke out for his impertinence in that moment was their very public setting.

"My dear, you look absolutely radiant tonight," the duke murmured.

Lady Elizabeth jerked her hand back at the first opportunity and looked pointedly away from the duke, rubbing his kiss away on her skirts. "*You* were admitted to Almack's?" Lady Elizabeth said, disbelieving.

Something truly frightening glinted in Oxley's eyes at that, and his reptilian smile deepened.

"Indeed," he said smoothly. "I am a particular acquaintance of several of the patronesses' husbands."

Minerva's opinion of the patronesses plummeted even further. Sometimes being a penniless orphan of middling birth was a blessing, for she truly felt sorry for all the young women who were herded through these doors, no better than cattle at market, to be snatched up by men like Oxley. The Duchess of Montford's estimation of Almack's social worth—that they'd escape Oxley's clutches here—had been entirely too optimistic.

Marlowe snorted at this, and the duke's smile grew hard. "You are welcome to accompany me into the ballroom, Lady Elizabeth. With your companion, of course," he said, his eyes sliding over Minerva. She fervently willed him to look elsewhere.

"That, I am sure, would be highly irregular," Lord Marlowe drawled.

"Something of which you are an expert, no doubt," Oxley retorted. "But surely, as Lady Elizabeth is my fiancée and as she is in the company of her duenna, there can be no question of irregularity. I shall return her to your doorstep before one."

"I am *not* . . ." Lady Elizabeth began hotly, but her brother interrupted her.

"Fiancée?" Marlowe asked, looking completely surprised by the news. Minerva wanted to cheer him for it. "Surely you are mistaken."

Oxley's eyes narrowed. "The banns have been read," he said through gritted teeth.

"Indeed," Marlowe said, politely disbelieving.

"At the parish church in West Barming," Oxley gritted out.

"I see. Well, until my father has confirmed such an occurrence, I am afraid I must play my sister's dragon. I do hope you understand, Poxley."

Oxley's expression made it clear that he didn't, but he held his tongue.

Marlowe stepped closer to Oxley and lowered his voice. "And should I hear any rumor that ties my sister's name to yours before we have properly settled this business, I shall personally remove your tongue from your mouth. With relish," he said pleasantly.

The duke looked livid underneath all of his paint. "I shall remember your insolence on my wedding night, Viscount," he hissed.

Minerva started forward to confront the duke herself as the threat carried to their ears. She felt outraged enough to cosh the dreadful man over the head with her reticule, and only Lady Elizabeth's hand on her arm restrained her from doing so.

But she needn't have bothered. Lord Marlowe's insouciance dropped away completely at the duke's words, revealing a burning fury that made even Oxley look uneasy.

"Perhaps I'll have your tongue now," the viscount growled, "and damn the audience."

She decided to stand aside and let Marlowe do his worst. He did look rather magnificent when he was filled with righteous indignation. "We *are* alone for the moment," Minerva said helpfully.

Oxley wisely stepped backward a few steps, though this put his back against the corridor wall. Marlowe followed after him, flexing the fingers of his right hand in a manner that presaged violence. Marlowe seemed past reining in, and Minerva would have felt sorry for Oxley, had the man not been such an utter reprobate.

But then a gaggle of pastel-colored young misses poured into the corridor, giggling and gossiping on their way to the retiring room, and the tension broke between the two men. The violence went out of Marlowe, and he stepped away from the duke.

Oxley removed himself from the wall with as much dignity as he could—which was not much, considering—and straightened the lapels of his coat and the tilt of his wig before giving a final sniff of disdain.

"I am sure the earl will be in contact with you regarding the matter," Oxley said haughtily. "I shall no doubt see you soon."

Marlowe's smile was wolfish. "You should hope otherwise, Your Grace."

The duke paused at the threat before making a judicious retreat toward the ballroom. Minerva watched him go with a mixture of triumph and dread.

"Well, *that* was certainly interesting," Lady Elizabeth said briskly when they were alone once more, though she was still distressingly pale. "I take it back. You've not grown boring at all, Evie. Cast out from Almack's and assaulted in the hallways. Is it always so exciting when you go out?"

"It usually ends in a duel, or at least a satisfying brawl," he said, and Minerva wasn't certain he was lying. "But I manfully restrained myself tonight."

"No need to on my account," Lady Elizabeth said. "I would have not minded in the least if you had broken his nose."

Marlowe glanced at Minerva, as if awaiting her judgment. She sighed. "I don't think I would have either."

Marlowe looked inordinately pleased by her admission. "My governess, condoning such a public display. Be certain the twins don't get wind of how bloodthirsty you can be."

My governess. She chose to ignore his teasing. "If anyone deserves a broken nose, I expect it is His Grace."

"Oh, Evie, what are we going to do?" Lady Elizabeth cried, moving closer to her brother. He put a comforting arm around her shoulders. "If Poxley has already found me in London, Father will be right behind. I cannot marry him."

"You won't," Marlowe said, his jaw firming with resolution. "Don't worry; I've not yet begun to fight—but fight I will. Lord knows I've had the practice."

Oh, yes, Minerva rather liked this fiery permutation of the viscount. She liked him too much, judging from the little frisson of pleasure that went through her at his fiercely protective expression.

And judging from the way he'd handled the duke just then, Minerva was starting to believe he *could* protect his sister after all. If anything, he was too stubborn to fail, and would as soon call Oxley out and shoot the blackguard in his attributes before he allowed the marriage. Such a way of solving the problem was a bit medieval, but it would be effective. Minerva hoped it wouldn't come to that, however, for she'd grown too fond of the viscount's head to see it blown off in a duel.

Though, *fond*? She couldn't even fool herself anymore into thinking it was mere fondness, could she?

Looking back on it, even from that first confrontation in the ditch in Barming, there had been a spark. She'd presumed it due merely to the spectacular irritation she'd felt toward him. Yet she'd been irritated before, and it had never felt like that, like every nerve ending was on fire, every sense heightened, and the world around her drawn with sharp, exhilarating clarity. And it kept on happening every time she was in the viscount's company, even when the irritation had faded. He had somehow bewitched her.

And now, watching him with that fierce determination to protect his sister still lingering on his face as he escorted them both to their carriage, she felt herself falling even deeper under his spell. For all of his idiosyncrasies, his love and loyalty for those he cared about—his twins, his sisters and friends, even Mrs. Chips and the meddling Duchess of Montford—burned so bright and hot it was nearly blinding. And Minerva didn't merely admire it. She *wanted* it. She wanted *him*.

As if that could ever happen, for all of the reasons she'd already listed in her head a hundred times over since the start of the night. Governess, viscount. Daughter of a sailor, son of an earl. Poetry lover, composer of bawdy limericks.

She was sure there were more, but all she could think as he lifted her back into his carriage as if she were a true lady and not an imposter in a borrowed dress was, *God, God, oh God.*

For he was going to break her heart someday, wasn't he?

Chapter Twelve

In Which The Earl Of Barming Does Not— And Absolutely Will Never— Win Father Of The Year

AND THEN—AS IF *ALMACK'S* HADN'T been horrible enough—the Earl of Barming stormed into Marlowe's library one morning a week later. Marlowe had known it was only a matter of time after the contretemps with Poxley at the Assembly Rooms, but he'd been hoping for a miracle. Or at least a wreck on the King's Highway to delay the inevitable for a little while longer.

It wasn't all bad news, however, for Marlowe was pleasantly surprised to find that the earl had grown old in the near decade since he'd last set eyes on the man. Gray streaked his hair, wrinkles lined his face, and there was a definite hunch in his spine that had not been there before. Marlowe almost—*almost*—felt sorry for the man.

Until he opened his mouth.

"Where is my daughter?" Barming demanded tersely, jerking off his gloves and glaring around the room as if Betsy might be hiding behind one of the chairs.

"Father, I can't tell you how lovely it is to see you," Marlowe murmured. Because it wasn't. At all. He slouched at his desk with as much insolence as he could muster. Which was a great deal.

Barming's eyes narrowed. "I don't have time for your games. What have you done with Elizabeth?"

"Today? Very little, as she is most likely still abed," he replied laconically. Then he stiffened as he caught sight of the parade of Barming servants passing by the open library door with suspiciously large pieces of luggage. His stepmother followed in their wake and seemed to be attempting to issue orders to Mrs. Chips, whose eyebrow was twitching at a worrying rate.

He shuddered inwardly and sat up from his slouch in alarm. He didn't like where this was going.

"Father, what are all of those servants doing with all of that luggage?" he asked, though he was fairly certain of the answer and how much he was not going to like it.

"We have come to stay until we sort out this business with your sister," the earl informed him haughtily.

"And *your* London residence?" he inquired, though he knew very well the earl had rented it out for the Season.

The earl glared at him for bringing up the subject of his finances, however obliquely, but Marlowe had no time to gloat over hitting a nerve. Barming moving into his household? It would never do. For one, it was likely to end in murder. For another . . . well, it was *likely to end in murder.*

Marlowe used to think of his father as some kind of giant, immortal and omnipotent, and he'd spent his early years terrified of incurring the earl's wrath, while simultaneously defying him at every turn. He'd not known the meaning of self-preservation. It wasn't until he'd returned from his first year of Cambridge that he discovered he'd grown past the earl in height and breadth by several inches. So great was his father's power over him, however, he hadn't even noticed this sea change until the earl had raised a fist to him for one infraction or another, and Marlowe had bloodied his nose effortlessly in return.

Marlowe had been as shocked as the earl.

His father had never raised another hand to him. And

when, the following summer, he'd discovered that the earl had transferred his aggression to Betsy—not Evander, never Evander—he'd put a permanent stop to that with some well-placed and well-meant threats. His father had schooled him well in the art of intimidation, and though Montford and Sebastian had long since disabused Marlowe of his practice of bullying his peers as an effective way of making friends, he was more than happy to intimidate the hell out of Barming. He was grateful that Betsy was too young to remember.

The earl had never forgiven Marlowe for fighting back, and so he'd taken out his anger on his heir in other ways: verbal thrashings, the withholding of funds (which never worked, since Marlowe had inherited his own fortune from his maternal grandmother—yet another sore point with the earl), and his unrelenting disapproval of him writ large for all society to see. It was a disapproval that seemed ever more justified, especially after Marlowe's public feud with old Manwaring that had led to his holiday on the Peninsula with Sebastian. But that was just fine with Marlowe. He didn't want the bastard's forgiveness or approval, and he certainly didn't want society's.

The worst, though, was when Caroline and Evander's betrayal was laid at his feet by the earl. It was the last conversation he'd ever had with the man until the present moment, in fact, just after they'd laid Evander to rest in the family mausoleum. The earl had run on and on about Marlowe's culpability, how this never would have happened if he'd not run off to the war, if he'd been more of a man and less of a wastrel, etcetera, etcetera, until Marlowe thought his head might explode.

Marlowe had waited until his father had stopped for a breath—a long, long wait—and then calmly informed the earl that Evander had been bedding Caro behind his back since they were fifteen, a revelation that his wife had been sure to share with him before she'd run off and gotten herself killed. Then he'd taken the twins and Mrs. Chips and decamped for London and tried very, very hard to have nothing to do with his family ever again.

Clearly, that had not worked, for the earl was now invading his home as if it were his right. *And* the countess . . .

Ugh.

His father had not married the current Lady Barming for her weak chin, featherbrain, myopia, or vacuous disposition. But she had come with a generous dowry, one that the earl had apparently finally run to ground. Hence Barming's desire to sell his daughter to Poxley's tender mercies.

It boggled the mind how the union of the earl and countess had produced a daughter like Betsy, who, while a bit exasperating, was a likable human being, even after sixteen years under the earl's thumb. It would have broken a lesser mortal—had nearly broken *him*. But if Betsy had inherited anything other than her looks from her Leighton ancestry (thank hell she had, for even her broad shoulders and roman nose were improvements over her mother's chin—or lack thereof), it was the Leighton pigheadedness. She was simply too stubborn to be as miserable and insufferable as her parents.

Marlowe was surprised she hadn't run away sooner.

But then, just when he thought the day couldn't get any worse, Uncle Ashley lumbered in behind the earl, winded and sweating prodigiously. Marlowe should have known the glutton would turn up like a bad penny, since he never strayed far from his brother's purse strings. In this case, Marlowe suspected his uncle had come to enjoy the spectacle and his sideboard—and kitchens—more than anything else.

The man was undoubtedly a Leighton, with his brown eyes and berserker build, but he'd run to fat from decades of dissipation and utter purposelessness. Marlowe's stomach further soured watching his uncle turn sideways to fit his belly through the doorway. He had the sudden, horrible realization that *that* could have been him, had he continued down his road of self-loathing and debauchery.

Marlowe liked to think he would have reformed, however, before it became necessary to wear a girdle.

Not that it was helping his uncle's impressive girth—*that* was well past rectifying. And so was the man's wardrobe. It seemed that age and a spreading waistline had not broken Ashley's taste for extravagance. He'd been a legendary macaroni in his day, but that day was long past. Now he was just a beached whale in stays and a gold-threaded frock coat that could have housed a regiment of soldiers underneath it.

Uncle Ashley toddled to the nearest settee and collapsed upon it, causing the inner coils to screech and the legs to creak worryingly. He sighed in exhaustion, pulled a lace handkerchief from his breast pocket, and wiped the sweat from his jowls. He waved his ham hock of an arm in Marlowe's general direction when he was done.

"Pour me a draught, won't you, Evie? I'm devilish parched. Thought we'd never arrive," Uncle Ashley drawled.

Well, some things never changed.

Barming looked upon Uncle Ashley's dramatic entrance with open disgust. Uncle Ashley was supremely unconcerned with his brother's opinion, however. It was one of the few things Marlowe had always admired about his uncle—the man's complete imperturbability. He was the one person on earth who seemed totally immune to the earl, content to be both a shameless hanger-on and a permanent thorn in the man's side.

It probably helped that Uncle Ashley was sober only when he slept, though Marlowe suspected that even that was a rare occurrence.

Marlowe silently congratulated his uncle for taking the wind out of the earl's sails so thoroughly with his entrance.

Perhaps he was not so cross with Uncle Ashley's presence after all, for at least he distracted the earl. Feeling magnanimous, he poured his uncle some port—without bothering to ask if the earl wanted the same.

The earl just glared at him and resumed his diatribe. "Your influence over Elizabeth is entirely unacceptable. I will not allow you to ruin her the same way you have your own daughters."

Marlowe delivered his uncle's port and tried very hard not to punch his father as he returned to his seat. "Elizabeth came here of her own volition and without my foreknowledge. And if by ruin, you mean protecting her from a ridiculously unsuitable marriage to the Duke of Oxley, then, by damn, I am guilty. She's sixteen, Father."

"Poxley Oxley!" Uncle Ashley blustered into his port, turning toward the earl with his eyes popped wide. He looked like a startled toad. "The devil you say!"

The earl glared at his brother impatiently. "You were there when the banns were read, Ashley."

"Was I?" Uncle Ashley said, his face screwing up thoughtfully as he searched his memory. It didn't seem to work, for he eventually shrugged and took another sip of port. "Don't recall it at all." Which was hardly surprising, considering Marlowe had never seen his uncle stay awake during a Sunday service in his life. "Last I heard about Poxley, he were run out of a nunnery in Soho for nearly killing one of 'em. Can't say as I like the thought of him marrying our little Betsy."

Marlowe had also heard that same tale—and so had the earl, judging by his promptly dismissive snort and wandering eyes. "Lies, I'm sure. Besides, what care I for some tart?"

"No, you care only for the duke's deep pockets," Marlowe muttered.

The earl's scowl deepened. "The marriage contracts have been signed. I won't have you cocking things up in the final hour, Marlowe."

"If you're short on funds, all you need do is ask me for a loan," Marlowe returned silkily.

When Marlowe was ten, the look the earl gave him at that moment would have sent him into fits of terror, as it usually presaged a backhanded blow at the very least. Now Marlowe just quirked an eyebrow and smiled at his father, daring him to do his worst.

The earl seemed determined not to lose their battle of wills, however. He changed tack. "The duke informed me of your rather rude behavior at Almack's. He's not best pleased with his future wife at the moment. I'll not have him calling off the arrangement, so I have invited him over to dine tonight."

"Have you indeed?" Marlowe drawled boredly while inwardly seething. And he'd thought the day couldn't possibly get any worse.

"We must salvage the mess you have made as best we can."

"Must we?"

"Don't play the fool with me, my boy," the earl bit out. "You've not a leg to stand on, and you know it. Elizabeth will marry Oxley, and that is an end to it."

"Your compassion for your daughter is touching, Father."

The earl waved a dismissive hand. "She'll be a wealthy duchess. Far more than the strumpet could ever hope to achieve otherwise."

Marlowe was glad Betsy had not left her rooms yet, so that she might be spared the words out of her father's mouth. "I'm sure the fathers of Poxley's three dead wives thought the same thing," he murmured.

"You are the last person who should cast stones on account of rumor and innuendo," the earl pronounced.

"The moral high ground suits you even less than it does me, Father," he said pleasantly. "But by all means, let us have the fellow over to dine. Shockingly, my appetite fled the premises not long after you arrived anyway. Though I'm sure Uncle here will have no trouble with his digestion."

Uncle Ashley slapped his belly and gave Marlowe a wry grin. "You know me too well, nephew. My belly's survived this long in this family; a little meal with Poxley ain't going to put me off my feed. I shall enjoy the spectacle, I'm sure."

The earl transferred his wrath in his brother's direction, but Uncle Ashley merely finished off his port in response.

"I hope I don't fail to entertain, then," Marlowe murmured, for if Uncle Ashley wanted a spectacle, he'd damned well give him one.

On his list of things he'd rather not inflict upon himself, dining with Poxley Oxley rated just below stabbing himself in the eyeball with a dessert spoon, but if his father was playing his hand now, Marlowe was more than ready to play his own. He'd thought he'd have a little more time to finesse his ammunition against Poxley, but he could work with what he had.

In fact, the more he thought about it, the more he liked the idea of dining with Oxley, since it meant less effort on his part to run the bastard to ground. Better men than the duke—much, much better men than the duke—had run screaming for the hills after dining *en famille* with the Leightons.

And just in case that wasn't enough, Marlowe knew just who to invite tonight to rid himself of Poxley forever. Thank hell that little tip from Sebastian had panned out the way it had. He was going to enjoy every minute of this evening. And with any luck, he'd have the lot of them—Poxley, Barming, the countess, and even Uncle Ashley (if he could fit)—out of his house by morning.

Chapter Thirteen

In Which The Viscount Hosts A Dinner Party

THE LAST TIME MINERVA HAD been asked to dine at the table of her employer had been when Lady Blundersmith had needed her to even out the numbers. Minerva had had to endure an entire evening talking about furuncles with an eighty-year-old hypochondriacal lord. It had been one of the most painful conversations of her life, but worse still was knowing that if she'd put a foot wrong in front of Lady Blundersmith's company, she'd have been out on the streets by morning.

She hardly feared the same happening now, since the viscount, owing to some perversity of character, seemed to like her best when she was being insubordinate. The black mood that had descended over the household the moment the earl had descended upon the townhouse did nothing to assuage her nerves, however—or the knowledge that the Duke of Oxley was to be in attendance as well. She could only hope that the viscount had found some way around his sister's predicament. Of course, the likelihood of the viscount successfully disentangling his sister from the arrangement over the soup course was very low, but stranger things had happened since she had joined the household.

Minerva suspected that the night would be an interesting one, if nothing else.

Armed in the sapphire gown, she entered the drawing room that evening to find it empty of all but Marlowe, his sister, and a weak-chinned woman who could be none other than the Countess of Barming. One look at the countess, and Minerva knew that all of Lady Elizabeth's complaints about her mother had been accurate . . . and that Lady Elizabeth had been fortunate to inherit her handsome looks from her father's side of the family.

The countess sat on the edge of her seat with the rigid posture of someone who had been forced to balance books on her head during most of her childhood, peering out at the world through her lorgnette. She seemed to be trying to make up for her lack of chin and poor eyesight, however, with the obscene amount of gold and diamonds gilding her gown. The glare was nearly blinding in the candlelight.

From the way Marlowe's eyes were half closed, he was either trying to protect his vision from the glare or was bored out of his mind by the countess's monologue on why her modiste was the best in London.

Minerva suspected the latter, knowing him. Or both. It was a very powerful glare.

However, for a woman who was remarkably oblivious to the true reason the earl had brought her up from West Barming (she seemed to be under the impression it was so she could shop on Bond Street, from what Minerva could glean from her chatter) and almost blind, the countess amazingly recognized Minerva before Marlowe could get through his languid introductions.

"Why, aren't you Belinda's girl?" the countess said, scrutinizing her from top to toe through her lens.

Minerva's heart sank at the name as she rose from her curtsy.

The viscount perked up visibly at this. Apparently, she

was more interesting than modistes.

"Belinda? Who's Belinda?" he asked with poorly concealed delight.

"Lady Blundersmith," the countess said. "A dear friend of mine."

Marlowe looked Minerva over with a bemused expression, obviously waiting for further explanation. Minerva quirked an eyebrow at him and said nothing, just to see what he would do. His bemusement quickly gave way to a peevish frown when he realized she wasn't going to give him any answers.

The countess, however, seemed more than happy to air all of Minerva's secrets. She waved her lorgnette at Minerva. "You're the one she sacked, aren't you, gel? Whatever are you doing here?"

"She's my governess," Marlowe said briskly. He turned back to Minerva. "What does she mean, you were sacked? And what the devil were you doing working for old Blunderbuss, Miss Jones?"

"Earning a living, my lord," she said without bothering to hide her irritation. She might have been infatuated with him—Lord knew why—but that didn't mean she'd let him tease her in front of mixed company. "I was Lady Blundersmith's companion for five years before I went to West Barming."

"Five years," Marlowe breathed, looking both horrified and grudgingly impressed. "How are you not in Bedlam?"

She'd often wondered the same thing.

The countess was not impressed at all. She glared at Marlowe through her lens. "Just what are you implying about Belinda, Evelyn?"

The viscount visibly gritted his teeth at the use of *his* Christian name. "I ain't implying nothing," he muttered, suddenly all of five years old.

The countess sniffed and turned her lens back on Minerva. She frowned at her with deepening suspicion. "I'm sure Belly had a perfectly good reason for the sacking," she said in a tone that made it clear she'd found Minerva sorely wanting.

Then suddenly, out of the corner of her eye, for she couldn't seem to make herself stop *noticing* him, Minerva saw Marlowe's whole face light up with unholy glee. She held her breath, fearing that he'd finally remembered their first true encounter.

He had, God help her. "You were at the Montford Ball when Sherry and I . . ." He made a complicated hand gesture that Minerva took to represent two grown men rolling in sponge cake. "*You* were the little wallflower old Blunderbuss nearly flattened."

The blood she could feel rushing into her cheeks was only fractionally due to embarrassment. The rest was from pure vexation. Truly. How could she have fallen for such an absolute, utter oaf?

"Little wallflower," she said flatly.

Lady Elizabeth seemed the only one in the room who had any idea how near Minerva was to exploding. But instead of being concerned, the girl just laughed merrily.

Meanwhile, Lady Barming continued to examine her through her lens with the intensity of someone searching for nits. Not even Countess Lieven had made her feel so awkward. This felt more like the morning she'd stood in the middle of the headmistress's office after the viscount's bungled housebreaking—the *second* time she'd been sacked.

She thought longingly of her bedroom, far, far removed from what was shaping up to be an excruciating evening.

"I feel certain Belly told me why she dismissed you," the countess mused. "Some dreadful unpleasantness, I'm sure. How you managed to secure a post in my stepson's household is quite beyond me."

"Have you met your stepson, my lady?" she countered.

Lady Barming sniffed at Minerva's cheek and lowered her lorgnette. She turned to the viscount. "Is there such a dearth of servants in London that you must hire this impertinent creature? Whatever is she doing here at this hour anyway?"

The viscount gave a long-suffering sigh. "You insisted upon having another female at the dinner table, Stepmother. I could have Mrs. Chips take Miss Jones's place, if you would prefer."

Mrs. Chips, who was pouring the countess's sherry at the sideboard across the room, looked as horrified at this prospect as Lady Barming.

Or at least her left eyebrow did.

The countess warily accepted her drink from the housekeeper and sniffed it suspiciously. "Really, Evelyn, you must hire a proper staff," she finally said. "A governess at the dinner table, and your poor housekeeper serving drinks like a common footman. It is all very irregular."

Mrs. Chips's eyebrow rose even higher as she glanced pointedly at the viscount. On this subject, it seemed that she and the countess were in agreement. Apparently a valet and a couple of footmen and grooms were not enough staff for her tastes.

"And what have we here?" interrupted a deep voice at Minerva's back.

Startled, she spun around to find the most enormous man she'd ever seen. He put even Lady Blundersmith's girth to shame. He turned sideways, too wide to fit through the doorway otherwise, and squeezed himself in. He then proceeded to shuffle toward her with a blatant leer on his face. He had the Leighton hair and eyes and looked like a much older version of the viscount—had the viscount continued down his road of dissipation and excess . . . *and* consumed a whole roast pig every evening for about two decades.

She tried to gather her chin from the floor, since she was sure that was where it was at the present moment.

The man's beady brown eyes took her measure, and then took it again. "She's a tasty little morsel underneath all that drab," he declared. Really, the utter . . . "You always did have an eye, Evie. Caro were a prime article, and I can't blame you one bit for having your head turned arse to ankles over that one. It weren't your fault she were a lying, faithless bi—"

"This is the *governess*, uncle," Marlowe cut in, his cheeks a bit pink and his jaw tight. "Of my *children*. I'll thank you to keep a civil tongue tonight. Miss Jones, this is my father's brother, the Honorable Ashley Leighton." Marlowe sounded extremely dubious about the accuracy of *that* particular courtesy title.

Uncle Ashley's leer only increased. Minerva, quite recovered from her surprise, stared him down with a cool look she'd reserved for her most recalcitrant students (i.e. the twins). If the viscount's family insisted on being rude, she'd damn well serve it back to them in spades.

Uncle Ashley's leer turned into a delighted smile at her glare . . . though it was hard to be sure underneath so many layers of blubber. He finally seemed to lose interest in trying to disconcert her and waddled farther into the room. She was shocked the buttons on his waistcoat didn't fly across the room when he settled himself next to Lady Barming, the chair groaning ominously beneath him. He snapped two meaty fingers at Mrs. Chips and gestured toward a stool on the other side of the room.

Minerva nearly gasped at his effrontery and half expected Mrs. Chips to chuck the decanter of sherry at his head. The housekeeper looked as impenetrable as ever, but she took her time fetching the stool and setting it at the man's feet, her eyes like flint shards. *Someone* was going to receive cold tea and stale biscuits in the morning.

Uncle Ashley waved her away, unbothered, and heaved a gouty leg on top of the stool. The only one who didn't look disgusted at the sight of the swollen appendage was Lady Barming, and that was only because she was too blind to see it.

Minerva, who still found herself standing in the middle of the room, finally took her own seat next to Lady Elizabeth. It put her farthest from Uncle Ashley's leg.

Tasty morsel indeed. From the look of the man's waistline, he was not even being metaphorical. She had the horrible suspicion that he'd consume her for a midday snack if given half the chance, and still have room for pudding in the evening.

"Nevertheless, my boy," Uncle Ashley continued after tossing back the sherry Mrs. Chips had handed him in one go, "you do know how to find 'em." He held his glass out to the housekeeper for more. Mrs. Chips's eye began to spasm.

"*If* he knew how to find a proper staff," the countess intoned with a distasteful look at Mrs. Chips.

"That weren't what I were talking about," Uncle Ashley muttered.

Minerva decided not to hold back, as no one else seemed to be bothering. She turned to the viscount. "Do you and your uncle talk about your conquests at every family gathering?"

"Only the interesting ones," he replied. He gave his uncle a warning look. "Play nice, you old goat, or I'll ban you from the evening's entertainment."

Uncle Ashley brightened. "Entertainment, eh? Anything to my taste?" He licked his lips suggestively and eyed Minerva.

Oh, the man was a pig.

The viscount just grinned cryptically. "Very much so, Uncle."

"Entertainment? Lud, I did not know there would be entertainment!" the countess cried in alarm. "I must be up early to catch my modiste for a consultation. I shall have a new wardrobe out of this trip, if nothing else."

Minerva had never known a mother's love, but it hardly seemed as if it would feel good to know one's mother cared about her new frocks more than her own child's pending marriage to a blackguard. From the way Lady Elizabeth's shoulders slumped next to her in defeat, Minerva suspected the girl would agree with her.

"Don't worry, Stepmother, the entertainment shall commence at the evening meal. You shall be in your bed before ten," the viscount assured her. "And out the door before dawn, if all goes well," he muttered in a voice so low that only Minerva was able to hear it.

This didn't seem to mollify Lady Barming. "Entertainment *during* the meal? I've never heard of such."

Neither had Minerva. She could only guess what Marlowe had planned.

"Never heard of what?" demanded yet another new voice at the doorway, and from one glance she knew it could only be the Earl of Barming. Aside from the gray in his hair and the angry wrinkles lining his face, he looked exactly like his son, just on a slightly smaller and meaner scale. But whereas his son's brown eyes danced with life, the earl's were hard and cruel, and the tight line of his mouth spoke eloquently of a man who rarely smiled. He strode into the room as if he owned it and surveyed all of its occupants with a frown.

Minerva felt Lady Elizabeth stiffen next to her and watched the countess fidget with her lorgnette. Even Uncle Ashley straightened his bulk as much as he could, as if he too were unwillingly disturbed by the earl's presence.

Only Marlowe seemed unaffected, slouching casually as ever in a banyan, Pymm's influence completely forsaken for the night. But Minerva knew it was all an act from one glance at the viscount's eyes. Minerva had seen the same calculation in her father's when he'd talked about the French Navy. It was the look of a man facing his bitterest adversary.

"So nice of you to join us, Father," the viscount said with false sincerity.

The earl's disdainful look swept around the room, fell onto Minerva, and paused. She held her breath, feeling even more apprehensive than she had in Oxley's company, and wondered if the earl might not notice her if she stayed still enough.

She began to understand why Marlowe had buried himself in drink and excess for so much of his life.

"Who is that?" the earl demanded.

"Miss Jones. The governess," the viscount said breezily.

The earl sneered and immediately dismissed her from his notice. She didn't know whether to be indignant or relieved at the slight. At least the countess and Uncle Ashley had insulted her to her face.

Lady Elizabeth tensed further at Minerva's side when the Duke of Oxley, bewigged, painted, and looking even more unsavory than he had at Almack's, entered behind Lord Barming.

"Your Grace! You can't imagine how pleased I am to see you." The viscount sounded just the opposite, however.

The duke gave Marlowe a grim look before bowing over the countess's extended hand with stiff civility. He did the same to Lady Elizabeth, though she winced at his overzealous grip. He ignored Minerva entirely, and Minerva couldn't muster up anything but relief at the cut. The man made her nauseous.

Lady Elizabeth wiped her hand against her skirts, as she'd done at Almack's, and didn't bother to hide her disgust. Minerva didn't blame her. If the duke had kissed her hand, she would have scrubbed it for hours, then doused it with spirits for good measure just to make sure all traces of him were gone.

The earl's eyes narrowed on his daughter, no doubt devising some future retribution for her display. Minerva couldn't help but squeeze the girl's hand in silent support—the one Oxley *hadn't* touched.

"Shall we dine, then, or are we expected to cook our

own food in this house?" the earl demanded of his son.

"Momentarily, Father. We are still one guest short," Marlowe replied much too brightly.

The earl's brow creased with consternation. "I've not invited anyone else."

"No, but I have. It is my house after all, and since you invited Poxley,"—Uncle Ashley snickered at this; Oxley's wrinkled cheeks pinked with indignation beneath the paint—"I thought I'd invite someone as well to keep him company."

"I do wish your guest were a female, Evelyn," the countess opined, oblivious to the tension in the room, "for even with your *person*—" she peered disdainfully through her looking glass at Minerva, "the numbers are still dreadfully uneven."

Marlowe smiled at the countess. "I'm sorry to disappoint, Stepmother, but needs must tip the scale even further against the ladies tonight."

The countess wrinkled her nose in dismay.

"What do you mean, keep *me* company, Marlowe?" the duke growled suspiciously.

Marlowe gave Oxley a wolf's grin. Oh, he was definitely up to something. Minerva exchanged a hopeful glance with Lady Elizabeth, but from her bewildered look, the girl seemed as oblivious to her brother's plans as Minerva was. "Don't worry, Poxley. I think you'll be well pleased with my guest."

Marlowe's cocked eyebrow dared the man to say otherwise. Oxley just gritted his teeth at the viscount's continued mispronunciation of his title, his neck beginning to flush an angry red where it was not caked in paint or speckled by lesions.

Those lesions were very worrying.

As if on cue, Mrs. Chips, who had slipped out of the room sometime after Uncle Ashley's third glass of sherry, slipped back in with their final guest hot on her heels.

"A Mr. Soames has arrived, your lordship," Mrs. Chips intoned.

Minerva found herself gaping in shock for the second time that night at the sight of the new arrival.

Mr. Soames gifted the room with an elaborate bow fit for the royal court, though it wobbled dangerously on the upswing. The man had Marlowe's height but was built nearly twice as wide. He hadn't Uncle Ashley's impressive girth—who did?—but his belly was substantial enough to stretch the silk of a virulently red waistcoat to its limits. His stained cravat was tied in what appeared to be a Gordian knot, and his tailcoat of cheap black superfine looked as if it had been cut for a man half his size. His broad grin revealed a mouthful of yellowed teeth, and his carefully coiffed dark hair *a la Brutus* stank of penny pomade even from across the room.

Lady Barming squinted through her lens, as if she doubted what she was seeing. Which was obviously not a lot, since she'd not stormed out of the room in a righteous huff.

The earl glared at his son.

The duke gasped in horror and backed into the sideboard, nearly knocking the decanter to the floor.

Uncle Ashley finished his sherry with a rapturous sigh and signaled to Mrs. Chips for yet another.

"Thank you, Mrs. Chips," the viscount said breezily, crossing the room to greet the new arrival. It didn't escape Minerva's notice that it was a courtesy he'd not extended to the duke. "May I present my friend, Mr. Soames of Bow Street. Mr. Soames: my father and stepmother, the Earl and Countess of Barming; my sister Lady Elizabeth; the Honorable Mr. Ashley Leighton; and Miss Jones. Oh, and the Duke of Poxley."

Oxley's complexion took on a greenish cast beneath his cracking paint as Mr. Soames beamed in his direction, and a faint film of sweat began to coat the edges of his wig.

"Yer Gracefulness! Fancy seein' you here," Mr. Soames said. "This is what they call a commencement, for I were jus' finking about you today while I were visiting me cousin."

"You are acquainted! What a lovely *commencement* indeed!" Marlowe's look of delighted surprise was so exaggerated that Minerva thought even the myopic countess would realize how feigned it was, but her lens was still pointed at Mr. Soames's waistcoat. "I was unaware of your interest in Bow Street, Poxley. Surely this is how you know Mr. Soames?"

Oxley's greenish complexion had given way to red over the course of the viscount's words. It was nearly purple with rage by the time he opened his mouth to answer.

But Mr. Soames cut off whatever the duke would have said with a chuckle and a hearty slap to the back. The duke's legs nearly buckled from the blow.

"Oh, aye, we're old friends, Poxley and I," Mr. Soames said, rocking back on his heels and looking well pleased with himself. "'Is Gracefulness and I 'ave a business arraignment, doan we, gov?"

Oxley spluttered, glaring at the viscount as if he wanted to strangle him. "I have never seen this ruffian before in my life!" Oxley exclaimed.

Mr. Soames's broad grin grew even broader at this, but there was something hard-edged beneath his expression when he looked at the duke. It was the same look underneath Marlowe's veneer of calm amusement, as if they were both wolves circling their prey.

Well, Minerva had known the night would be anything but boring. She decided to follow Uncle Ashley's lead and sat back in her seat to enjoy the show. Mrs. Chips pressed a glass of sherry into her hands, as if reading her intentions and approving heartily of them.

"Ruffian!" Marlowe cried, seemingly taken aback at Oxley's accusation. "Surely you are mistaken, Duke. Mr.

Soames here is an officer of law and order in this fair city of ours."

"Jus' doin' me civilian duty, m'lord, an' 'appy to be 'ere tonight amongst such quality," Mr. Soames affirmed solemnly.

The viscount smiled at his guest. "Mr. Soames has done me a great favor, and I couldn't think of a better way to repay him than an intimate family dinner."

Marlowe could think of no better way to annoy his family, either. The earl looked as if he were one breath away from apoplexy.

The countess, on the other hand, looked as if she were still trying to work out how Mr. Soames could possibly exist. "You have a most fascinating accent," she said as she peered through her lorgnette. "What is it? Dutch? Belgian?"

"East London, Yer Excellency," Mr. Soames said, sweeping her another courtly bow.

The countess dropped her lorgnette into her lap. "Indeed!"

"An' I doan aim to be impotent, Yer Excellency, but I doan fink I've seen finer assets than yer own," he said, gesturing in the vicinity of the countess's bosoms. "Are they genuine?"

Uncle Ashley spluttered his sherry down the front of his cravat at this, and the viscount and Lady Elizabeth choked on horrified laughter.

The countess seemed to understand what Mr. Soames was truly referring to, however—her only show of astuteness since recognizing Minerva earlier. She touched the enormous diamonds around her neck with a haughty sniff. "Of course they're real."

"You've excruciating taste, Yer Excellency," Soames said, bowing once more.

The countess didn't know whether to be flattered or offended, judging by the constipated look on her face.

"If ever yer needin' an 'onest appraisal of value, I know a man in Covent Garden. 'E makes excellent paste for ladies such as yerself what might be in need of a little supplemental pin money, if ye takes me meaning."

"My stepmother only shops on Bond Street, Mr. Soames, and would never wear paste," Marlowe interrupted smoothly when the countess flushed with affront.

"Of course," Mr. Soames said breezily.

"And that necklace is an heirloom. If it were to be interfered with or *misplaced*, it would surely break my stepmother's heart," Marlowe continued, his easy manner laced with steel.

Mr. Soames's smile froze. "Of course," he repeated, less breezily this time, giving the necklace one last look of longing.

"What is your game, Marlowe?" the earl barked at his son. He looked as if he'd finally recovered enough from the shock of Mr. Soames's presence to continue to be as disagreeable as possible.

Marlowe's look of feigned innocence was so outrageous Minerva only barely held back a snort. Uncle Ashley didn't bother. "I truly don't know what you mean, Father. This is just an intimate meal among friends, is it not? I thought it a wonderful opportunity to invite Mr. Soames to join us and thank him for all of the wonderful work Bow Street does for the citizens of London. You've always been after me to perform my civic duty, after all."

"Me an' me fellow runners are benighted to serve, Vee-count," Mr. Soames declared agreeably.

Marlowe grinned. "Eloquent as always, Soames. Now I believe it's time to dine. Countess?" Marlowe said, offering his stepmother his arm.

Somehow, the earl ended up escorting Minerva to the table, though he looked the entire time as if he'd rather be having his teeth pulled. She would have felt insulted, but she was too entertained to do so. What had started off as a miserable evening had quickly become something else altogether. She had a feeling that Lady Elizabeth was going to find herself without a fiancé by the end of the evening. Whatever Mr. Soames held over Oxley had to be huge for the duke to even consider sitting down at the same table as the runner.

She had once again underestimated the viscount. She'd feared this dinner with Oxley might have meant Marlowe's capitulation to the marriage, but she should have known better. The night was going to end in a spectacular disaster, of that she had no doubt.

And if there was ever a doubt where the twins had inherited their penchant for wreaking havoc, the sight of Mr. Soames settling into his seat next to the Earl of Barming erased them all. She sought out the viscount at the head of the table and found him relaxed in his seat, wineglass poised carelessly in one hand, the picture of indolent amusement. He seemed completely immune to his father's glower and the duke's silent fuming. He caught her eye and gave her a guileless look as Mrs. Chips ladled cold pea soup into his bowl.

She groaned inwardly, for it seemed Mrs. Chips had devised the same menu she'd served to Minerva the first night of her employment. Pea soup and mutton were as much a call to arms for the housekeeper as the viscount's East London dinner guest. The vile combination meant that the housekeeper disliked their present houseguests as much as she did.

But it also meant that Minerva would be going to bed hungry.

Uncle Ashley and Mr. Soames attacked their bowls with alacrity. They were the only ones. The sound of their slurping was the only thing that broke the awkward silence that had descended over the table.

Minerva decided to give this disaster in the making a little kick and turned to Mr. Soames, waiting until he was between spoonfuls of soup to pose her question.

"So, Mr. Soames, how is it that you know the viscount?"

Mr. Soames spilled most of his next spoonful onto his waistcoat as he turned to her. He gave her a yellow grin, his eyes twinkling with some sort of secret delight. "Well, that's a bit of a tale, Miss Jones," he said loud enough for the whole table to hear. "The vee-count and meself share a mutinous friend in the Marquess of Manwaring."

"He came to the heroic rescue of one of the marchioness's dogs a few years ago," the viscount said dryly.

She was sure she didn't want to know.

"I didn't know Bow Street was in the habit of rescuing pets," Lady Elizabeth said from across the table, leaning as far away from Oxley as she could as she ran her spoon listlessly through the soup.

"It were a one-off, Yer Ladyness," Mr. Soames said. "The opportunity presented itself, an' I took it. 'Carpenter diem' an' all that. I'm out of the pet business these days, though, and on to more charitable indebtors."

"Rescuing animals seems *very* charitable of you, Mr. Soames," Minerva said, wondering where in the world this conversation would end up.

Mr. Soames was well pleased by the praise, judging from the way he flung his spoon through the air as he spoke. "Aye, but people 'elping people—and wot-not—is wot this great city of ours needs more of, an' that's the line of business I aim to pursue. Bow Street does good work, but there are too many criminals that woan ever be persecuted proper-like." He shot a pointed look at the duke, who was as green as his soup at the moment. "So I offer me services to wronged parties that woan see the renumeration they deserve through the courts."

"How very public minded of you, Mr. Soames," she said, impressed by his philanthropy. Perhaps she'd underestimated the man.

"I'm sure Mr. Soames is well compensated for his services," the viscount said, dry as dust, as he took a sip of his wine.

"I take a small percentage," Mr. Soames admitted, not looking the least bit ashamed. "I'm an entremanurial-minded fellow. I can't be doing charity work for free."

Well, perhaps she *hadn't* underestimated the man after all.

"God forbid," Marlowe agreed.

"Can't say as I doan enjoy the work, though," Soames continued after another slurp of his soup. "You meet all sorts. It's how I became acquainted with the duke 'ere, in fact."

"Oxley, I didn't know you too were so involved in charitable endeavors," Marlowe declared disingenuously.

Oxley, conspicuously silent since he'd sat down, went rigid, and the green beneath his thick maquillage quickly changed to scarlet. His soupspoon clanged hard against the porcelain bowl as he dropped it from a clenched fist. "I should call you out for this, Marlowe," the duke gritted out.

The viscount's grin developed a razor-sharp edge to it, and Minerva repressed a shiver. Nothing of the indolent aristocrat remained. This was the man who'd fought and won too many duels of honor to count.

Now she remembered why she was so taken with the man.

"Nothing would please me more," he said flatly.

The high color fled the duke's cheeks.

"My heavens! I shall need my salts tonight if you insist on dueling at the dinner table, Evelyn," the countess breathed, looking uncomfortably befuddled, sitting as she was between the two men.

"Our highness 'ere is one of my biggest contributors," Mr. Soames continued, as if oblivious to the tension in the air. "I felicitated 'is 'elp after a mutinous friend of ours lost 'er employment due to a viscous assault on 'er person."

"Why, how awful! And Bow Street cannot find her assailant?" Lady Barming cried, for she seemed the first one, surprisingly, to have muddled out Mr. Soames's meaning.

Mr. Soames's genial smile faded, and he fixed the duke with a hard look.

"I'm afraid the courts were unable to prosecute this particular villain through conventional means," Marlowe offered when Soames just continued to glare at the duke.

"This is why I despise London!" the countess declared, trading her lorgnette for a gold-encrusted fan and fluttering it frantically in front of her. "I should not feel safe shopping even on Bond Street after hearing such a sordid tale. I should only hope ruffians like that confine their activities to the lower orders where they belong."

"Aye," Soames said sagely. "My client *is* but a lowly businesswoman, Yer Ladyness, but she's an 'onest woman all the same, wot doan deserve wot's been done to her."

"How admirable of you to come to this poor unfortunate's aid, Your Grace," the countess said, turning her attention to her neighbor. "Even if she is in trade."

Oxley just gritted his teeth.

"I should like to help as well," Lady Barming continued, "so that she may recover enough to resume her work. Where was she employed, Mr. Soames? For I should like to write a very stern letter to its proprietor for letting this poor woman go."

"The White House, off Soho Square, Yer Ladyness," Mr. Soames said. "And thank ye for yer kindness."

It seemed the countess, who smiled benevolently at the runner, was the only one at the table who *didn't* know what the White House was. Even Lady Elizabeth seemed to recognize the name, judging from the way she choked on her wine.

The earl glanced from Mr. Soames to the viscount, as if he couldn't decide where to focus his rage. And he was angry, *very* angry, a large purple vein throbbing in his right temple and his fingers clutching his spoon so tightly the silver had started to bend.

"You will cease this game at once! How dare you invite this . . . opportunistic villain to the table!" the earl hissed at his son with quiet fury.

Marlowe merely lifted a bored brow. "*You* invited Poxley, not me."

The earl spluttered indignantly.

Uncle Ashley snorted in amusement.

The duke rose from the table, sweat pouring down his face and streaking through the maquillage, making it seem as if his face were melting off. His hands clenched at his sides as if he were barely holding himself back from crawling over the table and strangling his host. "I'll stand for this no longer, Marlowe. I've never been so insulted in all my life," he seethed.

"I'm the one who should feel insulted, as if anyone could ever think I'd let a man like *you* marry my sister," Marlowe returned.

Minerva's heart swelled at his words. She wanted to stand up and cheer, and when she glanced across the table at Lady Elizabeth, she looked as if she wanted to do the same.

"The arrangement has nothing to do with you," the duke snapped.

"On the contrary, it has everything to do with me," the viscount interrupted briskly, "since Mr. Soames has sold to me some extremely interesting documents indeed."

The duke's face went pea green once more. He shot daggers at Mr. Soames. "We had an arrangement!"

Mr. Soames just smirked. "Wot can I say? I 'ad a better offer elsewhere, an' I took it." His smirk faded. "Asides, Jenny's me cousin's sister-in-law. Family's family, and I've of a mind to 'ave you brought as low as you brought 'er."

"I'm a peer of the realm," Oxley sneered. "I hardly think a prostitute's allegations would send *me* to Newgate."

"Prostitute!" the countess cried, aghast, fanning herself vigorously. "Oh, lud. I hardly think this is appropriate conversation for the dinner table!"

"We've been talking about prostitutes for the past quarter hour, Mama," Lady Elizabeth said from Oxley's other side, not bothering to hide her delight in the proceedings. "What business did you think the White House was? A haberdasher's?"

The countess clutched her diamonds as if they could be contaminated by such low subject matter and glared at her daughter around Oxley's buttocks. "Elizabeth! An unwed lady doesn't speak of such things!" she gasped.

"But don't you think I should be better acquainted with my fiancé's hobbies?" Lady Elizabeth said much too sweetly. "You said it was important for a wife to pretend to share her husband's interests."

The countess moaned and swooned in her seat, her vinaigrette falling from limp fingers. Lady Elizabeth rolled her eyes and took another sip of her wine.

"I shouldn't worry about that, my dear," Marlowe said. "For I think that Poxley shall be going on an extended holiday very soon and, alas, shall be in no need of a wife after all."

"What have you done?" Oxley growled, rounding once more on the viscount.

Marlowe's smile was so implacably frosty that Minerva finally glimpsed the soldier who had survived the Peninsular Wars underneath all of his armor.

And in that moment, she had to wonder how much of his life was a performance. He played the court jester—the feckless sot—so well that very few people would ever suspect anything lay beneath the mask. She herself would have never guessed he had half a brain, much less hidden depths, had she not lived in such close quarters with him these past few months. His reasons for playing the fool were becoming a bit more obvious now that she'd met his extended family, however. She'd don as much armor as she could as well against such perniciousness.

But she wondered if she'd ever know who he truly was underneath all of his formidable defenses. She'd thought perhaps she was beginning to, but she had a horrible feeling she'd only scratched the surface. Though as she gazed at him in the candlelight—at his rich coffee eyes and unruly mahogany curls, his hawkish nose that had been broken one too many times, and those full, mobile lips that said and did such outrageous things—she felt oddly up to the challenge.

She was definitely, definitely doomed.

"The court of public opinion can be as powerful as Whitehall," Marlowe continued. "And I have to confess to being something of a philanthropist, just like Mr. Soames here. The *Times* was quite keen to acquire the documents Mr. Soames sold to me. I would suggest that you leave for Calais before the morning delivery. Though I don't think even France deserves the likes of you." The viscount's eyes glittered with triumph as he took a laconic sip of his wine, as calm and as unruffled at the chaos he'd orchestrated as if he'd been talking about the weather.

"You bastard!" the duke bellowed, launching himself forward over the countess's lap. The countess shrieked and fell out of her seat, knocking her half-finished bowl of pea soup with her fan. The greenish contents upended over the back of the duke's breeches as he punched the viscount in the face.

Marlowe's head jerked to one side from the force of the blow, but he was smirking when he turned back to the duke, despite the cut high on his cheekbone from the duke's pretentious signet ring. He didn't even bother to rise to his feet. "Shall you try that again?" he taunted. "I barely felt it."

The duke lunged at the viscount again and punched him in the jaw this time, but the viscount remained unmoved. It was more an insult than if he had met the duke's challenge. "I refuse to fight a coward like you, Poxley," he said with cool disdain.

"How dare . . ." Oxley strangled out as he went for the viscount once more.

Mr. Soames jumped from his seat, wiped the pea soup from his mouth with his sleeve, and stuffed a couple of bread rolls in his pockets before wading into the fray. He rounded the table faster than Minerva thought someone with such a prodigious belly could ever hope to move, stepped over the prone countess, and restrained the duke's spindly arms behind him.

"Unhand me, you pleb!" the duke snarled.

"As an officer of Bow Street, I'm afeard I can't obligate Yer Gracefulness. Attacking a man in 'is own home is a 'orrible breach of manners."

"Thank you, Soames," the viscount said, patting at the cut on his cheek.

"Jus' doin' me job, gov. I only wish I could stay for the main course."

"Another time, perhaps. See that you deposit him on the docks, as we discussed."

"It will be my great pleasure to obligate, my lord," Soames said grandly and kicked at the duke's knees to get him moving forward.

"I'll have your head, Marlowe!" Oxley bellowed as Soames marched the man out the door.

Only the countess's indignant pants broke the silence that followed, as Lady Elizabeth helped her mother back into her seat.

Mrs. Chips cleaned up the spilled soup and took away everyone's bowls with quiet efficiency, as if nothing untoward had happened.

The earl waited until Mrs. Chips had served the mutton course and left the table before he threw down his serviette and stood, as if only the presence of the servant had restrained him. Hands clenched at his side, he stalked over to Marlowe with a murderous look on his face.

Minerva heard Lady Elizabeth gasp, and even Uncle Ashley paused in the act of cutting up his meat. She began to truly worry for the first time all evening. Vile as he was, Oxley was hardly a physical match for Marlowe, but the earl was nearly as broad as his son and looked thrice as capable of doing violence.

Marlowe just stared up at his father with a vague amusement, as he'd done with Oxley, and waited.

When the earl backhanded him squarely across the cheek, Marlowe's head recoiled from the blow, and his lip began to bleed, but his expression never changed.

Marlowe dabbed at his lip, unimpressed. "*You're* getting old," he murmured.

The earl looked disgusted. "You have done so many things over the years to embarrass this family, I was rather used to the disappointment, but tonight . . . tonight has been a special hell."

"The only embarrassment is you selling your daughter to a deviant who almost certainly already killed three wives."

The countess gasped, as if it were the first time she'd heard of this. It probably was.

"Unfounded innuendo," the earl insisted.

"Doubtful. But my sister will not marry him."

"You've no leg to stand on, boy," the earl sneered. "The law is on my side. She'll marry where I say."

Marlowe looked unbothered by this technicality. "You may take legal recourse, by all means. Oxley will be long gone by then, but I'm sure you can find another titled reprobate to fill his shoes. Though even if you brought the magistrate and all of Bow Street to my door, Betsy shall be leaving this household over my dead body."

"That can be arranged," the earl bit out.

Marlowe gave his father a cold smile. "Please. Don't make threats you can't possibly mean, Father. It makes you look ridiculous. Given his appetites, Uncle Ashley is liable to die next week, leaving Cousin Eustace as your only heir—the one person on earth you hate more than me. You'd rather eat glass than have him inherit." Marlowe nodded apologetically at his uncle. "Pardon, Uncle."

Uncle Ashley waved a forkful of mutton dismissively. "No need for apologies, my boy, no need. You are not wrong."

"If only Evander had been born first!" the earl raged.

Marlowe shrugged. "Sorry to disappoint you, Father, but Evander *is* dead."

The earl scowled. "For which *you* deserve the blame."

Marlowe cocked his head to the side, a flicker of . . . something wary crossing his face. The earl had finally hit a mark, it seemed, enough to jar his son out of his easy nonchalance, and Minerva braced herself. "Do I? How, exactly, did you come to such a conclusion?" It sounded like a dare.

"You were *weak*!" Barming jeered. "Half the man your brother ever was. So pathetic he stole your wife right from under your own roof."

The tension in the room reached a fever pitch at this pronouncement. No one dared to move, much less breathe too loudly . . . except Uncle Ashley. "Well, *that* were direct," he muttered around his mouthful.

Minerva felt sick to her stomach at the earl's revelation. For though his expression was still carefully neutral, she could see the pain in Marlowe's eyes and the stiffening line of his shoulders. Oxley's comeuppance had been rather satisfying to witness, but this . . . *this* was getting truly ugly.

No wonder Betsy had run away. And no wonder Marlowe was so . . . Marlowe-ish. Minerva thought her father had been a cold fish, but he had nothing on the earl. For once, Lady Elizabeth hadn't committed gross exaggeration when she'd complained ad nauseum these past few weeks about how awful her family was. If anything, Betsy's accounts had been kinder than they deserved.

The Leightons made Minerva glad to be an orphan for

the first time in her life.

"Careful, Father," Marlowe warned.

The earl didn't listen. "You disgust me. A worthless cuckold raising and *ruining* another man's children . . ."

The moment the words left the earl's lips, Marlowe snapped. His careful neutrality gave way to a raw rage that she'd never before seen cross his face. It was like looking at a stranger. He rose from his seat, and before the earl could complete his vile thought, he laid the man out with a blow of such ferocity it lifted the earl off his feet and sent him sprawling back on the parquet floor.

The countess shrieked. Uncle Ashley choked on his mutton. Lady Elizabeth looked grimly satisfied.

Minerva herself felt as if her heart were about to beat itself out of her chest. Between the implication of the earl's words and the sight of his unconscious body on the floor, she rather thought she might be going into shock.

Marlowe stood over his father, shaking out his fist and breathing hard, face still contorted with rage.

"Well, I've never been so entertained, my lad," Uncle Ashley said, breaking the silence with false cheer. "I believe the finale was my favorite part. Been wanting to do that for years."

Marlowe gave his uncle an unimpressed look, but at least that horrible rage was gone from his eyes. He nudged his father with his boot. The earl slowly came around, looking dazed as he managed to raise himself up on his elbows.

"Say what you will about me, but never speak of my daughters," Marlowe said with quiet fury. "For I shall call you out, no matter the scandal it would cause, and I would *not* delope."

The earl looked as if he might actually continue the argument, but Marlowe's expression darkened, and his fist clenched again. The earl wisely shut his mouth and glanced away from his son.

"I'm sure you'll want to depart at daybreak," Marlowe

said in a tone that made it clear this wasn't a suggestion.

The earl's scowl deepened, but he didn't protest the edict.

The countess, however, was not so wise. "But my modiste! I have an appointment with her in the morning, and I simply must visit . . ." She trailed off when Marlowe turned his hard gaze in her direction. She slumped back in her seat in defeat.

"I believe we are done here, then." The viscount gave Minerva one long look before he executed a short, stiff bow toward the table at large. "Ladies, Uncle. I bid you good night."

With that, he stalked out of the room.

No one made a move to help the earl to his feet.

The countess turned to her daughter, looking heartsick. "So does this mean you *won't* be becoming a duchess? For I did so have my heart set on the loveliest Brussels lace for the ceremony."

Lady Elizabeth sighed and patted her mother's hand in consolation.

CHAPTER FOURTEEN

In Which The Viscount Miss Jones Seduces Miss Jones The Viscount

WHEN MINERVA RETURNED TO THE nursery that night, she found the twins still awake and playing spillikins, despite having tucked them in before the start of dinner. It was obvious having Lord Barming under the same roof was the reason they were unable to settle for the night, but she supposed she couldn't blame them. The last time their grandfather had been around, they'd been shipped off to West Barming School for Recalcitrant Young Ladies. That was enough to cow even the most intractable of souls.

She managed to coax them back into bed by promising them a chapter from *Gulliver's Travels*—a book they seemed to love despite its gruesome politics (though that was probably *why* they liked it)—but just as they were settling in, the viscount appeared at the door, looking weary and rumpled, his jawline already starting to reveal its bruises and the cut in his lip just beginning to scab over.

After all that had happened at dinner—all that had been revealed—she understood his mood and his desire to seek solace in his children. He had routed the duke, but the cost to himself had been high. He must have been used to his father's contempt—had even expected it to be rained down upon him—but she doubted that familiarity had made it any easier to bear the earl's vicious words. She barely resisted the urge to go to him and offer some sort of comfort, for he looked as if he needed it. But it was not her place. She doubted it ever would be, though she was beginning to wish it were.

When the girls caught sight of him, they jumped from their beds, decorum completely abandoned, and mobbed him. The weary look on the viscount's face immediately faded away, and his tense lips smiled gently as he held his children close. But then Beatrice looked up at her father and frowned. "Papa, what happened to your face?" Beatrice cried in alarm.

Marlowe touched his bruised jaw and split lip as if he'd just remembered the abuse he'd received and froze. "I tripped," he said.

"Tripped?" Beatrice said skeptically.

"Tripped and fell into a door." It was a ridiculous explanation, but Minerva supposed it was better than the truth.

"It must have been a very angry door," Bea said, her brow furrowed as if she still did not quite believe it.

"It was," he agreed. "And speaking of angry doors, I have good news. Your grandfather will be leaving tomorrow morning."

The twins both breathed a sigh of relief at this. "Can we have our reward, then?" Beatrice demanded after exchanging an excited look with her sister.

Marlowe fixed Minerva with a mock serious look. "Miss Jones, how did my daughters fare today?"

"Very well, my lord," she managed. They'd been so well behaved it had been disconcerting. "We did figures this morning"—both twins made retching sounds at the reminder—"and they both chose books to read for the afternoon."

"We've been ever so good today, Father," Bea said, gazing up at her father with her big brown eyes. "Just as you asked."

He sighed, as if greatly put upon. "I suppose that means we must have ices at Gunter's tomorrow after all."

The girls cheered and danced around their father, and something flipped inside Minerva's chest as she watched the viscount smile down at his gamboling children. He finally looked back at her, and his expression was a bit sheepish. "Miss Jones, I'm afraid I must enlist your services tomorrow for an expedition to Gunter's."

She pretended to think about it. "It's my day off, but I suppose I can make an exception if ices are involved." She'd resigned her days off to the dustbin ever since the Fountain Incident, but the prospect of spending the day with the twins and their father was not at all unappealing. In fact, she could think of few things she would like better.

She was definitely doomed.

The viscount clapped his hands together. "There. It is settled. Now, to bed with both of you before I change my mind."

The twins obeyed with more alacrity than Minerva ever managed to elicit from them and tucked themselves in while Minerva turned down the lamps and picked up their game.

"Will you read to us, Papa?" Bea asked wistfully, the picture of childish innocence, all swaddled in her bedclothes.

He cast Minerva a questioning glance, and she nodded, handing over the copy of *Gulliver's Travels*. He saw the title and smiled. "I love this one." Of course he did.

Minerva had never heard the viscount read to the twins before, but he was surprisingly good at it. She thought about retreating to her room, but she was not ready to leave his company quite yet, not after the revelations of the evening. She sat back and let the quiet words wash over her without really paying attention to their meaning.

Marlowe was even more extraordinary than she'd thought. His attentiveness toward the twins was indeed unusual for a father of any class, and especially one of the aristocracy, who normally left the rearing of children—particularly girl children—to a legion of nursemaids and governesses. After what she'd learned tonight, Marlowe's obvious affection for the twins was even more of a rarity. Few men of any class would have loved so unconditionally children who were not their own. Yet nothing in his manner toward them would have ever betrayed the truth of their birth.

If she hadn't already been infatuated, this revelation would have surely done it.

Soon his rumbling baritone had put the twins under, and he motioned toward the door. She followed him out into the moonlit hallway, away from the nursery door, and paused under a window. It was as if he were as reluctant to leave her company as she was his. He looked as if he might speak, stepping toward her into a shaft of moonlight, and Minerva, who was already wound tight after the tumult of the night, felt her heartbeat pick up at his approach. It quickly plummeted when he seemed to change his mind and stepped back into the shadows with a troubled frown.

"Well," he said, sounding reluctant, "I suppose I shall say goodnight. I must be up with the sun so I might chase my family back to the seventh circle of hell."

And a good riddance that would be. She'd hardly be surprised if that was precisely where they resided when not bedeviling Marlowe and his sisters. Though she thought she might, just a very little bit, miss Uncle Ashley. Once one looked past the gluttony . . . and the raging misogyny . . . he was wonderfully droll.

She opened her mouth to take her leave as well when she spied the gash set just above his left eyebrow, a remnant of the duke's assault that had escaped her notice before. Dark red blood welled up and caught in the moonlight as he shifted.

"You're injured," she said, reaching toward the wound.

Halfway there, she realized what she was doing, lost a bit of her courage, and ended up awkwardly grazing one of his sharp cheekbones.

She didn't think she imagined the gasp and widened eyes her touch elicited, but the moment was gone in a blink, too fast for her to be sure. Nevertheless, her heart began to race beyond her control.

His fingertips gingerly prodded the wound, and he grimaced. "Thought I'd tidied it earlier," he said gruffly.

"It's a nasty cut," she murmured, barely restraining herself from reaching out to him again. She was not searching for reasons to touch him. Not at all.

"'T'was a lucky punch," he groused, looking distinctly put out by the memory.

"You *let* both of them punch you," she reminded him.

"Like I said, lucky," he insisted.

"And then you let your father bait you."

"Contrary to what you may have heard, I do not make a habit of brawling," he said a bit defensively. "I leave that to the rest of my beloved family."

She couldn't help but snort. "The Marquess of Manwaring would certainly disagree."

He rolled his eyes, and she rolled hers right back. But at least his posture finally relaxed, the awkward mood having finally been broken by their banter. "I have already apologized for that," he declared. "And that weren't even a real fight. I pulled all of my punches."

He wasn't lying, considering the state of the earl after just one punch from his fist. It would have been a shame to inflict the same sort of damage upon the marquess's legendary countenance.

"You didn't pull your punch tonight."

"I lost my temper, but the bastard deserved it." He paused, cleared his throat, and gave her a guilty look that wasn't in the least bit sincere. "Pardon my French and all, Miss Jones."

"Well, he did deserve it after the terrible things he said," she continued, gauging his reaction.

A light went out of his eyes, his bantering mood vanishing as quickly as it had sprung up and his mouth growing taut at the edges. She immediately regretted reminding him.

"I'm sorry; I should not have brought it up," she said quietly, turning away once more.

He touched her arm to stop her from leaving, and a heated spark passed over her skin at the contact.

"No, no," he said quietly. "You should know the truth, I think, before . . ." He trailed off awkwardly, so different from his usual brashness. She could tell he was struggling with some great emotion, and she took a chance and patted his arm gently, offering as much consolation as she could without crossing that precarious line they seemed to be toeing around each other. She already suspected the truth anyway.

"I think I have some idea," she said. "His insinuations were rather to the point."

Marlowe released a long, pent-up breath, his shoulders slumped slightly and his expression bleak. She'd never seen him look so . . . small. Defeated. Human. She did not like it one bit.

"I had always planned to marry Caroline," he began haltingly, abandoning any attempt at his usual playful cant. "Her family lived on the neighboring estate, so the three of us grew up together—Caro, Evander, and I. When we were old enough, she made it clear that she would accept my suit, so when I was still at Cambridge, I proposed, and she accepted. I didn't want to wait, of course, but we agreed on a long engagement while I finished my studies. But then I was sent down with Sebastian—the marquess now—after a bit of trouble, and we were packed off to the Peninsula for our sins."

"Yes, I think I heard something about that," she said,

leaning against the wall and girding herself for the rest of the tale. She wasn't about to stop him, now that he'd begun.

He smiled, but without any humor behind it. "I'm sure you and half of England have. Some version of the story anyway," he said with a wry smile. "So I went to war, and though I loved her, I told her not to wait for me. I couldn't expect that of her. But she did."

He looked so baffled, as if he could still not believe Caroline had waited—that *anyone* would have waited—for him.

She would have. She squeezed his arm on impulse.

He sighed, shook his head as if to clear the memories, and stared down at her hand. "When I finally returned home, she welcomed me back with open arms, eager for our wedding. So I married her. Had I been in a better frame of mind, perhaps I could have seen the situation more clearly, but the war . . ."

He glanced up from his contemplation of her hand on his arm—she'd forgotten to move it, didn't *want* to—and she could see the anguish that was so often in her own eyes when she thought of all the losses she'd suffered—her father, Arthur. She could only imagine what he'd seen and done during the war. Perhaps he hadn't the poetic genius to put his experience into words, like Christopher Essex, but his eyes said it all.

"The war left me raw, Miss Jones," he said quietly. "You must understand, with all you've lost . . ."

"Yes, I do," she answered gravely.

His free hand suddenly decided to brush against her own, and she barely repressed a shiver. "Anyway, I married her, then shortly after discovered she was with child, and quite far along. *Definitely* not mine. Her modiste had done quite a good job of disguising it up until the vows were said," he muttered bitterly. "I could have forgiven her. I would have, had she wanted me to. I did love her."

He finally pulled his arm away from her grasp and turned

his body so that he was facing the window instead of her, as if he couldn't bear to look at her while he continued his tale.

"But she didn't love me. She never had. She was in love with Evander. Always had been, she said, even before I went off to war. The child . . . well, the children were his. She married me for the title . . . had hoped to marry Evander had I died in the war like I was supposed to. It was the reason she was so content with waiting." His lips quirked up cruelly at the edges, and a hard glint flashed in his eyes. "The title was at least one thing she loved more than my brother. And money. She loved my money."

It was one of the most horrible stories she'd ever heard. "Oh, I am sorry," she breathed.

He gave a shrug that was trying too hard to be nonchalant. "I think the war numbed me. I couldn't even muster up much anger at Evander. We'd fallen out long before that—like oil and water, we were, despite being identical—but I still loved him. And Caroline didn't manage to break my heart completely until after the twins were born. I could get over the affair. What marriage these days is ever about love anyway?"

She would have vehemently denied his reasoning if she'd thought he would listen to her, but she didn't think he'd care to right now. Not when he was pouring out his heart to her.

"But the twins . . . well, she wanted nothing to do with them, and *that* broke my heart. She stayed only long enough to recover from the birth before flitting off to the Continent with my brother." He huffed out a breath and turned back to face her with a shrug. "They were drowned crossing the Channel. And that was the end of that."

"Hardly the end."

He turned to her, eyes fierce. "The end, Miss Jones. Before tonight no one knew the truth but my father, and only because Evander was indiscreet enough to tell him.

I've never even told Sebastian or Montford. The twins are mine. They are my daughters, and I love them as much as any father has ever loved his children."

Well. He had nothing to prove to her on that score. His heart was as broad as those shoulders of his, of that she had no doubt. He just had so little faith in himself sometimes, and it made her want to scream at him. Instead, she laid her hand on his cheek, because she couldn't keep herself from touching him anymore. Damn the line between them. This night had only confirmed what she'd been trying to deny for weeks now.

He was the most complicated, ridiculous, compelling man she'd ever met, and she *wanted* him, damn the consequences.

"I know you do," she said just as fiercely. "And I'd never tell anyone."

"I know you wouldn't, Miss Jones," he murmured, all deep and rumbling like thunder on the horizon, and she shivered.

She was not mistaken in thinking that they had come to be standing rather close—close enough for her to feel his breath on her cheekbone as he looked down at her with those rich brown eyes. Close enough for her to feel that resonant voice in the marrow of her bones.

In fact, it was fair to say that he was looming a bit, so near to her that she had to tilt her head back to meet his gaze. They'd been doing quite a lot of this close conversation for some time now, if she was being perfectly honest with herself, but she was surprised how little she minded. He'd ceased to intimidate her long ago.

And besides, it was a fairly chilly spring evening, and they'd been conversing in the hallway for quite a while now, and he was so warm and . . . broad . . . and he smelled so very nice, of leather and bay rum, sandalwood and India ink . . .

The thwack of her head against the wall behind her tore

her out of her stupor, and her hand finally dropped from his cheek—she'd forgotten she'd even had it there. He'd loomed, and she'd tilted . . . and tilted some more, until her head had encountered the obstruction. It wasn't enough to hurt, but it did sober her up a bit.

What was she doing, skulking about in the shadowy hallway exchanging intimate secrets with the viscount?

She'd nearly found the wherewithal to put some distance between them when one of those large, warm, ink-stained hands of his—why *were* they always ink-stained?—grasped her forearm, as if to steady her, though she was in no danger of falling.

His touch, and his murmured, "Are you injured, Miss Jones?" in that deep, growling baritone of his, made all of the good sense flee her mind once more.

Oh, she knew precisely what she was doing skulking about with the viscount. It was what she'd wanted to do since the night of their Almack's misadventure, though she still wasn't certain the viscount was aware of her licentious designs upon his person.

"You're the injured one," she finally managed to breathe, and reached out once again toward his face. He caught her hand before it could touch the wound and brought it back to her side . . .

But he didn't let it go. Her heart sped up at this small intimacy, but she tried to contain herself. The viscount was often thoughtlessly tactile with people. It didn't have to mean anything if he kept holding her hand. But . . .

She would never know what devil possessed her in that moment to push her luck, but in retrospect she'd blame the hand-holding. "I might have something in my room to clean it," she blurted.

His eyes widened a bit more, and his chest rose and fell a little faster than before. That banked fire she sometimes thought she saw deep in his eyes flared to life. He wasn't so oblivious after all, then. He leaned in close, and for a moment she thought . . .

"No," he said a bit harshly, jerking his head away, though he didn't release her hand.

Her stomach did not feel as if it had been punched at all. Nor did her cheeks heat with shame. Of course he said no. What had she been thinking?

"Of course," she murmured, looking anywhere but at him. "Oh God, what am I even . . ." She groaned softly and attempted to pull away, hoping to preserve at least a modicum of dignity.

But he wouldn't let her. He just gripped her hand even harder. She glanced up at him in surprise. Something tentative in his heavy-lidded eyes made her think he was as out of his depth as she was in that moment.

"I mean," he said slowly, haltingly, clearing his throat, "that . . . my rooms would be a bit better for . . . wound cleaning and . . . um, whatnot."

Oh. *Oh.*

Her already-pounding heart kicked forward into a gallop.

"You could . . ." he began, gesturing vaguely down the corridor with his free hand.

"Yes. Yes, of course," she murmured back, hoping all of the gesturing meant what she thought it meant.

He looked rather stunned, as if he couldn't believe she'd agreed.

She couldn't believe it either.

"Well, then," he said, and cleared his throat yet again.

"Yes, well," she answered just as eloquently.

He gave a short, firm nod and started walking down the corridor, still holding her hand firmly, as if he didn't want to take a chance of misplacing her along the way. It was an unnecessary concern. She had made her decision, even though she'd never thought anything would ever actually happen with the viscount.

She was glad to be mistaken.

Unless he *was* just taking her to his rooms to tend to his wound. It was a very real possibility with the viscount. Despite their loaded exchange and hand-holding, it was all still worrisomely ambiguous. Marlowe was, if anything, a wild card, and she could have very easily imagined the heat in his eyes and the innuendo in his invitation. He hadn't even tried to kiss her yet, so by the time they actually did reach his rooms on the opposite side of the house, she'd prepared herself for the possibility that she was just as likely to be employed as his nursemaid as taken to his bed.

His bedroom was decorated in deep, masculine greens and blues and dark woods. It was neat and clean, almost stark in its simplicity, and not at all as she had imagined. She'd expected a space as careless, cluttered, and chaotic as the viscount, but she was beginning to suspect that the viscount only pretended to be those things when it suited him.

The massive four-poster's bedding had been turned down for the night by the maid, with a gas lamp lit on the nightstand and a fire roaring in the grate. Plush orientals defined a small seating area near the fire, and he led her there and rather awkwardly placed her on the settee before disappearing into one of the adjoining chambers.

She was beginning to wonder what she had gotten herself into when he returned to the settee armed with toweling and a small medical kit. He sat beside her and cleared his throat.

There seemed to be a lot of throat clearing going on tonight.

So she was here to merely patch him up after all. She tried not to show her disappointment as she took the supplies from him and set to work. She dabbed at his wound with the clean toweling and a bit of ointment, and if she leaned a little too near him, then that was her prerogative.

"This probably needs stitches," she said.

"I've had worse," he murmured, his breath glancing off

her forehead.

She paused in her half-hearted dabbing, and her heart started racing again. At some point he'd inched his body forward until his thigh and breast pressed against her, hot and hard and insistent. She'd not even noticed until the deed was done, and she began to wonder if she had underestimated Lord Marlowe once again. She seemed to do that quite a lot.

She lowered her trembling hand, tossing the toweling aside, and Marlowe quickly seized it in his own.

"My lord . . ."

"Marlowe," he interrupted gruffly.

She looked up from their joined hands to his eyes and just barely held back her gasp. There was no misinterpreting the heat in his glance now.

"Call me Marlowe," he insisted.

She couldn't contain her smile, and neither could he. They grinned at each other.

"Well, I'd give you permission too, but you already call me Minerva when it suits you, *Evelyn*."

He grimaced at the taunt. "I'll ask for permission properly if you never call me that again. Evelyn is my father's name."

Ah. "Well, then I promise never to call you that again. Shall you sack me if I tell you how much of a horse's arse your father is?"

His eyes practically glittered with amusement. "I'll give you a raise," he said, then grew a bit somber. "Though I do regret losing my temper tonight. Minerva, I . . ."

"You needn't pardon anything, for I would have lost my temper long ago," she said, and laid her free hand on his cheek, and it was as if that one touch finally burst some dam inside of him, for on a soft sigh, he raised their joined hands to his lips and kissed her knuckles gently . . . then her palm and the inside of her wrist, slowly, painstakingly, as if savoring the taste. If she had any doubts before that he wanted her, or her purpose here in his rooms long after the witching hour, they were erased at the raw hunger she now saw in those intense brown eyes.

When he was done kissing her hand, she cupped his chin and pulled him toward her until their foreheads touched. Their breaths thundered against one another in the meager space between their lips, chests heaving, bodies trembling with electrical current.

She savored the moment of tension, this calm before a storm that she now knew to be inevitable. She took in the scent of him, the heat and strength of him, and knew a desire so profound she thought she might burst from it. No one, not even Essex in his most coy of poems, had ever engendered this want in her, this physical ache. This itch to touch and taste and dig, dig, dig, down to the very heart of him.

That it was the Viscount Marlowe, of all people, who had inspired these appetites was still rather alarming. For the longest time, she hadn't thought she'd even liked him. But *oh*, she liked him. More than *liked*.

"This is not supposed to happen yet," he murmured against her lips.

Yet? She had no idea what he meant, but it didn't sound promising. This was *definitely* supposed to happen.

"What are you waiting for?" She thought she'd been about as brazen as she could get without actually removing her clothing. Though she would consider doing so if it would move things along.

His lips, surprisingly soft and tasting of red wine and mint, grazed her own, and she gasped.

"I need to tell you, explain to you . . ." His brow furrowed, as if he were trying to recall something, but he soon gave up and went back to teasing her mouth. "I can't even think straight anymore. You've mucked it all up in my brainbox," he murmured. "We are being very naughty, Minerva. Very naughty."

His voice was as rich and earthy as the sherry she'd drunk earlier, and she shivered from it. "I think you like being naughty, my lord."

He groaned. "I do. Damn the proper order of things. Damn it all to hell. I want to kiss you, Minerva; I've wanted to kiss you for ages."

She pulled away from him with a frown, and he gripped her hand as if still afraid she would disappear. "Does it look like I am stopping you?" she said in exasperation. "I thought I was the one who was supposed to be the tease."

After a moment of wide-eyed surprise, Marlowe grinned in that devilish way of his that had started all of this mess in the first place, and her heart went from a gallop to an all-out sprint.

"I'll show you a tease," he growled.

That electric current between them traveled down her spine, straight into her lower belly, at the sound of his velvet voice. She was pretty sure that was a threat, but before she could figure it out, his lips were on hers, and there was nothing teasing about what followed.

The one thing that she'd never doubted about Marlowe was that he was a sensualist, but even she was taken aback by his . . . mastery. Just two seconds into the kiss, he'd already surpassed all the passionate moments Arthur and she had ever shared combined.

And that was before any tongue was involved.

By the time he coaxed her lips apart and delved inside, her bones had melted and her skin was humming with pleasure—and he had yet to even lay a hand on her. He was so very good at this that she began to suspect that he'd been the one seducing her all night, not the other way around. Oblivious her foot. He knew exactly what he was doing the moment he'd taken his hand in hers.

Then he touched her waist—her waist, still very much clothed—and her brain began to melt right alongside her body. She gasped against his mouth as his fingers tangled in her hair, pulling it from its pins, then moaned when his hand wandered to the underside of her breast.

Then she was sinking into something soft, though she'd not even noticed she'd moved. She opened her eyes after a few breathless moments, her senses returning enough to focus on more than her body's reaction, and found herself lying against the pillows of the settee. His face hovered a few inches from her own, his hawkish features thrown into stark relief in the shadows cast by the firelight. She felt his hands on her and looked down to discover he was already halfway through the buttons on the front of her bodice.

Somehow he'd already managed to shed his banyan and cravat, and she ran her hands over his broad shoulders and felt the firm, taut lines of muscle and sinew underneath the loose linen shirt. She shivered at the heat arcing down her spine. Finally she was allowed to touch him, all of him, and it felt even better than she'd ever allowed herself to imagine.

She trailed her hand down his chest, all the way to the hem of his shirt, then underneath to the warm, bare skin beneath, and he sucked in a breath and paused in his work on her bodice. His eyes were practically glittering when they met hers, and his expression was even more intent, though there was a hint of a smirk at the edge of those lips. "Oh, you'd better be sure, Minerva," he murmured. "The things I plan to do to you."

She tugged on the band of his breeches in lieu of a verbal response—oh, she was very sure—and grazed her fingertips across his exposed hip bone.

He groaned, tore through the rest of her buttons, and jerked her gown down her legs and over her ankles, leaving her in her shift and the pantaloons that had once flown high on Poseidon's trident. He tossed the gown behind him, barely missing the fire, and then stood up, looming over her as he made quick work of his boots, never taking his hungry eyes off her body.

She tried to stand as well, with some odd notion that she might help him in his haphazard frenzy to undress, but he just urged her back down and fell to his knees in front of her, still half-clothed. In the lust-fueled fog that filled her mind, she was at a loss as to what exactly he was doing until she felt him gripping her ankles and tugging off her slippers. Then her stockings. Then, before her brain could quite catch up, she felt his hot, rough fingers against her bare legs, loosening her pantaloons as he went and pulling them off so that she was totally bare from the waist down.

And for the first time that night, she began to panic. She'd certainly never gotten this far with Arthur—she was not sure Arthur would have ever even known to go this far in the first place. She had a feeling Arthur would have done all of his business in bed, in the dark, and under multiple layers of blankets and nightclothes. But not Marlowe. She didn't think even she had the imagination for what Marlowe intended to do to her.

She was, however, becoming more convinced by the minute that Marlowe's breeches were not coming off anytime soon. Instead, he busied himself pushing her knees apart and settling between them, staring at that naked place between her legs currently being highlighted by the firelight as if it were the most fascinating thing he'd ever seen.

She could feel herself blush from head to toe and attempted to shut her legs. He wouldn't let her, instead running his hands up and over her thighs soothingly until she'd no choice but to relax. It felt too good to do otherwise.

The moment he felt the tension go out of her, however, he gripped her naked backside and pulled her closer to the edge of the settee with a wicked grin. She slumped into the pillows at her back with a surprised yelp. "What on earth are you—" she gasped out.

She couldn't finish what she was saying—couldn't remember *language*, really—as his hands wandered down her thighs, to her knees, then traced upward and *in*, his blunt, calloused fingertips tickling the sensitive skin leading to . . .

He raised his head from his survey of her bare flesh and cocked an eyebrow, as if waiting for her to continue her protest. But all the words were caught in her throat now as his fingers hovered just a hair's breadth away from *that* spot.

His devil's smirk gave him away however. He knew she was beyond speech.

"A third time pass'd my hand on marble turn'd / As warm as woman's secret flesh interred," he murmured, breath hot on her fevered skin.

Wait, did he just quote Essex at her naked bits?

"You . . ." she began, raising herself on her elbows, but again she was cut off. By his mouth. And his tongue. On said bits.

Ah, so *that* was what Essex meant with that line. Though she didn't know exactly how she felt about hearing her favorite poet quoted to her—such a strange intersection between the man whose words she loved and the man whose . . .

Well, she definitely, *definitely* loved Marlowe's tongue at the moment.

Then she stopped thinking of Essex, or anything besides the wet, hot feel of his lips, teeth, and tongue caressing and teasing her in just the right spot. That spot she'd discovered on her own years ago, but never once had imagined having *this* done to it.

How could she never have imagined such a glorious thing?

She gripped his hair and tugged a little, urging him on, and he moaned in response, apparently liking the rough treatment. He pushed his tongue inside of her and proceeded to tease her in the lewdest manner yet of the evening. She gripped his hair even tighter, and still he didn't complain. In fact, her abuse only seemed to spur him on, and suddenly one finger, then two, were playing inside of her, and she cried out at the novel sensations.

She'd certainly never done *that*.

He lifted his head and met her eyes. His mouth and chin were obscenely wet, and his brown eyes were glazed over and unfocused with something that looked very much like bliss. His expression only made her feel even hotter, even with the loss of that lovely tongue of his, but when he licked his lips, as if savoring the taste of her, and did something incendiary with his thumb down below, she nearly tumbled over the edge.

"Tease," she said, breathless.

He smirked at her and lowered his head once more, licking a long, wet, heated strip up and over that little bundle of nerves at the same time as he sped up the motion of his fingers inside of her.

Minerva came long and hard, back arching and toes curling, her vision going white, letting out a loud, embarrassingly high-pitched wail. He continued to toy with her until she could bear no more. She tugged on his hair to bring him back up for a kiss, and he obeyed with alacrity, licking her lips open the same way he'd licked her . . . well, her *other* lips open. She tasted herself on him, salty sweet.

She was distracted yet again when she noticed one of his arms reaching inside his breeches. She was unable to see exactly what he was doing down there from her angle on the settee, but the hazy, unfocused look in his eyes, the flush of his cheeks, and his labored breaths gave her a fair idea.

She reached for his falls, but he stilled her hands, a wild look coming over his face. "Not this time, not until . . ." He panted, unable to continue, and instead buried his head in the crook of her shoulder, his hand working himself so vigorously his whole body trembled atop hers.

Seconds later, he stiffened and moaned, sending a renewed spark of heat through her at the raw sensuality of the moment. Then he moved his lips to her ear and whispered, "*Then burn'd did she, and follow her I burn'd.*"

It was the most erotic—and bewildering—thing that had ever happened to her in her life. She wondered for a moment whether she was stuck in a dream only Lady Hedonist could have scripted, but then she felt Marlowe shift her on top of him, his arms warm and strong around her torso, his breath ragged and sweet against her ear, and she knew this was too real to be a dream.

She lifted her head. He was watching her, his expression still dazed and perhaps a little wary. She almost laughed at the bird's nest he'd—*she'd*—made of his hair and the look of lazy satisfaction on his countenance. God, he was rather *beautiful* like this, even with the bump on his nose, and she wanted to say a thousand things, ask him a million questions—especially the ones that mattered most at the moment.

What did this mean? Was he in love with her? Because she was rather horrifyingly certain now that she was in love with him.

But all that came out of her mouth was, "We didn't even make it to the bed," for surely she wouldn't be expected to be able to think straight after *that*.

He just laughed as if she'd said the most delightful thing, and pulled her down for a kiss. Then another. And another.

She definitely stopped thinking at all after that.

Chapter Fifteen

In Which Miss Jones Finds Out

IT TOOK SEVERAL MORE KISSES, the promise of a long talk on the morrow, and finally a threat or two before she'd convinced Marlowe to let her return to her room alone. He'd wanted to accompany her across the house, but she'd thought it a terrible idea. Neither of them looked anywhere near presentable, and if they were intercepted together by anyone at such a late hour, there would be questions they couldn't answer.

Better for her to go alone. They'd already risked too much in coming together to his rooms in the first place.

This dalliance business was certainly not for the faint of heart. He was right to want to talk the next day—even though he'd been strangely cagey when he'd suggested it—but she was too tired and too bewildered to undertake the endeavor at the moment. She needed time alone to sort out in her mind what had happened between them before she saw him again. She'd hardly thought the consequences of her brash actions through, and she desperately hoped she'd not come to regret them.

He'd stopped short of fully taking her, and she didn't know whether to feel relieved or worried about the implications. But she *was* confused. Neither of them had made any declarations, and though she suspected he might be in love with her, she couldn't be sure. She needed to hear the words. More than that, she needed to know his intentions, for even if he did love her, she feared that might not be enough for this to end in anything but complete disaster.

They definitely needed to talk. But she wanted to be fully conscious for such an undertaking, in case—*when*—he said something she didn't like. She didn't want to leave him, or the children, or Lady Elizabeth . . . or even Mrs. Chips. She'd grown to love not only the viscount but also every aspect of her life here. For the first time in her life, she felt as if she were part of a family, and it was going to break her heart if she had to say goodbye.

But she would if she had to. Marlowe had a dim view of matrimony at best, and even if that were not the case, it seemed presumptuous of her, even now, to think that a penniless woman in her position could ever even hope to marry a nobleman, no matter how unconventional he seemed to be. And contrary to what had just occurred between them, she was not prepared to be his mistress, no matter how much she wanted him.

So caught up in her increasingly uneasy thoughts, she almost shrieked when she rounded a corner and collided with Lady Elizabeth, who dropped the books in her hands to the floor with a gasp.

Glad for the shadowy hallway, Minerva could feel her face flame scarlet as she crouched down and scrambled to gather up the fallen books. She'd thought that by now she'd be well beyond mortification, considering what the viscount had just done to her, but running into his sister after hours spent in his arms had not figured into her plans.

She straightened, shoved the books back into Lady Elizabeth's arms, and tried to make a quick escape before the girl could realize how untoward it was for the governess to be skulking about the hallway near the viscount's rooms before dawn.

But of course she'd never be so lucky. She could tell the

moment the girl figured it out, for her eyebrows almost disappeared into her hairline. Even worse, only seconds later, Lady Elizabeth's expression of shock quickly metamorphosed into a cross between a knowing smirk and relief.

"Oh," she breathed. "*Oh!*"

"Lady Elizabeth . . ."

"But this is brilliant," the girl whisper-cried, looking as pleased as when she'd discovered Christopher Essex had published a new poem. "Finally! I avow, I was about to resort to extremes if something didn't happen soon."

It was Minerva's turn to be shocked. "You know?"

Lady Elizabeth gave her a look of incredulity. "Darling, you are both as transparent as glass."

"But . . . we are always fighting . . ."

"You mean flirting, don't you? Good grapes, it's been absolutely painful to watch the pair of you. Thank heavens my brother has come to his senses and seduced you as he should have months ago."

"Lady Elizabeth!" Minerva cried reprovingly.

She shrugged, unrepentant. "As I said, it's been *excruciating*. I didn't think Evie would ever tell you the truth. I assured him it would all work out if he did, and see how right I was? I would write a torrid novel about Essex's happy ending if Evie weren't my brother." She shuddered. "I have *definitely* learned my lesson on that score. Lady Hedonist is on permanent holiday."

It was probably the late hour, Minerva's troubled thoughts, and the rather mind-altering bliss the viscount had given her not too long ago that were making it so difficult to follow the thread of Lady Elizabeth's ramble . . . well, more difficult than usual. "What are you talking about?"

Lady Elizabeth smirked. "*You've* had a long night, haven't you?"

Minerva blushed again. To be teased by a sixteen-year-old about one's . . . *torrid* night *with said sixteen-year-old's brother* was far too much to bear at four in the morning.

"Betsy!" She tried her best to sound convincingly stern.

Lady Elizabeth sighed but relented. "I'm talking about Evie being Christopher Essex, of course. I told him, if he were to ever truly secure your affections, he was going to have to tell you. I mean, he's been absolutely *ridiculous* about it. You have me to thank for . . . Miss Jones? Minerva? Are you quite all right?"

Minerva squinted up through the gloom at a hovering Lady Elizabeth, wondering when she had collapsed on the window seat. She couldn't remember doing so . . . couldn't, in fact, remember the past minute or so of her life at all. She couldn't remember when it had gotten so cold either. It was as if all the warmth in her body had been extinguished as quickly as a flame doused with water.

"I'm sorry; what did you say?" she managed.

Betsy's expression fell, and her normally rosy skin looked suddenly ashen in the weak moonlight. "He didn't tell you, did he?"

"Tell me what? For I could have sworn I heard you say that your brother, Lord Marlowe, is Christopher Essex. But that can't be right, can it?"

Betsy looked stricken, collapsing next to her on the bench, burying her face in her hands. "Now I've done it. *Lud*, Evie's going to kill me."

"Not if I kill him first," Minerva muttered out of lips numb with shock. "But it can't be true."

Even as the words came out, she knew it *was* true. Obvious, even. The way he'd teased her for her poetry collection. His Bodleian-inspired library no true dullard would ever bother with. His facile manipulation of language. His stupid, *stupid* limericks. Lady Elizabeth's sudden, inexplicable disinterest in Essex.

His *ink-stained* fingers.

The evidence was there. But she had been too stupid,

too self-absorbed . . . too *infatuated* . . . to put the pieces together.

Even tonight—he had practically taunted her with his verse as he'd seduced her. Oh, how he must have been laughing at her the whole time.

"Oh, God, he's Christopher Essex!" she breathed.

But why? *Why* would he do this? He was not a cruel man. Even now she couldn't believe this, not after she'd witnessed his love for his children, his sisters. Yet everything they'd shared—everything they'd done—every wild, hopeful thought she'd allowed herself afterward . . .

Minerva felt like the biggest fool for hoping, for even *thinking* the word marriage not five minutes before—that it might be a possibility, however slim. He desired her in the basest of physical ways, that much was clear, but beyond that, she wondered if he had *any* tender feelings for her.

She remembered how scornful she'd been when she'd thought Lady Elizabeth to be the viscount's mistress, how much better she'd thought herself in her moral righteousness. Except Minerva was that girl, wasn't she? Even worse, she'd not even realized it until now, for she'd thought herself *special*. But she wasn't. How could she be, when the viscount had kept such an essential secret from her—teased her with it—for months?

She'd once scoffed at the idea of feeling real physical pain from a broken heart in every bad poem she'd ever read—even in the good ones (Oh, *God*, Essex!)—but that was before this moment. She could barely take a breath through the agony in her breast, and she gripped Lady Elizabeth's hand for fear of drowning in it.

She hated Lord Marlowe for making her feel such pain.

No, she was entirely certain that she *loved* him, which was even worse.

CHAPTER SIXTEEN

In Which The Viscount Suspects Something Is Amiss

MARLOWE HAD NOT PLANNED ON seducing his governess the night before, but then again, he was fairly certain it had been the other way around. He'd been rather powerless in the face of Minerva's intent, for there was only so much he could bear before giving in to what was so freely offered. He had been resolved to wait to declare his intentions until after he'd declared a few other rather crucial things (i.e. his poetic alter ego), but his resolution had been no match for her soft gray eyes and gentle lips.

In the light of morning, the satisfaction he'd felt at the conclusion of last evening was beginning to give way to his concern over how Minerva would react to his confession. He could put it off no longer. He'd had a taste of her, and it had only confirmed his growing conviction that his governess would suit much better as his wife—more than merely suit, it seemed, as the physical alchemy between them had been undeniable, better than he could have ever dreamed.

And they'd not even completed the union. That was one act he couldn't bring himself to share with her until he'd given her all of his truths. For if she were to reject him—a prospect he couldn't ignore, however painful it might be to think about—he would not have compromised her irrevocably. He cared too much for her to be so careless, even in the heat of the moment.

But he'd not held back otherwise. He'd slaked his own lust as surely as he had slaked hers, in the only way he'd dared, his senses buried in the honey scent of her. And even after he'd sent her off to her own room, just the thought of her, bared before him—the lingering taste of her upon his lips, the scent of her still in his nose—was enough to make it necessary to bring himself off yet again. God, she'd reduced him to a randy adolescent.

He'd not slept so deeply in months, though, despite his bruised face and scraped knuckles.

But now that he was conscious, the thought of the day to come—of the look on her face when she discovered that he had concealed so much of himself from her—made him uneasy. He was not naive enough to even *hope* he'd emerge unscathed, but surely she would come around. Eventually. Maybe.

The first sign that something was wrong came after he'd packed off the earl and countess in acrimonious silence and found himself alone at the breakfast table. Betsy had taken to joining him regularly since she'd discovered his secret, even though she found mornings abhorrent, so her absence was a bit unusual. He would have been concerned the earl had tied her up and hidden her among his luggage . . . but he'd checked the coach from top to toe himself before he'd allowed it to depart. (He'd given up underestimating his father's villainy.)

But even after an hour had passed and he'd finished all of his papers and an entire pot of tea on his own, Betsy had not appeared. He decided not to be alarmed. She was, as a sixteen-year-old female of noble birth, naturally inclined to lie in, and just because he'd become accustomed to her company in recent days, it didn't mean it was guaranteed.

After the night before—and dealing with her mother all of yesterday besides—she couldn't be blamed for wanting some time to herself.

The second sign something was wrong, however, was when he emerged from his library in the early afternoon and realized the twins had not visited him all day. They usually managed to slip Minerva's grasp and interrupt his work by now. In fact, he'd seen no sign of life from the nursery at all today. He'd decided to put off his conversation with Minerva for the evening after the twins were asleep (he was *not* stalling), but he'd still expected to see her at some point during the day, since they were all meant to go to Gunter's to celebrate routing his father and Poxley. He was beginning to wonder what the devil was going on.

The third and most worrying sign came when he ventured up to the nursery in search of some answers and found his daughters sitting at their table, quiet, subdued, and *conjugating Latin* under Mrs. Chips's stern eye, Minerva nowhere to be found. The three of them seemed determined to ignore him completely, and it sent a chill of foreboding down his spine. One thing he had always been able to count on was his daughters' preference for his company over their Latin.

Something was dreadfully, dreadfully wrong.

He ordered Mrs. Chips out into the hallway—the same hallway in which he'd bared his soul to Minerva only the previous night—and his housekeeper closed the door behind her with a snap that seemed a little bit more aggressive than usual.

"Where is Miss Jones?" he asked, the feeling of dread in his bones deepening when Mrs. Chips's eyebrow began to spasm.

"She has left your employment, my lord," Mrs. Chips said with so little venom in her tone that he knew she was incandescently furious with him.

His heart dropped to his toes. No, *no*, this could not be

happening. "What do you mean she's left?" he demanded when he managed to find his voice again.

Mrs. Chips sniffed, unimpressed with his dramatics. "Just that. She has gone. She took off before your family, in the company of Dr. Lucas."

"What!" he cried. She may as well have punched him in the gut.

"You must talk to Lady Elizabeth," Mrs. Chips said haughtily, lifting her chin in that proud way of hers that signaled an end to the matter. "She may be able to shed more light on the situation than I."

He didn't like the sound of that one bit.

Chippers clearly felt it was improper for her to speak further on the matter. Not that she needed to—the judgment on her twitching brow was speech enough. "Now if you'll excuse me, someone must mind your daughters," she said as she marched away, "now that you've run off their keeper."

Well, perhaps she *would* speak further on the matter, then.

Marlowe took himself off to his sister's rooms in a daze, a thousand black scenarios running through his head. He felt sick to his stomach, for the one scenario that he could not immediately dismiss was one in which Minerva regretted what had happened between them enough to leave. But to run away with Lucas? It seemed extreme, even for his governess at her most histrionic.

Surely she knew him well enough to know he would not entice her further if she could not return his affections. He had put an end to their night before their actions became any more intimate, after all, and made it clear he wished to talk with her before things progressed further.

Had she taken his words—his caution—as a rejection? Had she left thinking he wanted nothing more from her than a few stolen moments? That *he* regretted it? Surely she could not think so poorly of him, not after all they'd been through together.

Perhaps he had been too vague after all. Yet he couldn't bear to declare himself without complete honesty between them, and he hadn't been prepared to broach that subject last night, not after all that had happened. He'd already been wrung dry by his father's acrimony.

Marlowe found his sister in her room scribbling away at her desk, and one look at her guilty expression was enough to confirm Mrs. Chips's horrible words.

"Why the devil did Miss Jones leave in the company of Dr. Lucas this morning?" he demanded without delay.

Betsy looked everywhere but at him as she set down her quill to answer. "She has gone to Montford's, and she didn't wish to take a hack. I had a footman fetch Dr. Lucas to escort her, for I feared for her safety."

"And why, pray tell, did she not take *my* carriage?"

Betsy grimaced. "She was unwilling to avail herself of anything belonging to you at that particular moment," she said carefully.

He collapsed on the edge of his sister's bed. It was even worse than he had imagined. He knew he never should have let Minerva go alone to her room last night. He should have made her stay with him, and damn the consequences.

"What did she say?" he asked, distraught.

Betsy's cheeks grew ruddy, and her guilty look deepened. "I . . . er, I believe you need to ask her that?" she said in a strangled voice.

He straightened from his slouch, suspicious of his sister's manner. "You know something."

"What? *No* . . . That's ridiculous! Good grapes, how could you even . . ." she spluttered, looking as if she might bolt from the room at any moment. "I didn't do . . . This is *not* my fault!" she finished in a tone that made it clear she thought otherwise.

His suspicion deepened. "I didn't say it was," he murmured.

Betsy glared at him. "You should really talk to her. She said she was going to accept the post the duchess offered her, so I assume she hasn't eloped to Gretna Green with the doctor or anything so dire. He just gave her a ride."

"Don't even tease!" Marlowe huffed, rising from the bed. He'd not even considered Minerva might do something so rash as elope. With *Whiskers*. But now that Betsy had suggested it, he could think of nothing else.

Betsy's eyes were wide with alarm as she watched his pained reaction. "*Please* go talk to her, Evie. I shan't say any more on the subject, but I'm sure with significant groveling, you might win her back."

"The fact that you think I need to win her back at all is not comforting in the least," he muttered. He stalked toward the door, stopped, and fixed his sister with a scowl that promised retribution. "Don't think I won't find out what you've done, Elizabeth. I know the look of a guilty conscience well enough."

Betsy's cheeks were leeched of color, and he left her to marinate in wary anticipation of her punishment. He'd deal with his sister later. For now, he had a governess to hunt down.

CHAPTER SEVENTEEN

In Which The Viscount Finds Out That Miss Jones Found Out

IT WAS TESTIMONY TO THE level of Minerva's anguish that not even the notoriously nosy duchess had demanded much of an explanation when she found Minerva on the doorstep at dawn. Her Grace had taken one look at her and merely shown her to a bedroom, ordered her a pot of tea, and left her to her misery.

Minerva was still upset far into the afternoon, but the mortifying tears seemed to be past, at least, and she was steady enough to receive the doctor in one of the duchess's drawing rooms when he returned as promised to check on her. She was hardly in the mood for company, but she owed him some explanation after having taken him from his bed at such a ridiculous hour of the morning. She certainly hadn't been in any shape to explain herself during the carriage ride earlier.

"What has he done?" Inigo immediately demanded as he strode into the room, clasping her hands.

Of course he'd guessed that it was Marlowe at the bottom of this. What else would drive her from her employment in such a dramatic manner?

She sighed. "It was a . . . misunderstanding," she finally settled on. Which seemed like the biggest understatement of her life, though it was accurate. She had misunderstood so much—the viscount, their flirtation, her place in his life. All of it seemed like lies to her now.

"It must have been a rather serious misunderstanding," he murmured, "to have driven you out in the street."

She rolled her eyes at his dramatics. "I'm hardly homeless. The duchess has taken me in. I'm to be governess to her sisters."

"Ah," he said, looking as dubious as he had when he'd learned she was governessing for the viscount's daughters. But she was grateful he said no more on the subject, for she didn't think she could have borne him questioning her decision. She couldn't go back to Marlowe.

"Do I need to call the viscount out?" he asked, only half joking.

When tears began to fall down her face in response, his wry look collapsed into dismay. "Oh, God, I do!"

"No, of course not. He did nothing I did not want."

This made Inigo look even more alarmed.

"Minerva . . ."

"And nothing that would warrant a *duel*, for heaven's sake. It was just a misunderstanding," she said firmly, wiping away her tears.

He looked as if he were steeling himself for some dire task as he spoke his next words. "If you are compromised . . ."

She broke away from him with a groan and crossed the room. Of course he was worried, and of course he would want to fix it, no matter the cost to himself.

"If you *are*," he insisted, "Minerva . . . please consider the offer I have made in the past. It still stands. We are friends, and you were Arthur's dearest companion . . ."

"You are too noble for your own good," she said. "But I'm not compromised in any way that would necessitate marriage. Only my heart is wounded."

"Nevertheless . . ."

"But we don't love each other enough for marriage, Inigo," she interrupted gently. "It wouldn't be fair to either of us, so please stop asking. You say you want to heed your brother's wishes, but I think that's an excuse."

"What are you talking about?" Inigo demanded, furrowing his brow.

He was going to make her say it—say *her* name—wasn't he? "You never stopped loving Yvette."

Inigo looked blank with shock for a moment, and then positively crushed with anguish at the mention of the girl he'd once loved. Minerva almost regretted bringing up the subject, but Inigo needed the truth—they both needed the truth so that they would not keep returning to this ridiculous subject. It was a disservice to both of them, a way for them to cling to ghosts long dead.

"We are friends, Inigo, family even. But marrying each other . . . pretending someday that this would work between us . . . was just a way for us to avoid trying again. We both lost the people we loved, and it *was* so tempting to simply accept your offer. But now . . ."

Comprehension dawned beneath his old grief. "You're in love with *Marlowe*."

"Dreadfully, I'm afraid." Angry and heartsick as she was at the viscount, she couldn't deny the accusation.

"We would have had a good life together," Inigo insisted stubbornly.

"I know."

He sighed. "But it wouldn't have been enough." He paused, and the look in his eyes was so sad her heart ached for him. "The thing is, I don't think anything, *anyone* will ever be enough. I miss her, Minerva."

She damned convention and wrapped her arms around her friend, wanting to absorb some of his grief. She thought of Arthur and of the tragic, beautiful Yvette who'd ruined Inigo for anyone else. Minerva's heart had healed long ago, but she feared Inigo's never would. He'd loved Yvette with an intensity that eclipsed anything she'd ever felt for his brother.

She thought she could understand his pain now, though.

After a while, his stiff muscles relaxed into her embrace, and he sighed in defeat. "Anything you need," he murmured.

"I know," she began soothingly only to be cut off by an angry, too familiar baritone across the room.

"*Anything*, is it?" the voice growled. "What the devil is going on here?"

Minerva broke away from Inigo and turned to the intruder with a resigned sigh. Marlowe stood in the doorway, chest heaving and color high, his hair at sixes and sevens and his face mottled in the cuts and bruises from the night before. It was as if he'd rolled out of bed—and wasn't *that* a thought to make her blush down to her toes, considering what had happened the night before—and sprinted across Mayfair to confront her.

He looked more out of control than she'd ever seen him before, even when he'd been confronting his horrid father. His brown eyes were glinting like garnets in the afternoon light, filled with anger and something panicked and wild and desperate. His presence had always seemed to fill up a room, but now he seemed even bigger, more overwhelming, his mask cracked enough that those parts of him he'd kept so well hidden were bleeding through.

Gazing at him as he stood there practically vibrating with emotion, she thought how *obvious* it was, now that she knew. How much sense that it made, even though only a day ago she would have never imagined him capable of voluntarily writing a business letter, much less a heroic couplet.

Facing him now, knowing the truth, the anger and humiliation and crushing hurt she'd pushed away to talk to Inigo came rushing back. She didn't care how magnificent Marlowe looked at the moment, glowering at

Inigo with his wild hair and fierce expression. She didn't care how transcendent, how loved, he'd made her feel last night, before everything had come crashing down around her. He'd lied to her. He'd toyed with her for weeks . . . months, even.

And for all that every part of him was now achingly familiar—the hawkish nose broken one too many times; the way that one patch of hair on his crown always curled straight toward the heavens no matter how many times he tried to flatten it down with his restless hands; the breadth of his shoulders and that sleek bit of clavicle that always seemed to peek out despite even Pymm's best efforts to keep his master cinched and buttoned up—for all of that, it was as if she were staring at a stranger.

"What are you doing here?" she demanded. And when he ignored her words and continued to glare malevolently at Inigo, she snapped. If he wished to have it out with her, then so be it. But she'd be damned if he took out his wrath on Inigo. "Don't you dare," she seethed. "Inigo was just leaving."

Inigo's brow lifted, as if he didn't like that idea at all. She patted his arm in reassurance, and she heard something that sounded like a growl issue from Marlowe's throat.

She rolled her eyes. "I'll be fine."

Inigo cast Marlowe a skeptical glare. "Are you sure?"

She gave him a humorless smile. "I'm sure. But I don't know if *he* will be after I'm done with him."

Inigo snorted with satisfaction, squeezed her hand, and started for the door. He paused next to Marlowe and gave him a stern look. "If you hurt her any further than you already have, I'll have your head. I don't care who you are," he said with grim promise.

Marlowe's eyes widened in surprised confusion, then narrowed suspiciously on the doctor's retreating back. His hands clenched into fists at his sides, as if he would have liked nothing better than to pummel the doctor into oblivion.

When Inigo was gone, Marlowe stalked back to the door and shut it with ominous intent before turning once more to Minerva.

"What the devil is going on? Why are you here, Minerva? I thought after . . ." He broke off, at a loss. Clearly he didn't know what she'd discovered, why she'd run.

"Lady Elizabeth did not tell you?"

His brow creased in confusion. "Tell me what? She wouldn't say a bloody thing, save that you had come here. And now I find you embracing *him*, and I have no clue why. I thought . . ."

How dare he sound as if *he* were the injured party, as if he truly cared. "What business is that of yours?"

Her words shook him out of his momentary stupor. "It is entirely my business. Now that we've . . ." He cleared his throat and made a vague gesture.

She feigned surprise. "Really? Why was I not informed that I would become your property after sharing such intimacies? And why am I not surprised you've kept such an important piece of information from me," she sneered.

"I don't know what you're talking about," he bit out, visibly frustrated.

"Betsy *told me*," she said with quiet venom, too angry to even scream at the moment. "She didn't mean to, but it just slipped out when she caught me coming from your room last night."

His cheekbones flushed at that last bit. So did Minerva's. "Told you what?" he demanded. Behind his confusion, though, he looked vaguely uneasy, as if he suspected what was coming but didn't want to face it.

"I know who you are, *Christopher*," she hissed.

All of the color drained from his face.

After a very, very long silence, he finally had the nerve to open his mouth again. "I was going to tell you," he began, but her sharp look was enough to make him stop.

"When? After you'd tired of making a fool of me?"

"What? No! That was never my intention." He looked so shocked at the accusation that she could almost believe him. Almost.

"I don't believe you, for I certainly *feel* like a fool. Were you laughing the whole time at me?"

"No, I would never," he insisted hoarsely. He closed the distance between them and caught her up in his arms. They were warm and strong and felt so good that she wished—God, how she wished—she could stay there. But she couldn't, not now. Perhaps not ever again. She pushed against his chest, but he tightened his hold around her waist. "Minerva, *please*."

"I'm warning you," Minerva breathed, red-faced and furious. "Let me go."

He looked as if he would comply, for whatever he was, he was not a man who would manhandle a woman when she wished to be free. But he hesitated just a fraction of a second too long for her liking, so she lashed out. Her foot connected with his shin, and he stumbled away from her, cursing from the pain. His knee connected with a footstool next to them, and he lost his footing, flailing his arms for purchase. They alighted on Minerva's shoulders—of course they did—and he took her down with him.

He landed flat on his back on a divan, and Minerva fell against him, her breasts crashing against his chest, her legs tangling with his own long, unruly limbs. Minerva squirmed on top of him until she was sitting astride his chest, breathless with anger and something else she was unwilling to acknowledge at the moment. She stared down at him sternly, refusing to allow his proximity to muddle her resolve against him.

"You were laughing at me," she whispered.

"What?" he asked, bewildered by the accusation.

"You quoted him to me," she insisted. "While you made love to me. How were you not laughing at me?"

"*Him*? I *am* Essex!" he cried. "I was quoting *me*. I was quoting the words I wrote about *you*."

"What?"

"'The Alabaster Hip.' I wrote it about you. How I feel about you," he said earnestly.

If he'd thought she'd be gratified by the knowledge, he was sorely mistaken. "You are joking."

"I never meant it to be published," he said a bit sheepishly, sensing he had made yet another tactical error. "But after the fountain, I had a bit of an inspiration . . ." He trailed off as his eyes followed the angry flush rising up her neck and into her cheeks.

She was starting to reach that unnamable place beyond anger. She didn't know it was possible to feel so much, so intensely, and still manage to remain conscious.

"You . . . you wrote a poem about my *hip*," she cried. She suddenly felt very small. And very used. Her voice quavered, and she hated him even more for making her feel so vulnerable. "You have played a game with me. As you do with everyone. You toy with people, Marlowe. It is what you do best. I don't know why I ever thought . . . "

She bit her bottom lip and started to get up. She refused to let him know how much she'd come to care for him.

He reached out, grabbed her wrists, and pulled her back down. "Why you ever thought what?" he asked.

"Nothing. It's nothing."

"Please, Minerva. *Please* let me explain . . ."

"No!" She renewed her attempts to free herself, but she only succeeded in rubbing against him in a manner that sent the air out of them both. She shifted more cautiously, but suddenly there was no denying the hard press of his erection against her stomach.

"Oh," she said with a sigh, her eyes going wide.

He released her shoulders abruptly as if burned and gazed up at her with something akin to desperation, his breathing becoming labored, his eyes unfocused with that same look he'd had last night.

She could feel the heat of him beneath her, the barely leashed animal strength of his powerful body she'd become so familiar with. She could smell the clean, sandalwood smell of him, and her mind drifted, unbidden, to the pleasure he'd given her. Suddenly it was difficult to remember precisely why she was so angry at him, just as she'd feared would happen if she let him too near. Then he rocked his hips against hers, his hand wandering down to one of her breasts, and her mind went white-hot.

"Minerva, Minerva," he murmured, caressing her as she slowly melted. She could feel her body softening, trembling, molding itself to his.

He ran his hands through her hair and kissed her forehead, her eyes, her cheeks, her lips. She threw her head back, and his mouth found her throat.

He did care. How could he not, to touch her so, with such contrition and reverence?

Yet how could she trust him?

She forced herself to focus on the knifing pain in her heart when those damning words had slipped from Lady Elizabeth's mouth and she'd realized how much he'd played her for a fool. *I'm talking about Evie being Christopher Essex, of course,* Betsy had said, as if she'd always known the truth, as if Minerva should have known as well.

As if it were nothing and hadn't shattered Minerva's entire world.

She shoved at him desperately, and he could do nothing but release her, even though he looked as if he itched to do just the opposite. She pushed off him and stood up, straightening the bodice of her dress and smoothing down her wild hair.

"Minerva . . ."

She held up her hand. "You lied to me, Marlowe. And you seduced me."

"Did I?" he growled. "I rather thought we seduced each

other."

She glared at him. "Perhaps," she allowed. "But I have never lied to you. I have never kept anything from you. And you . . . I feel I hardly know who you are. At any time, you could have told me, before . . . last night, but you were too much of a coward, weren't you? You knew how I felt about Essex. We had so many conversations about him, and yet you did nothing but tease and deflect during all of them. I wonder if you ever would have told me, if it was only the foulest luck that Lady Elizabeth happened to do so."

"Foulest luck indeed," he muttered. "I would have told you *today*, Minerva."

"I don't think I believe you," she said softly. "I don't think any part of you is sincere."

"Oh, I am sincere. Do you think I would be here now if I were not sincere? Do you think I would have given you so much of myself last night if I were not sincere?" he demanded.

She flushed at his words and felt her heart flip in her chest.

"Last night was not a whim, Minerva. Good God, is that the sort of man you think I am?" he cried.

"I don't know the sort of man you are!" she retorted. "For you've kept a very large part of who you are from me!"

He ran his hands through his hair in his frustration, but all she could focus on were the ink stains on his fingers. So *obvious* now. "You won't even let me explain!"

"What is to explain?" she demanded. "And what makes you think I want to hear anything you have to say?"

His shoulders slumped at this, and his expression crumbled, as if he were finally losing heart. He stared at the space between their bodies, the violent light in his eyes dimming. "Will you never forgive me?" he asked quietly.

"Why should I?"

He balled his hands into fists at his sides and closed his eyes, as if attempting to block out the world. "I would answer that question if I thought you'd listen," he murmured. "But you won't. Not now. Perhaps not ever. But it was never my intention to hurt you."

"Then you failed spectacularly."

He shook his head and bit out a laugh without humor. "It is not the first time." He turned to leave. He paused at the doorway and looked back at her with an expression she could not interpret. "Shall you marry *him*, then?"

She didn't even pretend not to know what he was talking about. She knew she should simply tell him the truth, for it was a lie that had brought them to this horrible place. But she was just angry enough to want to hurt him any way he could. "Perhaps," she said. "But if I did, it would be none of your affair."

From the look of agony that flickered across his expression, she might as well have struck him. It probably would have hurt him less.

He left without another word.

He deserved it, she told herself long after he'd gone. He *deserved* to feel the same hurt she did. But she could never quite convince her heart of this as she lay awake in her bed that night, afraid to sleep. For all she saw when she closed her eyes was that terrible look on his face as he walked away from her.

CHAPTER EIGHTEEN

In Which Marlowe Broods Over His Poor Life Choices

"WELL, YOU LOOK LIKE HELL warmed over, old boy."

Marlowe groaned at the very familiar and far too cheerful voice at his back. He'd not counted on any company when he'd set off this morning for Tattersall's in the hopes of cheering himself up with some prime horseflesh, especially not that of his erstwhile friend. He'd not seen Sebastian since he'd first come out of his fever months ago, when the marquess had delivered a scolding of epic proportions over Marlowe's idiocy. Marlowe had taken the reproof with good grace, knowing he'd deserved it for his hypocrisy, if nothing else.

He'd delivered a similar scolding to Sebastian after Sebastian's unfortunate encounter with Sir Oliver's hired bullyboys. The difference had been that the blame for Sebastian's brush with death had fallen squarely on Sir Oliver's shoulders, while Marlowe's had been entirely his own doing. Sebastian had been very clear on that point and on Marlowe's need to curb his excesses—which was rich, since Sebastian had been an even worse wastrel before his marriage than Marlowe ever was.

Yet it hadn't made Sebastian's admonitions any less true.

It was just his luck that Sebastian had to catch him at his lowest yet again. But Sebastian had always been annoying like that.

He turned and gifted Sebastian with his best scowl. "What the devil are you doing here?" he demanded. "Thought you were moldering in the country these days." He took in Sebastian's inexpressibles and squinted. "And what are you wearing?"

Sebastian shrugged, undaunted by Marlowe's black mood. "I'm in London on business. Called round your house, and old Chippers directed me here. And these," he said, gesturing melodramatically toward his legs, "are plaid trousers, and they're all the crack."

Someone would definitely not be allowed in Almack's. "But you're not even remotely Scottish," Marlowe grumbled.

Sebastian shuddered. "Fashion advice from a man who once wore a dressing gown to the Duchess of Delacourt's ball."

Sebastian had a point. It had not been Marlowe's finest hour. But then again, neither had it been Sebastian's, who'd been going through his chartreuse period. For all that Sebastian worshipped at the feet of Brummell, the man had a horrible addiction to bright colors.

"Chartreuse," was all he had to say about that.

Sebastian paled, his blue eyes widening as if Marlowe had kicked a puppy in front of him. "Low blow, old boy, low blow. That was a decade ago. I was young and impressionable and in the hands of a charlatan tailor. You promised never to use that unfortunate month of my life against me."

"Did I?" he said dryly.

Sebastian narrowed his eyes, as if he was tempted to pursue the argument, but he held his tongue. "Tell me what's wrong. You only come to Tatt's when you're in a sulk."

Marlowe sighed. Ever since Sebastian's marriage, all the

man ever wanted to talk about were *feelings*. He was as bad as Montford. Marlowe lay the blame for this travesty entirely at the feet of Astrid and Katherine. They had ruined his friends. *Ruined*.

He turned his attention to the horse in front of him and made a show of inspecting his teeth. "'M not in a sulk," he muttered. Sulkily.

"You're in a massive sulk. Is it your father? Is he still being a nuisance?"

"When is he not?"

"So not the earl, then. Is it the twins? I heard they were well in hand these days with that governess of yours."

Marlowe shuddered at the reminder. "How the devil do you know this?"

"Montford, naturally," Sebastian said blithely. "Someone has to keep me informed, since my best mate hardly ever writes to me."

Guilt pricked him in the chest. Between the twins, Minerva, his father, and Betsy, he'd failed rather spectacularly at being a good friend. But he had to admit to himself that part of his lack of response to Sebastian's letters had been intentional.

Marlowe still hadn't forgiven his best mate for jumping ship on him for country life. He understood why Sebastian had done it—to steer clear of the London scandalmongers, who'd had nothing better to do than decry Sebastian's elopement with his uncle's widow—but he hadn't liked it. For so long, it had been the two of them against the rest of the world. When Sebastian had married Katherine, Marlowe had felt like he'd lost his better half. He'd hidden his resentment, knowing it was unfair of him, but it had malingered inside for months.

Montford's defection with Astrid years earlier had been hard enough, but to lose Sebastian to the marriage noose so soon afterward had been a blow. Even during Marlowe's brief, disastrous marriage to Caro, Sebastian had never been far removed. But then Lady Manwaring had to go and drag her new husband off to rusticate in the country—a fate Sebastian would have once thought worse than death. And while of course Sebastian had invited him to visit, Marlowe had never brought himself to accept.

But now, seeing Sebastian again after so many months apart, Marlowe was surprised to find that his admittedly juvenile resentment was gone. It seemed that he'd finally come to terms with the loss of his boon companion. Sebastian was no less his best mate than he'd ever been. He saw that plainly now, gazing into his friend's concerned eyes—concerned but content eyes. Katherine had healed Sebastian in a way that Marlowe had never been able to. And he couldn't begrudge him that.

He was happy for Sebastian; of course he was. The fool had mooned after Katherine forever, and while Marlowe had, of course, little faith in love, much less the marriage state, even he recognized how good Katherine was for his friend. He would never have encouraged the match with his ridiculous ploy at the Montford Ball had he not.

And he had to even grudgingly admit that Astrid was a good match for the duke. The stick up the man's backside only rarely made an appearance these days.

But Marlowe could not deny that it was hard to bear witness to the wedded bliss of his two best mates. Hard to stomach. For *he* had once been that happy with Caro, and it had all turned out to be a lie. And now . . . now *he* had lied—or at least heavily edited the details—and he feared that brief glimpse of happiness he'd had with Minerva was forever lost to him. Wouldn't Montford's and Sebastian's relationships similarly crumble one day? Wouldn't the romance soon be stripped down by time and a thousand little betrayals?

Or was it just Marlowe? Was he just that unlovable? That contemptible? He wasn't sure which truth would be worse. He'd cocked things up with Minerva before they'd barely begun—wasn't that further proof that he was simply not built for that sort of love?

"You two are worse than gossiping fishwives," Marlowe muttered. "I blame your wives entirely."

Sebastian grimaced. "You are really in a dudgeon, aren't you? What, has the governess finally scarpered? Is that it? To her credit, she's lasted longer than the other ones. I thought perhaps she'd finally tamed the little beasties."

He knew Sebastian was just joking, but as usual, his friend had blundered upon the truth of the matter. He tried valiantly to keep his expression blank, but he didn't succeed. Whatever Sebastian read in Marlowe's face made his eyes pop wide. "I'm right, aren't I? You're sulking over the governess."

He could hold his peace no longer. "She's decamped to Montford's."

Sebastian's eyes grew even wider, and he looked vaguely nauseated. "Monty's? How could she think *that* an improvement over your household? It's absolutely crawling with Honeywells."

Marlowe abandoned even the pretense of looking at the horse and stalked out of the stables, Sebastian at his heels. He'd find no consolation at Tattersall's today. "Astrid's made a project of her," he hedged.

"The poor girl," Sebastian murmured.

Marlowe snorted. Poor indeed. Miss Jones would land on her feet, of that he had no doubt. With Dr. Lucas, in all likelihood.

He couldn't say the same for himself. "Don't worry about her. If Astrid has her way, Minerva . . . Miss Jones will be married to Dr. Lucas before the month is out."

"Lucas!" Sebastian cried in disgust. "The devil you say! First Katie, now your governess. Has the man no shame?"

Sebastian's aversion to the sawbones was legendary, ever since the man had had the audacity to pursue Katherine after she was widowed . . . though Marlowe was convinced that Dr. Lucas's tendre for Katherine existed more in Sebastian's own jealous mind than in actual fact. The doctor's pursuit of Minerva, however, was very annoyingly real.

"It's those damn whiskers of his," Sebastian was muttering to himself. "Demmed if I know how he makes those look so bloody attractive."

Marlowe had to grudgingly agree with Sebastian. The doctor had spectacular facial hair. And profile. And figure. And damn fine eyes . . . if one found impossibly blue and commanding things attractive. Which droves of women did. Hell, if he went in for that sort of thing, *he'd* be after Dr. Lucas as well. The man even appreciated good whisky.

He'd not stood a chance with Minerva, had he? Not even after that night . . . a mistake, she'd no doubt call it. A moment of madness for which the stoic Dr. Lucas was the antidote. He'd expected her to be angry, but not this. And he'd never foreseen her finding out before he could tell her himself—though he probably should have.

Hours. He'd been *hours* away from his confession. She would have been upset, but at least he'd have the hope of salvaging the situation. Now he didn't even have that.

God, she'd never forgive him.

That dull ache he'd been fighting all morning rose up inside his breast with renewed intensity.

Sebastian looked a bit bemused by his rather extreme reaction, but he clapped him once more on the shoulder companionably. "It's a blow, to be sure. But one can't begrudge your Miss Jones the match, I suppose. Better a doctor's wife than a governess the rest of her days."

Or his viscountess. But he was not about to confess his impossible infatuation to Sebastian in the middle of Tatt's. Especially now, when Minerva had made it clear she was done with him. Better Sebastian never know. He'd never hear the end of it. He sighed. "I suppose you're right."

"Course I am. Now let us go to White's for a meal,"

Sebastian said. "I need a bloody fillet and a good glass of claret to fortify me. Katie has me eating nothing but rabbit food these days. Being in such proximity to the livestock has addled her brainbox. She categorically refuses to allow pork of any sort on our table, owing to her attachment to that damn pig of Astrid's she adopted."

Marlowe shuddered at the mention of Petunia. Then he shuddered again at the plight of his friend's larder. The marchioness had Sebastian thoroughly and utterly whipped.

At least Marlowe had the good sense to fall in love with a woman who had a healthy appetite for things that had once had a pulse. For someone so small, Minerva could really murder a good cut of beef.

He sighed yet again. He had a feeling he was thoroughly and utterly whipped as well, to be daydreaming about the eating habits of a woman who wanted nothing more to do with him.

"Let us hope she doesn't adopt a cow, then," he offered to Sebastian, and they took themselves off to the club to further commiserate.

CHAPTER NINETEEN

In Which The Twins Brood Over Marlowe's Poor Life Choices

MARLOWE HAD KNOWN PYMM WASN'T going to work out the day the valet had tried to dispose of his banyans in the dustbin, but Mrs. Chips's foreboding eyebrows had insisted that he keep the man. She'd had enough trouble finding decent staff willing to work for him, and she was certainly not prepared to lose a valet who had once been employed by George IV. Marlowe rather doubted the man's résumé (for Prinny would have never tolerated a crier like Pymm), but he had learned years ago not to cross Mrs. Chips.

Besides, who was he to deny Chippers her dream of running a household with a full staff (sans butler, as Marlowe highly doubted she would ever cede so much of her powers to a man) and a properly turned-out employer? His housekeeper had been starting to molder without anyone but the poor little chambermaid to terrorize. Thus he had, in the past few weeks, endured far too many trips to the tailor and days wearing proper footwear than he was entirely comfortable with.

But entering his chambers after his luncheon with Sebastian to find the valet in tears, surrounded by the remains of his wardrobe, really was the last straw. He'd sack Pymm, see if he wouldn't, for if any man under this roof was going to weep, it was going to be Marlowe, damn it.

But then he really took in *why* Pymm was weeping and decided to hold off on the sacking.

Coats, waistcoats, cravats, and breeches lay murdered at the valet's feet, cut into ribbons by a pair of marauding shears. Pymm cradled his newest acquisition—a navy cutaway with gold buttons and a full skirt that Marlowe had to grudgingly admit was rather dashing—to his chest as he glanced at his master with mournful, tear-filled eyes. "My lord, we have been burgled! Shall I . . . shall I call for the magistrate?"

Marlowe snorted, knowing very well who the culprits were, and clapped Pymm on the shoulder in a brusque show of comfort. The reedy man lurched forward a few steps and gasped.

"Don't panic, Pymm. We'll sort it out. No need to involve the magistrate over a few pieces of cloth."

Pymm looked like he disagreed mightily with this assessment of the situation but held his tongue.

Then Marlowe spotted his banyans—or what was left of them—among the carnage, and he began to understand Pymm's pain. Fortunately, he was wearing his favorite Chinese red silk since he'd been too down in the mouth to bother getting properly dressed for the trip to Tatt's that morning, but it didn't lessen the blow of losing the rest of his collection.

"Who would have dared, my lord?" Pymm breathed.

Oh, he knew exactly who had dared. This had the twins' handiwork all over it. He would be meting out some sort of punishment for this desecration, though he suspected he knew what had provoked it—knew he probably deserved this. They'd been quite clear on whom they blamed for Minerva's departure.

After reassuring Pymm that the world was not going to end and promising (while gritting his teeth) a future trip to the tailor to replace his entire wardrobe, Marlowe made his way to the nursery.

He found Beatrice on her bed, looking far too innocent as she turned a page of her book, pointedly ignoring him. There was no sign of Laura, but he supposed that in this case, a bit of dividing and conquering might be in order. He tended to forget what he was punishing them for when two pairs of big brown eyes were staring mournfully up at him.

"You have cut up my entire wardrobe," he said without preamble. Another advantage to cornering Beatrice alone. He never had to worry about delicacy around her the way he did around Laura.

Bea gave a nonchalant shrug but didn't deny it. She flicked to another page.

He tried again. "Poor Mr. Pymm is in tears over it, so I hope you're happy."

Bea, who had immediately (and inexplicably) taken to Pymm, looked a bit distressed over this, but not enough to apologize.

"*You* made Miss Jones leave, Father," she countered.

His hope that this was about something other than the giant hole in both of their lives fled. He sat dejectedly on the edge of the bed. "I know," he said and sighed.

"We quite liked her, you know. And we thought . . . well, that you liked her too."

"I did. I do." So very much. "I didn't want her to leave. But she is very cross with me right now."

Bea rolled her eyes as if that were obvious. "She found out you were Christopher Essex, didn't she?"

He'd thought he'd learned not to underestimate his daughters, but apparently he still did. "How did you know?"

Bea gave him a pitying look. "We're nearly ten, Father. We're very good at what we do. Besides which, we've lived with you all our lives. Of course we know how much you love to write."

"Of course you do," he said softly, wondering how he ever thought he could fool his daughters.

"But it was a shock to Miss Jones to find out. You know how much she loves your poetry," Bea scolded.

"I know, Bea. You might have spared my banyans, though," he grumbled.

"I cut them up first," she declared unrepentantly.

"Of course," he muttered.

"It was Laura's idea," she finally admitted, the concrete proof he needed to confirm his long-held suspicions that the quiet, sly Laura was the true mastermind of their little schemes, Bea merely the blunt instrument. "She's very mad at you. She's been mad at you for a long time, but you've really gone and done it now."

"You shouldn't do everything Laura says," he said. "But you're not mad at me too?"

Bea shrugged. "Not especially. Because I know you'll fix everything. You came for us at that dreadful school. You fixed Auntie Betsy's problems and Uncle Sebastian's, when Aunt Katherine wouldn't marry him. I know you'll get Miss Jones back."

Again he had underestimated her. He pulled Bea into his arms and held on tight. Pymm's tears must have been catching, for suddenly moisture welled in his eyes. Soft and fluffy indeed. Bea hugged him back with a resigned sigh, her embrace firm and sure, comforting him when it should have been the other way around.

"You sound so certain, Bea," he managed to wobble out.

"Of course I am. Even when you make a mistake, you always fix it." She pulled away and fixed him with a sober look. "I know this because you make a *lot* of mistakes."

He gave a hoarse laugh and pulled her back into his arms. "You have such faith in me, Bea. I don't know if I deserve it."

"You do, because you are the best father in the world."

He didn't know where Bea had inherited her more

agreeable disposition, for it certainly hadn't come from either of her parents. But he must have done something right to have received such absolution from Bea.

His heart melted completely, though he could hardly agree with such an optimistic pronouncement. Something told him that Laura wouldn't either. Laura hadn't Bea's stubborn optimism or capacity to forgive so easily. She had, he was afraid, taken entirely after him.

He'd have to try a little harder with Laura. He'd known since he'd retrieved them from West Barming that his battle to heal Laura's wounds was an uphill one. But Minerva's departure had undone all of the progress he'd made these past few months.

"I think Laura might have it right," he admitted.

"She doesn't," Bea said briskly and turned back to her book, nudging him on his way with her toes. "Now, I'm truly busy reading, Papa. Perhaps you might go find Laura and beg her forgiveness."

He stood. "Imp, don't think you won't be punished for my banyans."

"As long as you fix things with Miss Jones, I don't care," she said primly.

"I will do my best. Where *is* your sister, by the way?"

Bea paused, and her expression went blank—the same look she always had when she was feeling guilty about something.

He felt the first stirrings of unease.

"Well, actually," she began slowly, cringing slightly, "she might have, maybe, *possibly*, run away."

His heart sank with dread.

☾

THE DESPERATE HORROR that had gripped Marlowe the moment he realized Bea's words were true was worse than anything he'd felt before. Nothing had come close, not even his time on the Peninsula shooting at

Frenchmen or Caroline's betrayal and subsequent death. Even when he'd woken from his fever and discovered the earl had taken the twins away, he'd not felt half so panicked, for he'd at least known they were relatively safe in that horrid school, if not happy.

This time, however, he *didn't* know if Laura were safe, could barely even *think* through the terror of imagining his nine-year-old daughter lost on the streets of London, cold and afraid—or even worse, snatched up by some opportunistic blackguard, never to be seen again.

He barely even remembered the journey to Montford House, Laura's alleged destination, or how he managed to navigate the streets on his horse without trampling someone. Even though it was only a few blocks, a thousand horrible things could have happened to a little girl between his house and the duke's. Every alleyway he passed by, his heart was in his throat, for he was half expecting to see his daughter's broken corpse lying in the detritus.

An overreaction, his mind said, yet he couldn't seem to convince his heart of this. Even Mayfair wasn't immune to the rampant crime that infested the city—he knew this all too well.

When Marlowe reached Montford House, he pushed past the staid Stallings before the butler had the door even halfway open. All he was aware of after that was a blur of movement and a raised voice—*his* raised voice, he'd realize much, much later, shouting for Laura like a lunatic.

Stallings looked terrified of him as he scurried away to fetch his employers. Only a few seconds passed before Montford was there with Astrid on his heels, both of them taking Marlowe by the arm to calm him down. He only barely resisted the urge to buck them off and rampage the hallways, but one last shred of sanity told him this would be a horrible idea. He tried to steady his breathing, though it was impossible. For some reason, stepping inside of Montford House had made Laura's disappearance even more real.

Finally their jumble of words began to penetrate the panicked haze in his brain.

". . . just sent a footman to tell you Laura is here," Astrid was saying soothingly. "Miss Jones found her sleeping in her bed."

He felt no relief, not yet, and let Astrid pull him down the hallway. "Is she hurt?" he demanded. "Where is she?"

"She is perfectly fine. They're in the parlor having biscuits," Astrid soothed.

Marlowe didn't realize he was holding his breath until he finally saw Laura, sitting on a divan next to Minerva. He released it in a gust, feeling light-headed. She was munching on a biscuit, looking a bit rumpled and teary, but otherwise unharmed. He wobbled where he stood, relief and inexplicable grief flooding through him with the force of a blow.

Laura's face contorted with a mixture of guilt and defiance when she saw him standing in the doorway. Something of his grief must have shown in his expression, however, for the defiance in her gaze quickly dropped away, replaced immediately by tears.

He stumbled like a drunkard to the divan and swept her up in his arms. For the first time in days—months, really—Laura clung to him without reservation.

"You frightened me to death," he murmured into her hair, inhaling the soft lilac scent of her. "I thought something had happened to you."

"I'm sorry, Papa," she said, sobbing into his cravat. "I didn't mean to make you cry."

He realized for the first time that his cheeks and throat were wet, his eyes clouded over with tears. He must have been crying for some time without even knowing it. "Of course I'm crying," he said, rocking her back and forth. "I love you so much, and I couldn't find you anywhere."

"But I was just here with Miss Jones."

"I see that now," he whispered, and he smiled at Minerva in silent gratitude, though he could manage no more for his governess at the moment. She seemed to realize this, for she just nodded at him in solemn concern and didn't even try to speak.

He held Laura while she cried—while both of them cried, to be honest—and he wasn't certain how much time had passed when he finally came back to the world. At some point, Minerva and the others left the room and closed the door behind them to give them their privacy, for which he was grateful. He couldn't stomach any other company, not while he had so much to mend with Laura.

He waited a few more minutes until Laura's sobbing breaths had evened out, her small body finally relaxing against his own, before he began what he was sure was going to be a painful conversation.

"Why did you run away, Laura?"

"I told you, I wanted to see Miss Jones," she insisted muzzily. He couldn't really blame her, since he wanted to do much the same thing nearly every hour of every day, but he knew that Laura's behavior was about much more than the loss of her governess.

"There were other ways of going about that, darling," he said gently. "The streets are dangerous. You could have been trampled by a carriage or lost your way." Or much, much worse, he thought to himself grimly.

She made a noncommittal noise to this and shifted in his arms.

"I know you've been angry with me, Laura, and angrier still since Miss Jones left. I'm sorry."

"I wasn't angry with you," she said in a very small voice.

"My wardrobe would disagree," he said wryly. "And it is understandable if you were . . ."

"But I *wasn't*," she insisted, looking up at him through tear-swollen eyes. "I was just . . . frightened. I hate it when people leave. I hate it most of all when *you* leave. And then you almost died. We were sent away, and we didn't even know if you were alive or dead. I still feel scared all the time; I just can't help myself. What if you die? What if you leave us again or send us away? I don't think I could bear it."

His heart felt bruised in his chest as he realized how little these past few halcyon weeks had gone toward healing the careless wounds he'd inflicted upon his daughters.

Marlowe had always wanted to give to the twins what he had never had. A happy childhood, and a father who loved them unconditionally. Of course, the latter was true, would always be true. Yet it seemed his sins of the past nine years had at last caught up with him.

Had he made his children happy? He'd thought he had, or at least he'd tried his best at the time. The best clothes, the best toys, the best nursemaids and governesses—though none of those had ever stayed for long. Yet how often had he left them—for months on end sometimes—gallivanting across the countryside with Sebastian or locked away brooding over a verse or just simply in his cups . . . always in his cups?

At the nadir of Marlowe's black mood, even the thought of his beloved daughters had not been enough to sober him up, and the only kindness he'd been able to grant them was his absence. He could not have borne for them to see him brought so low, even though he knew they hated it when he was away. No amount of fatherly embraces or fancy gifts had ever been able to bring the twins out of their sulks after one of his long absences. Only time had softened their hearts.

The ghosts would always be there: his father's abuse and contempt; the horrors he'd faced in the war (the senselessness of it all underneath the thin veneer of patriotic duty); and a homecoming to a wife he'd loved all his life but barely knew, a wife who'd betrayed him in the most brutal way possible—she'd broken his heart as surely as the war had broken his spirit.

But he didn't feel so broken anymore, not even after Minerva's defection, and that was something. It had taken his protracted illness and nearly losing his daughters to his father's maneuverings to snap him out of his self-destruction, and he hoped it wasn't too late.

He'd failed his daughters spectacularly, but he didn't plan on failing them any longer. He'd damaged one of the few things in the world that he gave a damn about anymore: his daughters' trust in him. The wound could be repaired, perhaps, but the scar would always remain. He'd never wanted that sort of pain for his daughters.

"Never," he said fiercely, "I'll never send you away. And I won't leave you like I did in the past. When I did that, Laura, when I went away, it was because . . . well, because I was very sad, and I didn't want you or Bea to see me like that. But I see now that I shouldn't have done that."

Laura's brow creased thoughtfully, considering his explanation. "Why were you sad? Was it about our mother?"

Marlowe's eyes leaked a little more, and his heart suffered a pang. His daughters were too clever for their own good. Or maybe just clever enough. "Yes," he said honestly. "And other things. But I'm through with all that. You're right. I almost died last winter, and I'll never forgive myself for scaring you like that, or letting you be taken from me."

She looked a bit mollified. "It was horrible, Papa."

"I know. And I promise I'll never be so foolish again." He paused and decided on total honesty. Laura deserved nothing less. "But sometimes people do get sick or hurt, and sometimes people die. I can't promise you that this will never happen."

"I know *that*, Papa," she said impatiently. "I'm just afraid that now Miss Jones is gone, you'll be sad and go out and get yourself hurt again."

"I won't, darling. I might be sad she's gone—of course I'm sad—but I won't hurt myself. Please don't be afraid anymore."

She nodded and tightened her arms around his neck, sniffling into his shoulder. "I believe you."

He sighed with relief.

"But I suppose I am a *bit* cross at you about Miss Jones," she finally said with a bit of her old hauteur.

"I thought you might be," he said dryly. "I'm rather cross at myself. And so is Miss Jones."

"So what are we going to do about it?"

He wished he had a bloody clue about that. But one thing he now knew for sure was that his brooding had to end . . . and that he wasn't going to give up on his governess without a fight.

CHAPTER TWENTY

In Which Bathing In The Thames Enjoys A Surge In Popularity In Early 1820s London

THE PROPRIETORS AND PATRONS OF the Royal Waterloo Bath, one of the more unique attractions upon the Thames (aside from the bobbing rubbish, mudlarks, and sewage), swore by the manifold health benefits of the river water that flowed through its pioneering pump rooms. For just two guineas for the entire Season, one could soak up these dubious benefits in a private chamber aboard the ship—if one were male, of course, and possessed of such liquid funds.

One of those privileged few who could have afforded the exorbitant seasonal fee of the Royal Waterloo, had he been so inclined, was the Viscount Marlowe. But he'd determined when the pleasure barge had first opened that he'd set neither big nor little toe on board. He knew exactly where the dustman dumped the contents of his household privies, after all, and had no desire to bathe in the same place.

His opinion on the matter, which he was shocked to learn was among the minority (for even the fastidious Montford had a membership), seemed to be validated after his involuntary swim near the London docks and subsequent illness. No one would ever be able to convince him that ingesting buckets of the brackish waters hadn't had a deleterious effect on his constitution. And it was probably not a coincidence that the Royal Waterloo Bath tended to stay upstream from the more insalubrious shores of southeast London, where raw sewage was one of the least offensive effluvia seasoning the river.

This tale, however, has nothing whatsoever to do with the Royal Waterloo Bath—at the present moment settled into its moorings on the Waterloo Bridge after a day's brisk trade—and very little to do with the docks, the site of the viscount's own personal waterloo months earlier.

But this tale has everything to do with the lone figure, swathed in shadows and the occasional, ominous flash of lightning, struggling to cross the mildly toxic waters of said docks in a leaky dinghy. His destination: the rotting cesspool that was Jacob's Island, in the crotch of Bermondsey, on the other side of the river. It was a particularly foul place at the best of times, but when the river was at low ebb, as it was at present, the tidal ditches that marked its eastern boundaries overflowed with the best the Thames had to offer: carcasses—mostly animal, occasionally human—excrement, and the stinking red dye of the nearby tanneries.

Even the most avid of bathers probably would have avoided those particular waters. But it was doubtful that anyone with the luxury to even consider a leisurely soak would have set foot in the Jacob's Island rookery. Its old, rotted accommodations tended to attract the more criminally minded class, or those who were simply too poor to hope for better than a home that stank of death, violence, and pickling animal hides.

The occupant of the dinghy, who belonged to the former class of prospective inhabitants, was taking advantage of the foul weather to sneak onto Albion's shores once more after an involuntary absence. The rookery was hardly this villain's first choice of bolt-hole, but when one relocated to a place like Jacob's Island, one tended to have no other options.

What was left of his fortune had been spent in actually getting himself back to London, and so affording a hot meal, much less reclaiming his former London residence—or at the very least a proper Bond Street Hotel—was simply not in the cards. Not yet, anyway, though he had plans to regain what he'd lost.

Oh yes, he'd reclaim his fortune, and in the meantime he'd exact his revenge on the man who had destroyed his life. He'd waited a long time to see to it that the pompous bastard suffered, and now that he was finally in London, nothing was going to stop him. Not the grueling journey back, spent like an animal in a smuggler's hold. Not the endless bribes and threats he'd had to issue, or the men he'd disposed of along the way. Not that damned storm on the Channel that had nearly capsized his ship. And certainly not a leaky dinghy already half-sunk beneath him.

When he had restored his fortune, he was going to find the bloody little mudlark who'd sold him this leaking death trap and string him up by his testicles. The whelp couldn't have been more than ten, and by the look of him too hungry to be much of a challenge.

Oh, he'd find him and make him sing. A dirty, fatherless thing like that wouldn't be missed.

But even this particular villain couldn't blame the easterly pull of the ebbing tide, or the resistance one naturally encountered when paddling upstream, on the enterprising young boat seller. Those things he blamed on a higher power who, apparently, was in league with his nemesis to make his life a misery. The universe was out to get him, but he'd be damned if he'd let it defeat him now.

Lightning flashed in the sky, illuminating an old dock just a few lengths ahead, swaying in the tide upon waterlogged stilts like a drunkard trying to remain upright. The villain aimed his craft in its direction, but a few strokes later, the dinghy gave a final gurgle as its bow sank below the water, leaving him floating in the fragrant shallows with two useless oars and a sodden bag of belongings.

"God d—"

The heavens chose at that moment to roll with a deafening cannon blast of thunder, drowning out the villain's final word just in time. Perhaps he should have taken such a portentous coincidence as proof that a higher power did indeed dislike him very much, especially when he cursed in such an ungodly manner.

But he didn't.

He cast aside his oars, heaved his earthly possessions on one shoulder, and began to tread water in the direction of the vaguely piscine, vaguely gangrenous smell of the rookery.

His first contact with the slimy bottom of the shallows was heralded by another flash of lightning, illuminating once more the dilapidated dock and rotting ditches lining the edge of the river. Thunder began to roll seconds later as he trudged through the mire, his mood growing even darker than it had been during his long journey in the smuggler's hold.

It had seemed like an eternity since he'd last stepped foot on English soil, an eternity since he'd smelled the . . . well, not so fresh air wafting off the Thames. He'd have to find himself a new pair of boots, since he doubted the stink would ever come out of the old pair after such a dunking.

But just that thought was enough to reignite his anger, for he hadn't the blunt to buy new boots, did he? He barely had the blunt to fund his plans for revenge against *that man*. That odious, self-righteous prig who'd ruined him and driven him from his own home.

It had taken some time, but he would see to it that the man paid for daring to cross him. For taking away all that was his.

And all over a *woman*.

A woman that was rightfully his, at that. After he'd

seen to his revenge, he'd make sure she never escaped his clutches again. It was the least he deserved for the trouble she'd caused him, after all. Even God was certain to agree with his claim.

God did not, in fact, agree, and our villain might have picked up on this from the rolling thunder and crack of lightning directly over his head. But he was too distracted to notice such ominous portents, as a sudden surge in the knee-deep shallows knocked him off his feet. He stumbled forward, tripped over something much too gelatinous to be a rock, and fell facedown and nose deep in the muddy embankment.

He cursed the heavens once more—again, something he might not have done had he known they were cursing him right back—and scraped the foul-smelling muck from his face.

Oh, how that smug fool would pay!

CHAPTER TWENTY-ONE

In Which Miss Jones Takes Tea With The Duchess

EVEN AFTER THE DISRUPTIONS CAUSED by various Leightons over the past few days, the Duchess of Montford had miraculously demanded no explanations of Minerva, allowing her to settle in to her new life—such as it was, with both Miss Honeywells currently in Rylestone Green with their other sister. But Minerva knew that the duchess's rabid curiosity could only be contained for so long.

She suspected that her stay of execution was finally over when she received a summons to tea the day after Laura had found her way across Mayfair. She entered the main drawing room to find Lady Manwaring sitting with the duchess and sighed inwardly. The wives of Marlowe's two best friends would definitely want an accounting, and while she knew they deserved one, she was not looking forward to it, especially after yesterday.

Seeing how distraught Laura had been—how distraught the viscount was over his daughter's pain—she regretted leaving so hastily. She'd not even bothered to say goodbye to the twins, and it was obvious they were suffering for it. She'd not realized how attached they had become to her.

Or how attached she'd become. She missed them dreadfully.

Worse still, she missed the viscount. And she had no idea what she was going to do about it.

"Ah, Miss Jones!" the duchess said, brightening when she spotted Minerva. "I have invited the Marchioness of Manwaring to join us."

Minerva could see why the Marquess of Manwaring had nearly called out his best friend over the marchioness. She was even more beautiful than Minerva remembered her being at that long-ago ball, with her moonbeam hair and bright green eyes. There was a softening around the edges that Minerva suspected had something to do with a happy domestic life.

Which didn't make Minerva jealous whatsoever. Yet if ever she wanted to know what a woman in love with her husband looked like, she didn't need to go any farther than the duchess's drawing room.

And she did not need such a reminder, thank you very much, especially since she doubted she'd ever get to enjoy the same.

The marchioness inclined her head in greeting. "You were Lady Blundersmith's companion, weren't you?"

"I was," she said, surprised she'd been recognized yet again.

"How horrid for you," the marchioness said with a bit of a smirk.

Minerva choked on her tea. "Don't I know it," she finally managed.

The marchioness's smile widened, and she turned to the duchess. "I like her."

"Miss Jones is also particular friends with Dr. Lucas," the duchess said, sending Minerva a sly look.

The marchioness smiled agreeably. "Dr. Lucas is one of my favorite people. How do you know him?"

"I was to marry his brother, but Arthur died in the war."

Lady Manwaring's expression fell. "Oh, I'm sorry to hear

that. I think he's mentioned his brother once or twice."

"Speaking of marriage, we should really find poor Dr. Lucas a wife," the duchess said as she handed Minerva her tea. "And one who is not in love with one of my husband's best friends."

Well, the duchess had certainly cut to the chase. Minerva nearly dropped the contents of her cup into her skirts. She could feel the damning heat rise immediately in her cheeks and her heart begin to race with agitation.

She of course had known of Inigo's brief tendre for the marchioness, whom he saw as a kindred spirit when it came to their charitable endeavors, so she was quite clear on what the duchess was intimating there. It was the other implication that left her so dumbfounded. It was foolish to assume the duchess had not come to her own conclusions after the past two days, yet how the duchess could have deduced such a thing when Minerva had said nothing on the matter was quite beyond her comprehension.

"I'm not . . . don't be absurd . . . *what?*" she spluttered.

The duchess just gave her an arch look.

Minerva should have heeded all of Marlowe's warnings about the Duchess of Montford. The woman was a menace. She sighed in resignation and sat back in her seat. "How did you know?"

The duchess tsked. "I've known since I found you half up Poseidon's thigh."

The marchioness choked on her tea. The duchess patted her friend on the back. "That's a story for later, Katherine. The important thing was the way Miss Jones and Marlowe made calf's eyes at each other the whole time—when he wasn't staring at her legs. As if I wouldn't notice what they were up to."

"And Inigo?" Minerva demanded.

The duchess looked at Minerva as if she were an idiot. "A gentleman does not ask for a private audience with a lady to discuss the weather. Though he was hardly in tears when he left. I doubt any hearts have been broken . . . well, I suppose I can't say that. *Someone* left the house in tears that day."

Minerva decided to ignore that last part because she knew very well the duchess was painting it brown. Marlowe, in tears? Over her? Ridiculous. Though he had looked rather destroyed yesterday when he'd come to fetch Laura.

"Inigo is a friend," she said firmly. "He's long thought it his duty to marry me himself, but I think we have finally agreed that it could never work."

"Which leaves Marlowe," the duchess pressed. "You have been upset since you arrived, and I thought it best not to demand an explanation. But after all that has happened, I simply must know what is going on."

"I wouldn't even try to prevaricate," Lady Manwaring said wryly. "The duchess shall have it out of you one way or another. It just depends on how painful you make it for yourself."

Minerva sighed and took the marchioness's advice. "The viscount kept something from me that was rather significant. I had to find it out from Lady Elizabeth, and now I feel . . ."

"Betrayed?" the duchess offered.

"And humiliated. He made a fool out of me, and just when . . ."

The duchess and marchioness both looked much too interested in how she might finish that sentence.

"Just when I was beginning to think he truly cared for me."

"I'm fairly certain you're not wrong to think he cares, judging by Marlowe's behavior these past few weeks," the duchess remarked. "And that terribly transparent ode he wrote in the *Morning Chronicle*."

This time Minerva was the one to choke on her tea. Luckily most of it landed back in her cup. She set it aside and gaped at the duchess, who looked very pleased with herself.

"You know!" Minerva cried.

"Of course I know. Had it out of Montford on our honeymoon. He's horribly easy to break if you know where to press."

"I would rather not know what you and your husband get up to in the bedroom, thank you," the marchioness interrupted primly.

"Who said it was only in the bedroom?" the duchess murmured.

Lady Manwaring rolled her eyes at her friend, then looked uneasily at the divan upon which she was sitting, as if she suspected it to be the site of one of the ducal couple's non-bedroom trysts. "But what is it you know, Astrid? Why do I have the feeling I am the only one here who doesn't?"

The duchess turned to her friend with a pitying look. "You really must do a better job of wrangling your husband, my dear. He should have told you ages ago that Marlowe has a secret profession."

The marchioness looked from the duchess to Minerva and back again, clearly disbelieving as she began to piece the threads of the conversation together. "No!" she breathed.

"Oh, yes," the duchess said. "Marlowe is Christopher Essex."

"But . . . no! Marlowe?" Lady Manwaring looked positively poleaxed.

"Marlowe," Her Grace confirmed.

The marchioness collapsed against her seat as if she'd been struck by a cricket bat. It was exactly how Minerva had felt for the past two days.

"Marlowe is Christopher Essex," Lady Manwaring said slowly, as if trying to convince herself. "The author of *Le Chevalier d'Amour* and *The Hedonist*. The most celebrated poet in Britain. *Marlowe,* who wears a banyan all day because he can't be bothered to get properly dressed. Who massacres the English language nearly every time he opens his mouth. *That* Marlowe."

"That Marlowe," the duchess affirmed.

Something else seemed to click in place for Lady Manwaring. She turned to Minerva. "'The Alabaster Hip' is about you?"

Silence.

"What? No! Of course it's not," Minerva spluttered, thankful she hadn't even attempted another go at her tea.

The duchess frowned at her. "Of course it's about you. Knew it immediately—he must have written it right after your little contretemps in the fountain. Where he did, in fact, see your hips."

"What?" she cried, outraged that she could once again feel the heat of her mortification practically pouring into her face. "He did no such thing . . ."

"Oh, my dear, we *all* did," the duchess said with a pitying smile. "And you do indeed have lovely alabaster skin. I can attest that his comparison is completely accurate."

Minerva wasn't quite sure whether to thank Her Grace or storm out of the room in a dudgeon. She settled on pinching the bridge of her nose to warn away her burgeoning headache.

"'The Alabaster Hip' is not about me," she insisted, though she knew it was a lie. Marlowe had confessed it himself, though she was trying her hardest not to think about that particular conversation.

Or those brief, searing moments when those honied words of the ode had dripped from the viscount's lips as he lowered his head between her legs. When she'd discovered the truth, those words had seemed a mockery. But if they weren't, if he were being sincere . . .

Minerva was not sure she was prepared to entertain the possibility. She was just so angry, so hurt.

He'd squeezed his way past all of her defenses since the

day he'd picked her up off the side of the road. She'd been so determined not to like him at all, but then she'd witnessed firsthand his love for his daughters, the way he'd defended his sister against his own father, his fondness for Mrs. Chips, and even all of his singular quirks of character that should have annoyed her instead of charmed . . .

She'd thought she'd finally come to know the viscount's true self underneath all of his ridiculous banyans and fool's act. But it had turned out she didn't know him at all. She was not prepared to forgive him. Not yet.

"It's not about me," Minerva insisted, a little less vociferously this time. "And even if it is, it changes nothing. He should have told me. Before . . ."

Lady Manwaring's austere features softened, and she reached out and squeezed Minerva's hand in sympathy.

"Whether you forgive him or not, you shall have my support," the duchess declared. "I'm of the firm opinion that a woman should not depend upon a man for her happiness, much less marry one she cannot be certain of. I shall not matchmake."

The marchioness gave her friend a look of disbelief. "You? Not matchmake?"

"Stuff," the duchess said dismissively. "You and Sebastian were a special circumstance. It was literally excruciating to watch the two of you moon about, pretending to despise each other and playing all that dreary Beethoven. It was my duty to intervene. For the good of England."

"Dreary? Beethoven?" Lady Manwaring cried, appalled.

"Do you know how many times I had to listen to Sebastian play the *Pathetique* in this very drawing room? I had to insist that Montford move the pianoforte back to Sebastian's lodgings before I took a hammer to it."

The marchioness looked as if she might respond to that, but just then, Stallings, the Montford butler, swept into the room. He presented a card to the duchess with a bow. "A Lady Blundersmith to see you, Your Grace," he said impassively.

Minerva groaned inwardly. Of all the residents of London, she could think of only one other she'd rather see less.

The duchess grimaced. "Lawks, that woman has called upon me for days. I can't imagine what she should want. I suppose I'd better receive her this time."

Stallings disappeared, and Minerva took this as her cue to leave. She stood up.

"Where are *you* going?" the duchess asked, motioning her to sit down. "You must stay. We're not done discussing the viscount."

"But Lady Blundersmith . . ."

"If I have to endure the next half hour, I demand that you do as well." The duchess's grin was practically feral. "Besides, if she sees *you* having tea with me, she's liable to swoon."

The prospect of having one over on Lady Blundersmith *was* rather appealing. The woman had been rather vicious when she'd cast Minerva out without references. The look on her face when she discovered Minerva having tea with the duchess was sure to be worth the discomfort of her company. And Lord knew Minerva could do with some entertainment.

She sat back down. "So long as she doesn't swoon on me," she muttered.

Lady Blundersmith swooped into the room seconds later in a haze of violet taffeta and lavender toilette water. She was no less monumental than she had been nearly two years ago, her bosom jutting out ahead of the rest of her like the prow of a ship. After Minerva's encounter with the Honorable Mister Ashley Leighton, however, Lady Blundersmith seemed a bit less daunting.

Then Minerva remembered what it felt like to be trapped beneath all of that taffeta and bosom, the stink of lavender barely masking the more odorous emanations of a lady who claimed immersing any part of herself in soap and water was unhygienic.

Minerva shuddered at the memory. Then she shuddered again when she noticed the small, mousy woman in gray trailing behind Lady Blundersmith, a stack of cards in one hand and the lady's smelling salts in the other. Ah, Lady Blundersmith's latest victim. There but for the grace of God . . . or rather Christopher Essex, in Minerva's case.

Lady Blundersmith was halfway through the usual pleasantries when she spotted Minerva. The constipated look on her face was something to be savored, making even the necessity of curtsying to the lady worth it.

"And I believe you know Miss Jones," the duchess said, looking equally pleased with needling her unwanted caller.

"Indeed," Lady Blundersmith said stiffly, lowering herself upon an unoccupied settee. It groaned under the weight, bowing inward ever so slightly. Her anonymous companion hovered anxiously behind her employer and nearly jumped when Lady Blundersmith snapped her fingers for her smelling salts.

"I wonder how you have come to be acquainted with a *person* like Miss Jones, Your Grace," Lady Blundersmith said with no effort to conceal her disapproval. "I do hope you haven't been foolish enough to employ her."

The duchess had, in fact, done just that. But Her Grace stared in utter disdain at her visitor. "Miss Jones is a dear friend, Lady Blundersmith. I'm sure I don't know what you mean to insinuate."

Lady Blundersmith's eyes widened at this very clear set down, then they narrowed upon Minerva suspiciously, as if she'd enchanted the duchess somehow.

Minerva just gazed back at her former employer serenely, though inwardly she was awash with gratitude and a fair bit of disbelief over the duchess's words. She'd expected the duchess to explain how she had indeed hired her for a governess, not to claim her as a friend. The duchess had made it clear several times that she thought of Minerva in those terms, despite their brief acquaintance and disparity of station, but Minerva hadn't really dared to believe her. It was one thing to invite her to tea (mostly, Minerva suspected, to stave off boredom by prying into Marlowe's affairs), but it was quite another to defend Minerva to her peers.

Lady Blundersmith harrumphed and leaned back against the settee. It gave another alarming creak under the shifting weight. She turned to the marchioness and said with remarkably less enthusiasm, "Lady Manwaring, I did not know you were in town."

The marchioness, who had abandoned her relaxed posture for a more rigid one now that they were not alone, just inclined her head rather coldly at Lady Blundersmith. "My husband had business to attend to, and I thought it an opportunity to visit friends."

It was clear from her tone Lady Manwaring didn't consider Lady Blundersmith among them, which was unsurprising, considering the way the older woman's face had spasmed at the mention of the marquess. Lady Manwaring's elopement was still, it seemed, the subject of much contention among polite society, and it was clear Lady Blundersmith had allied herself with the high sticklers who disapproved.

Ironic, considering Lady Blundersmith's own Gretna Green marriage years ago. Though Minerva supposed Lady Blundersmith had spent her life since then doing everything in her power to distance herself from her own youthful folly—even convincing herself that it had never happened.

"Shall I call for a fresh pot, Lady Blundersmith?" the duchess inserted smoothly, diverting attention away from the marchioness.

Lady Blundersmith waved away the suggestion. "You're too kind, but I'm afraid I can't stay long, Your Grace."

"That *is* a pity," the duchess said with a sincerity Minerva doubted.

"It's a miracle I've finally caught you at home, and just in time, as well."

"I am intrigued at your urgency, Lady Blundersmith," the duchess murmured into her tea.

Lady Blundersmith snapped her fingers again, and her companion jumped and fumbled with the stack of cards in her hands. They fell into the folds of Lady Blundersmith's taffeta skirts, and with a panicked yelp, the companion dove in after them. Lady Blundersmith swatted her away with her fan and plucked the cards from her skirts. She handed them back to the companion, swatted at her again, and ordered her to deliver one to the duchess.

The duchess read the card, snorted quietly, and handed it over to the marchioness, who gave it a bemused look and passed it on to Minerva. She soon discovered the reason behind the duchess's snort—and Lady Blundersmith's dagger-like stare in her direction. It read:

> *The Ladies' League Against Lewd and Lascivious Literature and Letters invites you to its first annual Rally Against the Corruption of Public Virtue and Literary Vice in Hyde Park on Saturday, April 2, at three in the afternoon. Interested parties may bring offending material to be disposed of forthwith.*
>
> *Tea and Light Refreshment will be provided.*
>
> *LLALLLL is grateful for the patronage of Her Grace, the Duchess of Delacourt; The Right Honorable, the Countess of Carlisle; the Right Honorable, the Viscountess Blundersmith; and Lady Emily Benwick.*

"Your aunt, Lady Benwick, was sure you wouldn't be interested," Lady Blundersmith began, "but I assured Emily that just couldn't possibly be true. As your standing among the ton is without question, you must certainly be interested in setting an example for decency and virtue all of us may admire."

"You are correct, Lady Blundersmith. I should like nothing so much in the world as for everyone to be decent," the duchess responded with a completely straight face. "Do you not wish the same, Katherine?"

"It seems my mother does," she said, referring to Lady Carlisle. "And to think I almost didn't come up from the country. I might have missed this," the marchioness continued with a sweetness that only Lady Blundersmith seemed to buy.

"And the festivities are to be tomorrow," the duchess murmured. "So soon, Lady B?"

"Not soon enough!" Lady Blundersmith said rather querulously, waving her salts through the air. "After that dreadful man published his latest travesty, action must be taken, before all of our daughters are lost to perdition."

"Speak of the devil," the duchess murmured beneath her breath.

"But to which dreadful man do you refer?" Lady Manwaring asked, all innocence. "There seem to be so many of them these days."

"Why, that Essex fellow, of course. *Most* unsavory. The Ladies' League Against Lewd and Lascivious Literature and Letters is quite determined to end his influence upon our impressionable young ladies—and to see to it that those who promote his filth are dealt with."

It was quite obvious by the look she threw in Minerva's direction whom Lady Blundersmith considered a promoter of filth.

Minerva had the sudden urge to hurl her teacup at Lady Blundersmith's head. How dare the woman! How dare all the members of this league for their ridiculous crusade. It was clear Essex was this absurd Ladies' League's main target, and that would just not do. She didn't care how angry she was at the viscount—his poetry deserved to be celebrated, not censored by ignorant puritans.

"I do hope you're taking Byron to task as well," Her Grace said.

"Of course," Lady Blundersmith sniffed.

"And Shelley. Both of them. Oh, and that horrid Mr. de Quincy. He'll have all the debutantes eating opium if given half the chance," the duchess continued avidly.

"What about that Blake fellow?" Lady Manwaring added.

The duchess waved that suggestion away. "Poor man is a bedlamite. I shouldn't think it in good taste to crucify the infirm."

Lady Blundersmith had no idea how to respond to that. From the way her eyes were beginning to narrow, there was a possibility that she was beginning to catch on to her hostess's poorly veiled irony, but Minerva doubted this. Lady Blundersmith wouldn't recognize sarcasm if it hit her on the head and dragged her across the room. It was why Minerva had lasted a full five years before getting sacked.

The duchess set down her teacup and smiled so sunnily at Lady Blundersmith that Minerva knew immediately she was up to something. "I am positively intrigued, Lady Blundersmith. You may certainly expect me at Hyde Park tomorrow. I wouldn't miss it for the world."

Lady Blundersmith's confusion cleared. She looked delighted. "I knew Lady Benwick was mistaken about you, Your Grace. I myself was beginning to think—with the company you keep"—another damning glance in Minerva's direction—"that you wouldn't be interested in our endeavor."

"I am so interested in it I could scream," the duchess declared brightly.

Lady Blundersmith looked taken aback by the rather enthusiastic response. "Yes. Well. Certainly *that* won't be necessary."

THE MOMENT LADY Blundersmith steered her way from the room, the duchess's grin faded into a scowl, then into something grimly calculating.

"How do you feel about a stroll in Hyde Park tomorrow?" she mused.

"I can think of nothing better," Lady Manwaring murmured.

The duchess turned to Minerva. "Miss Jones? Shall you join us as well?"

Minerva remembered the way she had been unceremoniously cast from Lady Blundersmith's household without a reference because the lady disagreed with her reading material. If not for Inigo's aid in helping her to secure the position at West Barming—however loathsome it had turned out to be—she would have been out on the streets. Over *poetry*.

Many in her position would have probably given in to their employers' demands—life for a paid companion was precarious enough, with only the goodwill of people like Lady Blundersmith upon which to rely. But her life—her future—was so grim a prospect anyway that she had been unable to surrender what little autonomy was left to her. She had so few things she could call her own, but one of them was her mind. She'd not endure a life in which that most sacred part of her was imprisoned. She would not censor her mind *or* her reading material.

Nor would she let others do so simply because they didn't understand it.

"I may be furious with the viscount, but I'll not allow old biddies like Lady Blundersmith to speak ill of his genius," Minerva said firmly.

The duchess, pleased with her response, set down her teacup decisively and stood. "I must pay some calls, then, and muster the troops. We'll not let Aunt Emily get away with this."

Minerva almost felt sorry for Lady Benwick, for the

duchess's current expression was precisely the same one Minerva's father used to wear when staring down a target with his gun in hand—as if he were imagining it was Napoleon's head.

Chapter Twenty-Two

In Which The Marquess And Marchioness Of Manwaring Bask In Domestic Bliss

After one last scratch behind Seamus's ear, Sebastian Sherbrook, the Marquess of Manwaring, the "Most Beautiful Man in London", according to the *Times*, and now happily married former scoundrel, sent off the three-legged Irish Setter to join the others at the hearth and patted the column of watch fobs crisscrossing his waistcoat with satisfaction. Finally, after nearly three years of scouring every crooked pawnbroker in the city, he'd found the last of his collection, lost to Sir Oliver's thuggish cohorts, at a shop in the Strand. He'd felt rather naked without them . . .

Though he had to admit he was rather fond of being naked these days.

Still, it was nice to have his beloved watch collection restored to him after all this time.

He sat down at his Broadwood's stool and plunked out the first notes of the *Opus 109*. Beethoven was only getting better with age. After a few more sessions of rehearsal, Sebastian would have the piece perfected enough to play for Katherine in celebration of her happy announcement.

Just when he thought his life couldn't be improved upon, something came along to make it even better. First his watch collection, and now a child on the way. The only thing that would make life utterly perfect would be seeing Marlowe as happy as he was. His best mate had looked even more melancholy than usual at Tatt's, and he wished he knew of something he could do to help.

The door swung open with a bang, and he jumped to his feet in surprise, as did the four dogs now lazing at the hearth. He half expected some long-lost creditor of his he'd forgotten to pay off to come storming in, but it was only his wife. Katherine stalked into the room, ripping her bonnet off and tossing it carelessly to one side, her cheeks flushed with color, her green eyes bright with excitement. She was in such a lather it was easy to figure out where she'd been all afternoon.

"And how is the duchess?" he asked, crossing to his wife and bussing her rosy cheeks before ceding ground to the dogs, who promptly mobbed her for attention.

"You'll never guess what I have learned," she said without bothering to answer his question, petting each of the dogs' heads in turn.

He blazed a path back through the fray to his wife, caught her around the waist, and led her over to the piano stool before the dogs could knock her over. She was in a delicate condition, after all.

"I'm not sure I want to know what you've been gossiping about over there to have you in such a state," he said dryly. "Dr. Whiskers has made it clear you are not to overexcite yourself."

She rolled her eyes and waved away his concern. "Nonsense. I feel perfectly fine. I'm with child, not the plague."

Despite his opinion of the man's whiskers, Sebastian thought Dr. Lucas was a damn fine sawbones, and his advice seemed perfectly reasonable. His wife obviously thought otherwise. But she looked better than she had in days—that is, *less* green—so he decided to hold his tongue . . . no matter how much he'd love to assist his wife in relaxing. Preferably in their bedroom. Sans watch fobs.

Penny butted her head against his knees in a demand that he cede ground, and he backed up a step to allow the dog her due. He—and his ankles—had learned the hard way not to ignore Penny's admonitions.

Katherine stroked Penny's lumpy head and proceeded to tell Sebastian the news, whether he cared to know it or not. "Miss Jones was there . . ."

"Who?"

"Miss Jones!" she huffed. "Marlowe's governess! Dr. Lucas's fiancée! Only she's not his fiancée at all. You had that all wrong. And she's been staying at Montford House."

"Marlowe might have mentioned it," he said.

She scowled up at him. "Well, *you* didn't mention *that* part to me. I have a feeling you haven't mentioned a great deal about Marlowe," she accused.

Something told him he needed to tread very carefully. "I have no idea what you are talking about."

She shook her head as if disgusted with him. "Miss Jones! The viscount! Did you not think it strange that Marlowe's governess is now living with the duchess?"

"I . . ."

"And did you not think," she continued, her tone hardening a little, "in the nearly two years of our association . . ."

"Association!" he scoffed. "We have more than an association!"

Her eyes narrowed. That was never a good sign. "In the past two years," she repeated, "did you never think to mention the fact that the drunken, debauched scoundrel you call a best mate is, in fact, the most celebrated poet in all of Europe?"

Oh. That.

Yes, well, he supposed that had been a rather huge omission on his part.

"Er, the subject never arose?" he tried.

She smacked his arm in irritation. She had definitely been friends with Astrid Honeywell for far too long.

He rubbed his injury—or lack thereof, since he'd hardly felt it—with rather more vigor than it warranted and tried to look as innocent as he could. "Perhaps I should have mentioned it, but it's been a busy few years . . ."

"Not that busy."

". . .and Marlowe rather plays the whole Essex business close to his chest. As far as I know, only his publisher, Montford, and I know he is Christopher Essex. And, besides, it really isn't my secret to tell, is it."

She harrumphed, not looking mollified in the least. "Astrid knew."

He sent a prayer up to the heavens for Montford's poor, beleaguered soul. "Of course she knows. She doubtless beat every single secret out of Monty on their wedding night."

Her eyes narrowed even more. "I would hope I didn't need to do the same."

Well. He'd talked himself straight into that particular quagmire.

He redirected the conversation before he could do any more damage. "Yes, Marlowe is Essex, but perhaps we should keep that to ourselves. He is very set on his anonymity."

She only looked even more disgruntled. "Of course I'm not going to tell anyone. What do you take me for?"

"My beloved wife?"

Her expression softened. "Good answer."

He sighed in relief.

"But that doesn't mean I'm not mad at you for not telling me." Damn. "Or the fact that Marlowe and Miss Jones are engaged in a clandestine love affair."

Huh. That was something *he* hadn't known.

Sebastian had to sit down after that revelation. He fumbled his way to the settee and collapsed onto the cushions.

He couldn't speak for several long seconds, but at last he managed a weak, "What?"

"Marlowe and his governess," Katherine repeated slowly. "But he did not tell you this? Apparently he seduced her but failed to inform her that he was also Christopher Essex."

He tried to wrap his head around this information and failed. "I am cast to sea, my dear," he finally said.

She rolled her eyes. "I don't know why I'm surprised."

"Why should she care if he's Christopher Essex or not?"

She looked at him as if she couldn't believe she'd married such an imbecile. "If the man I loved withheld such crucial information from me, I would have his head."

He made a note to himself never to fib to his wife.

"Besides, Miss Jones is a Misstopher," Katherine added. "Needless to say, she has not taken Marlowe's subterfuge well."

He grinned at this new piece of information. Marlowe and a *Misstopher*. It was so wonderfully fitting. And hilarious.

"Well, I suppose a broken affair does explain why Marlowe was so positively morose the other day. He always was a hopeless case when he was in love," he said.

Katherine sighed, looking a bit overwhelmed. "I'm still getting used to the idea that Marlowe is Essex. Marlowe *in love* may be more than I can bear to imagine at the moment."

Sebastian always forgot that Katherine had not known Marlowe for very long. She had not lived through the Caro Years and had only caught the tail end of its disastrous aftermath. But Sebastian had been by his friend's side through all of Marlowe's many permutations, and though he made light of it at present, he was also very worried. Caro had nearly broken the man, and Sebastian honestly didn't think Marlowe would recover from another broken heart.

This Miss Jones had better watch herself, or he'd be very cross with her for hurting his friend. Very cross indeed.

"I didn't say he was in love," he said carefully. "Just that he might be."

"Then you must pay him a call tomorrow and get to the bottom of the matter," Katherine said briskly. Well, he'd walked into that one. She had definitely been hanging about the duchess for too long to be so determined to meddle. "Astrid is sending round Montford as well."

"Of course she is," he murmured.

She was not pleased with his reluctance. "Don't you want your friend to be happy?"

"Of course I do. But I have not even met this Miss Jones to know if I should even encourage such a match."

"She is splendid," Katherine replied with certainty. "I would not pursue this if I didn't think she was worthy. Even the twins like her."

It was hard to argue with such a recommendation. As far as Sebastian could tell from their horrible habit of setting caretakers' sheds on fire, the twins didn't like anyone.

Hmmm. Perhaps the twins' approval was *not* the best way to assess the governess's virtues.

But if this love affair were indeed the root of Marlowe's melancholia, then Sebastian supposed he'd better investigate. The chance that this Miss Jones might be the one to finally give Marlowe and his daughters a proper, happy ending was too significant to ignore. Though he was rather certain Marlowe was not going to thank him for meddling.

Which was exactly what the man deserved, now that Sebastian thought about it, after meddling in *his* affairs at the Montford Ball. He'd lost a lovely pair of boots to that cake.

"I shall consider the matter," Sebastian said.

She lifted her eyebrow.

He sighed in resignation. "And visit Marlowe on the morrow. But *only* to ascertain his intentions."

She looked grudgingly satisfied with his plans, so he took the opportunity to sweep her up in his arms, plunk himself on the piano stool, and set her on his lap. He wrapped his arms around her waist and cradled her belly, burying his nose in the nape of her neck.

"Now, I do believe it is time for a duet, my lady wife," he murmured.

CHAPTER TWENTY-THREE

In Which Lady Benwick Launches A Crusade Against Excellence In British Letters

THE LADIES' LEAGUE AGAINST LEWD and Lascivious Literature and Letters was born into existence the day Lady Emily Benwick opened up her daughter Davina's commonplace book, left by mistake on the parlor settee, and found a work in progress dubiously titled "Le Cockerel d'Amour." Half expecting some sort of childish fairy tale featuring an enchanted rooster (for Davina had always been overly fond of her Perrault as a child), Lady Benwick decided to see what sort of nonsense her daughter spent her time on these days and sat down to read.

After arriving at a passage in which the heroine fell to her knees at the poet's feet and began to fumble with the falls of his breeches, breast "heaving with passionate intent," Lady Benwick slammed the book shut and took to her fainting couch while her blood cooled and her mind cleared.

So, *not* about an enchanted rooster, after all.

She may or may not have also encountered the phrase "erect member" somewhere in her perusal, but she chose to forget that particular trauma entirely.

Just to make sure she had not just suffered a fever dream, Lady Benwick glanced inside the journal when she had recovered enough to bear the review. The story, in her daughter's unmistakable hand, with all of its alarming carnality, once more assaulted her eyeballs.

Before she could come across another scarring turn of phrase, she flipped farther along in the book and found several sheets of foolscap folded between the pages. It was another sensational bit of dreck, but this one was penned by someone calling herself Lady Hedonist. Lady Benwick made the mistake of reading a full page of the tale, featuring one Mr. Essex's misadventures with a woman of extremely loose virtue in the back of a carriage. She dropped it from her fingers, scalded by the indecency contained within.

She'd not even known half those things were physically possible in a bed, much less a moving conveyance.

She didn't want to know.

And she most certainly didn't want her daughter exposed to such filthy, vile pornography. *Cockerels* were the very least of Lady Hedonist's comprehensively indecent repertoire.

After copious tears, one ruined ball gown, and the threat of a Portuguese nunnery (despite her firmly antipapist stance), Lady Benwick soon had the whole sordid business out of her daughter. Davina admitted belonging to a secret confederacy of young women who called themselves Misstophers—and who apparently spent their days trading obscenities when not swooning over the poet's verse.

It was even worse than Lady Benwick could have imagined. She'd encouraged her daughter's friendships, blithely assuming that all young ladies spent their days as they were supposed to: gossiping about fashion and the marriage mart. Yet all the while, they'd been engaged in this disgusting diversion.

It was not to be borne.

Davina wisely did not ask what her mother thought she had been doing in her room for so many hours every day. She hadn't *that* many letters to write. Nor did she admit to the stack of old commonplaces she kept hidden under the loose floorboard beneath her bed . . . nor her secret ambition to become a sensational novelist. She knew her mother well enough to know that the very idea of her daughter with so common an occupation would send her on an even worse rampage than the Misstopher smut ever could.

Davina dreamed of the day she was married to a man—any man, really, as long as he didn't beat her (her standards were quite low these days)—if only that she might escape her mother's iron fist. She also would have been quite at peace with Lady Benwick's premature death, but that was a bit of wishful thinking she didn't plan on ever sharing with anyone. If her mother got wind of it, Lady Benwick would live for another fifty years just to spite her.

Lady Benwick confiscated Davina's journal and any volume of suspect literature in the house (i.e. all of it except the Fordyce) and consigned them that very same afternoon to the fireplace. Realizing she was beaten, Davina put up a token fight, all the while scheming to secure the rest of her hidden writings from her mother's reign of terror. Though she was rather cross about losing Lady Hedonist's masterpiece (it had taken months to acquire it), sacrifices had to be made for the Misstopher Cause.

Lady Benwick would have dropped the matter entirely after the commonplace book was destroyed and Davina seemed so properly chastised. She was horrified by her daughter's behavior, of course, but she hardly wanted to make public her own failings as a mother. No daughter of *hers* was going to be exposed as a Misstopher. But then . . .

Then in one of her searches of her daughter's room, long after the commonplace journal had been destroyed but not long enough to assuage her suspicions completely, Lady Benwick came across *the book* on one of the shelves. *The book* that had launched Davina's entire fascination with Christopher Essex one fateful summer: a copy of *Le Che-*

valier d'Amour hidden in the pages of Sir Thomas More's *Utopia* she had pinched from Rylestone Hall before it had burnt to the ground.

Lady Benwick had always wondered why her daughter was so interested in More. Now she knew, as *Le Chevalier* dropped out of *Utopia* and fell on Lady Benwick's toes.

One glance at the nameplate in the front was enough to push Lady Benwick over the edge.

From the Library of A. Honeywell

She should have known Astrid was behind her daughter's disgraceful behavior. That woman corrupted everything she touched. What Astrid must have done to tempt Montford into marriage didn't even bear thinking about. *Davina* should have snagged the duke, not Lady Benwick's meddlesome, bluestocking niece. She'd never forgive Astrid for that, or that tart Alice Honeywell for eloping with her beloved son to Gretna Green.

The Honeywells had ruined her life for the last time. She would take a stand against all of the licentiousness that had infected London society since the Duchess of Montford's arrival—or die trying.

Thus Lady Benwick's crusade was launched.

She promptly paid calls on all of her acquaintance and proceeded to lament over tea the poetic scourge that held the young ladies of the ton in its thrall.

Many of Lady Benwick's acquaintance demurred when asked to join her fledging cause, however, their own copies of *Le Chevalier*—or even a covertly acquired work by Lady Hedonist herself—tucked under their own pillows awaiting an airing. But she soon found kindred spirits in the Duchess of Delacourt, who hated all poetry on principle; Lady Carlisle, who publicly endorsed any cause that ruined the fun of young ladies; and even the notoriously enfeebled Lady Blundersmith, whose own former servant had turned out to be a rabid Misstopher.

Lady Benwick had become even more committed than

ever after learning Lady Blundersmith's story, for if ladies' companions had grown so bold, then the disease was even more advanced that she'd first thought.

She feared for England.

Spurred on by such esteemed patronage, matrons across the city began intercepting their daughters' correspondence and raiding their writing desks, uncovering a vast conspiracy of Misstopher writers and readers that rivaled any secret cabal of spies Napoleon could have ever mustered against the British Crown.

But "The Alabaster Hip" was the final straw. The streets of London were in a state of upheaval not seen since the Victory Parade of 1815 the day that lewdly melodramatic abomination appeared in the *Chronicle*—hardly surprising, given that rag was as far from good, old-fashioned Tory conservatism as one could get.

After some intense soul-searching—and the discovery of the *Chronicle* in Davina's stocking drawer—Lady Benwick and the other members of the newly minted LLALLLL decided that Hyde Park would be the ideal venue for their rally. Despite some concern for the level of decorum involved (mostly voiced by perplexed spouses who had long ago resigned themselves to their wives' dominion on matters of social reform—as long as they had their clubs and mistresses to retreat to), the crusaders were undeterred in their zeal.

On the Saturday afternoon in question, daughters were rounded up, libraries and stocking drawers were ransacked, and liveried servants were mobilized to provide an endless supply of tea and finger foods to the attendees. Even Bow Street was engaged (by the aforementioned spouses, who had wisely decamped to their clubs for the duration) to keep out the common rabble, while the supporters of the LLALLLL attempted to teach all of England an Important Moral Lesson—or at least the parts of England that mattered, which didn't extend beyond the Bow Street

Runners' present perimeter. Obviously.

Lady Benwick was, of course, at the front of this vanguard, her daughter at one elbow and the very perplexed Vicar of Rylestone Green (whose summons to speak at the rally had been so waterlogged by the journey north he thought that, from the few legible words that had remained, he'd been invited to a literary salon celebrating Essex) at the other.

Concerned mothers and recalcitrant daughters milled in front of an empty wooden stage, decorated in bunting made from the finest fabrics London drapers had to offer (for there was no need to look cheap even when engaged in political activism, according to the Duchess of Delacourt). A giant mound of insupportable material—journals, broadsheets, leather-bound commonplace books, and an overwhelming abundance of the offending issue of the *Morning Chronicle*—continued to expand in front of the stage as Misstophers, poor, unwilling worshippers upon the altar of the LLALLLL, were forced to give over their collections.

Though she'd managed to secrete away most of her own cache despite her mother's purge, Davina Benwick looked suitably cowed for appearance's sake as she threw a copy of *The Italian Poem* on the heap. It wasn't her favorite work, but it was still a reluctant sacrifice. She, along with the rest of the young ladies in attendance, hoped for a miracle to stop the LLALLLL's machinations, but it seemed unlikely to come, as Lady Benwick had already directed a servant to douse the pile of books and papers in whale oil (for what better way to destroy something than to burn it?).

But then the Duchess of Montford's carriage pulled up, along with a steady stream of uninvited latecomers. Lady Benwick could feel her blood pressure start to rise. Lady Blundersmith waddled up to her side, fluttering her fan as if it were boiling outside and not a chilly spring day. She looked much too self-satisfied for Lady Benwick's peace of mind.

"What have you done, Belinda?" Lady Benwick demanded.

"Did I not tell you?" Lady Blundersmith crowed. "I visited Montford House just yesterday, and the duchess pledged her support. I told you she would come if we just asked, Emily. It's a coup to have her influence for our cause."

Lady Benwick thought it was a coup, all right, and that Lady Blundersmith was an old fool to have ever approached the duchess. She knew her niece all too well, and the ducal carriage was not a welcome sight. When she spied the bobbing tower of Madame la Duchesse de St. Aignan's wig inside another approaching conveyance, she groaned inwardly and hurried along the servant with the oil before any of the new arrivals could even think about interfering.

No one was going to stop her book burning—certainly not a Honeywell.

CHAPTER TWENTY-FOUR

The Bonfire Of The Misstophers

WHEN MINERVA AGREED TO AID the duchess in her protest against the LLALLLL, she had not counted upon the placards. But the duchess had insisted—had even made Minerva stay up well past midnight to help paint them. And though she entirely agreed with the need to take a stand against censorship, she felt ridiculous as she tromped through the lawn with her sign. The duchess and Lady Elizabeth, however, were proudly brandishing their own placards, as if they were the latest fashionable accoutrements.

Perhaps if her placard read anything other than "Misstophers Unite," she would have felt much better about the whole situation. But somehow she'd been stuck with the blasted thing when Lady Elizabeth had accidentally taken up Minerva's much more morally instructive (and much less mortifying) "Censorship Is Tyranny" for her own. She would have even preferred the duchess's "Boycott Benwick," but she had a feeling that Her Grace was particularly settled upon her choice of signage.

But then Minerva saw the pyre of books and broadsheets towering in the middle of the lawn, and suddenly the placard didn't seem like such an insane idea after all. She raised hers up a little higher. She'd be a Misstopher, damn it, if that was what it took to counter the LLALLLL's tyranny.

"Surely they cannot mean to burn that," Lady Elizabeth breathed, gasping as a servant doused the gigantic pyre in oil.

"I believe that is exactly what they intend," the duchess muttered, her cheeks flushing with fury. "The utter gall."

Minerva could not agree more, though she was beginning to be rather concerned for Hyde Park. The sheer amount of literature in that pile was rather alarming. She wouldn't be surprised if the LLALLLL ended up burning the entire park down.

"I was n-n-n-not aware l-l-l-literary salons took p-p-place in Hyde P-P-P-Park," stuttered a man's voice behind them. "And, oh d-d-d-dear, what are you d-d-d-doing with all of those b-b-b-books, Lady B-B-B-Benwick?"

Minerva turned with her companions to observe a slight, balding man with a clerical collar holding a clutch of books to his breast. He was flanked on one side by a formidably sized matron in black bombazine, an austere onyx necklace, and a scowl, and a younger woman in a chartreuse gown festooned with a thousand miniature bows, who looked as if she'd rather be anywhere else.

The man just looked perplexed.

When the trio spotted them, the women looked even more constipated. The man gaped like a fish and began to fumble his stack of books.

"Aunt Emily! Cousin Davina!" Astrid declared brightly—too brightly. "And Vicar! How lovely to see you in London on such a gorgeous day."

It was cold, windy, and overcast.

The women exchanged insincere curtsies all around, and the nearly undetectable bob of the duchess's head skirted the bounds of politesse. Minerva, who had become well acquainted with relatives who loathed each other these past few weeks, wondered if she should seek shelter behind her placard for the war to come.

"Duchess," Aunt Emily said, looking as if she'd rather be run through than be forced to acknowledge Astrid's title, "I didn't take you for a supporter of moral decency."

Well, then. The gauntlet seemed well and truly thrown.

Astrid's broad smile took on a reptilian edge, and she twisted her placard until the message faced her aunt. Minerva had already learned what to do when she spotted that look on the duchess: step away, brace for impact, and above all else, enjoy the show. Minerva hoped Lady Benwick knew what she was getting into.

"You know how fond I am of fire, Aunt, considering the fate of my former home," the duchess said. "I fully intend to be entertained this afternoon. I daresay the world has not seen a decent book burning since Voltaire's time."

"B-b-b, b-b-b, b-b-book b-b-b-burning!" the vicar cried, eyeing the burgeoning pyre with trepidation, as if just realizing what it was. He hugged his pile of books even closer to his breast and began to tremble. "I thought we w-w-were v-v-vi . . . v-visi . . . v-v-v- . . . *attending* a l-l-literary salon!"

Aunt Emily patted the vicar's hand. "Do not concern yourself, Mr. Fawkes. We are only burning the wicked ones. Surely *your* collection is safe."

The vicar paled, obviously realizing just how far from a literary salon he was. "W-w-w-what w-w-w-wicked b-b-b-books?"

"Well, that horrid Wollstonecraft woman for one, and Lord Byron. And Essex, of course. That man has led far too many sensible girls to perdition with his overwrought sentiment." Lady Benwick cast her daughter a withering stare. Davina's face turned the same shade as her dress, and she looked everywhere but at her mother.

The vicar's already pale face lost all the rest of its color, and he tightened his hold on his books until his knuckles were white, taking a surreptitious step away from Lady Benwick.

"E-E-Essex, L-L-Lady B-B-Benwick? Are you qu-qu-quite sure . . . that is . . . h-h-his w-w-words, and h-h-his . . . p-p-p-passion . . ." Lady Benwick raised an eyebrow, and he immediately abandoned with a whimper wherever that thought was heading. "I-I-I really w-w-was expecting to . . ."

"Have a nice chin wag about 'The Alabaster Hip'?" Astrid interrupted brightly, her eyes locked with her aunt's. They were both smiling, but the daggers in their eyes could have pierced the tough hide of a boar. "Wasn't it divinely romantic, Mr. Fawkes? I think it Essex's best short work since the sonnets."

The vicar glanced from the duchess to Lady Benwick and back again, looking about five seconds away from casting up his accounts all over his book collection. Minerva didn't blame him. She would rather eat her bonnet than be stuck between that particular rock and hard place.

The vicar cleared his throat and sidled toward the duchess in increments. It seemed to be as courageous a stand as the vicar was likely to make.

"And should you and your library find yourself at loose ends in the city, Vicar, please call upon Montford and me," the duchess continued. "*We* have no need to burn books. Our supply of coal . . . and our library . . . is quite limitless."

The vicar's taut shoulders seemed to unspool a little at that, and he edged even closer to the duchess.

Lady Benwick narrowed her eyes at the duchess, then at the vicar's stack of books, and harrumphed when he attempted to cover the titles on the spine with his sleeve.

"Surely you cannot endorse such scandalous, morally corrupt verse, Vicar," Lady Benwick declared. "I have invited you here particularly to *speak out* against such sin."

The vicar's shoulders tensed again, his expression growing hunted. "I-I-I thought I w-w-was to d-d-d-deliver a sp-sp-speech on the religious imagery in *Le Chevalier d'Amour.*"

"Yes," Lady Benwick said, looking at the vicar as if he were dim-witted. "On such imagery being unwholesome and wicked."

"B-b-b-but I-I-I qu-quite liked it," the vicar said.

Both of Lady Benwick's eyebrows shot up at that.

"Pfft, of course you did, my boy," Madame la Duchesse de St. Aignan, the duchess's other aunt, said, toddling up behind the vicar and looking even more . . . spectacular than she had during the lady's brief visit to Montford House this morning. She wore a brocade gown that looked as if it had last had an airing at Louis XVI's doomed court, with crinolines nearly as wide as she was tall and so many jewels sewn into the bust that it sagged on her shriveled bosom to an alarming degree. On her face was an equally alarming amount of maquillage that rivaled even Oxley's, and on her head perched a towering reddish-brown wig with pin curls piled the height of a French croquembouche.

For a moment Minerva thought the mass of matching russet curls in Madame la Duchesse's arms was part of her wig, perhaps some sort of elaborate train, but then it moved, and from the cacophony of curls popped a pair of eyes, floppy ears, and a snout that looked as flat as an airless accordion.

Madame la Duchesse playfully thwacked the vicar across the back of the knees with her cane, despite the dog in her arms. The vicar yelped and nearly spilled his books on the damp ground. "I myself liked the naughty bits. I swear that Essex fellow has a predilection for dewy flesh and a well-turned hip unmatched by anyone but my sweet Billy," she said. She swayed a bit leeward as a large gust of wind hit her.

Minerva coughed at this.

"Aunt Anabel," the duchess greeted with a wide grin, pulling the woman upright once more, "we've been looking everywhere for you."

Aunt Anabel gave Hyde Park at large a dismissive sniff. "Hard to find anything of note in this crowd of philistines. It is Voltaire all over again."

"That's what *I* said," Astrid declared.

Aunt Anabel's rheumy eyes finally landed on Lady Benwick, and she didn't bother to disguise her snort of disgust. "Emily," she said grudgingly, "I should have known you'd be among this godforsaken rabble."

"Madame la Duchesse," Lady Benwick choked out, having even more trouble with this greeting than she'd had with Astrid's (for the day Anabel Honeywell had married a French duc had been a grim one indeed in the Benwick household). "I should have known you'd be here encouraging Astrid in her folly."

"And who is this beauty, then?" Lady Elizabeth said with delight, scratching Aunt Anabel's dog behind its ears, completely ignoring Lady Benwick.

"Ain't she a pretty thing?" Aunt Anabel agreed. Somehow she managed to cover both of the mongrel's ears with her hands despite the cane. She only wobbled slightly without the support. "She's illegitimate," she said in a stage whisper. "Her sire were a three-legged Irish setter. We don't talk about it around her, or my own dear, sensitive Billy. It gives the poor duc the vapors."

In that moment, Minerva came to the realization that Madame la Duchesse was completely, barking mad.

She suspected all Honeywells were.

"I think it reminds him too much of when Lord Cavan came to Versailles," Madame la Duchesse mused. "Poor Billy went out of his head with jealousy, which I can hardly blame him. That fellow were a strapping specimen, and when I had him down to his altogether . . ."

"Aunt Anabel, I believe Betsy wanted to know your lovely friend's name," the duchess interrupted in a very timely manner.

Aunt Anabel looked at her niece as if she were an imbecile. "I told you. Lord Cavan. Irish Earl from Cork or Kerry or some such. And he *was* lovely all over. Especially his coc—"

"The dog, Aunt!" Astrid inserted loudly, valiantly restraining herself from bursting into laughter at the piqued look on Lady Benwick's face.

"Oh! Why didn't you say so, gel?" Aunt Anabel demanded rather crossly of Lady Elizabeth.

Minerva thought Lady Elizabeth had.

"It's Mademoiselle Clare in honor of her *mixed nationality*." Aunt Anabel whispered the last two words and covered the dog's ears once more.

The dog sneezed through her puggish nose, causing Madame la Duchesse to startle so violently she dropped the poor beast and pitched sideways into her niece.

Mademoiselle landed with a smooth grace, obviously used to her owner's feebleness, shook out her russet curls, and padded over to the unlit pyre in the middle of the lawn. She pulled out a copy of the *Morning Chronicle* and began to tear it to shreds with her vicious little teeth.

Aunt Anabel tugged on the leather lead attached to Mademoiselle's collar, both of which seemed to be encrusted with enough jewels to feed the poor of London for at least a decade. "Naughty creature! Do not molest the *Chronicle*! I will not have a Tory troglodyte for a pet!" she scolded.

Mademoiselle padded back, sat on her haunches, and began gnawing on Aunt Anabel's cane instead.

"I should give you to Emily," Aunt Anabel cooed down at her pet. "You two can eat all the Essex you want together."

Lady Benwick sniffed, and as if on cue, Mademoiselle abandoned her cane and bounded to her paws at the haughty sound. Her body stiffening and the curly russet hair on her back rising like a cat's, she began to growl in Lady Benwick's general direction.

The woman eyed the dog balefully, then narrowed her

eyes at the duchess and her placard.

"You are not welcome here today, Astrid."

Astrid produced Lady Blundersmith's invitation and waved it in front of her aunt. "Oh, but I was specifically invited. And I took it upon myself to invite a few others. I do hope that is acceptable," she said, gesturing to the rapidly growing crowd of ladies with placards behind her.

"It is *not* acceptable, and if you cause any trouble today . . ." Lady Benwick began.

Mademoiselle's growls turned to outright barks when Aunt Emily took one step closer to the duchess.

"Trouble? *Moi?*" the duchess cried, sounding shocked by the accusation. "I wouldn't dare."

"*I* would," Aunt Anabel muttered.

"So would I," Lady Elizabeth said, and Madame la Duchesse looked at the young woman approvingly.

"Besides, you are the one causing trouble, Aunt Emily. Surely you're not truly considering lighting that pile ablaze," the duchess continued.

"Of course I am."

"But that's absolute madness!" the duchess cried.

"It is *not*. Someone must take a stand against such inflammatory literature, lest our whole society is corrupted."

"By *poetry?*"

"'To forbid us anything is to make us have a mind for it,'" Madame la Duchesse pronounced crisply.

"That was actually very well put, Aunt Anabel," the duchess said approvingly.

"It had better be. That were Montaigne," she muttered. "Not that Emily even knows who that is."

"If he's French," Lady Benwick sneered, "then I am sure I don't want to know. Now if you'll excuse me, I have a meeting to call to order." Then she snapped her fingers, and the servant who had just doused the pile of literature in oil dropped a lit taper before anyone could stop him. The pyre immediately ignited with a whoosh and crackle, nearly taking off the poor man's eyebrows.

Minerva, along with the duchess and her followers, cried out in dismay at the carnage. The rate at which the books and assorted papers went up in flames was alarming, and soon the bonfire raged at least twenty feet in the air. Several of the more excitable ladies of the LLALLLL (including Lady Blundersmith, of course) gasped and reached for their salts, and everyone widened the perimeter around the inferno.

The Misstophers began to wail.

CHAPTER TWENTY-FIVE

In Which The Duke And The Marquess Stage An Intervention

SINCE LAURA HAD RUN AWAY, forcing them to confront the cracks in their relationship, things had been easier between Marlowe and his daughters. The loss of their favorite governess had shaken them all, but they weren't broken. Only this morning, a frog in the cook's soup pot had created quite the stir, and Marlowe accepted it as the peace offering he knew it to be. Had his daughters stopped their mischief altogether, he would have been more worried.

He was less sure that his staff would recover, however. Pymm had nearly broken down in tears again that morning at the sight of Marlowe donning the red silk banyan—the only survivor of the massacre. He'd have to brave the tailor's soon before his valet died of melancholia, but there was only so much torture he could bear in one week. He was putting off the visit for as long as he dared.

Mrs. Chips was also making her displeasure with him known. He'd had lukewarm tea ever since Minerva had left, pea soup and stale bread at every luncheon, and a horrifying quantity of mutton at the dinner table. He was too afraid to say anything, however. Chippers had even taken to scowling at him, and this was such an unprecedented display of emotion that he'd adopted a policy of avoidance and nonconfrontation when it came to his housekeeper, lest she snap and abscond to Cornwall for good.

He hadn't even thought Chippers *liked* Minerva.

Marlowe knew he should have told Minerva long ago he was Christopher Essex, but by the time he'd realized he wanted something more between them, he'd been too frightened of her response—justifiably so, seeing as how she'd popped off to Montford's in a pique the moment she'd discovered his secret.

Besides, her infatuation with Essex, while not as horrifying as a commonplacer's (he still shuddered at the mere thought of Lady Hedonist and *the wand*), had made him uncomfortable. How could he ever live up to her expectations? He was, in reality, just a man—a deeply flawed man. He'd written his last poem about his governess's hip, for God's sake. That was hardly the mark of the romantic man of letters Minerva had cast in Essex's role.

He didn't know if Minerva would ever forgive him, or even if she should. Even discounting the whole Essex debacle, he was a bad bet all around, and she knew this too well.

But he'd not given up.

After their last acrimonious encounter at Montford's and all of the palaver with his girls, however, he'd thought it best to regroup and let her anger cool. In the meantime, he had vowed to write her a sonnet so incredibly moving and passionate that she'd fall into his arms, all of his sins forgiven.

He thought the plan was a sound one in theory. She liked Essex—she liked Essex perhaps more than she'd ever liked the viscount. *But* . . .

One night and half a day since he'd begun, he'd not produced a word.

And that was how Sebastian found him, slumped over his library desk, staring at a blank page.

He should have smelled the ambush the moment Montford—dressed in an uncharacteristically shiny silver cutaway, no doubt influenced by Sebastian's dubious sartorial advice—stepped into the library on Sebastian's heels. But he was distracted by the cask of Honeywell Reserve Sebastian's bulldog valet, Crick, was setting upon the sideboard.

He definitely should have cried foul when Montford, who'd sworn off Honeywell Ale for reasons he refused to explain (though Marlowe had inveigled most of the tale of Rylestone Green's Annual Foot and Ale Race of 1817 out of Newcomb years ago), began matching Sebastian's rather advanced pace. But two pints in—all that Marlowe would allow himself these days, despite the reserve being the nectar of the gods—and the loose, relaxed banter among the three of them had lulled him into a false sense of complacency.

"So, Marlowe," Sebastian began in his most disingenuous tone that always foretold trouble, "what the devil is going on with your governess?"

Marlowe choked on his mouthful of ale. He really should have seen this coming.

"I have no idea what you're talking about."

His friends' twin glares made it clear that he would not be getting off so easily.

"Oh, no," Sebastian said. "After the massive bolloxing you gave me when I was courting Katherine, there is no way I am going to pass up the opportunity to return the favor."

"My staff is still cleaning the cake from the ballroom ceiling, by the way," Montford said dryly.

Marlowe snorted. "Playing Katherine's swain was your dear wife's idea, Monty. I were only doing what I was told."

Sebastian's head turned sharply toward the duke, eyes wide with shock. "Astrid's idea? I should have known."

Marlowe rolled his eyes. How had Sebastian *not* figured

out that one? "You really should have, Sherry. Just like it was her idea, and the marchioness's, I'm sure, that you ambush me today."

Neither man was able to meet his eyes or deny the claim. The sheepish look on their faces would have been hilarious had Marlowe not been so annoyed at them.

"Look here, old thing," Sebastian finally said after polishing off his third pint, "you saved me from losing Katie, so forgive me for wanting to return the favor. If you are as enamored of Miss Jones as I am of my wife, then I cannot, in good conscience, allow you to withdraw from the field without even a fight."

Marlowe wasn't, but the last thing he needed was his friends' well-intentioned interference. It would be the cake fight all over again.

"She wants nothing to do with me," he muttered, "and for good reason. I lied to her about so many things she can never forgive me."

Both of his friends looked shocked that he'd not even tried to deny his infatuation. But what use was in denying it, when it was true?

Montford cleared his throat, awkward as ever. "I'm not entirely sure that is true. Astrid says the woman talks of nothing else but you. Well, ranting might be a more appropriate word for it."

"See?" cried Sebastian. "She wouldn't be so passionately vocal about it if she didn't still care."

"Yes, well, you've not heard the whole story," Marlowe muttered, and then he proceeded to tell them, if only to demonstrate how futile their mission was.

When he was done with his tale, Sebastian and the duke both downed another pint of reserve with desperate enthusiasm.

"Only you," drawled the duke, after emitting a very unducal belch, "would find yourself in such a ludicrous, tangled mire."

"Thank you both for your concern," he growled. "Now, if you'll leave me to my misery."

Sebastian and Montford exchanged glances and seemed to come to some sort of conclusion. It seemed to be, shockingly, in favor of following Marlowe's request . . . though it seemed the duke's and the marquess's consumption of Honeywell Reserve may have been a little too heavy-handed to allow them to follow through with their decision, as Marlowe soon discovered.

"Well, at least I can tell Katie we tried," Sebastian said on a hiccough. He rose to his feet but wobbled so badly he had to sit down again.

"I suppose I should see what Astrid's getting up to," the duke said with a resigned sigh. He too tried to rise to his feet but failed. "She's been on the warpath. Apparently some rather dreadful ladies' association is protesting today in Hyde Park, and my wife is determined to protest the protesters."

"The Ladies' League Against Lewd and Lascivious Literature and Letters," Sebastian drawled. "Or is it Letters and Literature? Unfortunately—or fortunately, I'm not sure which—my own wife is too under the weather today to accompany the duchess. But your sister and Miss Jones, I hear, are attending with the duchess."

Marlowe had wondered why Betsy had been so eager to visit the duchess today. "She's not my Miss Jones," he muttered. "What the devil are they protesting, then?"

"The Ladies' League is protesting you, old boy," Sebastian said. "Essex, Byron, de Quincy, Wollstonecraft, the Shelleys—any halfway decent bit of literature, as far as I can tell. The duchess and Miss Jones are having none of it, though."

"They made *signs*," Montford said mournfully, having Crick refill his glass in lieu of departing.

Marlowe brightened a bit at this information. The fact that Minerva was throwing her lot in with the duchess gave him hope. Surely if she didn't plan on forgiving him this century, she would not be so willing to support Essex so publicly.

"One more for the road," Sebastian said, signaling for Crick, "and then I really must be off."

Montford toasted vaguely in Sebastian's direction at such a clever idea, and Marlowe rolled his eyes. He should have known it wouldn't be so easy to get rid of them.

But before the duke and the marquess could start their last pint, Mrs. Chips appeared at the door and announced a very unexpected visitor . . . after flinging a quick glare in her employer's direction, as she'd done every day since Minerva's departure.

Dr. Lucas, of all people, swept into the room, looking unsurprised to find Montford and Sebastian in attendance. Marlowe was too exhausted—and a bit squiffy from his two pints—to even object to the man's intrusion, though he did send a token scowl the man's way. It seemed to have little effect, however, as the Doctor didn't so much as cringe.

"Whiskers!" Sebastian cried, swaying in his seat, waving his fourth pint at the man. Montford cleared his throat loudly in admonition, and Sebastian grimaced. "That is, er, Dr. Lucas," he amended.

Doctor Lucas ignored the marquess entirely, as he usually did, and after a brief nod at Marlowe, turned to the duke. "I have been summoned to Hyde Park," he said. "There is some concern that the ladies gathered may soon be in need of medical assistance, and I thought you might want to know."

Montford gusted out a sigh. "If my wife has started a riot . . ."

"I think it is the enormous fire the Ladies' League has lit in the middle of the park, rather than the duchess, that is a cause for concern," the doctor said.

Oh, good God.

"A fire! For what purpose?" the duke cried, wobbling to his feet and nearly spilling the rest of his ale. The man really could not hold his liquor. No wonder he'd always been so abstemious.

"Apparently they've decided to burn books," the doctor said, accepting a pint of ale from Crick. After a suspicious sniff, he took a small sip. Obviously deciding it was worthy of his palate, he polished off the pint in one long draught. Marlowe was rather impressed at the display. And hated the man just a little less for his obvious good taste. "This is excellent, by the way," the doctor added.

Sebastian shot up from his seat, incensed and only staggering a little. "They're burning *your* books, Marlowe!" he cried.

"Surely not," he bit out. Such an act of censorship was inconceivable.

"*Your* books?" Dr. Lucas asked, turning to Marlowe with a puzzled look.

Marlowe sent Sebastian a withering glance for his drunken outburst. But he could see no purpose in not telling the sawbones the truth, considering that everyone—and their dogs—seemed to know his secret these days. What good had it done him to remain anonymous anyway?

"I am Christopher Essex," he gritted out.

Dr. Lucas remained silent for a long, long moment, then held out his glass for Crick to refill. "I believe I shall have another drink."

When the doctor had made it halfway through his second pint, he seemed recovered from his shock enough to speak. "No wonder Minerva is so angry at you. She found out who you were, didn't she?"

"Got it in one," Marlowe muttered into the bottom of his glass.

"Well, I'm sure she'll come around," the doctor said brusquely. "Minerva's temper always burns hot and quick, but she is a very forgiving sort in the end."

Marlowe gave Dr. Lucas an astonished look. "What? Why are you . . . But I thought . . . surely you want Minerva for yourself!" he cried.

Dr. Lucas smiled wryly at him. "We are friends. That is all. I thought perhaps we might wed, when it seemed as if neither of us would ever find a more suitable match, but it is out of the question now."

"You think *I* am a more suitable match?" he spluttered.

Dr. Lucas fixed him with a scathing look. "I admit to having extreme doubts. But as much as you pretend otherwise, I know you are a decent enough fellow. And now that I know you are Christopher Essex . . . well, it explains many things. Besides, how could I ever compete with the poet himself for a Misstopher's affections?"

"That little minx . . ." Marlowe muttered, feeling a mixture of fury and relief at the doctor's revelations. "She had me convinced she would marry you just to spite me."

"Ah, so she's *not* yet reached the forgiving stage," Dr. Lucas said sagely.

"It will take a bloody miracle," Marlowe said.

"Or," Sebastian pronounced dramatically, with the look of someone who'd just had a brilliant idea, "a Grand Gesture."

"The ale has pickled your wits," Marlowe said. He didn't even want to know what Sebastian might mean.

"I agree with Sebastian," the duke said. Then for some unfathomable reason, he staggered to his feet and began to unbutton his cutaway jacket.

"What are you doing?" Marlowe cried.

The duke wobbled dangerously as he tried to strip off the sleeves, and Crick finally interceded to help.

"You can't very well make a Grand Gesture in a banyan," Montford said, sounding a bit slurred around his vowels. He thanked Crick as he took his jacket in hand and held it out to Marlowe. "And since you lost the rest of your wardrobe, I propose a trade."

"You are drunk," Marlowe declared.

"Maybe a little," Montford admitted, swaying on his feet.

"Maybe a lot, but I agree with Monty," Sebastian said, which of course he did. He was even more bosky than the duke. Grand Gestures indeed. "If you go to the park in your dressing gown to rescue the fair maiden, it will not go over well."

"Rescue the . . . ? Good God, what do you think they're doing in the park that anyone needs rescuing?" he cried.

"Apparently trying to burn it down," Dr. Lucas said into his pint.

"Not sure if I'll be looking any more presentable in the jacket," Marlowe muttered.

"I shall pretend I didn't hear that," Sebastian said haughtily. "I helped Monty select the fabric myself.

"Shocking."

Sebastian glared. "It's Italian silk."

"Just wear the blasted thing," Montford grumbled, looking ready to fight Marlowe if he didn't agree.

Marlowe, who knew very well what the duke's fists felt like, especially when applied to his molars, began to reluctantly shrug his way out of his banyan and into the silk abomination.

FIFTEEN MINUTES LATER, Marlowe gazed in utter dismay from Montford's open-air barouche as thirty-foot flames shot into the air down near the banks of the Serpentine, a crowd of rather belligerent-looking noblewomen gathered around the inferno arguing with each other.

Montford, whose notoriously weak constitution had been addled by the combination of the ale and the movement of his carriage, leaned against one wheel and wiped the bile from his mouth after emptying his stomach in the grass. "Seems Lucas is right about burning your writing," he said. "I can see the *Chronicle* from here."

"If ever there was the occasion for a Grand Gesture, I would think this qualifies," Sebastian pronounced, stepping out of the carriage and sipping from the pint he'd brought along for the ride, giving Montford a wide berth in case the man were sick all over him.

Dr. Lucas sighed heavily as he studied the scene before him. "I think I just spotted Lady Blundersmith fainting upon somebody. I suppose I'd better do my duty," he said without enthusiasm, polishing off the rest of his ale.

The doctor eyed the duke, perhaps hoping Montford might save him from his fate by being violently ill again, but the duke waved him on his way. The doctor's shoulders slumped.

The three of them watched in grave silence as the doctor march to his fate.

"Better him than me," Sebastian declared pityingly.

"I don't think I can do this," Marlowe murmured, turning to climb back into the barouche. Montford caught him by the collar and hauled him toward the bonfire.

"Buck up, man," the duke growled. "And after this is all over, I'll accompany you myself to the archbishop for a special license. We'll have you married before Monday."

"What?" Marlowe cried, turning to the duke, who'd obviously cast up all his brains along with the ale. "Special license? What are you even talking about?"

The duke glared at him, though his usual pompous authority was rather diminished by the red banyan and flushed cheeks. "I'm talking about you fixing this mess you've made once and for all, instead of all of this blasted brooding. Now go down there and win back your woman, for God's sake, Marlowe."

"Unless you *don't* want to wed Miss Jones," Sebastian murmured, staggering after them and looking far too amused with the proceedings for Marlowe's taste. "In which case, I don't know why we're even here."

"Of course I want to marry her. I am just not sure this is the best time to . . ."

"Nonsense, it is the perfect time," Montford said, shoving him onward.

"But look at all of them down there!" he protested. "It's like Corunna all over again."

"Grand Gestures deserve a grand audience," Sebastian declared, flinging his arms wide and spilling half his drink onto the lawn.

"Does that stage look like a gallows to you?" Marlowe asked. "Because it certainly looks like one to me. If this grand audience is burning my poetry, then they'd probably like nothing better than to string me up!"

Sebastian rounded on Marlowe with a growl of frustration, his amusement gone, and handed his drink off to Crick, who'd appeared out of nowhere. He placed his hands on Marlowe's shoulders and stared at him seriously. "Marlowe, I think it's about time someone told you the truth."

"What are you going on about?"

"Are you listening?" Sebastian demanded, leaning in close to him with such earnest entreaty that Marlowe started to feel even more apprehensive than he had staring down at the hoi polloi.

"Yes, I'm listening. How could I not be with you breathing all over me?" he snapped.

"Marlowe," Sebastian said, and paused dramatically, "you're a poet."

Good God, he was, wasn't he? He was a poet. He'd never let himself believe it, not really.

"I'm a bloody poet," he breathed.

"A damn good bloody poet," Sebastian confirmed. "And they're *burning your books.*"

The word he used in response to this was four-lettered and not likely to ever make it into any of his poems. "They are, aren't they?"

"Are you going to let this stand?"

"No, no, I'm not."

"And are you going to let Miss Jones get away without even trying?"

"No!" he cried. Though Marlowe rather doubted Minerva would appreciate a Grand Gesture of any kind. But then again, she *was* down there somewhere, standing unafraid against those who would denigrate his work. That was a gesture of a sort—one that made him hope as he'd not hoped in days.

The least he could do was show the same courage.

The last time he'd risked his heart, he'd had it shattered nearly beyond repair. It had taken years to piece it back together into some sort of working order, so risking it again was an absolutely terrifying prospect. He'd not thought he'd be able to survive another heartbreak. But after all he'd endured in the past week—losing Minerva, nearly losing Laura—he'd not fallen apart as he might have done even six months ago. He'd grown stronger and wiser these past few years without even realizing it. If he couldn't repair things with Minerva, he would be devastated, but he wouldn't break. He would not throw himself to his demons once more.

But if he had a chance to win Minerva back, he had to take it. And now seemed as good a time as any. He'd beg for another chance with her, and at the same time, he'd own up to who he was, as he should have done long ago. He'd thought he'd cast off his fears, but perhaps he'd merely suppressed them—pushed them deep down into the shadows, where they were lurking, unseen but toxic. What other honest explanation of his stubborn reluctance to claim Christopher Essex's works as his own?

He'd let fear control him for too long—and it had lost him the best thing that had ever happened to him.

Well, he'd be a coward no longer. He'd keep no secrets from the world or Minerva, and if he ended up making a cake of himself, well . . .

There was nothing new in that.

☾

HOURS LATER, MARLOWE awoke with a splitting headache, his hands bound to a chair, and absolutely no idea where he was. He should have known better than to take advice from his friends when they were all foxed on Honeywell Ale.

CHAPTER TWENTY-SIX

In Which The Viscount Makes A Grand Gesture

LADY BENWICK WORE SUCH A smug look as she ascended the stage that Minerva wished she could knock it off her face with her fist. She'd become worryingly bloodthirsty after living with Leightons for so long.

"Thank you to the ladies of the Ladies' League Against Lewd and Lascivious Literature and Letters for coming today in support of this worthy cause," Lady Benwick began.

There was a smattering of applause among the league's members, and a ripple of derisive snorts among the duchess's followers. Lady Benwick stubbornly ignored *that* side of the fire.

"Although it seems *many* here today have come to undermine the proceedings. The league seeks to save our daughters and our nation from the vulgar clutches of our modern poets and philosophers—and if some ladies present cannot see the clear danger in consuming such immoral rubbish, I suggest you are in the wrong place," she concluded huffily as the dissent from the duchess's ranks grew in decibels.

"The only danger I see, Emily, is your little temper tantrum burning down Hyde Park!" Madame la Duchesse boomed. She had a surprisingly loud voice for someone who looked as if her body were being held up entirely by stiff crinolines and sheer bullheadedness.

Lady Benwick's face grew an alarming shade of red as her composure began to fracture. "You're one to talk, Anabel," the woman hissed, as if the entire crowd couldn't very well hear her. "Since you burned down a castle last I saw you!"

"She has a point, Auntie," Astrid said to Madame la Duchesse. "Though I am worried less about Hyde Park and more about those poor books. Only tyrants and zealots burn books, Aunt Emily," she called out to the stage. "Have you even read any of the works you are immolating?"

"I don't need to read them to know they are a bad influence," Lady Benwick declared huffily. "Especially that horrid Christopher Essex—whom you foisted upon my poor, innocent Davina."

The duchess looked completely bewildered by the accusation. Lady Benwick indicated the gaggle of Misstophers penned in by their mothers, gazing longingly toward Astrid's side of the fire. Davina, who was attempting to hide among them despite her garish gown, flushed and looked everywhere but at her mother and cousin.

"You have turned her into a sensational novelist!" Lady Benwick finished with the same weight she might have used to accuse her daughter of murder.

"God forbid," Minerva muttered.

"Now if you would be so good as to let me continue," Lady Benwick said haughtily.

Astrid nodded regally. "I shouldn't dream of interrupting you again, Aunt. I haven't been so diverted in years."

Lady Benwick gave her niece a suspicious look before attempting to repair the dignity she'd lost during her argument. She turned back to her followers with a huff.

"Today we have gathered to take a stand against indecency in modern letters and to rescue our daughters from their own ignorant adulation. Where better to consign the immoral, inflammatory works of libertine thinkers than to the flames?" she intoned, gesturing toward the burning pyre in an obviously rehearsed manner.

A few of the LLALLLL clapped politely. Most of them gazed at the pyre in alarm and took a few steps back. The flames were getting even higher.

"To bolster our righteous mission, I have invited the Reverend Mr. Fawkes, Vicar of Rylestone Green, to say a few words today," Lady Benwick continued doggedly. "He graciously agreed to travel all the way from Yorkshire to support our cause. Vicar?"

Mr. Fawkes, drifting uneasily in a no-man's-land between the LLALLLL and the duchess's ladies, blanched at the summoning and the smattering of half-hearted applause that followed. The poor man looked torn between mounting the stage and fleeing the city, but Lady Benwick's gaze, which had turned threatening when she saw the vicar's hesitation, finally spurred the man from his paralysis. He climbed the steps of the platform with the reluctance of a French noble heading for the guillotine.

When Lady Benwick moved to relieve him of his clutch of books, however, he clung to them, white-knuckled, until she was forced to give up with ill-concealed consternation. She stepped to the rear of the stage, looking nonplussed by the vicar's truculence.

The last of the applause dwindled, and the vicar cleared his throat several times, gazing uneasily from one side of the fire to the other. He tucked his books under one arm and tugged at his clerical collar as if it were choking him.

"I . . . I m-m-m-must a-admit, m-m-m-my understanding of this . . . er . . . g-g-g-gathering . . . that is to say . . . the, er, sp-sp-speech I had p-p-p-prep-p-p-pared is p-p-p-p-perhaps n-n-n-not exactly what the L-L-L-Ladies' L-L-L-League A-A-A-Against . . . er L-L-L-Lewd a-a-a-and L-L-La, L-L-L . . . that is, the L-L-L-Ladies'

L-L-L-League h-h-h-had in m-m-m-mind."

He looked toward the duchess imploringly. "So we are sure this is n-n-n-not a l-l-l-l-l-l-literary salon, then?" he finally asked a bit desperately. "B-b-b-because I h-h-h-had a rather l-l-l-lovely sp-sp-speech p-p-p-p-prepared on the subject of Christopher Essex . . ."

Lady Benwick cleared her throat pointedly.

He glanced sidelong at her and renewed his grip on his books, paling even further at her expression. "B-b-b-but as you, L-L-L-Lady B-B-B-Benwick, are such a r-r-r-rich m-m-member—er, I-I-I-I m-m-m-mean, a *r-r-r-richly v-v-v-valued* m-m-member of m-m-my congregation, I shall endeavor to r-r-r-revise m-m-my sp-sp-speech accordingly."

Lady Benwick looked somewhat mollified until the silence following the declaration began to draw itself out. The crowd on both sides of the bonfire began to fidget with impatience as the vicar struggled to formulate his next words—even more so than usual.

Lady Benwick stared at the back of the vicar's head as if he'd grown horns.

The vicar looked even more disheartened as the minutes passed and the words wouldn't come. Finally, he managed, rather half-heartedly: "Well, if it's cr-cr-criticism you are w-w-w-wanting, then, I-I-I-I have to say I didn't r-r-really care for *The I-I-Italian P-P-P-Poem*. I-I-It is b-b-by far Essex's l-l-least successful work in m-m-my estimation. N-n-n-not that it w-w-w-wasn't b-b-better than m-m-most," he hastened on, "b-b-b-but I-I just didn't enjoy it as m-m-much as *Le Chevalier* o-o-or *The H-H-H-Hedonist* . . ." He trailed off, winced at Lady Benwick's frown, and wiped his sweating brow with his handkerchief.

Lady Benwick shook her head and pinched the bridge of her nose as if struck with a headache, and the LLALLLL members began murmuring indignantly among themselves.

The Misstophers looked as if they grudgingly agreed with the vicar's assessment. Minerva certainly did. *The Italian Poem* was by far her least favorite as well.

"I believe there has been a misunderstanding, Vicar," Lady Benwick finally said, stepping forward.

The vicar took a subtle step away from her, out of arm's reach, which Minerva thought very wise of him. "I-I-I-I c-c-c-couldn't agree m-m-m-more," he murmured warily.

"Don't worry, Mr. Fawkes," Astrid called out through her laughter. "You shall still have Montford's patronage. And I agree with you about *The Italian Poem*. It was not nearly saucy enough."

The vicar's face went beet red, and he glanced uneasily at the fuming Lady Benwick. "That is n-n-n-not why I d-d-didn't . . . that is . . . it w-w-w-was the imagery . . . and . . . er, the b-b-bit about the Etruscans I f-f-f-found somewhat l-l-lacking . . . anyway, Essex is m-m-more than just the . . . er, the saucy b-b-b-bits, Duchess. H-h-h-his genius l-l-l-lies in . . ."

He was cut off by Lady Benwick's rather less than subtle nudge to his side.

"But h-h-how about I-I-I speak on Lord Byron?" the vicar tried. "I-I-I am sure I c-c-could f-f-find l-l-l-loads of h-h-h-horrid things to say about him, Lady Benwick."

Lady Benwick didn't look as if she appreciated the vicar's gesture.

"I think you've said enough," she bit out through gritted teeth.

"I think you've all said enough," growled a new voice—well, it was new to the moment, but not to Minerva. Her heart turned over in her chest as she watched Marlowe himself push through the duchess's picket line, the Duke of Montford, the Marquess of Manwaring, and—for some unfathomable reason—Inigo flanking him and eyeing the bonfire incredulously.

For some other unfathomable reason beyond Minerva's

comprehension, the duke seemed to be wearing Marlowe's favorite red silk banyan, while Marlowe himself wore a tailored cutaway jacket that fit his broad shoulders like a glove. The silver fabric was a bit over the top, more suited to the sartorial splendor of the marquess, but he looked . . .

He looked dashing. Handsome, even, in a wild-haired, dramatic sort of way as he stalked up to the stage on his long legs and glared out at the gathering.

"What do you think you're doing?" Lady Benwick cried.

"What do *you* think you're doing, madam?" he shot back, gesturing at the bonfire. He looked outraged, but beneath that, Minerva could see the injury. It couldn't have been easy to watch a pyre that was fueled mostly by his own works burn to the ground, and her heart hurt for the poet in him in that moment. She was still so angry at him—and confused and unnerved by his sudden appearance—but she mourned his creative loss.

"How dare you engage in such philistine censorship," he declared.

"Philistine!" Lady Benwick cried. "How dare you, Lord Marlowe. What matter is it of yours what we burn?"

Minerva could see his next words written all over his face before he could speak them, and her heart nearly beat out of her chest with apprehension.

He wouldn't, surely he wouldn't.

For a split second, a look of utter terror flashed across his face, before it was strong-armed into oblivion by his dogged determination.

He *would*. He was going to do it. She didn't know whether to be proud of him or infuriated. To admit to a half-hostile crowd *now* what he couldn't admit to her for months . . . well, she didn't know how it made her feel, but it certainly wasn't anything good.

"It matters to me, madam, because *I* am Christopher Essex," he declared.

The crowd let out a collective gasp. The Misstophers, suddenly galvanized, thrust past their mothers and crowded at the bottom of the stage, tittering and moaning among themselves. Many of the LLALLLL took to their smelling salts once again, including Lady Blundersmith, who looked seconds away from collapsing upon her companion. The vicar, who had been standing awkwardly between Marlowe and Lady Benwick, gazed raptly at the viscount, as bowled over as any Misstopher, while the duchess's supporters let out an encouraging cheer.

Lady Benwick looked as if she might cast up her accounts—or shove Marlowe off the stage and into the bonfire, if given half the chance.

"You!" Lady Benwick scoffed in disbelief. "The Viscount Marlowe? *You* are Christopher Essex?"

"Evelyn Christopher Leighton, Viscount Marlowe. My mother's family name was Essex, and if you are not bloody well convinced, you may ask my publisher," he ground out.

Lady Benwick recovered enough from the shock to send a quelling look to the Misstophers—among them her own daughter—who were attempting to ascend the stage to mob the poet.

Marlowe glanced at the young ladies warily before turning his attention to the rest of the assembled throng. He seemed to be looking for something . . . someone, and Minerva began to have a really bad feeling about what was to come.

He finally found what he was looking for, and Minerva felt her cheeks flush, for his eyes had landed on her and seemed to have no intention of budging.

"I am Christopher Essex," he declared again, as if anyone *hadn't* heard him the first time, and . . . oh, god, he was going to make a speech. "Someone told me recently how much of a coward I have been to hide behind my pen all these years, and she was right."

Was she? She was beginning to doubt that very much.

"I was a coward about so many things," he continued, never taking his eyes off her. "And cowardice and fear have never led anywhere worthwhile." He gestured toward the bonfire to underscore his words. "Most of all, I was afraid of my own heart—and the fear has cost me so very dearly." The Misstophers moaned at the devastating words, but Minerva just felt her cheeks get even hotter and her heart beat even faster as Marlowe continued to look at her so imploringly.

Damn it, he was saying such lovely things, but at the same time she hated what a spectacle it all was. Didn't he know how little she would want to be the center of attention? Didn't he know how mortified his Grand Gesture would make her feel?

"Minerva, please forgive me."

Apparently, he didn't. She wanted to hide behind her placard as all eyes began to turn in her direction.

She supposed that many women would be flattered by the public declaration—by the high romance of the moment (especially the Misstophers, who were all glaring green daggers at her)—but all she could feel was a rising hysteria. What the devil did he think he was doing?

He seemed to falter slightly after this, as if he'd lost the train of his thought—or had guessed her mood. She tried to command him with her eyes to stop, but he barreled onward after Montford and Manwaring gave him encouraging gestures from the sidelines.

Well, at least now she knew who had put him up to this.

Lady Elizabeth, who had looked smugly pleased by the viscount's declaration at first, now looked between Marlowe and Minerva with growing alarm. "Oh, good grapes," she muttered. "He's cocking it up even more, isn't he?"

Minerva's throat was too tight for her to respond at all.

"Burn them if you must," he said of the unholy pyre. "They're all rubbish. Here is the only truth . . ."

Oh, dear Lord. She covered her face with her hand.

"'I speak not, I trace not, I breathe not thy name,'" he began, though he had, in fact, just spoken her name. In front of the most judgmental biddies of the ton. On a stage. In Hyde Park. "'There is grief in the sound, there is guilt in the fame; / But the tear that now burns on my cheek may impart / The deep thoughts that dwell in that silence of heart.'"

She wanted to simultaneously sink into the ground, smack him across the cheek, and kiss him on the mouth. He was quoting poetry at her.

Good Lord, he had finally cracked completely.

Never in her wildest imagination had she ever dreamed of Lord Marlowe, of all people, reciting anything other than a bawdy limerick to anyone. Ever. But that was before she knew he was the most celebrated poet in the whole kingdom, wasn't it? Here he was, unafraid and unabashed, speaking verse with an eloquence of tongue not even the smoothest of orators could have rivaled.

She couldn't help the flash of heat his earnest entreaty inspired inside, despite her general mortification. This would have been the point in the novel that the heroine would have fallen into the hero's contrite arms, bowled over by the sheer romance of the moment. But she certainly didn't feel like a heroine, and she . . .

Well, she hated novels.

And besides . . .

Besides, he wasn't even quoting himself at the moment. He was quoting Byron. Bloody *Byron*. And he knew—he *knew* how she felt about Byron.

It was, to her, the last straw in a mountain of last straws. He couldn't even be bothered to declare himself in his own words—he had to borrow someone else's.

She had complained to him last she saw him that she didn't know who he was. Well, the inverse had been proven today—he knew *her* very little if he thought this public spectacle was going to earn him anything but another black mark.

She wished she were the sort of girl who could ignore the grievances between them and the mortification she felt at being singled out in such a public venue, throw herself in his arms, and live happily ever after. But she wasn't. All the eyes on her, in judgment or jealousy, made her skin crawl.

"'Too brief for our passion, too long for our peace . . .'" he continued, oblivious to her distress, and suddenly she couldn't bear to hear another word.

She dropped her picket and turned away from the stage, the fire, the whole preposterous production. Carefully avoiding meeting anyone's eyes, she wove her way through the crowd and into the shrubbery, her only goal to hide until it was all over.

As ill-conceived and unwanted as his public declaration was, though, it gave her a modicum of hope. Perhaps he did love her. Perhaps he could be interested in her for more than his mistress—but the hope was very small, indeed, for when it came down to it, how could he love her when he hadn't even trusted her to tell her who he was?

MEANWHILE, IN THE SHRUBBERY...

JEM HIGGINS LOVED his wife—a rare occurrence indeed in this day and age. He also wisely loved the same things his wife did, including her sister, Jenny, who was still an employee of White House, a nunnery off Soho Square Jem's wife had (mostly) left behind upon their marriage.

At least, Jenny *had* been gainfully employed there— and surprisingly happy in her profession—until her last encounter with the Duke of Plagues, as Oxley was known fondly among the bawdy houses of St. Giles and Soho. *That* had not ended well, for now the poor girl was tucked up with Jem and his wife, too ill to get out of bed most days and suffering from something far worse than the cuts and bruises she had first received from that monster.

It was for this reason that Jem found himself crouched in the shrubbery behind a mob of angry noblewomen, watching half the inventory of London's bookshops burn to ashes as he awaited his quarry. Jenny needed a doctor, one of the proper ones who didn't cut hair or pull teeth for a living—or brew up backroom potions that were more likely to kill than heal—and she would have had one with the blood money Oxley had been obliged to give them, if not for Petey Soames.

He knew he never should have agreed to Soames's scheme to "invest" the duke's money at the races, but he'd always been hopeless when it came to saying no to his cousin. Granted, Jem hardly understood what the man was going on about half the time, but Soames always made it seem as if paradise awaited them both at the end, if only Jem would trust him just a little bit longer.

One would have thought Jem might have learned better by now, but alas, Soames and his silver tongue were just as hard to resist as when the two of them had been children picking pockets in Covent Garden (or rather, when Jem had been picking pockets, and Soames had put himself in charge of guarding their take).

Jem never thought he'd actually miss the days when his cousin's schemes were of the more illicit variety. But Soames now fancied himself a reformed officer of the law, and the only halfway interesting thing the man did these days was strong-arm money from coves like Oxley and lay a few hopeless wagers at the tracks.

That whole episode with the marchioness and her demon dog had left an impression on more than just his cousin's ankles.

Jem, however, couldn't afford Soames's new perspective on life, not with a wife and a sick sister-in-law to support.

And if that meant finding a little side job to make up for the funds lost at Newmarket, then that was what he would do.

The one upshot to working a job without Soames was that he wouldn't have to split the proceeds . . . or be cajoled into another trip to the races even farther afield than bloody Suffolk.

Soames had been the brains behind their little extracurriculars, however, and Jem wasn't so sure what his cousin would have thought of the man who had hired him . . . or what he'd hired him for.

Jem had never been involved in anything more nefarious than a bit of light house burgling, a few low-profile swindles, and the occasional blackmail scheme. The worst thing he'd done was that ill-fated dognapping that still had him jumping halfway to Hampstead Heath every time he heard a dog bark. He'd certainly never even considered abducting an actual human, yet that was what his current employer wanted. The prize—twenty pounds sterling—was rather too tempting to pass up.

Besides which, his quarry was a rich nob, of the same caliber as the Duke of Plagues himself, and no doubt deserved a lot worse than to be abducted. Jem hadn't the highest opinion of the Upper Ten Thousand. He'd spent too many nights standing guard at the White House doors to have little more than contempt left for its high-flying patrons.

And honestly, anyone who'd spend good English coin at his tailor upon a silver jacket *that* hideous was committing a criminal act in Jem's opinion. It was even worse than Soames's ridiculous red waistcoats.

He'd been following the nob in the silver jacket all day as he'd been instructed, waiting for just the right moment to snatch him. But the bloody man had been annoyingly social today, rushing about the city with his cronies—one of which Jem recognized with no little alarm as the

Marquess of Manwaring—and then attending that . . . whatever *that* was about in Hyde Park.

Jem shook his head at the sight of the burning pyre beyond the shrubbery and the mob of highborn women milling around it as if they were at an afternoon tea. It was all inexplicably strange to Jem's mind.

When he was really short on funds during the winter, he'd pinch the occasional book to burn from old Geordie's shop down on the corner, for a little added warmth in the stove. But he'd never heard of nobs burning books *for fun*, and he'd certainly never heard of nobs' wives doing so in the middle of the day in Hyde Park.

It seemed like something they'd do in France, though. The French, in Jem's humble opinion, had a lot of strange habits he'd never understand, but he knew Englishwomen seemed to love them. Jem was beginning to suspect, however, that highborn females of *any* nationality were even more mystifying a breed.

But this . . . *this* was a special kind of insanity. Jem couldn't read, but *he* wouldn't burn an Essex poem, even if it were the coldest day of the year, any more than he'd burn the Bard's. His wife loved Essex, and he had taken to memorizing the man's verse whenever he happened to hear it. Reciting "The Alabaster Hip" to the missus had led to many bliss-filled nights in recent memory.

Jem could only conclude that the women intent on destroying such genius had never had a bliss-filled night in their lives.

The nob in the silver jacket must have had the same idea, for he didn't look well pleased as he took to the stage. Jem wasn't well pleased either, for he had spotted his *cousin*, of all people, among the officers of Bow Street sent to keep the plebs away while the ladies had their bizarre little soiree.

Jem didn't dare move from the bit of shrubbery he'd found, in case Soames found him out before he'd done the job. The distance made it impossible to hear what his quarry was going on about after he'd all but knocked that old biddy off the platform and started speaking. But it couldn't be good, considering the noise the crowd had begun to make.

One particular lady—one of the sensible ones who seemed to be protesting the protest (though perhaps *sensible* wasn't the right word)—didn't seem a bit pleased with whatever the nob was spouting, however. She stalked off through the bewildered throng, past the fire burning high with books and broadsheets, and right toward where Jem crouched in the bushes.

The nob ended his speech abruptly and started after her.

The good news was that his quarry was now heading in his direction.

The bad news was that so was the lady.

Jem scratched his head at this conundrum.

AND THEN, A FEW STEPS FROM JEM'S BIT OF SHRUBBERY . . .

MINERVA DIDN'T GET far in the maze of greenery before Marlowe found her. She couldn't say she was surprised he had followed her, but she was certainly in no mood to make things easy for him. For even if her initial anger had cooled over the past few days, it still smoldered in her heart. And this spectacle—as well intentioned as it seemed to be—had done nothing to win her over.

"Where do you think you're going?" he growled out to her, stepping in front of her in his ridiculous silver jacket. As if he had any right to be angry at her.

"As far from you as I can get," she muttered.

He looked at her with frustration and hurt. "What the devil do you want of me, then?" he cried, spreading his arms wide. "What must I do to prove myself to you?"

"Certainly not make a scene before half the ton," she shot back. She tried to move around him, but he blocked her path. She huffed and walked in the other direction.

"A scene?" he bit out as he stalked after her, his long legs quickly overtaking her once more. "Minerva, please! It was meant to be a Grand Gesture."

"For whom?"

"I did it for you."

She snorted. "Unlikely."

He snarled at her and then did something unexpected. He seized her in his arms and crushed her against him, which was getting to be a bad habit of his. He glared down at her, eyes shining, breath ragged. "Do you know how hard that was for me? To declare myself in front of all of those people?" he bit out.

She thought she might have some idea considering how jealously he'd guarded his secret for years, but he was holding her so tightly—and his body felt so good against her own—that she was quite at a loss to respond. She gave a little incoherent grunt, because that was all she could manage.

"Do you know how you make me feel every second of every day, Minerva?" he asked.

"No, actually, I don't," she said honestly. "I have no idea what you truly feel for me." Which was entirely the problem.

He looked startled by her words—incredulous. As if he couldn't believe she didn't know. Suddenly his lips covered hers, as if to prove something to her, and he was kissing her as if his life depended on it. It made her lips ache and her body turn from floundering noodle into fiery inferno in the space of a few seconds.

Damn him. She gave a token struggle, but soon she was melting into his kisses. What choice had she when her body had turned into an inferno, after all? She twined her arms around his neck and held on for dear life as his mouth went to her ear and stayed there.

"Do you know how much I want you, Minerva? To finish what we began the other night?" he murmured, clutching her around the back with one hand, the other traveling up her leg and under her skirt.

She gasped. Was he going to . . . ? Dear God, Marlowe was going to ravish her right here, in the shrubbery. And she . . .

She couldn't allow it.

She could forgive him for not telling her he was Essex. She probably already had. But during their time apart, she'd thought long and hard about all that had happened between them . . . and all that hadn't.

She wouldn't regret the pleasure he'd brought her, but she'd been so hasty in her capitulation, so blinded by her physical attraction for him, that she'd ignored what had never been acknowledged between them. In all of the words spoken, all of their banter, arguments, and soul-baring over the past few months, neither one of them had ever spoken of love—except now, sort of, through borrowed verse. But it did nothing to assuage her doubts.

To be fair, she hadn't declared herself either, but how could she now, when he'd already laid her bare, stripped her to the bone?

She didn't doubt his regard for her on the physical level—he'd been attracted to her from the very beginning, hadn't he? He'd called her a fey creature, which was about as unsubtle as one could get, now that she thought about it. But she was afraid his regard ended there, that he wanted her for a lover and nothing else.

For some women—many women in a similarly precarious position as hers—that would have been a perfectly acceptable arrangement, but she was simply not built to be a mistress. She may have been a pragmatist about most things in life, but in matters of the heart, she was distressingly romantic.

She wanted him to love her enough to marry her, despite their disparate stations in life, and if that wasn't something he could offer her, then it was best they went their separate ways before they hurt each other even more.

"No!" she said, pushing him away firmly. "This is not enough."

He looked confused and hurt by her rejection. "Then what will satisfy you? My heart on a spit?" he demanded, frustrated.

"I won't be your kept woman," she bit out, finally acknowledging the elephant between them as much as she dared.

He looked poleaxed by the declaration. "Kept . . . what are you talking about?" he cried, sounding utterly mystified.

"I won't," she insisted, turning from him, unable to bear his bewildered, wide-eyed look. "It is not a life that could ever make me happy."

He spun her around to face him once more, and he looked down at her with an anguished expression. "How could you ever think . . . Minerva, that is not what I want from you."

"Then what? What do you want from me?" she cried. "Because you've never told me."

It was as close to begging as she could get without completely losing her pride. Even so, she hated how pathetic she sounded.

His expression softened, as if he finally—*finally*—understood her, and something like hope lit his big brown eyes. The knot of fear in her gut started to unravel a little at his gentle smile, and she began to hope as she had never let herself hope these past few days that he'd say the words she longed to hear.

"You've never let me," he retorted, without heat. "Minerva, I . . ."

But the words never came. Just as Marlowe opened his

mouth to speak, his gentle expression shifted into shock, and his eyes rolled into the back of his head. A moment later, he fell to the ground in a dead faint.

It took her a while to overcome her own astonishment enough to piece together what had happened. She glanced from Marlowe's unconscious body to the tall, bony ruffian standing over him with a rock in his hand. The ruffian's eyes were popped wide, as if he too were surprised at how well his coshing had worked.

She opened her mouth to scream, but the man lurched forward and clapped a filthy hand over her lips.

"Quiet now, missy, or I'll do for ye what I've done for him," the man sneered.

If he thought to frighten her, then he had another thing coming. Just when she was finally getting somewhere with Marlowe, this villain had to interrupt. And at perhaps the most crucial moment of her life. Did he have any idea how annoying that was?

Powered by sheer exasperation, she managed to push him back and land a hard right hook to the ruffian's eye, just as the captain had taught her. He yelped and staggered back, looking rather horrified at her show of aggression.

It didn't deter the man for long, however, for he soon made good on his threat and coshed her over the head, just as he'd done to Marlowe.

And for a long time thereafter, she knew no more.

CHAPTER TWENTY-SEVEN

Meanwhile, Back At The Ladies' League Against Lewd And Lascivious Literature And Letters Rally

BETSY WATCHED AS HER BROTHER chased after Miss Jones and shook her head in exasperation. She didn't know whether to feel more proud or embarrassed of his performance. What he'd done had taken courage, but public speaking had never been his forte, poor man. He'd been far more coherent than the poor, stuttering vicar, of course, but not by much.

If she were Miss Jones, *she'd* probably have run away in mortification too. Grand Gestures, whether or not they were eloquently given, were fine for novels and epic poetry, but Betsy was not so sure they worked in reality, especially in front of this particularly contentious audience. Especially when delivered in such a spectacularly awkward fashion. Especially when Marlowe thought quoting *Byron* to a *Misstopher* was a good idea.

What had he been thinking?

Miss Jones and Marlowe slipped into the shrubbery bordering the mob, and this seemed to signal some sort of descent into total pandemonium around her. It was as if the mob had been holding its breath until the viscount—*Christopher Essex!* the biddies and Misstophers whisper-cried as he'd passed them by—was out of sight.

Betsy slipped to the edge of the crowd and took stock of the scene before her.

The duchess and her cronies stood on one side of the smoldering fire, looking smug at the rally's total disruption. The vicar seemed to have jumped ranks, cowering behind the Astrid's placard, clutching his books to his chest and sending an occasional worried glance across the fire.

Betsy followed the direction of his concerned look and landed on a fuming Lady Benwick, who was staring daggers at the duchess. Lady Blundersmith was in the midst of a swoon beside her, and Davina was trying half-heartedly to hold on to the woman before she could tumble into the fire.

The gaggle behind this vanguard looked vaguely confused, while their recalcitrant daughters gathered in a huddle near the abandoned stage, waxing poetic about Essex's exotic brown eyes, Roman nose, and avant-garde taste in fashion.

She snorted disdainfully. To think she had been one of *them* not so long ago. That was her idiotic *brother* they were mooning over.

She spied Montford, who was standing on the periphery with the marquess and Mr. Soames, wrapped in Marlowe's favorite red dressing gown, and she had an answer to her brother's sudden transformation into a peacocking fashion plate. They must have traded coats in the hope that Marlowe wouldn't look so ridiculous standing in front of this crowd in his banyan.

It hadn't worked. He'd still looked ridiculous.

She was just about to turn her attention back to the ladies—Lady Blundersmith seemed to have finally tumbled atop Davina—when she noticed the fourth man standing in attendance to the duke. It was Dr. Lucas, looking much too somber beneath his whiskers. He'd probably be standing with Lady Emily's bunch of moralists if he'd dared.

She wasn't sure why Dr. Lucas got her blood up so, but

she was certain that it had to do with Miss Jones. If he thought he could interfere, then Betsy would have something to say about it. Her brother was an idiot, and he still couldn't seem to get anything right when it came to Miss Jones, but she knew how much he truly loved the governess. After all he'd been through with the earl and Evander and that . . . that horrid, selfish Caroline, Marlowe deserved his happy ending, and Betsy was certain that was with Miss Jones.

Dr. Lucas only confused the issue. And it wasn't even as if he truly loved Miss Jones, not the way Evie did. The doctor was just too noble for his own good, blast him, wanting to do the right thing by his dead brother's fiancée.

Well, she'd be having none of it. He could take that nobility and shove it elsewhere.

She started in his direction, determined to stall him in case he tried to go after Miss Jones and ruin everything, but a piercing cry from the center of the mob brought her up short. Lady Benwick had stalked over to the enemy's side when Betsy wasn't looking and was attempting to rip the placard from the duchess's hands, apparently having abandoned all her dignity.

Aunt Anabel's dog, Mademoiselle Clare, had a vicious hold of the hem of Lady Benwick's bombazine gown, growling fiercely in between tugs. Aunt Anabel herself seemed to be encouraging the beast in her assault.

"How dare you engineer this ridiculous spectacle!" Lady Benwick was sneering at her niece.

The duchess pulled at her picket and said, as pleasantly as she could through gritted teeth, "*I* am not the one who lit a fire in Hyde Park."

Aunt Emily tugged back. "You set up that . . . that disreputable viscount to undermine everything."

"I assure you, I had no idea he would come here today. But it *was* a smashing performance. I'm sure your daughter loved it." Tug.

"You leave Davina out of this!" Tug.

"My cousin has the good sense to appreciate Essex's genius. It is such a departure, considering her abysmal taste in clothes, that I want to support her." Tug.

"By undermining me, her mother, and encouraging her to fill her head with filth!" Tug, *tug*.

Davina, who had finally managed to unearth herself from beneath Lady Blundersmith, glared at her mother's back.

"How you ever maneuvered your way into matrimony with a duke—and your *sister* into my son's bed!—is quite beyond my ken," Lady Benwick huffed. "You were embarrassment enough at Rylestone Green. Now you make fools of us all in London. I rue the day my sister, God rest her soul, eloped with a drunkard like Aloysius Honeywell. Not even in death has she stopped shaming this family."

Well, *that* seemed a bit harsh.

Astrid agreed, for her careful composure seemed to crack a little under her aunt's verbal assault. She looked heartsick and in enough distress that her husband seemed to sense it even at a distance. Montford began to rush to her side, looking a bit unsteady on his feet, but he didn't manage to reach her before the fight seemed to go out of her completely. Her grip on the placard's wooden post went slack just as Lady Benwick gave a massive yank.

To Betsy's eyes, though, the timing looked a bit suspect on the duchess's part.

Lady Benwick stumbled backward in surprise and tripped over Mademoiselle, who was still busy making mincemeat out of her hem. Both the dog and Lady Benwick squealed in distress, and as the lady brought up her arms in an effort to regain her balance, she smacked Aunt Anabel's cane right out from under her with the placard's long wooden handle, sending the poor lady's russet wig flying into the ether.

Things escalated rather quickly from there. Lady Benwick fell on her arse and somehow simultaneously managed to smack herself in the nose with the sign, sending blood cascading from her nose. The duke, who had been rushing to his wife's aid, caught sight of Lady Benwick's blood-streaked nose, turned the same color as Davina's chartreuse gown, and fell face forward onto the lawn.

Aunt Anabel, disoriented by the loss of her wig and hampered by the heavy weight of her ancient gown and one too many inches on her heeled slippers, began to tilt toward the open flames of the bonfire, the stiff whalebone underpinning of her paneled skirts the only thing slowing her descent.

Thankfully, the Marquess of Manwaring, trailing after the duke, caught Aunt Anabel just before she could go up in flames. The crowd sighed in collective relief and, in the case of the Misstophers (and most of the rest of the females in attendance), a bit of envy. Betsy couldn't blame them, for who *wouldn't* want to be saved from a fiery death by the handsomest man in London?

Aunt Anabel, apparently, for the old lady swatted the marquess with her cane as soon as she'd been set upright once more.

"I'm a married woman!" she blustered out, seemingly oblivious to having been seconds from immolation. She wagged her cane at him threateningly. He staggered back a few steps to avoid it and nearly tripped over the duke. "You had your chance, boy. If you want a bit of slap and tickle, I ain't available any longer."

The marquess looked as queasy at this insinuation as Betsy felt.

Aunt Anabel's rant was interrupted by yet another high-pitched yelp. This one issued from Davina, who was pointing toward the side of the fire where Aunt Anabel had nearly met her doom. An excruciatingly expensive bejeweled dog lead trailed toward the flames, and something reddish-brown and fluffy smoldered on top of a charred stack of *The Hedonist*.

"The dog!" Davina cried. "It's burning!"

The crowd shrieked in collective horror. Somewhere in the background, Lady Blundersmith collapsed once more. Dr. Lucas, who had just finished staunching Lady Benwick's bloody nose, sighed, his shoulders slumping in resignation, and made his way over to the fainted woman.

Betsy could only watch, sick to her stomach, as the marquess and Mr. Soames managed to fish the burning creature out of the flames with the fallen placard's handle.

Aunt Anabel stood at the sidelines demanding to know what all the fuss was about. With Davina and half the crowd calling out Mademoiselle's name and Lady Blundersmith looking peaky once more, it should have been obvious. But it seemed that Madame la Duchesse was as deaf as she was bald.

The smoldering mass of fur finally rolled to a stop right at Aunt Anabel's feet. She squinted at the ball of fire and poked at it with her cane. Her expression collapsed as she touched her bare scalp, as if just realizing the loss of her wig. She shook her cane in Lady Benwick's direction.

"That were imported all the way from Gibraltar, Emily. Pure thoroughbred horsehair."

Ah. It was only the wig. Betsy heaved a sigh of relief, as did the rest of the crowd.

"But where is Mademoiselle Clare then?" Davina cried.

Betsy followed the abandoned lead away from the fire to the hem of Lady Benwick's skirts, where it disappeared underneath. Something lumpy moved in the pile of bombazine, and moments later, a furry head emerged, peered around the gathered throng, and barked.

Lady Benwick, still half reclined on the ground and clutching a handkerchief to her nose, looked even more mortified underneath all of the blood on her face. She kicked out the interloper with her boot heel, much to Aunt Anabel's indignation. Mademoiselle retaliated by nipping at Lady Benwick's ankle until the stocking ripped, then bounded away toward her bald mistress.

(Mr. Soames tucked Mademoiselle's jeweled lead into his coat pocket when he thought no one was looking, whistling innocently and imagining all the red waistcoats he could buy off the proceeds.)

With all of the pandemonium underway, Betsy almost missed the ruffian carrying Miss Jones over one shoulder through the shrubbery, but luckily she looked up at just the right moment to catch him in the act.

Betsy had heard a rumor that the Duke of Montford had abducted Astrid Honeywell to Gretna Green in a similar manner, but the man carrying Miss Jones was too thin and too blond to be the viscount. Betsy hardly thought her brother would gag and bind Miss Jones's hands, either, even if he had decided to abscond with her to Scotland. Evie was frequently infuriating and had made epically poor choices when it came to his awkward courtship of Miss Jones, but some lines not even her brother crossed.

But if it were not Evie stealing away with Miss Jones, where the devil was he?

She broke away from the crowd and followed after the ruffian, just to make sure she'd not imagined it. She stopped at the edge of the maze of shrubbery and peered around the corner to see the stranger depositing Miss Jones into the bowels of an old coach. She caught sight of her brother slumped unconscious on the seat next to her just as the villain slammed the door shut. Before she could decide whether to go after them, however, the ruffian bounded into the driver's seat and whipped the cattle into motion, tearing off down the lane in a haze of dust.

This could not be good.

Heart in her throat, she rushed back toward the bonfire, but just as she rounded a corner, she ran straight into a wall of starched linen, gray superfine, and salt-and-pepper whiskers. She shrieked and jerked backward so violently she nearly sent herself sprawling.

Dr. Lucas caught her arm with a surprisingly capable grip and steadied her on her feet. He stared down at her in consternation through his much too serious, much too beautiful, blue eyes. Not for the first time did she think it a crime to waste such incredible eyes on a fuddy old doctor. Or that handsome countenance lurking beneath those atrocious whiskers, come to think of it.

"Lady Elizabeth . . ." he began.

"Someone's taken them!" she cried, for she had no time for the lecture about running off alone that he was sure to deliver if given half the chance.

His brow furrowed, and she wanted to groan. Even his confused look was far too attractive for her peace of mind. "What are you talking about?"

"Miss Jones and my brother. Someone has abducted them!"

Without waiting to see if he believed her, she rushed toward the bonfire. Fortunately, the worst seemed to be over. Most of the crowd had begun to retreat to their carriages. The duke was just coming around in his wife's arms, and the marquess and Mr. Soames had taken it upon themselves, along with the rest of the Bow Street officers, to douse the bonfire's flames with buckets hauled up from the Serpentine.

And Mademoiselle was in the midst of a strategic assault upon the smoldering remains of Aunt Anabel's wig.

Once Betsy managed to wrangle Montford's and the others' attention, she told her tale, and then again when Aunt Anabel tapped her shin with her cane. "Speak up, gel, I ain't a mind reader."

"Are you sure you saw your brother in that coach?" the duke demanded after the second telling, though his authority was severely undermined from his position languishing on the lawn in his wife's arms.

Betsy wanted to scream. "Yes. He looked unconscious."

"But who the devil would abduct them?" the marquess

asked, his beautiful face fraught with concern.

The duchess proposed they investigate the Ladies' League Against Lewd and Lascivious Literature and Letters, in case one of them was so enraged by Christopher Essex's public unmasking that they'd decided to abscond with him.

Only Astrid's husband dared contradict her theory, pointing out the fact that Lady Benwick (who was making a strategic, if slightly bloody, retreat to her carriage with her daughter and an extremely unhappy-looking vicar in tow) had been breaking her nose at the time of the abduction.

The duchess then pointed out that a woman capable of organizing a mass book burning was more than capable of hiring a ruffian to abduct the viscount. The duke then pointed out that Lady Benwick could have had no idea the viscount was Essex, much less that he would appear here today. The duchess then retorted that it wouldn't be the first time her aunt's crusade against Honeywells had seemed supernatural in its scope.

Aunt Anabel blamed the Essex-mad Misstophers—until Betsy pointed out the abductor had definitely been a tall, male ne'er-do-well and not a gaggle of sixteen-year-old girls—while the marquess wondered if Barming could be behind it.

It was Soames, of all people, who hit upon the most likely perpetrator, for it seemed as if a certain poxy duke had arrived back in London just a few days ago, in spite of the viscount's ultimatum.

"What the devil is Poxley doing back in the city?" the marquess demanded. "And why did you not inform us sooner, Soames?"

Soames had that same shifty look he'd worn when he'd had his eyes on the Countess' diamonds the night of the ill-fated dinner party. "I were going to as soon as I 'ad collected on a few of his outstanding debts," he hedged.

"Of course," Montford said dryly. "If the viscount or Miss Jones has come to harm while you were busy extorting the duke, I will throw you on a boat bound to New South Wales myself. I've done it before, and I'll do it again."

Mr. Soames wisely kept his mouth shut and stayed a sizable distance from Montford after that.

CHAPTER TWENTY-EIGHT

In Which A Villain Is Confronted

A SHORT WHILE LATER, THE DUKE and the marquess were packing off the women in the duchess's coach and piling into Montford's open barouche with Dr. Lucas and Mr. Soames, intent on their mission to extricate Marlowe and Miss Jones from Poxley's clutches.

Betsy discontentedly watched the barouche leave in a haze of dust. She turned back to the duchess and Aunt Anabel, who was pulling a spare wig from underneath the seat and fixing it on her bald head at a jaunty angle. Mademoiselle happily chewed on the remains of the old wig at their feet.

"I can't believe they're sending us home. Just like that. He's my brother, and I'm the one who saw what happened to them," Betsy muttered.

Astrid smirked. "Who says we're going home?" She tapped on the carriage roof and directed Newcomb to Oxley's residence. Newcomb, who was always agreeable to any plan that might vex the duke, was more than happy to oblige. "My husband is as mad as Aunt Emily if he thinks to leave me out of this excitement."

Betsy privately thought her brother's abduction a much more serious matter than a mere "excitement," but she held her tongue, since Astrid's goal was roughly the same as hers.

It was doubtless indicative of the sort of marriage the duke and duchess led that Montford didn't even look surprised when Astrid's carriage pulled up behind the barouche at Oxley's palatial London residence just as the men were stepping down into the street.

He helped his wife from the coach with a long-suffering look. She swatted at his arm. "Don't give me that look. This is the most fun we've had in years. I refuse to sit at home and knit, or whatever dutiful little wives do while their husbands are out having an adventure," Astrid said.

"Never fear," he muttered. "No one would ever mistake you for a dutiful wife."

She swatted his arm again, and Betsy hoped that one day she could find a husband as resilient as the duke.

The duke wisely said nothing more and offered his wife his arm, leading the charge to Oxley's front door.

The footman who answered Montford's rather pointed knocks was as handsome and conceited as was typical of the breed, with a well-turned ankle, gold-buttoned livery, and snowy-white wig. He looked unsurprised to find seven people and a dog on the doorstep . . . but then again he *was* employed by Oxley, and Betsy didn't even want to imagine the things that went on under this roof. The footman obviously recognized Mr. Soames, however, from the look of disdain he sent him.

"May I help you?" the man asked with chilly politeness.

"We are here to see the Duke of Oxley," Montford said, equally frigid.

The footman produced a silver salver out of nowhere and waited wordlessly until Montford finally caught on to what the man was after. He reluctantly produced his calling card and dropped it on the salver, looking as if he couldn't quite wrap his head around the footman's impudence. The footman turned to the marquess next for his card, passed over Mr. Soames rather pointedly, and stopped on Dr. Lucas. Once he'd collected his spoils, he shut the door in their faces.

"The utter cheek!" the duke said, aghast.

"I rather liked him," the marquess murmured with a wry grin, clearly enjoying himself at his friend's expense.

"Is this how you mean to rescue my brother and Miss Jones? By standing on Poxley's stoop?" Betsy demanded, unimpressed by the progress they'd made . . . or rather, the lack thereof.

"He caught poor Montford off guard," the duchess answered briskly. "He's not used to anyone being insolent to him but me. He needs time to regroup."

Montford gave his wife, then the door, a stern look, then went to flip the knocker again. He was beaten to it by the footman, who swung open the door just as the duke was reaching for it. Montford just caught himself before he could stumble. The footman peered down his nose at the lot of them. "His Grace is not at home," he intoned solemnly.

Madame la Duchesse had apparently had enough, however, for she shoved Mademoiselle into Montford's arms, swatted the footman on his finely turned calves with her stick, and toddled into the foyer, her spare wig—champagne pink and two feet tall—listing to port side. "It's been a long day, young man. I suggest you take us to the duke before I shove my cane up your ar—"

"He is in his bedchamber," the footman interjected quickly, dancing well out of Aunt Anabel's range, but not before she'd managed to land a swat on his backside. He yelped and rubbed at his injury, his cool expression finally breaking. "He's *indisposed*."

"I'll bet he is, the randy old codger," Aunt Anabel muttered, then commenced to terrify the rest of the household staff that had begun amassing as she cut a determined but extremely slow swath across the marbled entrance hall with her cane's aid. "I remember when his mother had 'im.

He weren't a year on this earth before he were molesting his nursemaids."

Betsy wondered just how old Aunt Anabel was.

Madame la Duchesse waved her cane at a stout, well-dressed man coming down the grand staircase who could only be the butler. "You there, take us to His Grace's chambers immediately."

The butler eyed their whole group with a horrified expression. "All of you, madam?"

"That's Madame la Duchesse to you, sirrah," she said. "It might be French, but that don't mean it ain't real."

The butler was speechless.

"I have learned to do as she says, old boy," the marquess drawled. "It makes things much easier."

Aunt Anabel waved her cane at Manwaring, her expression softening. "You've always been my favorite. And not just because of your fine arse."

The marquess just grinned at her and gave her his leg. "I live to serve, Madame la Duchesse," he murmured.

The butler thought it best to concede defeat and led them up the staircase. For storming the lair of a villain, however, they moved at a rather glacial pace. But even Mr. Soames seemed to think it impolite to race ahead of Aunt Anabel, who was hampered by both the weight of her crinolines and her age.

The butler hesitated on the threshold of Oxley's bedchamber. "He really is indisposed," he said, casting a dubious glance Betsy's way. "And certainly not fit for a young lady's company."

"We shall be the judge of that," Montford said, his expression constipated as the ball of fluff in his arms steadily licked at his chin with its wet, pink tongue.

Mr. Soames took it upon himself to elbow the butler out of the way and threw open the door.

The smell of burning herbs, stale sweat, and something putrid assaulted Betsy's nostrils even from where she stood in the corridor. The duke turned green and gave Astrid a frantic look. The marquess withdrew a delicately laced kerchief and held it to his nose. Betsy suspected he'd been waiting for just this sort of opportunity to display it, the peacock. The duchess rolled her eyes at both men and stalked into the room with her aunt.

Betsy followed despite the foul miasma inside, determined to be there for the confrontation with her former fiancé. If he'd done something to her brother and Miss Jones, she'd know immediately from one glance at his smug face.

But the slim hope of finding Evie and Miss Jones at the duke's mercy soon dwindled to nil. Inside, all was dark and unbearably stuffy. The drapes were drawn, and a fire roared in the grate despite the warm weather. Upon the large four-poster bed, a lump stirred beneath lurid scarlet-colored bed linens. The smell grew even worse the closer they came to the bed, and she buried her nose in her sleeve, wishing she'd had one of the marquess's fiddly handkerchiefs.

Montford deposited Mademoiselle in his wife's arms and stalked to the draperies. He threw them back, sending light flooding into the room. The lump moaned in agony and muttered curses, and seconds later, a head as bald as Aunt Anabel's underneath her wig peeked out from underneath the bedclothes. Two angry, bloodshot eyes glared out from a face nearly unrecognizable as the one she'd last seen at that disastrous dinner party.

Poxley had not been a particularly agreeable-looking man even then, his countenance, even beneath the heavy maquillage, ravaged by too many years and too many vices. Now, however, he was ravaged all over with pestilential boils. When he propped himself up and the bedclothes fell down, revealing the reddish bumps and boils continuing down over his torso, Betsy nearly cast up her accounts.

No wonder he'd worn so much lead paint.

Montford retched, and Betsy feared the weak-stomached duke might faint for the second time that day.

"What the hell are you lot doing in here?" Oxley demanded blearily. His eyes landed on Betsy and widened. He tugged the sheets up to his chin, which she counted a small mercy for all of their eyeballs.

"We've come for Marlowe and the governess," the marquess said through his handkerchief. "I don't suppose you have them tied up underneath your bed?"

Oxley didn't even try to dignify that with an answer.

"You are supposed to be abroad," Montford accused, breathing carefully through his mouth.

Oxley scowled. "I decided to return home. The viscount's threats mean little to me now. As you can see, there's no hiding it any longer," he said bitterly.

"What is wrong with you?" the duchess demanded, not bothering to hide her disgust.

"He's dipped his tallywacker in a contaminated well, I'd say," Aunt Anabel observed. "Hoisted upon your own petard after all these years, eh, Poxley?"

Poxley looked at Aunt Anabel askance. "Is that . . . are you . . . Anabel Honeywell? You're *still* alive? Why are *you* here?"

"I am the Duchesse de St. Aignan to *you*, boy. And never mind why I'm here. Where is the viscount?"

"Tallywacker?" Betsy asked, because, really, someone had to.

Dr. Lucas blushed next to her.

Aunt Anabel waved her cane in the general direction of the duke's nether regions. "His tackle, gel. He has the French Disease. Had it some time by the look of it. Would have given it to you too, had your brother not sent him packing."

Now she was the one to turn green.

Despite her parents' best efforts to censor her education in such matters, Betsy knew precisely what the French Disease was. She felt something break inside her, for despite everything her father had put her through, she had never really been able to believe he didn't love her somewhere deep inside his rusted heart.

But this—*this* was irrefutable proof otherwise. He didn't love her. He didn't even loathe her as he did Evelyn, and this absence of emotion seemed even crueler somehow. Barming would have sold her to a man who would have killed her, whether it had been through violence or this slow, agonizing disease.

"You were going to marry him?" Dr. Lucas exclaimed, sounding as appalled as she felt.

"Not willingly," she gritted out.

"He'll not be marrying another woman by the time I'm finished with him," Montford growled out.

Oxley looked unimpressed at the duke's posturing. "Do your worst, Montford," he said, scratching at a sore on his face. "I shall not be alive to care. And as for the viscount, I have no idea to what you are referring. Nor do I care. Now good day."

"We ain't goin' nowheres until ye give us proper answers. Ye may be all poxy, but that don't mean ye can't of solsticed an abduction," Mr. Soames said cryptically.

"I haven't a bloody idea what you just said," Oxley said with withering contempt.

"Nor I," the marquess murmured.

Montford sighed. "You could have paid someone to abduct the viscount," he clarified.

Oxley snorted. "If I paid anyone to do anything, it would be to kill the viscount outright. Besides, how would I fund such a scheme? Between the Continent and this one"—he stabbed a poxy finger at Soames—"extorting me, where would I find the blunt for it?"

"I ain't extortioned you," Mr. Soames lied with a haughty sniff.

"No, you just send around your bullyboy. Only this

morning, that ruffian who claims to be your cousin came lurking around demanding money. I had my staff run him off, but not before he stole my coach and two of my best horses."

Mr. Soames went a bit shifty eyed at this.

"This wouldn't be the infamous Jem, would it?" the marquess drawled. "I've been meaning to ask after him, Soames, but it sounds as if he's just the same as ever."

"Do you think your cousin is involved in this, Soames?" the duke demanded.

Soames looked very reluctant to open his mouth, but one look at Aunt Anabel's cane had him rethinking his reticence. "We may or may not 'ave lost the gen'rous donation 'Is 'Ighness 'ere bestowed upon us. On the 'orses. It were only in a contempt to raise more blunt for our Jenny. It weren't my fault our pick went lame on the second turn . . ."

"Your point, Soames," Montford interrupted.

"My point is, Jem were sore over it an' wanted to find another job. 'E said 'e had an opportunity presentated to him by some old geezer 'e met down Jacob's Island way. Something about abductioning a nob. I says to him I wanted no part in it, as I am a legitimate businessman these days."

The marquess snorted his disbelief.

"I'm a reformed soul," Soames insisted, undaunted, eyeing Mademoiselle with no small amount of trepidation. "I learnt me lesson long ago."

Oxley just waved his hand around wearily. "There; you see I didn't take Marlowe or the woman. Obviously this Jem fellow did so. If you find my equipage and horses, kindly return them. Now if you don't mind, may I die in peace?"

"If I find out you had any involvement in this, Oxley," Montford growled, "I'll have your head."

"Please do," Oxley retorted, slumping back on his pillow.

"Better than this slow end."

As they left the residence, Betsy almost felt sorry for the man . . . until she remembered what a loathsome pig he was. She'd leave the sainthood to Dr. Lucas, who'd arranged with Oxley's butler to return the following day in a more doctorly capacity. He really was too noble for his own good. And she didn't admire him in the least for it.

Not in the least.

Soon enough, they found themselves precisely where they'd started, on Oxley's stoop with the footman slamming the door behind them.

"Well, Poxley's finally lived up to expectation," Manwaring said dryly. Which was rather cold, considering the man's sorry state, but not, Betsy thought, undeserved, all things considered.

That, upstairs in that putrid bedchamber—*that* could have been her fate, if not for her brother. She shivered and wondered if she'd ever feel warm again.

"As educational as that was," the duchess said, handing off Mademoiselle to her aunt, "we are no closer to locating Marlowe and Miss Jones."

"I've an idea where they are, Yer Gracefulness," Soames said grudgingly. "I 'ave . . . er, that is, *Jem* 'as a bolt-hole in the rookery, an' I'd wager that's where we'll find 'em."

"You shouldn't be wagering on anything, Soames," Montford snapped, then sighed grimly. "Jacob's Island? Must we really?"

"I'm afraid we must," Manwaring said, slapping his friend's back.

The duke turned to his wife. "I suppose there's nothing I can say to stop you coming along, is there?"

"Oh, there probably is," the duchess said breezily, "but I doubt you'll think of it soon enough."

Montford turned to Betsy, but she just arched her brow at him, and he didn't even bother trying to change her mind.

"There's one thing I don't understand, though," the marquess said as they retreated to the carriages.

"Just one?" Montford muttered.

Manwaring ignored his friend. "If Poxley isn't behind this, then who is?"

CHAPTER TWENTY-NINE

In Which Another Villain Is Confronted

MARLOWE THOUGHT IT BANG OUT of order that someone had the audacity to rouse him from the first decent doze he'd had in days by screaming in his ear. He attempted to turn away from the noise and seek refuge under his pillow, but for some reason he couldn't move his arms.

The twins had taken after him so much in the mischief department that he thought it likely his present immobility was part of one of their more elaborate pranks (they still *were* rather cross with him for chasing off Minerva). And if that were the case, he was really going to have to put his foot down the next time the duchess tried to foist off her sisters onto his household. The Honeywells had given his girls entirely too many ideas when it came to troublemaking. The twins were no saints, but Bea and Laura would have never thought to tie someone up before those misanthropes corrupted them. Probably. Hopefully.

In fact, he'd have words with Astrid that very day—just as soon as he woke up. Which would not be anytime soon, despite all of the shouting. And the dull throb in his skull—though he didn't recall going on a bender. He was rather certain, in fact, that he'd resolved not to do so just the night before. But Minerva Jones did have the unfortunate effect of making him forgo his nobler resolutions to himself. Hence why he could very well have drowned himself in a bottle, despite his intentions otherwise. His heart was taking her repudiations rather poorly, after all.

He'd never known a hangover to feel quite like this before, however—as if he'd been coshed over the head with a cricket bat and then trampled by a pack of wild dogs. And he'd certainly never experienced a hangover that kept bashing itself against his shins with all the concentrated fury of a woodpecker on the trail of a wily ant.

He squinted his eyes open and found weak afternoon light pouring into the room from a window half-covered in faded newsprint. The dull throb in his skull immediately spread into the back of his eyeballs, and he groaned in misery.

As he was fairly sure the windows of his bedchamber were paned in glass, he came to the swift conclusion that he was not there. In fact, judging from the stained and crumbling plaster walls, the half-rotted floorboards beneath his boots, and the much too familiar stench of the Thames nearby, he was not even in Mayfair anymore.

He was also, much to his bewilderment, bound to a chair—though whoever had done so was obviously an idiot, since he'd not even bothered to tie up Marlowe's legs. And his *daughters* could tie better knots than the ones binding his wrists behind him, for with just a few tugs he could already feel them start to give.

It was a sad testament to his life thus far that he'd regained consciousness in worse situations than this. When he was eight, the earl had pulled him from his slumber to mete out punishment for some imagined transgression—likely Evander's doing—and he'd not been able to sit down for a week afterward. His first year at Harrow, the older boys had yanked him from his bed for a trip to the privies—an initiation he would have gladly forgone—and the stench in his hair had lingered for days.

In Spain, he'd come around after a battle to find himself a prisoner in a French camp, and though he'd managed to escape a few days later, the intervening time had not been pleasant. He still lost sleep whenever his unconscious mind touched on those carefully suppressed memories, even after all these years.

Then there had been that morning he'd woken up to find his wife had run off with his brother, leaving him with a careless note and month-old twins. That memory, worse in many ways than that of his brief imprisonment, was nothing, however, compared to coming out of his fever to discover his daughters had been taken from him by the earl.

So waking up to miserable situations was rather old hat to him, though the present one was rather unique in his experience. He just hoped he lived through it unscathed. Or mostly unscathed, since he suspected a concussion rather than a hangover was to blame for his brainbox's current incapacitation.

He closed his eyes again to block out the light and concentrated on loosening the knots around his wrists.

Suddenly, the kicking and shouting recommenced, sending a lancing pain through both temples and shins. He groaned and cracked his reluctant eyes open once more, turning his spinning head to the right just enough to spot his tormentor.

He'd admit to a few idle daydreams over the past few miserable days, featuring Minerva Jones tied up and at his mercy (or, honestly, vice versa; he wasn't picky), but this was not quite what he'd had in mind. His imagination had featured a lot less clothes and scowling on Minerva's part . . . and perhaps a feather bed and a few declarations of forgiveness and undying love thrown in for good measure.

What he hadn't imagined was having Minerva tied to a chair beside him in a derelict ruin that stank of rot and sewage. Somewhere along the way she'd lost half the pins in her hair, so most of that long selkie pelt was falling down her shoulders. Her redingote looked rumpled and dusty, and one of the faux militaristic epaulettes that he'd thought made her look rather like a female martinet had been ripped off. But other than that, the smudge of dirt on her nose, and the fact that she was as stuck to her chair as he was, she seemed to be unharmed.

In an extremely bad mood, but unharmed.

"Finally!" she said, scowling at him through her fallen hair.

It was comforting—and a bit daunting—to know that being abducted and tied up did nothing to dampen her temper. Though he did think he detected a bit of worry behind her flashing eyes. "I've been trying to rouse you for ages."

She made it sound like it was his fault he'd been unconscious, though he felt rather confident that for once it wasn't.

"What the devil happened?" he managed, though even speaking softly made his head spin and his stomach churn.

"We've been abducted, obviously," she snapped.

It *was* a bit obvious, he supposed, but she didn't have to look at him as if he were an idiot. "Yes, but why? How?"

"Why? I haven't a clue, though I'm guessing it's your fault somehow," she accused.

He snorted and then wished he hadn't, for it made the throbbing in his head even worse. "Of course it is," he muttered.

"As for how, do you not remember?" she continued, sounding a bit worried underneath all of that venom.

He thought as hard as he could until his head felt as if it were about to launch itself to the moon. The last thing he recalled was arguing with her in the shrubbery along the Serpentine, and the smell of burning trees and leather, and . . .

Dear God, the *bonfire*. His *books*. That *speech*. He remembered everything now.

He flushed all over with renewed embarrassment. He'd never been comfortable speaking in front of large groups, much less making a public declaration.

Which had been rather thoroughly rejected—a caveat for going against his instincts if there ever was one.

He blamed Sebastian. And Montford. Definitely Montford with all of that talk of special licenses and grand romantic gestures. How could he have ever taken advice from a man who had wooed his bride by winning a drunken footrace?

He cleared his throat and looked everywhere but at Minerva. "The last thing I remember was chasing you into the shrubbery after you rejected me in front of the entire world." If he sounded a little bitter, then that was because he was.

She growled at him and looked as if she wanted to kick his shins again. He shifted his legs away from her just in case.

"I did not . . . For the love of . . . Are you sulking *now*?"

"I'm not sulking," he said, even though it wasn't the least bit true. "But that *is* the last thing I recall. *You* wanted to know."

She sighed. "Fine. You followed me into the shrubbery, and a ruffian came out of nowhere and coshed you on the head. I tried to run away, but he coshed me too, put us both in a carriage, and drove us here. We're on the South Bank, I believe."

Marlowe's blood began to boil with fury at her recounting of events. "Did he hurt you?"

"My hand's a bit bruised from punching him in the face, and I've a knot on my head, but other than that, I'm fine."

His blood boiled even hotter. No one was allowed to manhandle Minerva. Besides himself, of course.

But at least she'd managed a decent bit of resistance. He didn't doubt the potency of her right hook. She was a hellcat, after all.

"Now it's your turn to explain what you've done to land us in this mess," she snapped.

Well, that seemed unfair of her. But she was always quick to judgment. "Why do you think this is my fault?"

She looked at him incredulously. "Since I've met you, you've had me sacked, written a poem about my *hip*, blackmailed a duke, and had a prizefight with your own father over the dinner table."

"I was entirely justified in my actions—other than the sacking, of course," he finished contritely when the look she leveled on him could have frozen hell. "And the hip."

"My point is," she gritted out, "you're the one with the long list of enemies, not me."

He understood that she had every right to be angry right now, but she was being entirely unfair. His list of enemies was very short, thank you very much, as it contained only one name—Poxley—and the man was probably halfway to Egypt by now. Old Manwaring was dead—may his soul rot in hell—and as far as Marlowe was concerned, his fight with the French had ended with the Treaty of Paris.

And while he and his father felt a mutual antipathy, the earl would never stoop to hiring a third party to abduct him. The earl's assaults were mostly verbal these days, and when they weren't, they tended to involve his fists. Obviously. Barming would be satisfied with nothing less than injuring Marlowe by his own hand, not someone else's. He was refreshingly predictable that way.

Marlowe had no time to defend against her accusations, however, before the villain himself descended upon them.

"Already cavorting with another woman, I see. I knew you were never deserving of Miss Honeywell," a voice boomed from the doorway at his back, cutting their argument short.

Marlowe didn't know whether he was relieved or annoyed by the interruption, since he and Minerva were finally making progress (i.e. speaking to each other). But he was certainly confused at the mention of Miss Honeywell. He knew a handful of females with that particular surname, but none of them had anything to do with him, last he'd checked.

Marlowe craned his neck around to find a short, paunchy man with a smattering of scraggly brown hair combed over the crown of his head marching in his direction, eyes glittering with a fury bordering on madness.

Definitely not Poxley, then.

The man was grinning victoriously at Marlowe, but that grin faded, and his confident swagger faltered shortly after Marlowe turned his head.

"Who the hell are you?" the man squeaked out in dismay, his once glittering eyes now wide with shock. "*You're not Montford.*"

"No, I'm not," Marlowe said, as thoroughly baffled by this turn of events as his captor. He gave Miranda a quick, smug grin. "I told you it weren't about me."

She just rolled her eyes.

He turned back to the squat little man. "And I'd like to know who the bloody hell *you* are, if you wouldn't mind."

The man's face reddened in rage, and he stomped back to the door, bellowing for someone named Jem. He then stomped around the room for a moment in a temper, kicking at the cracked plaster and muttering to himself before turning back to them and glowering, as if it were *their* fault he'd kidnapped the wrong people.

A few moments later, a tall, weedy man with greasy blond hair and a swelling eye barreled into the room, skidding to a stop next to the other man.

"Wot's it, gov?" the man—who must have been the aforementioned Jem—shot out breathlessly, side-eyeing Minerva with trepidation and giving her chair a wide berth.

"You!" Minerva breathed, struggling against her bonds as

if ready to pounce upon the man.

Jem jumped back a few steps and touched his injured eye.

Minerva shot Marlowe a dark look. "He's the one who coshed us over the head."

"It weren't personal. Just following orders, missy," the man said rather querulously, holding up his hands placatingly.

"No, *not* following orders at all, you . . . you *imbecile!*" the paunchy man raged.

"Wot!" Jem looked totally baffled.

The man jabbed his finger at Marlowe with such violence Marlowe was rather surprised the air around it didn't shatter. "That is not the Duke of Montford!"

"Wot?" Jem cried, bafflement swiftly giving way to alarm. "But that's not right now, is it? 'Cause you said as how 'is nibs were the tall one with dark hair in the silver jacket, and 'e were the only one in a silver jacket as far as I could see."

Marlowe groaned. He'd known the minute he'd put on his friend's jacket that he'd been making a horrible sartorial blunder, but he'd never dreamed that it would come to *this*.

"Are ye sure it ain't him?" Jem asked hopefully.

The man just glared at his associate.

Jem turned to Marlowe instead with an imploring look—as if Marlowe could, perhaps, make himself into the right person with enough incentive.

"I'm fairly certain I'm not the Duke of Montford," Marlowe drawled. "But I *am* wearing his jacket."

Jem looked somewhat mollified that he'd gotten that much correct, until he glanced at his furious companion. His expression crumbled. "Does that mean I woan be gettin' the rest of my blunt?"

The man growled and stalked in Marlowe's direction without answering, pulling a pistol from the back of his breeches. *That* rather changed the game . . . and in a way Marlowe was sure to loathe.

"Who are you?" the man demanded, pointing the gun at Marlowe's head as he neared.

The smell of something foul assaulted Marlowe's nostrils—foul and familiar. He had more than a passing acquaintance with the sewer-ripe stench of the Thames at low tide after his ill-fated bath in it last winter, but it was not an acquaintance he'd wanted to pursue. He was fairly certain that the odor was emanating from their captor, for the closer he came, the more the stench intensified.

"What's that horrible smell?" he demanded, breathing through his mouth.

The man faltered back a few steps and glared down accusingly at his boots, his ruddy complexion darkening even further.

Marlowe looked to Minerva, who seemed a bit green about the gills as well, but he wasn't sure if it was from the smell or the pistol. Marlowe himself was a bit concerned about the latter, of course, considering it was trained on his head, but he had no intention of letting harm befall his governess. If the odorous little man so much as touched a hair on her head, Marlowe wasn't going to be held accountable for his actions.

As for Jem's manhandling . . .

Marlowe fixed the stringy Jem with a look that made all of the color drain from his face, his Adam's apple working up and down nervously.

"Don't try to turn the subject," the paunchy man said. "Who are you?"

"I am the Viscount Marlowe," he declared with as much authority as he could muster with a head wound and bound wrists.

Minerva snorted next to him.

Well, apparently not even the appearance of their abductors *and a gun* were enough to scare her out of her righteous indignation.

The lunatic looked between them with a furrowed brow. "Then he's *not* the Viscount Marlowe?" he demanded.

Minerva scowled at him. "He's Christopher Essex apparently," she said reproachfully.

Marlowe guffawed. He had to question her decision to continue their argument while an obvious lunatic waved a gun in their faces. "Are we really going to have this out now, Minerva? In the middle of our bloody abduction?"

She shrugged and refused to meet his eyes. "Why not? It's obvious they've abducted the wrong person. They wanted Montford, not you."

"This is true." Marlowe glanced at his captor. "What did you want with the duke anyway?"

The man looked two seconds from full-on apoplexy, as if offended to his core that they shouldn't already know. "He *ruined me*! Had the courts send me to New South Wales simply because of a *woman*. Do you know what it's like there?"

Marlowe's coshed brain finally slotted the pieces together. "You're Lightfoot, aren't you?" he breathed. "You abducted Astrid and tried to force her to marry you!"

"The girl didn't know what was best for her . . ." the man muttered miserably.

Minerva made a loud, disparaging sound at this.

"How the devil did you make it back here from Australia?" Marlowe asked, because he'd really like to know. It was . . . impressive. And a bit alarming. Montford had always told him how insane Lightfoot had been, but he'd not truly believed his friend until now. The man certainly had the eyes of a lunatic.

"Stop trying to change the subject," Lightfoot barked. "Whoever you are, you're wearing the duke's jacket. Is this some elaborate scheme of his? Has he discovered I am returned and sent you as bait to flush me out?"

Marlowe was rather impressed at the extent of the man's

paranoia. "Nothing like that, I can assure you. He loaned it to me."

"Ha! Likely story. If you are indeed *Christopher Essex*—which I highly doubt—there is no way the pompous Duke of Montford would loan you anything, much less associate with the likes of you," Lightfoot declared.

Well, that was just not on. Marlowe had spent the entire afternoon battling dragons masquerading as bombazine-clad society matrons intent on burning England's literary establishment to the ground. He didn't really feel up to defending himself against felonious ex-brewers who were one step away from Bedlam.

"So you don't like my poetry?" he taunted.

"I prefer prose," Lightfoot growled. "Now tell me what the duke is planning."

He sighed. The man was certainly tenacious in his delusions. "Last I heard? He was planning on visiting the archbishop to petition for a special license."

Lightfoot looked baffled. "How can that be? Is he not wed to Miss Honeywell?" A strange gleam came into his eyes at the possibility that Astrid was still unwed.

As much as the duchess annoyed him sometimes, Marlowe shuddered on her behalf. Lightfoot was just . . .

No. God, no.

"He was to accompany me to the archbishop," he amended.

"What?" Minerva cried.

He could feel his cheeks heat. He'd not exactly planned out how he was going to climb back into her good graces after his latest failure at Hyde Park, much less propose marriage. He certainly hadn't expected to do so when they were both tied to chairs by a lunatic with a grudge. But he had learned his lesson about dragging his feet where Minerva was concerned.

"We meant to go today," he said defensively. "After that business in Hyde Park—though *that* was wishful thinking, wasn't it? I suppose he wouldn't go there *now*, not without me. It's not as if he's the one who is planning on proposing marriage . . ." He trailed off and squirmed in his seat at the look of utter incredulity on Minerva's face.

"Are you . . . are you asking . . . ?"

"Yes?" he prompted.

"Are you proposing . . . marriage? To me? Right now?" Her voice had started off soft but had ended up alarmingly shrill at the end.

This was not a good sign.

But the sudden loosening in the ropes around his wrists was. His last contortion had finally managed to unravel the final knot. They'd apparently been abducted by rank amateurs. It was rather insulting how easy it had been to free himself. He thought it best to bide his time, however, until he found his way around the pistol. If the idiots had even managed to load it properly.

"I might be. Yes, I am," he said.

"Now. In the middle of our abduction?" She sounded extremely unimpressed.

He scowled at her. "Well, should I wait? Perhaps *after* they've shot us and thrown our bodies into the Thames?" She winced at that. "Someone said to me quite recently, in fact, that I was a coward for not telling you the truth sooner . . ."

"You *didn't* tell me," she interrupted hotly. "I *found out*! From your sister! After you seduced me under false pretenses!"

Ugh. She was never going to let that go. "Forgive me for being caught up in the moment with the woman I love. Besides, whatever you believe, I *did* plan to tell you that morning, but you ran away." He squeezed his eyes shut and tried to tamp down his irritation, and he surreptitiously shucked the ropes from his wrists. "And I have never hid who I truly am from you. I just happen to write a few poems under a *nom de plume*."

He grimaced inwardly at this rather weak justification, but when he opened his eyes, Minerva was staring at him with wide eyes, her expression softened to something almost tender. He was so used to seeing her in a temper these days that the look totally confounded him. "What? What happened?" he demanded. "What did I say?"

"The woman you love?" she asked softly.

Oh. *Oh.* He could feel his body heat all over from that tone in her voice, a tone he'd not heard from her since she'd been beneath him on his bedroom settee.

"Yes, of course the woman I love," he said gruffly, feeling quite at the end of his tether. "What the devil do you think I've been trying to tell you all this time? And today, when I made an arse of myself in front of the entire ton?" Not that *that* was anything new.

"You've never once said that," she murmured, looking rather uncertain. "That you love me."

"Have I not? And how can it not be perfectly obvious? Of course, *of course* I love you."

She huffed a breath and wrinkled her nose, looking remarkably unconvinced, even after he'd just torn his heart out and laid it at her feet. Again. "Well, it's not obvious to me. I thought . . . well, I don't know what I thought. And your little spectacle today did nothing to convince me you were so . . . committed."

He guffawed in disbelief. "Are you joking?"

She glared at him. "Byron? *Really?*"

"How is my recitation of one of the most romantic poems ever written not enough of a declaration?"

She just pursed her lips and refused to meet his eyes. As if he should be able to read her mind on the matter.

He looked to his two captors for guidance before he remembered how stupid an idea that was, all things considered. Lightfoot was just glancing between the two of them as if *they* were the lunatics, but Jem scratched his head in consideration and shrugged.

"Well, you are a poet, ain't ya? In me 'umble experience, birds want their fellows to write their own bit of verse, not poach some other bloke's."

The scarlet flush that came over Minerva's cheeks said that Jem knew significantly more about women than he knew about knot tying.

"You're upset I didn't write my own poem?" Marlowe hoarsed out, gobsmacked.

Her flush deepened, and she bit at her bottom lip as if trying to hold herself back. Finally she seemed to break, exhaling and flashing stormy eyes at him. "Well, you *are* bloody Christopher Essex. You can write an ode to my hip, but not *one* decent love poem?"

"Told you, mate," Jem said smugly.

Marlowe shook his head in disbelief at Minerva's . . . ridiculousness. What should he have expected, though, from a woman who was just as obsessed with Essex as his sister had been before the incest had gotten in the way?

But then again, she did have a point. He should have used his own words. It was yet another way he had failed in not only giving Minerva what she deserved but also conquering his own poetic demons. He hadn't known it was possible to feel any worse than he had in the days following Minerva's decampment, but in that moment, with a probable concussion, a gun to his head, and yet another reminder of his complete failure as a man *and* a poet, he found that it was indeed very possible.

"I tried," he said quietly. "I was going to write the greatest love poem in the history of humankind, but I couldn't. I haven't been able to write anything other than that damnable ode in months, Minerva." Years, really. "And besides, I was in a bit of a rush this morning, and the words . . . there are no words, Minerva, that could ever possibly come close to expressing how much I love and adore you. But I shall try, for the rest of my life, to find them."

Minerva's expression crumbled, and her eyes welled with

tears. He straightened in his chair in alarm at her reaction. He must have said the wrong thing yet again, or, God forbid, not enough.

"Those. *Those* are the words. The perfect words," she said as the tears fell down her face.

Oh, thank bloody hell.

His cheeks may or may not have also felt suspiciously damp at the moment, but he felt entirely justified in indulging himself. Minerva had not made things easy for him, and he had a feeling he'd merely won the battle and not the war.

"So does that mean you forgive me?" Let it not be said he wasn't willing to capitalize on the moment.

She smiled at him tremulously, but before she could give him a proper answer, the deafening report of a pistol echoed through the room and his aching head.

He shifted his attention back to Lightfoot—he'd nearly forgotten the little rat was still there at all—and found the man glaring at him with a smoking gun in his meaty hand.

"Enough!" Lightfoot growled. "I don't know who you think you are . . ."

"Oh, I think *that* has been well established by now, don't you?" he drawled, flexing his fingers at his back.

"But this . . . ridiculous pantomime has gone on long enough! If you have nothing useful to tell me about the duke, then I have no further need of you. Jem, shoot them and dump them in the river."

"Wot?" Jem cried, alarmed. "I weren't paid to do no murderin'."

"You'll do as I say if you want to see a single pound."

Jem snorted. "Doan fink I will, mate. Now I'll be havin' the rest of me money, and be on me way."

Lightfoot rounded on Jem and shoved the gun in the man's face. Jem's eyes popped wide in surprise, as if he'd not expected this particular turn of events, and he raised his hands in surrender.

"You won't be having the rest of anything unless you do as I say. Now shoot them before I shoot you!" Lightfoot snarled.

"Why doan you just shoot 'em yerself and leave me out of it?" Jem cried.

Lightfoot paused and looked worryingly thoughtful, as if such a novel idea had never occurred to him.

Marlowe cursed Jem silently. Just when he'd begun to like the lad.

He supposed it was time to make his move, since it looked as if Lightfoot was inclined to take Jem's advice. But before he could rise out of his seat, Lightfoot stumbled on Minerva's outstretched leg as he stalked toward Marlowe.

The villain floundered in the air, arms windmilling, then fell in an awkward sprawl on top of Minerva, knocking her chair backward. She let out a pained cry as her bound hands were pinned beneath the combined weight of her body and Lightfoot's.

Indignant, Marlowe sprang to his feet and jerked Lightfoot from Minerva, knocking the pistol out of the man's paw at the same time. He nearly recoiled at the sewer stench that clung to Lightfoot's person—the man must have bathed in the shallows to smell so rotten. He swung Lightfoot around by the collar and punched him in the jaw, breathing through his mouth the whole time.

Lightfoot's eyes rolled into the back of his head, and he collapsed to the floor in a dead faint. Marlowe quickly took up his discarded rope and bound the man's arms behind his back, this time with some proper knots, before he let himself relax. All in all, it was a bit of an anticlimax.

Minerva cried out in alarm, and when he glanced up, he discovered Jem had retrieved the pistol. The man aimed the gun in his direction, his arms trembling so badly Marlowe was afraid he'd press the trigger by accident.

"'E didn't say nofink about no murder!" Jem cried.

Marlowe raised his hands and stepped away from Lightfoot. "I believe you, Jem."

"'E wanted the Duke of Montford brought 'ere is all I knows. And I only done it for the blunt. Our Jenny needs a proper doctor, and I figured one duke done it to her, another duke can pay. You nobs are all the same to me. But I ain't no murderer."

This was beginning to sound horribly familiar.

"You wouldn't be talking about Jenny Turner of the White House off Soho Square?"

Jem blanched. "Wot! How'd you know?"

"I believe we have a mutual friend. Mr. Soames."

Jem's expression darkened. "How do you know my cousin?"

"Never mind that. But I thought Soames had collected quite enough funds for Jenny's injuries."

Jem snorted. "'E did, but then 'e said we could double it at the races."

Oh, good Lord. "That didn't go to plan, then?"

Jem shook his head.

"And you went along with it?"

Jem nodded, his face flaming.

Good God, the imbeciles. Though Sebastian *had* warned him.

"Did Soames put you up to this?" he demanded. He'd kill the runner if he were involved in this madness.

Jem shook his head. "'E weren't interested. Claims 'e's a legitimate businessman these days."

That was painting it a bit brown, but he had to commend Soames for drawing the line at abduction-for-hire. It certainly hadn't done him any favors before. "I hate to use Soames as a paragon for anything, but perhaps you might try to emulate your cousin."

"Emu-wot?"

Marlowe sighed. "I'll get Jenny the finest doctor in the city," he said grudgingly, for it was the least he could do for the poor girl. She obviously had no one sensible around her to care for her properly, judging by Soames's and Jem's recklessness.

Jem's expression brightened.

"But you have to stop pointing the gun at me first."

Jem startled as if he'd just remembered what he was holding in his hands. The gun wavered even more in Jem's grip, but for some reason the man seemed reluctant to comply.

Marlowe sighed. "You're no murderer, I can see that, Jem. But if you pull that trigger, you better be sure you kill me, because if you don't . . . well . . ." Marlowe gave Jem the same grin he'd given the French soldiers he'd met—and killed—on the battlefield. Jem paled. "You'd better run."

Jem swallowed nervously.

"Far, far away," he continued.

Jem dropped the gun and ran toward the door. It was the first intelligent thing he'd done all day.

He didn't get far, however, for at that exact moment, the door crashed inward, and Soames himself barreled straight into his cousin. They fell to the floor in a tangled, cursing heap. The boards creaked alarmingly under their weight, and Marlowe braced himself just in case the whole room collapsed.

Montford and Sebastian hurtled through the door next, with the duchess hot on their heels. Her expression was suspiciously bright as she took in the scene. She was no doubt relishing every minute of this misadventure, though when she caught sight of Lightfoot, her good humor faded into disgust. "Oh, not him again!" she cried.

Marlowe should have been more surprised to see them, but his head hurt too much to question their appearance.

"We heard a shot. Is anyone injured?" Sebastian asked.

Marlowe glanced at the unconscious Lightfoot and toed him a bit with his boot. "No."

"Speak for yourself," Minerva grouched. "My hands feel as if two people fell on them . . . Oh, wait! Two people *did* fall on them. And if someone doesn't untie me this instant, there will be consequences."

Oh, good Lord—*Minerva*. And she was using her governess voice. That did not bode well. In his defense, he'd not forgotten Minerva in the fracas so much as concentrated on disarming the enemy before further injury could befall her, but he doubted she would see it that way. She'd been left bound to an upended chair for much too long.

He righted Minerva's chair and grinned down at her, hoping to divert her wrath at the very least. "Is that a promise?"

She blushed and glared at him in wordless eloquence, and his heart felt light with happiness at the sight of her, whole and hopping mad. He decided to seize the moment before she had full use of her extremities—just in case she'd decided to take a swing at *his* eye—and pecked her on the lips. It lasted a fraction of a second, but it still sent a deliciously electric thrill down his spine.

It was enough to still her protests. She gaped at him in stunned silence as he reached around and undid her knots. When he was through, he pulled her to her feet and examined her hands. The skin around her wrists seemed a little abraded—for which Jem would pay in some creative way—but he could see no cuts or bruises.

Someone cleared a throat, and he turned his head to find Montford and Sebastian holding up a slumped Lightfoot between them, the duchess beaming in their direction. He realized he must have been examining Minerva's hands for longer than he'd thought.

She did have lovely hands, though, so he thought himself quite justified.

"It seems you didn't need our help after all," Montford rumbled, looking slightly put upon. "Though why Lightfoot would kidnap you in the first place . . ."

Marlowe scowled at his friend and jerked out of the blasted silver jacket. He balled it up and threw it at the duke. "I told you I looked ridiculous in it. I looked like *you!*"

Montford fumbled to catch the jacket, releasing his hold on Lightfoot and startling Sebastian so badly that the marquess's grip faltered and the villain crashed face-first to the floor once more. They all stared down at the fallen man in consternation for a moment but decided to let him lie.

"Ridiculous?" Montford blustered. "*I* am ridiculous? Why, I . . ."

Astrid patted her husband's arm consolingly. "I think it's a splendid jacket. A bit more . . . *reflective* a fabric choice than your usual, though."

Montford turned his scowl on to Sebastian. "I am *never* inviting you along to my tailor's again."

Sebastian just shrugged and propped his foot on Lightfoot's backside. "You are letting a man who wears scarlet banyans and Jerusalem sandals shame your wardrobe, Monty."

"*I* am allowed to wear banyans and sandals. *I* am an eccentric poet," Marlowe proclaimed.

Sebastian's brow rose, and his mouth twitched. "Oh? Is *that* the reason? I thought it was from being punched in the brainbox one too many times during the war."

Before he could formulate a suitably cutting retort, there was a commotion in the hallway, featuring a high-pitched voice that was far too familiar. He groaned inwardly and braced himself. Seconds later, Betsy flew into the room with a russet-colored dog barking hysterically at her bootheels. A harassed-looking Dr. Lucas stumbled in behind her, with Astrid's dotty Aunt Anabel hanging off his arm, looking bound for the Bourbon court.

Betsy threw herself into Marlowe's arms with a cry of relief. He hugged his sister close and glowered at the doctor over her shoulder. Lucas, the only halfway sensible one of the lot, should have known better than to allow Betsy to accompany them to a rookery. The doctor just shrugged helplessly. "I tried to stop her."

"But I was having none of it," Betsy said crisply, pulling away from Marlowe and grinning broadly. "I wanted to make sure you were all right with my own eyes. Since *I* was the one who figured out you were abducted in the first place." She glared at Montford and Sebastian as if daring them to contradict her claim.

Both men wisely held their tongues.

Betsy broke away from him and threw herself at Minerva next, lifting the smaller woman off her feet and spinning her around. It was exactly what Marlowe had wished to do, but he was afraid if he tried to spin anyone around at this point, he was liable to faint. He supposed their reconciliation would have to wait for another day. But there *would* be a reconciliation now, of that he had no doubt.

Minerva looked up, met his eyes, and gave him a small smile, and his heart swelled with hope. It would have to be enough for now.

"As much fun as it's been, I suggest we depart the premises posthaste, before our carriages are stolen," the duke said, reluctantly hauling Lightfoot back to his feet with Sebastian's help and dragging him toward the door.

"Hold on," Sebastian said, abruptly dropping Lightfoot's legs. They thudded against the floorboards, and Lightfoot groaned in pain. (Everyone ignored him.) "What's happened to Soames and his cousin?"

Marlowe froze and glanced around the room, but no trace of the two ruffians remained. Damn. They'd doubtless skulked their way back across the river by now.

Well, it seemed the pair of them would live to bedevil London for another day, for Marlowe was much too tired—and concussed—to give a damn about chasing them down.

"And what in God's name is that smell?" Sebastian continued, wrinkling his nose as he glared down at Lightfoot's fragrant boots.

CHAPTER THIRTY

In Which Miss Jones Makes A Grand Gesture

Following the duchess of Montford's advice on any occasion was probably a terrible idea. When that advice included the midnight hour, a bit of light housebreaking, an ancient ladder, and a two-story climb, it was *definitely* a terrible idea. Horrible, even. Especially when one of the rungs of said ladder broke beneath Minerva's foot halfway up and she nearly plummeted to her doom.

She clung to the sides and glowered down into the midnight gloom, where the moonlight glinted off the duchess's red hair—the duchess, who was wearing *trousers*.

"I am going to die!" she hissed. "I told you this ladder looked rotten."

Astrid made some wild gesture with her hands that looked vaguely encouraging, though she had to abandon her steadying grip on the ladder to do so. Minerva clung even more desperately as the ladder wobbled. This was Poseidon all over again.

"You're almost there!" the duchess stage-whispered. "Don't turn coward now, Minerva Jones. You wanted a Grand Gesture; *this* is a Grand Gesture!"

"This is a terrible gesture," she muttered to herself, but

continued to climb.

At the present moment, in the middle of the night, in the middle of the *air*, Minerva wasn't sure how she had been so convinced of this plan's cleverness not six hours earlier. She blamed the duchess entirely.

After the debacle in the rookery with that horrid bedlamite, Mr. Lightfoot, the viscount had been suspiciously absent from her life. As if, after his public declaration and subsequent marriage proposal (while tied to a chair—and heavily concussed), he'd given up on her. She didn't think that was true, precisely, but the fight had definitely gone out of him. Which just wouldn't do.

He'd backed off, the idiot, just as she'd asked him to. It was, frankly, the last thing she'd expected him to do, and deep down the last thing she'd wanted. For now that the first blush of anger was behind her, she was clearheaded enough to realize that she'd forgiven him for his deception long ago. She'd only held on to her anger out of sheer stubbornness.

For a man who'd spent a decade keeping his avocation as a poet a secret—longer than that, even, with a father like the earl, who'd probably tried to beat the poetry out of him as a boy—announcing he was Christopher Essex to a largely hostile audience had to have been excruciating for him.

He'd always used words as a shield to hide behind, whether through the eloquence of Christopher Essex or the teasing, ironic cant favored by the viscount. He'd laid his soul bare as Essex, but his anonymity had made such truth telling easy. To do the same without hiding behind the public mask he'd so carefully cultivated as the feckless viscount couldn't have been easy for him to do.

Yet he'd done so, for her. In her utter mortification at the bonfire, it had been difficult to appreciate this, and she'd ended up scolding him for not only his public declaration but also for reciting Byron to her.

Well, she was still rather cross about *that*, but she understood now why he'd done so. Even after all that had transpired, she'd not truly connected the mercurial viscount she'd come to know with the poet who must have spent the last few years struggling for words—a poet who had just recently published a poem that was in large part a lamentation on his inability to write . . . in between all the bits about her dewy hips, of course.

Not until he'd explained to her that there were no words, that there never could be any words adequate to express his love for her, had she finally put all of the pieces of the puzzle together:

Lord Marlowe was Essex, who had, for years, written such profundity as to leave her and most of England half in love with him. But Essex was also Marlowe—a man she had started to love for all of his eccentricities months ago. Now, with the merging of his two identities, he was an even more complex creature than she could have ever fathomed. And one of the most unfathomable things about him was his tendre for her.

She'd been infuriated at first when she'd discovered he'd imagined her as the nymph in "The Alabaster Hip," but the fury had faded and left in its wake utter bafflement. How he could see anything nymphworthy in *her* was quite beyond her ken. It had seemed further proof to her that he was mocking her, as he'd mocked her from their first conversation in West Barming, with all his talk of fey creatures.

But now—now she was rather certain he'd been serious in his allusions. Even if she could never see herself as he apparently saw her, she realized he had never mocked her.

How could she compete, though? He'd declared his love for her in front of half the ton, and then done so again while at the mercy of a lunatic kidnapper. Even "The Alabaster Hip" had been a declaration, though she'd not known it at the time. All of these grand gestures, and she'd given him nothing in return but contempt. She didn't want to be the sort of person who punished the people they loved out of pettiness . . . though that was exactly the sort she was fast becoming when it came to Marlowe.

But just when she'd made up her mind to accept all he'd offered, he'd retreated. It was maddening, but it was not unjustified. Why should he continue to give so much when she refused to give anything in return?

It was her turn to make a Grand Gesture.

When Minerva had made the mistake of wondering aloud over tea if she should just climb into the viscount's bedroom window to confront him, she'd been joking, but the duchess, of course, had thought it a brilliant idea. And before Minerva's head could stop spinning, she'd somehow found herself agreeing to this nighttime misadventure.

Lord only knew what Astrid had told her husband—or done to him—to get him to let her leave Montford House in the dead of night with only Newcomb in attendance. Minerva suspected she didn't want to know.

Only the fear of climbing all the way back down the half-rotted ladder kept her from abandoning the mad scheme altogether and calling upon the viscount like a normal person in the morning instead. She was never listening to the duchess again.

When she pulled herself over the top of the ladder and onto a stone balcony, the impracticality of her plan only seemed to be confirmed. The room beyond was closed up tight, with no hint of life beyond its locked doors.

She sighed and leaned over the stone railing, searching for some glimpse of the duchess. She could just make out the shadow of her friend crouching among the shrubbery.

"He's not in his room!" she called down as loudly as she dared.

Whatever the duchess might have answered was drowned out by the deep voice behind her, so close to her ear it made her jump.

"Minerva?"

She spun around to find Marlowe standing practically on top of her, his large form temptingly warm despite the nip in the air. The balcony doors now stood open behind him, the dim light of a single gas lamp she'd not noticed before casting a weak glow across his broad shoulders. He wore nothing but an overlarge lawn shirt and inexpressibles, his dark curls in disarray, his feet bare.

"What are you doing?" He sounded curious but careful, his mouth turned up at the edges as if he were prepared to be amused by her and little else. His rich brown eyes caught the moonlight in a manner that, had she been Essex, she'd have waxed poetic about for several stanzas. But the only words she had at hand to describe them were beautiful . . .

And cautious. Her heart sank at the shuttered look he wore.

He was obviously done with wearing his heart on his sleeve, back to the indecipherable viscount she'd first met . . . though without even that incarnation's irreverence. This was the viscount who'd faced his family over the dinner table like a general going to battle. This was the viscount who still mourned his wife and brother despite their betrayal—this was the viscount who was used to getting hurt.

"I was attempting, rather poorly, to make a Grand Gesture," she muttered.

His brow furrowed in confusion, and he started to say something, but the sound of hushed, angry voices and the rustle of bushes below them caught the attention of them both. He leaned over the balcony's edge, and she followed suit. "Did you *climb* up here?" he asked, catching sight of the ladder. "And is that *Montford* carrying his wife out of my garden?"

"Yes," she said to the first question. "And that is very likely," she said to the second, as she watched the tall, shadowy form of the duke pass through the garden gate with a pouting duchess in his arms. Montford must have caught on to his wife's nighttime scheme and had come to fetch her home…or at least attempt to. He didn't seem to get very far before Astrid had successfully distracted him yet again. Minerva blushed and averted her eyes when the duke set his wife down and began to kiss her rather passionately on the other side of the gate.

Marlowe coughed and turned his attention back to the ladder, his cheeks suspiciously rosy as well. He frowned. "You climbed up that old thing?" he demanded rather disapprovingly. "You could have killed yourself."

She put her hands on her hips. This was not going at all as she'd envisioned it. "*You* scaled five stories without anything but a fever," she pointed out.

"The risk was acceptable."

And in his mad brain it would always be, for he'd do anything for his daughters, no matter how barmy. It was one of the things she loved best about him. But he always underestimated his own value. "So was this," she said firmly, for *she'd* do anything for *him*.

He gave her a skeptical look and turned on his heel to return to his bedchamber. She followed behind him and watched him pace rather awkwardly between the unlit fireplace and the escritoire. She noticed the small desk was cluttered with stacks of half-used foolscap, ruined quills, and empty inkpots. She peered inside the grate and could just make out a pile of balled-up papers waiting for incineration. Judging from these rather blatant clues and the ink staining his fingertips, he'd been writing—though it looked as if things had not been going well.

She could read other signs of his distress in the lamplight—dark bruises under his eyes and a tautness at the edges of his mouth that reminded her too much of his joyless father. He looked wan and even thinner than at their last meeting, as if his unhappiness were sucking the very marrow out of him—marrow he could scarce afford to lose.

He was not meant to be a skinny man, not with those massive shoulders and broad chest. But she supposed he would always be a man of extremes without someone to care for him properly.

Well, she planned on being that someone.

"I never gave you my answer," she said, gathering up her courage.

It took him a while to puzzle out what she was talking about, but when he did, he paused in his pacing. His shoulders slumped, and he began to fuss around his desktop, stacking papers and gathering up his quills.

"I thought I'd give you time to make your decision," he said, not meeting her eyes.

"I've not seen you in a week," she huffed.

"I thought it best not to torment myself—or you—until you had made up your mind."

Well, that sounded painfully self-pitying. But what did she expect, really, from a man who'd once written two volumes' worth of sonnets on heartbreak?

"Only if you didn't *want* me to accept your offer of marriage," she countered. "I assure you, I *could* reconsider, if it would torment you less."

The papers tumbled from his slack hands and all over his feet. He finally met her eyes for the first time all night. He looked ridiculously confused. "What?"

"I said, I would accept your offer. I would have done so after the abduction, but you ran off before I could get a word out." Granted, he'd not so much run off as been carried out by Inigo with a concussion, but he was not the only one given to hyperbole when feeling overemotional.

"*What?*" he repeated, dumbfounded, though there was a spark in his eyes that hadn't been there before.

"I don't know how to be any clearer. It's been a week since I've seen you, so I've had to resort to *this*. Climbing through windows as if I were a common thief . . . or a Leighton." He gave a weak smile at this. "Living with the duchess has done something horrible to me, Marlowe."

"You were climbing statuary long before Montford's," he pointed out. "But I still don't . . . Minerva, please, if you are toying with me, I could not bear it."

"I am perfectly sincere," she said crisply. "Though it seems *you* have given up on me."

"Never!" he said, his voice hoarse and so very, very contrite. "I was just busy . . ." He waved his hands at the escritoire, then at the littered fireplace, as if that would explain himself.

"Writing?"

He cleared his throat, his cheeks pink, his brow furrowed in consternation. "Attempting to, at least. Following Jem's sage advice. You wanted a poem."

She didn't know whether to be charmed or exasperated. "I don't need a poem, Marlowe. Just you."

He looked at her skeptically, determined to doubt her. She supposed she couldn't blame him. "Nevertheless, I wanted to be well armed before our next battle."

"Then let us have a treaty instead," she said, approaching him slowly, as she would a skittish animal. "I am done with this war between us."

A little bit more of the tension went out of his shoulders, but he still looked hesitant.

"I was so furious with you," she began. "But more furious with myself. Things . . . happened so quickly between us, and I was ready to give myself to you with no thought of consequences. I couldn't help but think the worst of your intentions after I discovered you were Essex."

"Well," he said gruffly, "I'll own they were never *that* honorable, Minerva. I wanted under your skirts from the moment we met."

Suddenly the room was much too warm. She'd forgotten how wonderfully frank he could be.

"But I never . . ." He cleared his throat and fixed her with such a tormented expression her heart flipped. "I never would have touched you that night had I not already made up my mind to wed you. My mistake was not making sure you wanted the same—*if* you could want the same after I told you everything. But I cocked things up, didn't I? That night you were so lovely, though, and I was so weak, and . . . I just *wanted* you, Minerva. I couldn't help myself."

Oh, good Lord, this *man*. Suddenly nothing mattered but being close to him and feeling those long, ink-stained fingers all over her skin, that deep, rumbling voice, full of nonsense and eloquence both, in her ear as he did wicked, wicked things. She wanted his warm embrace she'd known too fleetingly; she wanted to be engulfed entirely in bay rum and sandalwood and *Marlowe*—in miles of muscle and sinew and shockingly soft skin.

She'd wanted him too—still did. She stepped forward until they collided and stopped any more desperate words he might utter with a kiss.

He stiffened only momentarily before all of the stress and fatigue and unhappiness seemed to melt from his body, and then he began to return the kiss like a man who'd been denied water for too long, lips desperate and gasping and clumsy for more. His arms wrapped around her, sturdy and warm, and tightened their hold until no space remained between them, unwilling to part from her anytime soon.

When she finally managed to come up from air, dizzy with his kisses and half-mad for more, she said, "I'm sorry, Marlowe."

He was busy pressing kisses to her temple, behind her ears, and the edge of her jaw. "Hmm? Whatever for?" he murmured absently.

"For always being so quick to think the worst."

He paused for a moment, considering her words. He brought up his hands and cupped her face, tilted it upward so she had no choice but to meet his eyes. They were as soft as melted chocolate, and he looked . . . content, as she'd never seen before. And she realized that even at his most languid, there had always been a restlessness to him that had precluded him from ever being truly at peace. The restlessness was finally gone now, however, and her heart swelled even more at the thought that she was responsible for his peace.

"Nothing in your life had ever suggested it was a wise idea to think otherwise," he said gently. "I cannot fault you for protecting yourself, Minerva."

"You were only doing the same, weren't you?"

He grimaced and looked reluctant to answer her. She waited patiently, expectantly, her hands stroking the planes of his chest, until he finally gave in.

"My family—and Caroline—always ridiculed my poetry. I suppose it just became easier to hide it than to worry about what people might think of me. And after a while, it ceased to matter . . . until I met you. By the time I worked up the nerve to tell you, I'd lied to you for so long I knew you would hate me for it. You were right. I was trapped by my own cowardice."

She brought her hand up to the rough, unshaved surface of his cheek. "Well, you had one thing very wrong. I don't hate you. And by the by—other than your sisters, of course—your family is the absolute worst."

He grinned that devilish grin of his that never ceased to take away her good sense. "So will you have me, then?" he asked. "Will you be my wife and a mother to my daughters?"

"I could think of nothing I'd like so well," she said. "Though I am certain Laura and Beatrice shall have something to say about the latter."

"They have already made their opinion clear," he said. "They've threatened a coup unless I wooed you back. My wardrobe was the first casualty."

"Your banyans?"

"One survived—only because I was wearing it," he said ruefully. "You've won their hearts, just as you've won mine."

Well, then. How was she to argue with that? And how had he fooled her for so long, when he said such devastatingly perfect things as that? "Then I will marry you," she said firmly. "Now take me to bed. Properly this time."

He looked gobsmacked by her boldness, then positively ravenous. "Only if you're absolutely certain," he said, as if it pained him.

She pushed her way out of his embrace and gave him her sternest glare—which she doubted was very stern at all, considering how giddy she felt. "Surely the man who wrote *The Hedonist* would not be so reticent."

"The man who loves you would make sure," he countered, a wicked glint in his eyes despite his noble words. "And if it is the hedonist you're wanting tonight, I'm afraid I can't oblige. I'm rather in the mood to play the chevalier."

Ooh. *Well.* That sounded very promising indeed. "Canto three?"

"Canto three, verse five," he confirmed, closing the distance between them once more. A moment later, she was in his arms, her legs wrapped around his waist, and he was carrying her across the room toward his massive bed as if she weighed nothing at all. "In which the chevalier carries his Italian bride to the marriage bed."

"I'm not Italian," she countered, breathless.

He grinned down at her. "No, you're fey, aren't you?"

"Thought I was a nymph," she mock grumbled.

"You're *mine* is what you are," he growled.

She felt that growl all over. "You'll have no arguments from me."

"It's a bloody miracle, then," he murmured.

"Why, you . . ."

But before she could work herself up any further, he bit her bottom lip and ran his fingertips over just the right spot on her thigh, for through some magic unbeknownst to her, he'd already managed to find his way under her skirts. She couldn't help the moan that escaped her lips at his perfect touch.

"No pantaloons tonight?" he asked huskily.

"It is . . . a warm night," she managed between his caresses.

Marlowe's grin deepened even further, and he tossed her into the middle of the giant four-poster, then proceeded to crawl over her in a manner that reminded her of some exotic jungle cat, all sleek and rangy and intent on his prey. He made short work of her gown and slippers and seemed to delight in tormenting her as he slowly—much too slowly—rolled her stockings down her legs one by one, peppering her skin with kisses as he went.

She fought back by pulling at his lawn shirt until he was forced to pause his ministrations and shrug out of it, revealing for the first time his broad shoulders and bare torso for her delectation. She'd imagined too many times to count what he must look like beneath those untidy clothes of his, but the reality was more glorious. She ran her hands up his chest, tangling in the dark mat of curls dusting his belly and pectorals, sliding over the smooth skin of his shoulders and down the hard, sculpted planes of his back.

He was a beautiful man, a far cry from that drunken, bloated mess she'd first encountered two years ago. Yet that disparity made him even more attractive to her. His body was a bit beaten around the edges, filled with cracks and fissures that spoke of a lifetime of crushing disappointments and hard living. His beauty was hard-won and sometimes hard to spot beneath all of those masks he donned for the world. But she had spotted it and could not help but revel in it now as she ran her hands over that burning hot, naked flesh until he shuddered from her touch.

He caged her beneath him, arms and legs lightly pinning her in place, as if he was still concerned she planned to escape him, despite her roaming hands and boneless body. He leant over her and kissed her, openmouthed and fierce, and took one of her hands in his, guided it down to the front of his nankeens, and pressed. The feel of him, so hard and hot and . . . formidable sent a flash of heat straight to her core.

But when she reached for his falls to finally release him, he caught up her hands and pinned them above her head, looking halfway in agony.

"Not yet. Won't last a second if you do that," he breathed, as if it took every ounce of his remaining control to admit it.

She felt a thrill low in her belly at how undone he'd become in so short a time. She decided to press her luck. "But I want to see all of you this time. It's only fair."

She received no coherent reply to this other than a squeeze to her wrists and a roll of his hips against the most sensitive part of her.

He pulled away at last, but only to divest her of the rest of her clothing. She watched him with amazement as he worked at the strings on her shift with alarming dexterity. He was beyond good at this, and she wondered if she needed to be jealous of the other women upon whom he'd honed his skills. Then she decided she didn't care when he finally managed to strip away her shift and immediately sucked one of her nipples into his mouth.

He played with her body until she was in an agony of sensation, and just when she'd almost resorted to begging him, he finally allowed her to strip him of his nankeens and explore his body as he'd explored hers. She ran her hands over the sharp, eager jut of his hip bones, the sleek, plush flesh of his arse, and finally, the hard, hot length of him, heavy and alive against her palm. Just the barest of caresses, and he was moaning out her name, pressing her into the bedclothes and nudging himself between her legs.

"Minerva," he whispered, hot and desperate in her ear as he wrapped her legs around his waist, canting her hips until they were locked together. "Minerva," as if her name were the only word he remembered.

And when he finally pushed inside of her, she knew he had been right that day on Jacob's Island—*there were no words.* All she needed to know was in his eyes—unfocused, soft with adoration and bright with awe. And when he began to move, first gently, then with inexorable passion, ecstasy sparked, wild and electric, in his glance.

He never looked away from her, and when he tried to speak, his words were nonsensical, filthy rubbish. She reveled in it. Here he was, stripped bare of all of his words and masks, naked love and lust written in every line of his body, every thrust of his hips and caress of his hand, every kiss of his lips and stuttered exhalation of his lungs. He'd stopped hiding from her, and she vowed to herself in that moment to never make him regret it.

"I love you," she whispered, for though he'd said the words more than once, and though he must have known, she'd never said them back.

He may have proven words unnecessary by the worship in his eyes and body, but those particular words, from her heart to his, must have been very nice to hear indeed. He groaned, and his thrusts picked up and became just a touch more insistent. He angled his hips, shifted his hold on her body, and began to hit upon some spot inside of her that made her vision go bright at the edges and her body feel as if it were being struck by lightning.

Thought—much less words—became impossible for her after that. There was only the warm, animal heat of his body covering hers, the impossibly perfect fit of him inside of her, the sound of their broken breaths and uncontrollable moans—and then, when it had all become nearly too much, the blush-inducing, obscene slap of flesh against flesh.

At last, she crested, her whole body sparking and shuddering with ecstasy again and again, and she cried out in awe. It was even better than the pleasure he'd brought her before with his mouth, for she was surrounded by him entirely, held firm in his warm embrace and hot, desirous gaze.

He finally broke his careful vigil as he too found his release in the wake of her own, tucking his head into her shoulder with a groan. His body tensed and began to shake helplessly, and he spilled inside of her, his hands squeezing her hips with an intensity that stopped just short of too much.

"Mine," he murmured possessively into her shoulder, convincing her more than ever of his Viking ancestry.

She laughed and held on to him tightly, never wanting to let him go again. "Yes, and you're all mine." Every contradictory, unique bit of him.

⁂

MUCH, MUCH LATER, he rolled off to one side, her hand clasped tight in his, and they both panted, bodies limp with sated exhaustion.

"Chevalier indeed," she murmured when she finally worked up enough residual energy to speak again. She turned her head and gifted him with a lazy smile.

He looked well pleased with himself, staring in sleepy satisfaction at the ceiling, still half-breathless and painted over in sweat. "I do believe toward the end I was more hedonist than dashing French nobleman."

"I do believe you're right," she replied, feeling the wonderful, exhausted soreness in all of her muscles. "So, just out of curiosity, *did* you write me a poem?"

He laughed. "I knew you'd not let that lie. I can't believe I am marrying a Misstopher."

She didn't know she still had the capability of blushing after being had so thoroughly, but blush she did. But she didn't bother to deny his accusation. She'd never deny being a Misstopher again, for she *was*, through and through.

"I only wish to know if you are over your creative

malaise," she said primly, for even if she were a rabid Misstopher, she wasn't going to let him tease her too much without returning the gesture.

He saw through her immediately and snorted. "Creative malaise?" He propped himself up on his elbow and grinned down at her, running his fingers rather boldly over the curve of her hip. She shivered in response. "I believe those days are over. My muse has returned with a vengeance."

"Then you *have* written me a poem?"

His grin turned wolfish. "Indeed. Would you like to hear it?"

She narrowed her eyes, not quite trusting that grin or the playful glitter in his eyes. "Of course," she said.

He made a show of clearing his throat and composing the planes of his face into some semblance of proper gravitas.

Then he opened his mouth and spoke.

> *There once was a man from West Barming*
> *Who wrote rhymes the world found alarming*
> *Along came a girl*
> *Who thought him a churl*
> *'Til one day she found him most charming.*

Silence.

She finally found her voice. "You . . . You . . ."

"What?" he asked, all innocence, his eyes sparkling with mischief and just a bit of wariness—as if he expected her to attack him for his impertinence.

He was a wise man, for attack him she did . . .

But with a kiss, loud and inelegant, on his absurd mouth. He looked satisfyingly flummoxed.

"You say the most lovely things."

He laughed in delight. "Knew one day you'd come to appreciate my gift."

She most certainly did, and when he rolled on top of her

and she could feel another of his particular gifts prodding hot and hard at her hip once more, she appreciated him even more.

He must have read her thoughts, for his cheeks flushed adorably, and his grin turned a bit dangerous. His eyes went hooded as he began to move his own hips in a most delightful way, sending little bursts of pleasure through her with every slow, grinding drag against her core.

He started to pepper her face all over in kisses.

"First an ode, now a limerick," she mused through his kisses. "I wonder what can possibly be next."

"A fairy epic," he murmured.

She pulled away and stared at him incredulously. "Really?"

He furrowed his brow in irritation. "Why does no one believe I can write a fairy epic?"

"Oh, I don't doubt that you *can*. I just wonder if you *should*," she said pertly.

"Everyone's a critic," he said with a sigh, snuggling closer in her arms. "And you wonder why I didn't want anyone to know I was Essex."

She laughed and kissed his pouting forehead. "Fine. You may write a hundred fairy epics if you want. I'm just glad your muse has finally returned."

"Indeed she has," he said, smiling into her eyes and holding her close. "And I'll never lose her again."

The End

AUTHOR'S NOTE

DEAR READERS,
    For those who have noticed the (nearly two year) gap between my publication of *Virtuous Scoundrel* and *The Alabaster Hip*: thank you for your patience! I had a bit of writer's block, so I thought it only fitting to write a book about a character afflicted with a similar problem. I don't think my block was quite so angst-ridden as Marlowe's, but some days it felt like it came close. I am more than happy with the end result, however, and I hope you are too.

    One of the most intimidating things about tackling *The Alabaster Hip* was the development of Marlowe's poetic alter-ego, Christopher Essex. I am no poet, so I really fretted over writing some verse that was (passably) convincing for the time period. The poem, "The Alabaster Hip", is as good as it gets for me, and even then I relied heavily upon one of Keats's odes for a model. You're welcome to figure out which one.

    Another thing that helped me through (or distracted me from) the writing of this book was fanfiction. I am an unabashed, avid Fangirl Geek Extraordinaire, with so many 'ships I could form an armada, and so I got to wondering if a similar sort of subculture existed during the 19th century. I knew women (and men) were flinging themselves left, right and Chelsea at Lord Byron back in the day, but what were these people writing? Quite a lot, actually. The idea for my Misstophers grew out of all of this research—

and my own (unhealthy) obsession with contemporary fan culture. There is a wonderful article on the subject by Corin Throsby, called "Byron, Commonplacing, and Early Fan Culture" in the book, *Romanticism and Celebrity Culture, 1750-1850*, if anyone is interested.

Thank you for reading this final installment in Montford's, Sebastian's, and Marlowe's story. I've had so much fun writing these boys' happy endings. I'll be back soon for another excursion into Regency England, so stay tuned!

ABOUT THE AUTHOR

MAGGIE FENTON HAS BEEN A music teacher, a professional accompanist, a cheesemonger, a waitress, a line cook, and a college instructor...among other things. She has one master's degree in English literature and another master's degree in piano performance. She might try for a third if this writing thing doesn't work out. She also writes Victorian steampunk romance under the pseudonym Margaret Foxe. Visit *www.maggiefenton.com* for Maggie's latest news.

Printed in Great Britain
by Amazon